Hopeless!

A.M. Myers

Hopelessly Devoted
Bayou Devils MC
Book One

A.M. Myers

A.M. Myers

Hopelessly Devoted

The characters and events in this book are fictitious. Names, characters, places and plots are a product of the author's imagination. Any similarity to real persons, living or dead, is coincidental and not intended by the author.

Cover Design by Jay Aheer
Editing by Nicole Bailey
Proofreading by Julie Deaton

Copyright © 2017 by A.M. Myers

First Edition

All rights reserved. No part of this publication may be reproduced, distributed, or transmitted in any form or by any means, including photocopying, recording, or other electronic or mechanical methods, without the prior written permission of the publisher, except in the case of brief quotations embodied in critical reviews and certain other noncommercial uses permitted by copyright law.

A.M. Myers

Hopelessly Devoted

"She's not just a girl. She's the only evidence of God that I can find on this entire planet." - St. Elmo's Fire (1985), Dir. Joel Schumacher

A.M. Myers

Hopelessly Devoted

Prologue

My hands are fucking sweating like crazy, and I swear my heart is about to beat right out of my chest. Rubbing my hands on my jeans, I look down and grimace at the oil stains under my fingernails. Jesus Christ. This is only the biggest fucking night of my life, and I couldn't even remember to wash my damn hands? I grab the rag out of my back pocket and spit into it, doing my best to clean them before she gets here. Tonight has to be perfect. Weeks of preparation are leading up to one single moment that will change our lives, and I feel like I'm going to have a heart attack. I check my watch and take one last look around the back deck of the house I just bought for her today.

When she pulls up out front, the first things she'll see are the solar lights that I installed along the sidewalk into the backyard, lighting her way to me. Shit. Maybe I should have gotten the rose petals, too. They seemed so fucking cheesy on the shelves of the store but now I feel like I didn't do enough. Why the fuck didn't I get her rose petals? Running my hand over my hair, I look up at the twinkle lights that I strung across the patio, stretching the entire length of the deck above our heads. There are a shit ton of candles clumped together in groups all around me, casting a soft glow over the yard with the swing set where our kids will play one day.

Two years ago to the day, I was honorably discharged from the Army, and I thought my life was over. The shit I saw and did in theatre haunted me but not more than the one thing I didn't do. Just shy of two weeks before my tour ended, I was supposed to go out on a recon mission with my unit but the night before, I got sick. I wasn't going to let it stop me though, and I tried to power through, but when I passed out in the barracks, the decision was taken from me. They made me stay back and sent Coleman, my best friend out there, in my place. That was the last time I saw him. They were ambushed, and no one survived. He never should have been out there. I should be dead right now but I'm not, and because of me, his mother can never hold her son again, and his fiancée lost the love of her life.

I couldn't adjust. The quiet was the loudest thing I'd ever heard, tormenting me with my guilt. I couldn't just be. And then she walked into my life. She breezed into the shop where I was working, and as soon as I laid eyes on her, I was a goner. I couldn't get enough and soon, the silence was drowned out by her sweet voice and infectious laughter. For the first time in a year, I felt light and happy instead of weighed down by my mistakes. She's everything that I never even knew I wanted, and I'll do whatever it takes to make sure she's by my side forever.

I'm just a lucky bastard because, really, she could have any man on this planet. All she would have to do is smile in their direction and they'd follow her to the ends of the earth. And for some reason that I'll probably never understand, she chose me. She chose me, and she lit up my life in the most beautiful way possible. I'll never stop trying to make up for my failures. I'll never stop trying to be the man she deserves. That's why tonight has to go perfectly.

I take a deep breath and look around for a second time, wondering once again if there was more that I could have done, but before I can delve into my panic any further, she steps around the corner of the house and gasps. Her jaw pops open, and she covers it with her hand, looking all around me in wonder. My heart pounds a little harder, and I'm not sure how it hasn't broken a rib yet.

"Logan," she whispers as she slowly makes her way over to me, her blue gaze darting over everything again and again like she can't believe it's really here. She steps up to me and places her little hand on my chest. "What is all this? And where are we?"

"It's all for you, Baby," I tell her, placing my hand over hers and pressing it harder against my skin, loving her hands on me. Her touch is seared into my skin, imprinted into the very fiber of my bones, and there will never be another that makes me feel the way that she does. She giggles, and I can't stop the wide smile from stretching across my face as she looks around again.

"But why?" Wonder transforms her voice, making it whisper soft as she looks around the patio, trying to take in every minute detail that I spent the last few hours putting together. I take a deep breath and look around the space with her, trying to see it through her eyes. All these lights and candles seemed so perfect when I pictured it in my head, but now I'm wondering if the vision in my mind really translated well in real life. I was in such a dark place before her, and she was my light. She walked into the room, and the darkness didn't stand a single chance.

"Because I love you," I tell her, and her head whips back to me, dark hair fanning out in a veil around her. She smiles up at me and leans in for a kiss. I keep it sweet, making sure she can feel every ounce of love that I feel for her. When she pulls away, she smiles up at me again, happiness dancing in her eyes, and it takes my breath away. I want to beat my chest, show everyone that I'm the one that puts that look in her eyes. I want every single person on this earth to know that I'm the man that makes her that happy.

"I love you, too, but that still doesn't answer my first question."

"What was your first question?" I ask, my nerves affecting my ability to remember even a few moments ago. She laughs.

"Where are we?"

I smirk, loving that I was able to surprise her with this. "Oh, you mean the house."

"Yes, the house, Logan," she scoffs, trying to pull away but I wrap my arm around her hip and pull her into my body, leaning in, and kissing her cheek, right by her ear.

"I bought it for you," I whisper, and she gasps loudly, pushing against me, and I lean back. Her eyes are wide but she has a smile teasing her lips, almost like she doesn't want to get her hopes up.

"What?"

Spinning her around in my arms, I point her toward the sliding glass door at the back of the house and stand behind her, wrapping my arms around her waist as I rest my chin on her shoulder. "It's ours, Baby. Signed the papers today."

She shakes her head before leaning back into me and reaching up to run her fingers through my hair. "You're insane but I fucking love you for it."

Her hand slides down my cheek, scraping against the stubble, and I know it's time. I spin her back around and grab her hands, rubbing my thumb across the back of hers as I take a deep breath. "I have one more surprise for you."

"A house wasn't enough?" she asks, arching a brow, and I smile.

"Not quite."

"What is it?" She glances around the yard like she might find the surprise out there. She's so fucking cute. I take one more deep breath and release her hands, reaching into my pocket to pull out the diamond ring I saved six months of paychecks for, and drop to my knee. Her mouth pops open again for a second before tears form in her eyes. She bites down on her bottom lip as I grab her left hand.

"Sweetheart, I didn't ever think that I could be this happy but then you walked into my life and showed me just how wrong I was. You lit up my world and brought my tired, beaten down soul back to life. Will you make all my dreams come true and marry me?"

Tears fall down her cheeks as she lets her hand fall away, showing me her watery smile as she nods. "Yes, Logan. A thousand times, yes."

I slide the ring on her finger, warmth expanding in my chest at the sight of my ring on her hand. It feels so fucking right, and I can't stop myself from standing, and crushing her body to mine.

"I love you so much," she whispers into my neck, and I shudder, the impact of her words rocking through me.

"You're the only woman on this earth for me, Sophia. I love you. Always."

Hopelessly Devoted

Chapter One
Alison

Gravel crunches under my tires and dirt kicks up behind me as I pull into the rundown parking lot. My skin prickles with unease as I look around. After pulling into a parking spot at the very end of the lot, I throw the car in park, making sure my doors are locked as I reach for my phone to double-check the address he sent me. If it weren't for the line of cars all along the chain link fence covered by a flimsy green material that's obscuring my view, I would think this place was abandoned. After I confirm that this is, in fact, the right place, I look around in a desperate attempt to figure out where I am. Isn't this how all horror movies start? The stupid girl goes into the creepy place even though all her instincts are telling her to turn and run like hell, and then the next thing you know, someone is wearing her skin. At this point in any movie, I would be rolling my eyes and screaming at my TV, telling the girl to get out of there. And yet, here I am, sitting in my car and waiting for my date for the evening.

A sign hoisted up on a large pole in the corner of the lot catches my eye, and I groan when I see the name of the place. Mud Runner Obstacle Course. Seriously? My date, Troy, didn't tell me anything about where he was taking me, only sending me an address and telling me to meet him at five. Who even takes a girl to an obstacle course for a first date? First dates are supposed to be fun, flirty, and have a little edge of mystery. Me, running through an obstacle course and sweating my ass off while my date watches, does not sound fun or flirty to me. And while a good first date should leave you a little breathless, this was not what I had in mind. With a grumble, I grab my phone and check the time, relieved that I still have a few minutes to just relax before I have to go in there. I toss the phone back into the passenger seat and lean my head back on the headrest, letting my eyes drift closed.

    I hate this whole thing already, and I hate Mr. Klein, my boss, even more for making me do this. I can't believe I'm even in this position. Last week, I thought I was a shoe-in for the columnist's spot that opened up at the paper I work at. But when Mr. Klein called me into his office, it was to tell me that I was up against Chelsea – a woman who has only been at the paper for a year and has worked her way up on her knees, if you know what I mean. My boss, the disgusting pig that he is, came up with the idea to hold a little contest for us. We would each sign up for an online dating service, go on three dates, and write about them to best give him an idea of what our column would look like. If I didn't want this job so damn badly, I would have turned him down, but I've been working for so damn long, and the thought of just giving up killed me.

I've been a crime reporter at the Baton Rouge Times for the last five years, and I've worked my ass off to get to where I am. First, in high school so I could go to a good college, and then even more so in college so I could land my dream job. Since starting at the paper straight out of college, I put in countless hours to build a solid reputation for myself. I love my job, and I've learned so much and grown as a writer, but lately, something has been off. There is this stirring in my soul for more. So often, the only time someone sees me is after they've already become a victim. I'm the person that comes in and digs into their pain so I can tell the world about it, and after doing it for so long, I'd like to do more. I want to find a way to help people instead of hurting them more. I don't exactly know how I'd like to do that yet but I can't help but feel like the columnist position is exactly where I need to be to do it.

My phone chimes with the two-minute warning for my date, and I suck in a steadying breath as I peel my eyes open and grab it, shutting the alarm off. I glance up and scan the line of fence, looking for an entrance, and my gaze lands on a hulking figure standing near an opening that must be the entrance. Even this far away, I shrink back on instinct. Good lord, please tell me that man is not my date. He looks like he could crush me with his bare hands and not in a sexy, "oh, your muscles are so big" way. More like a "please put down the steroids, even your muscles have muscles" kind of way. Looking down at my phone again, I log into the dating website and read his profile one last time. His name is Troy, he's thirty-two, and a personal trainer. I roll my eyes and gaze at him through the windshield. A personal trainer who brought me to an obstacle course for our first date?

How original.

Glancing up once again at the behemoth I fear is waiting for me, I suck in a fortifying breath and turn off the car before stepping out into the dense Louisiana heat. Time to get this over with. Walking a little taller as I near the entrance, I remind myself that I've got this. Chelsea's writing is, at best, mediocre, and as long as Mr. Klein remains professional, this job is as good as mine.

Then again, I shouldn't rule out the possibility. He has been banging her right in his office for the past six months.

"Ali?" the giant asks as I draw near, his crystal blue eyes sparkling and a wide smile stretching across his face in greeting, and my fears are confirmed. I muster every ounce of politeness I can and extend my hand. Truthfully, it's not Troy's fault that I don't want to be here. Mr. Klein is the object of my anger, not him.

"You must be Troy," I say, pulling forward my professional side as my hand hangs in the air between us. "It's nice to meet you."

I expect him to shake my hand but instead, he wraps an arm around my shoulders, pulling me into his body and pinning my hand between us as he embraces me in the most awkward hug of all time. My body tenses up, and time seems to stall. I don't think I've ever been more uncomfortable in my life. Besides a few quick messages back and forth to set up this date, we haven't even spoken and he's holding me like we're old friends. When he finally releases me, I take a deep breath, the tension easing out of me slightly but I'm still on edge as he smiles at me, his gaze leisurely dropping down my body and back up again.

I force down the disgust trying to rise up inside me and remind myself why I'm here. If I leave now, I'll never get this job, and I'll be forced to read Chelsea go on about sex tips and how to give a perfect blow job twice a week. It would be hell.

"You ready to do this?" Troy asks, motioning to the gate behind him that leads to a massive obstacle course. Oh, hell no. I could maybe be a good sport if the guy had given me a heads up and told me to bring a change of clothes, but no. I'm standing here in a skirt and heels, and there is absolutely no way that I'm doing this. I'm about to answer him when two women stroll by, engrossed in conversation with each other. Both of them are covered, head to toe, in mud. It's smeared across their faces, caked in their hair, and stuck to their slim, toned bodies like a second skin. When I look back at him, he smiles at me again, almost reminding me of an eager puppy.

"Um…" I say, not sure how to break this to him, and his face falls.

"You're not into this at all, are you?" he asks, looking forlorn, and I actually feel bad.

"I'm sorry, it's just that I don't have anything else to change into." I point down to my skirt and heels like it should be obvious, and he nods. Understanding dawns, and he shakes his head, scrubbing his hand across his short blond hair.

"Shit. Yeah, I guess I should have mentioned that part."

I want to come back with some sarcastic remark but he looks so disappointed that I can't bring myself to do it. Plus, I need to go on this date no matter how badly I just want to go home and crawl into bed with a good book. If I don't, I don't get that job.

"I'm sorry. If I had known, I would have brought workout clothes."

He shakes his head, almost like he's brushing off his mood and smiles at me. "Naw, it's cool. I understand. We can still go grab dinner though. I know this great place."

"Okay," I say, breathing a sigh of relief that I don't have to run home and find another date to replace this one. "I'll meet you there. What's it called?"

"I'll text you the address."

I feel apprehensive about agreeing to follow him to another mystery destination but reluctantly agree before walking back to my car. As I slide into the seat and close the door, I let out a heavy sigh and lean my head back on the headrest. What a disaster. All I can do is hope that dinner goes better and I actually have something to write about. My phone chimes, and I grab it, expecting the address from Troy but instead smile at the text from my best friend, Izzy.

Izzy:
Where the hell are you?

Me:
Out on a date.

The text from Troy comes in right after I press send, and I program the address into my GPS before setting my phone in the cup holder and starting the car. Just as I'm getting ready to back out of my parking spot, my phone chimes again and I grab it.

Izzy:
Any good?

Me:
TBD. Standby.

Izzy and I have always had a system for getting out of bad dates, and I just have this sneaking suspicion that I'm going to need to use it tonight. Troy seems like an all right guy, I guess, but my not wanting to be here is making me less patient than usual. I back out of the parking spot and start driving toward the restaurant, my GPS guiding the way as I think about the last good date I had.

My love life has pretty much been on hold lately. I had a few "boyfriends" in high school and college but we were just having fun, and no one really hung around for long. Then, just before graduation, I met Adam. He'd been in town to see a few friends graduate and approached me in the coffee shop on campus and asked me out. Adam was so charming, and I was surprised by how quickly I fell for him. A year later, we were moving in together, and I saw us getting married someday. Everything wasn't perfect but I loved our life together, and I thought we were going somewhere; that we were growing together. Then two years ago, I came home early one day and walked in on him screwing the eighteen-year-old neighbor. I just stood there and watched them for a minute because I couldn't wrap my brain around what I was seeing. All the dreams that I had built in my head came crashing down around me. I moved all my stuff out that night, and Izzy let me stay with her until I was able to buy my house.

I was completely shattered, broken in a way that I didn't even recognize myself, and I promised that I would never let that happen again. And even though I've moved on with my life, I've stuck to my "no dating" policy. It drives Izzy up a wall because she's going out with someone new every weekend but I don't want to force something that should be natural. Izzy likes to play and have fun but I'm a relationship girl, and the way she lives her life never really appealed to me. She always wants to set me up with some guy she knows, and I love that girl but it drives me crazy.

Pulling to a stop, I'm drawn out of my thoughts, and I sigh as I turn off the car and grab my phone before stepping out. Troy waves at me from the door, and I smile, offering him a small wave as I shut the door and lock it. *I've got this*, I remind myself for what feels like the tenth time tonight and make my way to the door. When I reach him, he slips an arm around my back and guides me inside to the hostess stand. She smiles sweetly at us and grabs two menus before leading us to a table in the back. As we sit down, she sets a menu in front of each of us and fills up our water glasses before leaving.

"So, what is it that you do again?" he asks, pulling my attention away from the menu, and my growling stomach.

"I'm a reporter at the newspaper."

"Oh, man, I think I would go crazy if I had to sit at a desk all day long."

I nod, taking a sip of the water as I try to sneak peeks at the menu without being rude. "Yeah, it can make you a little stir crazy at times but I get up and go get water or something to stretch my legs. Plus, I'm out in the field a lot."

"I could give you some easy workouts you can do around your desk, if you want."

I picture standing up in the sea of cubicles and trying to do exercise moves as all the other reporters look on, and it makes me laugh. "No. Thank you, though."

He nods again and looks off to the side of our table as an awkward silence falls over us. Thankfully, the waiter appears so we don't suffer through it for long.

"Good evening. My name is Henry, and I'll be your server this evening. Can I get you folks started off with an appetizer?"

I smile up at Henry and start to tell him that I'd love some mozzarella sticks when Troy interrupts me.

"We'll just take two chef salads, please."

I blink in shock, and poor Henry looks to me for confirmation. When I try to tell him that I don't want the salad, Troy interrupts me again.

"That'll be all. Thank you." His voice is hard like he's angry or something, and for the life of me, I can't figure out why. Also, I don't really care anymore. I haven't even known this guy for an hour, and he's already hugged me and ordered for me like he knows me. And a salad? Seriously? Salad is the food before the food. Henry scurries off, and I turn to Troy, doing my best to remain calm.

It's not a big deal.

I can just eat real food when I get home.

"Trust me, you'll thank me later," Troy says, and I take another deep breath, feeling like my face is turning bright red from the anger simmering just under the surface. Just what the hell does he mean by that?

"Excuse me?"

"I'm just saying, Babe. If you stuck to salad and let me train you, you would be a knockout. You probably only need to lose five to ten pounds."

An explosion of anger rocks through me, and I do my best to not shoot a death glare at him. I'm not a big girl but I do have curves and up until this moment, I never thought that was a bad thing. Who the hell does he think he is and what happened to the sad guy that I left at the obstacle course? It's like he swapped bodies with someone. I take a drink of the water in front of me, and my hand shakes. I want to say something to him but I'm honestly so shocked that I can't find the words. He picks up on my anger though and holds his hands up.

"Hey, don't get mad. I'm just saying that if we worked a little bit of weight off you, you'd be a ten."

He winks, and I feel like I'm going to explode. I have to keep reminding myself that prison yard orange is so not my fucking color as I pull my phone out of my purse and fire off a text to Izzy.

Me:
911. Save me.

"Like how often a week do you eat junk food? I bet if you cleared that shit out of your diet, it would help a lot."

Izzy replies back immediately and saves me from launching across this table and throttling Troy and his oversized muscles with my bare hands.

Izzy:
On a scale of 1 – prison time, how bad is it?

Me:
25 to life.

I glance across the table at him, and he's still rambling on about my diet and me just going for a walk every now and then but I'm tuning him out. It's really for his own good. My phone rings, Izzy's picture popping up on my screen, and I let out a relieved sigh.

"I'm so sorry. I have to take this," I say, and he finally shuts his mouth, nodding at me. I answer the phone and immediately have to pull it away from my ear to avoid permanent damage.

"Ali!" Izzy screams into the phone, and the people at the tables surrounding us all turn to look with wide eyes.

"Izzy, are you okay? What's wrong?" If I didn't want to get out of here so badly, I would be laughing my ass off right now. She is so goddamn dramatic.

"I fell down the stairs, and I think my leg is broken. You have to come here!" she wails, adding in some fake tears that sound very convincing.

"Did you call an ambulance?"

"No, I need you. Please, Ali. It hurts so bad," she screams, and I grab my bag from the floor in preparation.

"Okay, Sweetie. I'm coming right now, okay? Just hang tight." I hang up the phone and look at Troy with an apologetic look. He looks genuinely concerned, and I bite my lip to hold back my laughter.

"I'm so sorry. I have to go."

"Of course, do you want me to drive you?" he asks, standing up to go with me.

"No, it's okay. You stay here and eat your dinner. We'll be fine," I tell him, standing, and rushing out of there with another quick "I'm sorry" as I race past him. As soon as I'm outside, I dial Izzy again, and when she answers the phone, I can hear the smile in her voice.

"How was that?"

"You're so over the top," I tell her, finally letting the laughter spill out, and she joins me.

"It got the job done, didn't it?"

"Yeah, just remind me to submit that little performance for an Oscar this year," I laugh, sliding into my car, and locking the door, thankful that my windows are tinted and no one can see me.

"I'd like to thank God, first and foremost, and of course my parents for always believing in me," she says, launching into a fake Oscar acceptance speech that makes me laugh even harder as I pull away from the curb.

"Over the top," I say again, interrupting her, and she laughs.

"So, what happened to make you use the 911?"

"I'll tell you all about it later. Right now, I'm gonna go home and drown myself in a bottle of wine."

She laughs again. "Okay. Drink a glass in my honor."

"Of course, you saved me. Love you, Girlie."

"Love you, too. Talk to you tomorrow."

I hang up and chuckle to myself as I remember Troy's face in the restaurant. I'm so glad we made up that silly little system. It's usually Izzy using it but I'm grateful that it was there when I needed it, too. I sigh as I drive back home, ready to get this whole thing over with. One date down, only two more to go.

A.M. Myers

Hopelessly Devoted

Chapter Two
Alison

"Hey, what are you up to tonight?" Izzy asks as soon as I answer the phone, and I lean back in the seat of my car and sigh.

"Another date."

"Interesting," she hums. "You're really living it up, huh?"

I let out a sharp laugh and shake my head. "No, not really."

"Oh, come on. You haven't gone out in over a year, and now you've had two dates in two days. Sounds like you're trying to get back on the horse to me."

Checking the time, I turn the car off and open the door. "I promise it's not what you think."

"What is it then?" she asks.

"I don't have time to explain it right now." I stop by the front door of the restaurant, and lean against the wall, hoping I can get her to drop this before my date gets here.

"Tough, missy. Start talking and leave nothing out."

"I really can't, Iz. I'm standing outside the restaurant right now, and my date will be here any second."

She huffs, and I imagine her crossing her arms over her chest and pouting, which makes me laugh. "Fine, but I want a full report this weekend. Capisce?"

"Yeah, yeah, I got it," I laugh. We wrap up the call, and I shove my phone back in my purse and turn to go in the restaurant.

"Are you Ali?" someone asks, and I look up, meeting warm brown eyes and a mop of curly brown hair.

"Zach?" I ask, and he smiles. He nods and holds his hand out to me. I shake it and relax a little. We're off to a good start, and while I don't get sparks or crazy butterflies when our hands touch, I do feel comfortable around him. When he releases me, he extends his hand out in front of him to indicate that I should go first, and I feel a little more of my stress melt away. He's perfectly nice, and for the first time since this assignment started, I don't feel like it's the worst thing ever.

A hostess greets us and grabs two menus before leading us to a table out on the patio with a reserved sign on it. There are other tables out here but they are all empty, and I can't help but feel like this was planned. I look over to Zach, who shrugs.

"I'm friends with the manager, and he owes me a favor," he says, a slight blush rising to his cheeks.

"That's really sweet. Thank you."

Hopelessly Devoted

He pulls my chair out for me and I sit while he goes to the other side, and the hostess sets the menus down in front of us. As she's filling up our water glasses, I take a quick look through the menu and decide on what I want. This is one of my favorite restaurants so I was happy when Zach recommended it. She asks for our drink orders, and after we rattle them off, she leaves.

"So," he says, and then his voice trails off and we both laugh, some of the first date awkwardness dissipating.

"I know I read it on your profile but tell me again what you do?" I ask, and he gives me an easy smile.

"I'm a manager at a clothing store right now."

"Right now?"

He nods, taking a sip of his water. "Yeah, I'm going to school to get my business degree."

"Oh, very cool."

"Yeah, what about you?"

The hostess comes back with my wine and Zach's beer, setting them down in front of each of us and leaving without a word.

"Well, I'm a crime reporter right now but I'm up for a columnist position so I'm really hoping that I get that."

The waitress appears at our table before he can say anything else, and we both order and hand her back our menus before she bustles off again.

"What do you want to write your column about?" he asks when she leaves, and I smile. I love talking about my work, and I could probably do it all through dinner if he let me, so this part is easy for me.

"I'm not sure yet. I'd love to find a way to help people, though. It'd be a nice change of pace from what I'm doing now."

"How do you mean?"

"Well, as a crime reporter, I kind of only show up when something bad has happened to someone. It's awful to dig into someone's pain like that, especially when it's still so raw."

He nods, looking thoughtfully off in the distance for a second. "Yeah, I guess I can see how that would be draining."

"It is," I tell him, nodding because he kind of hit the nail on the head. The stories I write do take a lot out of me. Listening to a father break down and sob in front of me after his daughter has been killed or watching a shop owner walk through the store that he spent his life building after someone broke in and robbed him sometimes takes every ounce of strength I can muster.

We chat casually, and I like that it's easy to talk to him. The waitress stops by the table and drops off the appetizer that Zach ordered, and I realize that it's one of my favorites. When she leaves, he slides the plate between us.

"They seriously have the best fried mozzarella I've ever had," he says, taking a piece at the same time that I do.

"I know. This is one of my favorite restaurants."

"Wow. Lucky guess."

I nod and take another bite of the food. "Did you grow up around here?" I ask, finding myself genuinely interested. We may not be right for each other romantically but there's no reason that we can't be friends. In fact, I think Zach and I could be good friends.

"Naw, I grew up in South Carolina near Charleston."

"Oh, what brought you over this way?" I ask, and he tenses up.

"A girl."

It's the only answer I get, and he's quiet for a few awkward moments. Glancing out at the river, I try to think of something to say but I'm not even sure what upset him. The waitress comes back with our dinners, and he seems to shake off whatever it was that was bothering him as we dig into the food.

"Are you going to LSU?" I ask, and he nods.

"Yeah, I have a life here now, and it seemed silly to go anywhere else."

I watch him for a moment, unsure if he's completely recovered from earlier. "Can I ask you something?"

He looks up and seems to think it over for a moment before nodding. "Yeah."

"Why did you wait so long to go to school?"

His gaze hardens right in front of me, and he clenches his teeth as I lean away from him, surprised by his reaction. "Because I was with this girl, my high school sweetheart, actually. And she wanted to go to school so I needed to work to support us. We had a whole plan, you know? She would go to school and then after she graduated, I would start classes, but instead, she started spreading her legs for one of the guys in her art class."

"Oh my god, that's terrible. I'm sorry." I know exactly how he feels, and I wouldn't wish it on anyone.

"We had a plan, you know? She was going to design jewelry, and I was gonna run the business but that wasn't good enough for her. Four years just flushed down the fucking drain." He's off on a tangent now, and I don't think I could get a word in if I tried.

"There was so much bullshit. I put up with it 'cause I loved her, and we were gonna have a life together but the little bitch only ever thought about herself. She was only concerned with what she wanted, and it didn't matter who she trampled in the goddamn process. Why couldn't she just break up with me if she wanted someone else?"

I try to say something but he just keeps talking, and I'm not even sure that he knows I'm here anymore. I tune out his ongoing rant as I start eating faster, trying to finish this up so I can leave. I'm sure that I look very lady-like right now as I shovel baked ziti into my mouth, but desperate times and all that. He was nice at first but this is really uncomfortable.

"It was like being with a child! She never did anything to help out around the house so on top of working my ass off to support us, I was also doing all the cleaning and cooking. Really, I was like a butler, except she occasionally had sex with me when she wasn't screwing the model from her class."

I try to keep my face neutral as he goes on ranting but each thing he says only adds to the awkwardness blanketing us right now. I believe that a relationship can survive after cheating but both people have to want it and work really hard at it. Listening to him, I have to wonder why he's still so hung up on her if their relationship was really as bad as he's describing. When Adam cheated on me, I was shattered, but in a way, I was thankful for it. His infidelity allowed me to see how lopsided our relationship had been and how much the way he treated me had taken out of me.

Adam wasn't intentionally cruel to me. He was just young and selfish. Adam only did what he wanted, and I was never a priority in his mind. It's amazing how much that can take out of a person, and it's taken me so long to find my way back to a version of myself that I was before he came into my life. Sometimes, I have to wonder if it's really worth it, and it's one of the reasons that I don't date. What's the point?

I would like to say that I'm too young to be so jaded but I fear that I am that jaded. My days are spent around all different kinds of people, and not a single one of them has caught my eye since our break-up. I haven't even spared a guy a second glance in over two years, and it might be that I'm just not cut out for relationships.

"How can a person be that selfish, you know? How can you spend that many years with a person, claim to love them but then treat them like that? I've never understood. If she wanted to be with someone else, she could have just broken up with me but no, she wanted to have her cake and eat it, too," he says, and I nod as I take a sip of wine and shove more food in my mouth.

Finally, I finish my meal and sit back, finishing off my wine and discreetly checking my phone, ready to call in Izzy again if I need to. Zach looks up from his meal and notices that I'm done and mercifully stops talking.

"You ready to get out of here?" he asks, looking sad at the possibility but I don't understand why. He just spent the last fifteen minutes complaining about his ex – in excruciating detail.

"I'm sorry. I've just got an early morning tomorrow so I should probably be going soon."

He smiles and nods. "Sure. No problem. Let me just go pay the check."

He sets his napkin down next to his plate and gets up. As I watch him walk back inside the restaurant, my phone buzzes in my hand with a text from Izzy.

Izzy:
How's the date?

Me:
Epic fail.

I sigh as I look out at the Mississippi River off in the distance. On the bright side, this date is better than last night's, and I only have one more left. I'm dreading it but excited to get this all over with so I can go win my new job. My phone buzzes again, and I laugh at Izzy's text.

Hopelessly Devoted

Izzy:
Need a rescue? I've been practicing ;)

Me:
No, I'm about to leave.

"Ready?" Zach asks, walking back up to the table, and I offer him a small smile as I stand and grab my bag. We're quiet as he walks me outside, and I stop in front of the restaurant, careful not to let him follow me to my car.

"Thank you for dinner, Zach. I had a nice time." Normally, I would feel bad about lying, but after last night's date and tonight, I'm really starting to be okay with it.

"Yeah, me, too. You're a really great listener." His gaze drops to my lips, and my whole body sparks in alarm. *Oh, please don't try to kiss me right now.* He doesn't take his eyes off my lips as he moves in, and at the last second, I turn, giving him my cheek instead. His lips brush against my skin, and I feel nothing. It could be a kiss from my grandmother from the lack of spark. When he pulls back again, he smiles widely at me.

"I'd love to do this again," he says, and I give him a tight smile.

"Call me," I reply, knowing damn well that I never gave him my number but I hope it takes him a little while to realize that so I can get out of here. He nods, and I turn, walking away from him quickly but not so quickly that he realizes I'm trying to flee from him. Once I get to my car, I unlock the door, and sink into the seat, letting out a heavy breath. One more date and then I can put this whole thing behind me.

You can do this, I remind myself as I start the car and head back home, looking forward to my big comfy couch and some trashy TV.

Hopelessly Devoted

Chapter Three
Alison

I don't feel like myself.

I step out of my car, hand my keys to the valet and look down at my red dress, wondering if it's nice enough for this place. One look at the opulent restaurant in front of me and I know I'm severely out of my element. Peeking inside, I'm assaulted by a massive amount of gold and it's leaning toward tacky. It looks like Liberace threw up in here. I'd much rather be at a little hole in the wall place than here. Give me a pair of jeans and a good steak and I'm good to go. My heels clink against the stone stairs that have got to be marble as I walk up to the grand double door entrance. It's like an out of body experience as I step inside and look to my left where a large seating area is. It's like that scene from *Pretty Woman* and I can feel everyone's eyes on me as they judge me.

I pull up the dating website on my phone and go through my date's information one last time, trying to commit it to memory so I don't accidentally call him Troy or Zach. I'm beyond thrilled that this is the last date but I have no idea how I'm going to write this article. A part of me just wants to give Mr. Klein what he wants and write that these past three days were so great, but the other part of me really, really wants to march into his office, tell him exactly where he can shove it in extreme detail, and storm out of the office with my head held high. Whatever I do, at least I won't have to do this anymore. My weekends can go back to me lounging on my couch in sweatpants.

Izzy will probably throw a fit.

She's so excited that she thinks I'm dating again. For the past three days, she's been sending me pictures of guys that she thinks I'll like, and I'm a little concerned that they've all come from her reject pile. Izzy may choose to drown her pain in between the sheets with various men but I do not. Not that I'm in pain, I just don't date. Then again, maybe it's time that I open myself up to the possibility again. At least, allow someone the opportunity to try and get close to me. Since the whole Adam debacle, it's like I've had a huge "Closed for Business" sign around my neck and guys usually don't even try.

"Alison James," a hostess calls from the desk in the lobby, and I look up. She smiles and motions for me to follow her. Standing, I reread over the info one last time. His name is Blake, he's thirty-six, and works as a real estate agent. I take a deep breath and nod, committing it to memory. As I follow her through the dining room, my nerves spike. Quiet murmurs of private conversations buzz around me, only interrupted by the sound of silverware gently clinking against plates, and I only feel more self-conscious. The people here are wealthy. One look in the parking lot will tell you that, and while I do okay for myself, I don't come anywhere near this level of money. Not that I really want to either. Looking around the dining room, everyone looks so uptight.

The hostess turns and starts heading toward a more private part of the restaurant, and I can't help but wonder how much it costs a guy to reserve a table back here. It can't be cheap. We approach one of the tables, and there is a man already waiting there with his back to me. I take a deep breath just as the hostess stops at the chair directly across from him and motions for me to sit.

Just don't let him be worse than date number one.

"Alison James, sir," the hostess says, giving him a polite smile, and he stands, turning toward me. He grins and winks before turning to the hostess and slipping her a fifty. Fifty bucks just for seating me? I knew this place was way out of my league.

"Thanks, Sweetheart," he says, smacking her on the ass as she walks by us, and I immediately want to spin around and follow her out. *Take me with you*, a little voice in my head screams like she's violating girl code by leaving me here. Jesus. I mean, who the hell smacks another woman's ass when he's on a date? He turns his attention to me, and I barely restrain myself from taking a step back.

"And, Ali, so nice to finally meet you, Babe. I have to say, your pictures don't do you justice." His brown eyes draw a line down my body, and he makes no effort to hide the fact that he's inspecting every part of me. How much longer do I have to be here? I shift under his gaze and look at my watch, the time moving painfully slow already.

"Nice to meet you, too," I force out, plastering a professional smile on my face that honestly hurts a little. He flashes me a glimpse of his overly bleached smile and brushes his blond hair back before motioning to my chair and sitting back down in his own. Seriously? He's not even going to pull my chair out for me?

"Please, have a seat." He doesn't even bother to look at me when he says it, his gaze glued to his phone, and I close my eyes and take a deep breath before sitting down in my chair and picking up the menu. Fuck this. If he wants to bring me to this place and flash his money around, I'm going to order the most expensive thing on the damn menu.

A waitress appears and I order wine, knowing damn well that I'm going to need it, and when she turns to leave, I want to grab her by the wrist and beg her to stay. I'll even cry if I have to. Instead, I watch her walk away and look back at my date, just knowing that this is going to be truly awful. His eyes are still on the waitress's ass, and I have to wait until she's completely out of view before he looks back to me, smiling. It feels so fake.

"Sorry, Honey," he says, not looking the least bit sorry, "I just appreciate beauty."

I bet you do, pig.

My eyes want to roll so badly that it physically hurts to keep them trained on him but I manage and force a smile to my face as I nod. This guy's going for the fucking gold in most atrocious date ever, and he's off to a good start. It's like someone took date one and two and mashed them together to create one super awful date to end this shitty experience.

"So, what do you do again, Baby?" he asks, and I barely hold back the cringe at all the pet names he's throwing around.

"I'm a crime reporter."

"Ah, that sounds terrible. I'm sure the pay sucks, too. I'm in real estate, and I gotta tell ya, Sweetheart, money is good."

Trying my best to remain polite, I force a tight smile and nod. "Good for you."

Only fifty more minutes.
Just last for another fifty minutes, Ali.

The waitress arrives with my wine, and I practically snatch it out of her hand, taking a large gulp before setting it back down. She gives me an understanding smile and leaves.

"I just sold this place yesterday for a couple mil. The commission on that is pretty sweet."

I smile and nod as I take another drink. I wonder if he thinks that I actually give a damn about how much money he makes. I literally couldn't care less and not just because I get the very strong feeling that he's a raging douchebag. He leans closer, resting his elbows on the table like he's going to tell me a secret, and winks.

"You like that? Depending on how well tonight goes, maybe we can go do a little shopping tomorrow and get you something sparkly."

I would like to say that I'm shocked but in the ten minutes I've been here, I've gotten a pretty good read on this guy, and I'm not sure that he could say much that would surprise me. I'm also fairly convinced that he thinks he's getting laid tonight. Yeah, that's not fucking happening.

"I don't really wear jewelry," I say, downing more wine, and wishing I could just get the bottle.

"Some new clothes then," he adds, looking down my body again. "Something sexy to wear when you're not at work."

"No, thank you," I grit out, losing my patience with all this.

"Don't be like that, Baby. Just trying to do something nice for you. Then again, I suppose you don't really care about the money, do you?"

Oh, shit, maybe he does have a brain cell. I'm about to respond to him when he holds his hand up and keeps going.

"I mean, of course you'll quit once you get married."

I take another sip of wine, torn between chugging the thing and making it last. "Why would you think that?"

"Because that's your job. Once you get married, it's all about taking care of him and giving him babies. You know, carrying on the family name."

I stare at him for a long moment, in total shock. I think my mouth is hanging open but I couldn't really tell you for sure because my body is numb. Did he…just call me a breeding machine? Because I'm fairly certain that's essentially what just came out of his mouth.

"Excuse me?"

"Sweetheart, you can get mad at me all you want but we both know it's the truth. Your purpose is to have kids. Honestly, with a body like that," he says, letting his eyes fall to my chest, "I don't know how you haven't been scooped up yet."

Yep, he called me a breeding machine.

"I see, so my main purpose in life is to be bred," I ask, my chest heaving in anger.

"Well, and raise them, of course. I know a lot of chicks get mad at me for this but it's the way it should be. The man goes to work and makes the money, and it's the woman's job to take care of the house and the kids. I guess I'm just an old fashioned kind of guy."

Or a dick.

I take another swig of my wine, so close to just chugging the rest of it but I have a feeling I'm going to want that last little bit because I don't think he's done.

"I don't know why love even has to be in the picture for you women. Just find someone who makes your cunt drip and do your part for the human race, ya know?"

Ah, there it is.

I take the last swig of wine and stand up, grabbing my bag. "Will you excuse me, please? I need to use the restroom."

He grins and nods. "Sure, Sweetheart."

I hustle into the bathroom and roll my eyes at the couch nicer than the one I have in my living room, pushed up against the wall. I sink down and pull my phone out, dialing Izzy's number.

"Hey, chick, what's up?" she asks.

"I'm on a date, and it's awful, Iz."

"Oh, do you need me to get you out of there again?" she asks, her voice brighter, and I shake my head.

"No, I'm in the bathroom right now. But, seriously, what do I do?"

"What did he do that's got you hiding in the bathroom?"

"Oh my god, he called me a breeding machine and straight up said that I'd quit my job when I got married so I could start popping out kids."

"Jesus Christ," she swears into the phone and then is silent for a moment. "Just get out of there, Ali. Like, right now."

"I can't do that. It's so rude, and I won't get the job."

"What the hell kind of job are you trying to get with this asshole?" she yells, and I pull the phone away from my ear for a moment.

"It's not with him, Iz. It's with the paper."

"What are you talking about?"

I sigh and go over to the door, peeking out to make sure he's not coming to check on me. "It's complicated."

She's quiet again for a moment, and then she sighs. "All right, just get out of there. Sneak out the back or something but just get out. Then tomorrow,

Carly and I are coming over and you're telling us everything, understand?"

"Yes, okay."

"I'm serious, Ali. No brushing over details. You tell us everything."

"Okay, I promise."

"Good, now run the hell away from this guy, and call me when you're home so I know that you're safe."

We hang up and I step out of the bathroom, still not sure if I can just leave. I want this job so damn bad, and I don't know what will happen if I bail out on a date this early. Will they still count it?

"Excuse me?" a pretty young woman asks from behind the bar.

"Yes?"

"Are you here with Mr. Lucas?"

"Yes, I am."

She nervously shifts her gaze, and my stomach rolls. "I just thought you should know that when I brought him another drink, he tried to get my number. I don't know if you're his girlfriend but I wanted to tell you that I'm not interested at all."

And just like that, my decision is made. The bartender shifts again in front of me, looking terrified. I feel bad for her and put my hand on her arm to calm her down a little. She looks young, in college maybe, and I'm sure this situation is really awkward for her. "We're on our first date and thank you so much for telling me. Do you think you could do me a favor?"

She nods, looking relieved. "Anything."

"Can you distract him so I can slip out of here unnoticed?"

"Absolutely. I'll take him another drink and flirt a little bit," she says, grabbing a glass, and filling it with whatever he's drinking.

"Thank you. And just a little word of advice, avoid that man like the plague."

She gives me a mock salute and balances the tray with his drink in her hand. "Will do. Have a good night."

I watch her go, and then make a beeline for the front door, handing the valet my slip as soon as I make it down the steps. As I wait for them to bring my car around, I continually glance over my shoulder, hoping that Blake doesn't come looking for me before the car gets here. When it finally pulls up and I'm still alone, I breathe a sigh of relief and say a mental thanks to that bartender. I drive away from the restaurant, worry knotting my stomach as I wonder if I've done enough to get this job or if I'm going to lose my dream because of Blake Lucas.

* * * *

I've got to be honest with you all, it's been awhile since I dated. And while I'd love to sit here and tell you that I met my soul mate and we're getting married next week, that's not what happened. This week did however make me think to try again, and I guess I can be thankful for that. But just not like this. After going through the process of online dating, I'm not sure how anyone meets a special someone online. It seems so exhausting. Most of all, you can't force these things. I am a big believer in fate, and when it's time for you to meet the person you're supposed to be with, it will happen. You shouldn't have to clench your teeth to get through dinner, and you certainly don't want to spend the entire evening looking for one redeemable quality in your date because you're so lonely that your whole body aches. Hold out. Love will find you when the time is right and then suddenly all of this will make sense. At least, I hope it will.

Tapping my pen against the table, I read through my article three more times before sighing. I start chewing on the cap and wonder if I should really send this in. I went through and documented my three dates in excruciating detail before ending it with my little message of hope, and I know that Mr. Klein is going to hate it. When he assigned this, he wanted something sexy and fun. If I send this in, I'm basically handing this job to Chelsea. But, on the other hand, I don't know that I could stomach lying and acting like this past week was a fun time for me. And what good would it do my readers if I lied?

After all three dates, I just feel like I'm done. I'm done with letting these guys walk all over me. From Mr. Klein to each of the dates, I've been sufficiently trampled by men, and I'm so goddamn sick of it. I'm mad at myself for even agreeing to this. That day in his office, I should have told Mr. Klein exactly where to shove it when he suggested this. Everyone in the office knows that promotion should be mine, and yet, I was subjected to this little "test." What will I do, though? If I send this in, tell my boss to shove it, and get fired, how will I support myself?

The doorbell rings, and I glance down the hallway toward the front door, remembering that Izzy and Carly are coming over as I toss my pen down and stand up. Taking one last look at my article, I sigh and close my computer, pushing it away from where I was sitting before going to the door, and flinging it open. I do my best to plaster a fake smile on my face but the moment Izzy sees me, her eyes narrow and she shakes her head.

"I don't think so, sister. That fake ass smile isn't convincing anyone," she says, and despite my sour mood, I can't help but laugh. She knows me so damn well, and she has absolutely no filter. If it pops into her head, it comes out of her mouth, and it's one of the reasons I love her so much. You never have to guess where you stand with Iz. If she's pissed, you'll know.

"Where's the wine?" she asks, shoving past me.

"Kitchen," I call over my shoulder. She's already halfway down the hallway, and I just shake my head and laugh again. Carly steps up and wraps me up in a hug. I feel a little of my stress melt away as she gives me a squeeze and releases me.

"I heard all about the article, Hon. It's absolute bullshit. Chelsea's boasting all over the office that she's got this in the bag, and I wanted to stab her with my heel."

I throw my head back and laugh, imagining Carly taking off her favorite four-inch black heels and digging them into Chelsea's arm. I met Carly Mills when she started working at the paper shortly after I did, and we became friends instantly. She's more mellow than Izzy, and I feel like she brings a balance to our group. "Well, that would make this whole thing a whole lot better."

"Ladies!" Izzy yells from my kitchen, and Carly and I both turn to look at her. "If you don't get in here, this bottle is going to be gone."

I chuckle as I shut the door and turn to Carly. "What's her deal tonight?"

"She's irritated that she doesn't know what's going on with you. And she was kind of excited that she thought you were starting to date again."

I just roll my eyes as we walk into the kitchen. Izzy's sitting at my kitchen table with a big smile on her face and full wine glasses in front of three chairs.

"You're impatient," I tell her, and she nods, sliding my glass closer to me as I sit down.

"Yes, I am. Now, drink and spill."

I eye the glass warily and look up at her again. "You didn't slip truth serum in here or something, did you?"

Her eyes light up, and I start laughing. "No, but do you know where I can get some?"

"No."

She pouts a little and scoots the glass a little closer. "Too bad."

My gaze flicks to Carly who just shakes her head with a smile on her face as she brings the glass to her lips and takes a sip. Sighing, I do the same and look back to Izzy.

"Come on, lady. I've been waiting for days!"

"You need a Xanax," I say, getting a little bit of pleasure from making her wait a little longer. Her eyes practically bug out of her head, and she looks like she's about to explode.

"Alison Marie James! Now." Her voice leaves no room for argument so I sigh and launch into telling them about the article and the first date.

"Idiot," Izzy snorts when I tell them the part about the obstacle course.

I nod and continue telling them about the rest of the date, and when I finish, Izzy's mouth is hanging open.

"Oh, no, he didn't," she seethes, and I nod.

"Yeah, that was pretty much my reaction. Hence, why I called you."

Shaking her head, she takes a big sip of wine. "Sweetie, if that had been me, I would have been calling you for bail money."

I point at her and nod. "I just reminded myself that orange was not my color."

"What about date number two?" Carly asks, hope in her eyes that maybe it wasn't as bad.

"Ah, date number two was Zach," I say and begin to tell them about the dinner from hell. When I finish, they're both giving me looks of sympathy.

"Well, that's fucking awkward," Izzy says, taking a sip of her wine, and I laugh.

"Uh, yeah, you can say that again. I don't think I've ever eaten that fast in my life."

"I would ask if date three was better but since you called me from the bathroom, I'm gonna say no."

"Yeah, no," I reply and begin telling them all about Blake. When I'm done, both of their mouths are hanging open, and they're silent.

"Je-sus," Izzy draws out before finishing off her glass of wine.

"I honestly have no words," Carly says, staring dumbly at the table, and I nod. That was about how I felt last night after I snuck out of the restaurant and came home. It was like a nightmare, and I started to question if it really happened.

"Who even does shit like that on a date and where the hell did you find these guys? I mean, how short do you have to be on brain cells to call a woman a breeding machine? Just give me their names and I'll make their lives a living hell, I swear to god," Izzy rants, and I just shake my head, knowing she needs to get it out of her system.

"Honestly, it doesn't matter now. I need to decide if I'm gonna play Mr. Klein's game or tell him to go screw himself."

"Did you already write the article?" Carly asks, and I nod.

"Yeah, but I don't know if I'm gonna send it in."

"Let me see it."

I grab my computer and open it up, the Word document still pulled up on the screen as I slide it over to her. She leans in closer to the screen and starts reading.

"And you," Izzy says, pointing at me as she narrows her eyes. "What the hell were you thinking going out with three fucking strangers without telling anyone? What if one of them had cut you up and put you in their freezer? How would we have known?"

I know she's got a point but I just wanted to get the whole damn thing over with, and I knew if I talked to them about it, I would be even more negative on my dates.

"I was careful," I tell her. I never let any of them know where I lived and always met them somewhere. They don't even have my phone number. The only way they can contact me is through the dating website.

"Um... no, you were the exact opposite of careful. You didn't tell either of us about this. You could have disappeared without a trace and we would have had no way of knowing where to start looking for you."

"Does it matter now, Iz? It's done and over with. Look. Here I am, safe and sound, in one piece."

"You got lucky," she huffs, crossing her arms over her chest for a second before uncrossing them and pouring herself some more wine.

"I really like it, Ali," Carly says, pushing the computer away, and I smile. Whenever someone tells me they like what I wrote, I can't help but grin. "But you're right. Mr. Klein is not gonna be happy with it."

"I'm trying to decide if I even care anymore," I say as I bring my glass to my lips.

"I hear you, Hon, but what the hell are you gonna do if you leave the paper?"

"And that right there is why I haven't sent it in yet."

She sighs and looks back to the computer for a second. "You know what, you'll find something. And if you quit or he fires you, you'll get scooped up quick."

I set my glass down and spin the stem between my fingers, focusing on the reflection of the glass on the table. "You really think I should do this?"

"Do you want to write something else?" she asks, arching a brow, and I know she already knows the answer to that. Even if I tried, I don't think I could. I've never lied to my readers, and I'm not going to start now.

"No."

"Then what other choice do you have?"

Taking a deep breath, I push the glass away and pull my computer toward me. With shaky hands, I pull up my email and quickly send the article off to my boss. After I push send, I grab my glass of wine again and drain it.

"I'm proud of you, Ali," Carly says, and I smile at her. "It's disgusting that he even suggested this for the two of you. Even at her best, Chelsea isn't half the writer that you are, and she shouldn't even be in the running for the job."

"Yeah, but you know why she is, right?" I ask, making a motion with my hand and mouth that gets the message across. Carly nods, and they both start laughing.

"Man, if I realized that was all it took, I would have become a partner years ago," Izzy says, referring to her job as a paralegal at a law office downtown, and we all laugh again.

"Maybe I should just quit," I say, feeling a little bolder than I did moments ago.

"And do what?" Izzy asks.

"I don't know what I want to do, I just know that I don't want to do this anymore."

"If it's meant to be," Carly says, quoting the article I just sent in, and I smile as I roll my eyes.

"Yeah, yeah, I know."

Chapter Four
Storm

I fucking hate hospitals.

My boots squeak on the linoleum floor as I stare down the hallway and make my way to her room, doing my best to push back the deluge of memories frantically trying to take over my mind. After that night, I swore I would never be back here, but for her, I would do just about anything. Everything about this place haunts me, from the sound of monitors beeping and loved ones crying to the smell of antiseptic. Each little thing like a demon hiding in the shadows, laying in wait to reach out and pull me back into that night and everything I lost.

The memories start to overwhelm me, and I have to stop, leaning back against the wall, and closing my eyes as I try to pull air into my body. Flashes of images, like a horror movie, roll through my brain, and I lean over, squeezing my eyes shut tighter like that might make them stop as I fist my hands on my knees.

"Sir, are you okay?" someone asks, and I snap back up into a standing position. The only thing worse than losing my shit is someone watching me do it. The woman in blue scrubs standing behind the nurses' station offers me a reassuring smile, and I clear my throat.

"Can you tell me which room Emma West is in?" I ask, and she nods, looking down at her computer.

"Are you family?"

"Yes," I answer without hesitation.

She looks up and smiles at me, her gaze trailing down my body. "Room 116."

"Thanks."

The sign at the end of the hallway instructs me to go left, and I walk off without another word, ready to see Emma and the babies so I can get the fuck out of here. I love that girl but I don't want to spend more time than I have to in this place. Once I find her room, I pause, taking a deep breath to push all my shit back down before I walk in there to see her. Emma's got eyes like a hawk, and if I go in there even a little bit upset, she'll fucking know it.

When I feel in control, I push the door open and close it quietly behind me. Emma's in the bed with a little bundle in each arm, and when I walk in, she looks up and grins at me. Nix is passed out in the chair next to her bed, his arms crossed over his chest, and his legs kicked out in front of him. I grimace at the awkward angle his neck is bent in, glad that I'm not him. That's gonna be one hell of a headache when he wakes up.

"Hey, stranger," Emma whispers and beams at me, happiness just rolling off of her in waves. My chest aches as I remember a time in my life when I knew what it was like to be that happy but I smile through it as I shove those feelings back down. I'm so used to this routine. Feel and shove it back down again and again. Over and over until maybe one day, it won't hurt so fucking bad just to be alive.

"Hey, sis. How you doing?" I never thought when I met this girl nine months ago that she'd become so important to me but she wormed her way into my heart without even trying. Hell, every single guy in the club is putty in her tiny little hands. Here we are, big bad bikers who take on assholes every day of the week without blinking an eye, and she's like the little sister we never realized we wanted. She asks for anything and we all jump to give it to her.

"We're good," she answers me, glancing down at the babies sleeping in her arms. "You wanna stay with me for a while so Nix can go get some food?"

"Absolutely."

"I'm fine," Nix grumbles from the chair, not even bothering to open his eyes, and I chuckle.

"Phoenix West, you haven't eaten in over twenty-four hours, and I can hear your stomach growling from here."

"You can not," he snorts and peeks open one eye to look up at her. She grins at him, and the love they have for each other is so obvious you would have to be blind to miss it.

"Go get some food," she says and looks to the door, but he just shakes his head.

"You haven't eaten either. I'll be fine."

"Well, will you go get me some food? And while you're there, get some for yourself."

He opens his eyes and sighs.

"Please?" she asks, adding in a little pout, and I hold back my laughter, knowing that he doesn't stand a chance. He sighs again and stands, leaning over her bed to kiss her forehead before looking down at his kids, and kissing her again.

"I love you. Be right back."

She nods. "Love you, Baby."

When he passes me, I hear his stomach growl loudly, and I start laughing. He would have starved himself to death if she hadn't made him leave. I move to the side of her bed and sink down into the chair that Nix just vacated as he steps out of the room and closes the door behind him. Looking up at her, I can't help but smile. She's fucking glowing.

"You look happy, little mama."

"I am," she says, her green eyes smiling down at me as she pulls her gaze away from the babies resting in her arms. "It's so crazy, though. It was only a year ago that I was scared to death of everything. When I looked in the mirror, I didn't recognize the person staring back at me and now look at me. I'm a wife and a mom, and I can't remember a time in my life when I was happier than I am right now. Life changes so fast and if you blink, you could miss it."

I nod, trying my best to swallow past the thump in my throat. She doesn't need to tell me that. I know all too well just how quickly life can throw you a curveball and fuck everything up. I shove it all back down again, disgusted with just how good I am at it.

"I'm just so thankful," she says, oblivious to my inner torture. "If it wasn't for Nix, you, and all the other guys, I wouldn't be here right now. You saved my life, Storm, and you saved my babies. I'll never be able to repay you for that."

"You don't got to repay me for anything, Darlin'." When I joined the club, Blaze, our president, and his son, Nix, hadn't spoken in years but after Blaze got shot, he knew he wanted to make changes in his life. He turned the club in a new direction and tried to reconcile with Nix but it wasn't easy. For a long time, their relationship was strained but Emma brought them together. When Nix came to Blaze for help, they bonded, and from the moment that I saw Nix and Emma together, I knew she was the one for him. I'd never seen him like he was with her, and in an instant, she became family to all of us.

"There isn't anything on this earth that me or any of those other guys wouldn't do for you and yours," I tell her. She smiles and shakes her head as a tear slips down her cheek.

"Damn hormones," she chuckles, looking down at the babies in her hands as she tries to wipe her cheek with her shoulder and misses completely.

Smiling, I stand from the chair and wipe her cheek with the back of my fingers, and she laughs again. "You gonna let me hold one of these kids?" I ask, motioning to the two little boys in her arms. She nods as the tears dry up.

"Which one do you want?"

"Shit, it don't matter," I laugh, reaching for the one farther away from me. They look so damn tiny, and I don't want to try and maneuver them too much.

"That's Grady," she says as I position him in the crook of my arm and sit back down in the chair. God, he looks so much like Nix that if Emma wasn't lyin' in a hospital bed, I would question if he was hers. Another memory nags at me, and this one is harder to shove back down. There was a time in my life when I looked forward to all this - marriage, kids, a family of my own.

"They look just like Nix, don't they?" she asks, and I look up, grateful for the distraction.

"They sure do. I was about to ask if you were sure they were yours."

She throws her head back and laughs. "Well, if the pain I'm feeling is any indication, I'm gonna say yes."

I nod and look back down at the baby in my arms, my chest tightening again. I imagined this moment so many times. Not with someone else's kid but with my own. I had a whole life planned out before it was ripped away from me.

"You ever think about having one of your own?" Emma asks softly, and I clear my throat, struggling to hold it together.

"Naw, not really in the cards for me."

I glance up at her, and she's staring at me, her head cocked to the side as she studies me. It makes me uncomfortable.

"I think you'd be an amazing dad."

"Yeah, am I just gonna conjure one out of thin air? I'm only one part of this equation," I say, trying to joke with her even though I'm right on the verge of losing my shit. Images of *her* flash through my head – my girl – but she's gone, and it's my fault. Because of my endless arrogance, I lost her forever.

"You'll find someone, Storm. You're too good of a guy to spend your life alone."

"Whatever you say, Em," I choke out. Thankfully, she doesn't say anything else, and I close my eyes, desperately grasping at my self-control. The pain in my chest intensifies, and I know I've got to get out of here. Just as I stand from my chair to hand Grady back to Emma, Nix walks in with a tray of food in his hand.

"You're in luck, Sweetheart," he says, setting the food down on the table, and Emma sniffs the air, her stomach growling.

"Is that bacon?"

"Bacon mac and cheese. The nurse was just bringing food for us, and I ran into her in the hall."

"Gimmie," she demands, and we both laugh as Nix takes Grady from my arms and transfers him to his little bed next to Emma's before doing the same with Corbin. I start to back away toward the door.

"I've got to get going but ya'll just let me know if you need anything, ya hear?"

Emma smiles softly, almost like she can see that I'm losing it but I know that's impossible. "We will. Tell everyone else we said hi?"

"You got it, little mama."

They say good-bye, and I duck out of the room, my breathing harsh as I stomp down the halls, needing to get out of this place before I suffocate. The last time I was here…

Shaking my head, I push that thought down and burst out of the double doors into the Louisiana sunshine. I walk to my bike and jump on, firing it up. The rumble of the engine drowns out some of my thoughts, and I'm able to breathe for the first time since I looked down at that little baby's face.

Pulling out of the parking lot, I let the road take away everything – all the pain, all the memories, and everything that pulls me down into the darkness where I now reside. It's not going to do me any fucking good to dwell on that shit so I just need to rebury it and move on. By the time I reach my house in Baton Rouge, I'm back to normal. Or as normal as I get, anyway.

Stomping up my front steps, I head for the door, and stop short when I see the plain white envelope leaning up against it. I glance around the neighborhood, my instincts telling me that something is up, but I don't see anything out of the ordinary. I reach down and grab it, ripping it open, and pulling out the contents. There is a three-inch thick stack of photos of me, doing everyday shit – washing my bike, hanging out at a bar with Kodiak, and driving one of the women we rescued to safety.

I flip through some more photos, getting angrier with each new photo. Someone has been following me for a while, and it pisses me the fuck off that I don't know why. This is so fucking bad. If any of the husbands or boyfriends we rescue these girls from ever found out where they are, they would be in grave danger.

Hopelessly Devoted

Stuffing the photos back into the envelope, I run to my bike, and shove the photos in my back pocket before starting it up and backing out of the driveway. As I race over to the clubhouse, I try to figure out who the fuck would be following me. It could be totally random. Just one of those guys trying to find his girl and he just happened to pick me. Either way, we've got to put an end to it. We won't let any of these bastards get close to their girls again.

Images of the last girl we saved flash through my mind, and I shudder when I think about the fact that we almost didn't get there in time. He came home early and caught her packing up. We usually always come early, just in case, but there was a huge accident and we got stuck in traffic. By the time we reached her, her whole body was covered in bruises, and he had left her for dead. We drove her two counties over to an emergency room, and we've got guards on her at all times until we can get her out of the state, but she's got a helluva long road to recovery.

I'd love to just end any man that puts his hand on a woman but we mostly stay on the right side of the law now. I met Blaze when I was working at the motorcycle shop that the club owns and for a while, I never really thought about joining. But after the night that I lost everything, Blaze came to me and explained that he wanted to take things in a new direction, become more legitimate. At the time, I had nothing else to live for. In the years since, I've gotten a sense of purpose from the work we do and the women we save, and I couldn't imagine doing anything else. Til they lay me in the ground, I'll do whatever I can to make sure these bastards never touch a woman again. There's a special place in hell for men like them.

Pulling into the compound, I clear my head of all the shit that I've seen in the five years that I've been a member of this club and pull into a parking spot. Kodiak is sitting on one of the picnic tables, smoking, and I nod to him as I turn my bike off and swing my leg over. As I walk over to him, I pull the envelope out of my pocket.

"You seen Blaze?" I ask, and he nods.

"In his office," he says, motioning to the clubhouse behind me. His gaze drops to the envelope in my hand before looking back up at me and blowing out a stream of smoke. "What ya got there?"

I look down at the envelope and shake my head. "Nothing good, man."

Without another word, he tosses his cigarette on the ground and stomps on it before following me into the clubhouse. Kodiak and I usually work together when we transport a victim, and he's a solid dude, always down for whatever needs to be done, and I know he's got my back. We walk inside and music is blaring over the speakers. Chance and Smith are sitting at the bar bullshitting, and Moose and Fuzz are playing pool off in the corner. I nod a hello to Chance, and he nods his head at me. I met Chance when we were kids, and after I joined up, he wanted to join, too. I'm not sure that he really had any idea what he was getting into but we both found our place here in the club. I make my way through the club and reach Blaze's office door, knocking.

"Yeah?" he calls out, and I shove it open, striding into the room as Kodiak pushes it closed behind him.

"We got a problem, boss," I say, and he looks up from the papers in front of him and pulls his glasses off, setting them on the desk. He studies me for just a second, his gaze lingering on the envelope in my hand.

"What kind of problem?"

I toss the envelope in front of him, and it lands on his desk with a thump. His brow shoots up in question as he grabs it and pulls out the photos. He starts flipping through them faster and faster until he tosses them back on the desk.

"Shit. Where did you get these?"

"My front porch."

Kodiak grabs the photos and starts flipping through them before tossing them back down and shaking his head. "Dude," he says, drawing the word out. We all know just how bad this could be.

"You got any ideas?" Blaze asks, and I wish I could give him a good answer.

"Not a goddamn clue. And whoever it is, is fucking good because I haven't noticed anyone hanging around."

"Boyfriend or husband?" Kodiak asks, echoing my thoughts from earlier.

Blaze looks down at the photos again as he scrubs his hand across his face. "Naw, I don't think so. If it was, why the fuck would they let you know they were watching you? If this was just about finding their girl, they would have stayed in the shadows."

I nod, agreeing with him. "You got any idea who it is?"

"Not off the top of my fucking head," he growls, and I know this is bothering him. He takes the safety of these women seriously - even more so since Emma was in danger.

"We got some enemies from the old days that might be coming for blood," Kodiak says, and Blaze nods.

"Yeah, I know."

"What do you want me to do?" I ask.

"Let me have Streak look into it. Just watch your back and maybe you should cool it on the rescues. We can't risk the girls," he says, and even though I hate it, I have to agree with him.

"Yeah, I hear ya, boss."

"Good," he shoots back, standing, and walking over to me. He shakes my hand and slaps me on the back as we head for the door. "I gotta get going but I'll let everyone know what's goin' on at church later. It's time for me to meet my grandkids."

I smirk at the proud smile on his face and hope that we figure out who the hell this is and fast. As I head back out to my bike, I stop and look toward the stairs, wondering if I should just crash here for a little bit. If I'm not going to be going on runs, I'll be cooped up at the house and that'll drive me fucking crazy. Sighing, I run a hand through my hair and shake my head before jumping on my bike and heading back to the house that's more like a jail cell.

Hopelessly Devoted

Chapter Five
Alison

"Hey, you heard anything yet?" Roy, my co-worker, asks, peeking over the half wall that divides our desks. I sigh and shake my head, tossing my pen down on the desk. I haven't been able to focus all morning as I wait to hear if the job is mine.

"No, not yet."

He lets out a heavy sigh, rolling his hazel eyes as he shakes his head. "Listen, everyone here knows that you should get that job, and we're all pulling for you. I have no idea what Klein is thinking with Chelsea."

"Oh, I think you know what he's thinking," I reply, shooting him a look, and he laughs.

"They really should be more discreet, shouldn't they?"

Chelsea started off in the mailroom a little over a year ago but she caught Mr. Klein's eye, and it wasn't long before she was moving up. Every single person in this office knows exactly what's going on when she goes in to "get her article approved." Not to mention that just last month, they weren't all that quiet in their activities.

I shrug. "He is the boss. What are any of us going to do about it?"

"I miss Mr. Carlyle. He never would have let this shit fly."

I nod in agreement. Mr. Carlyle was the one that originally hired me but he never had kids so when it came time to retire, he had no one to leave the paper to, and he had to sell. Since Mr. Klein took over two years ago, things have been steadily going downhill. Sadly, this paper is starting to resemble a sinking ship, and it may be time to jump.

"Honestly, I have a feeling that today might be my last."

"Honey, Carly showed me your article, and I don't blame you. Being pit against Chelsea, who doesn't know the difference between their, they're, and there, would have been enough but then to have to go on those dates? I'm surprised you're still sitting here."

Just as I'm about to agree with him, Mr. Klein pokes his head around the corner and motions me over. Sucking in a nervous breath, I stand and smooth my hands down my skirt. "Well, looks like it's time," I say to Roy, and he looks over at our boss before turning back to me and giving me a thumbs up.

"Good luck."

I scoff because he and I both know luck has nothing to do with it. Hell, every person in this office right now knows that I'm probably not getting this job. It feels a bit like I'm walking to the gallows as I make my way over to Mr. Klein and follow him to his office. People whisper or flash me encouraging smiles as I walk down the hallway, and something clicks into place inside me. No matter what happens with the job, I won't be working here anymore. One part of me is terrified but the other can't figure out what took me so long to do this. I haven't been happy here, and I'm so tired of not being happy.

Mr. Klein goes into his office first with me trailing behind him, and when he sits down behind his giant desk, he motions for me to sit in the one empty chair across from him. Chelsea looks up at me from the other chair, a smug smile on her face as she crosses her legs demurely and places her hands in her lap. It's hard to hold in my laughter at the sight of her trying to look proper when she's probably spent more time on her knees in this office than in a chair. I sink down in my chair and look to Mr. Klein, eager to get this over with.

"Well," Mr. Klein says, smiling widely as he runs a small comb through his salt and pepper hair, brushing it off to the side, "I first want to thank the both of you for all your hard work."

I bite my lip, dropping my gaze to my lap as I try to remain professional, but in my head, I'm like a teenage boy, twisting everything he says into sexual innuendos aimed at Chelsea. It's freeing, in a way, knowing that I'm done with this place.

"Both of your articles were excellent, and you certainly made the decision difficult for me," he continues, and I mentally shake off my inappropriateness. I'm only going to be employed here for a few more moments, the least I could do is act like a twenty-seven year old college-educated woman.

"Thank you, sir," Chelsea practically purrs, and I force a smile to my face as I nod in agreement. He leans back in his chair, folding his hands across his large stomach, the buttons of his vest straining and I worry that one's going to burst and take my eye out.

"With that said, I must say congratulations to Chelsea! Your article was exactly what I was looking for."

I can't hold back the laughter anymore, and both of them turn to look at me with puzzled expressions.

"Oh, I bet it was. Tell me, Chelsea, how do you read an article to someone with a dick in your mouth? You've really got to teach me that so I can snag the next promotion."

She gasps in shock, which only makes me laugh harder, and I look to Mr. Klein, whose face is bright red with anger.

"What the hell is wrong with you?" he seethes, glaring at me from behind his desk, his fat cheeks resembling tomatoes. I stand and cross my arms over my chest, and his gaze falls to my tits, his tongue poking out, and I consider ramming my heel into his eye.

"Me? Absolutely nothing. I'm just done with this bullshit. I'll go pack up my things."

He stands, arrogance rolling off him as he places his hands on the desk and leans forward, looking at me in disdain. "Miss James, that's enough. This is quite dramatic for just losing out on a promotion."

"You're absolutely right. If it was any other situation, this would be dramatic, but you and every other person in this office knows that I should have never been up against her. I'm the more talented writer, and the only reason I'm not a columnist right now is because she's the one sucking your cock."

He just stares at me in shock for a moment before pointing to the door and shouting, "Out."

"Oh, gladly," I shoot back, adrenaline racing through my veins as I spin to stomp out the door.

"You're fired, Alison, and you'll never work in this town again."

Stopping, I slowly turn back to him, hatred in my gaze as I glare at him. Anger is replacing the humor I found in this situation just moments ago, and all the frustration I've been feeling for the past year is about to come pouring out of me. "First off, you can't fire someone who just quit, and secondly, you're giving yourself far too much credit if you think that you have anywhere near that kind of influence. Mr. Carlyle did but you've taken what he spent his life building and run it into the ground because you're thinking with the wrong head."

I let my gaze fall to his crotch to make my point, and without another word, I turn and march out of his office with my head held high. Goddamn, it felt good to finally say all that to him. When I walk into the bullpen, Roy stands up and rushes over to me.

"That. Was. Epic," he says, grabbing my shoulders, and I laugh at his excitement, glancing around at the smiles in the room.

"You guys heard all that?"

"Well, his secretary may have 'accidentally' turned the intercom on, and we may have 'accidentally' heard every single word. And can I just say…" He trails off as he drops to his knees and fans the floor like I'm the Queen of England, and I laugh.

"Miss James," Mr. Klein barks out, and everyone turns to look at him, "you have five minutes to gather your things before security escorts you out."

I roll my eyes as I turn back to Roy and shrug. "Party's over."

I go to my desk and find a box already waiting for me. When I look up, Roy flashes me a smile, and I mouth a thank you to him. I peek around the room looking for Carly but don't see her anywhere. She had to do some research for her next article today, and she must not be back yet. Quickly packing up all my stuff, I start to feel a little sad that I won't get to work with these people anymore but when Mr. Klein huffs from the entrance to the bullpen, checking his watch in annoyance, that feeling goes away.

When my stuff is all packed, I grab my box and toss my purse inside before walking over to Roy, who kisses my cheek and wishes me luck. Just as I reach Mr. Klein, Kevin, the officer who runs the front desk, comes up behind him. He glances over his shoulder and snaps his fingers at him before pointing to me.

What a dick.

"Hey, Kevin. How's your little girl doing? She still in a cast?" I ask, ignoring Mr. Klein and his lack of manners. Kevin has always been so nice to me, and I like to stop and chat with him whenever I get a chance.

His daughter is in dance class and broke her leg about a month ago so I've been asking about her periodically.

Kevin smiles and nods. "Yeah, for a couple more weeks. She's already running all over the place though."

"I bet," I laugh.

"This is not a social visit. Escort Miss James out of the building now," Mr. Klein snaps, and Kevin starts to shoot a glare in his direction but I shake my head before I take off for the entrance. Kevin follows behind me, and I'm glad. There's no reason that he needs to lose his job today, too.

"You all right, Miss Ali?" Kevin asks when we're far enough away from Mr. Klein. I smile over at him and nod.

"Yeah, I'm good. This was my choice."

He nods. "Do you want help out to your car?"

"Oh, no. I don't want to get you in trouble. I can manage. Thank you, though."

"Anytime. I'll miss you around here."

"I'll miss you, too. If you ever need anything, don't hesitate to give me a call, okay?"

He nods before we say a quick good-bye, and I step out into the late morning sunshine, wondering what I should do now. I decide to head to my car and call Carly to fill her in on everything that happened. Once I deposit my box in the trunk, I slide into my seat and dial her number.

"Hey, what's up?" she asks as soon as she answers the phone.

"Oh, a whole lot. Where are you?"

"I'm at the coffee shop across the street. I wasn't ready to go back to work yet."

I frown because I know exactly how she feels. It's the same way I've been feeling for months. This job that I loved wasn't so fun anymore with Mr. Klein running things. "I'll be there in a couple minutes."

We hang up, and I climb out of my car, locking up before walking across the street to our favorite little coffee shop to hide out in. As soon as I walk in, I spot Carly at a back table, and she waves me over. When I sit down, she slides a coffee in my direction.

"When you called me, I ordered your favorite."

"Thank you. I needed this."

"That doesn't sound good. Tell me everything."

I sigh before launching into the whole story, pausing quite often so she can get her laughter under control, and when I finish, she's gaping at me.

"He's fucking delusional," she says, and I nod. "The man runs a small newspaper in Baton Rouge, Louisiana, and he thinks he's Walter fucking Cronkite."

"I think getting sucked off by Chelsea is inflating his ego a little."

"I can't believe you said that to him."

I shrug. "It was about damn time someone said it. How long has she been on her knees for him? Since she started there? And then she magically gets all these promotions? I don't think so."

"You're my spirit animal," she says, taking a sip of her coffee, and I laugh.

"Well, thank you, I think."

"So, what are you going to do now?"

I shrug and look out the window. It's a fantastic question, and I wish I had an answer for her but I don't. "That street corner looks nice," I say, nodding to the corner of the coffee shop, and she laughs.

"Uh, no. You're not hooking. You're a talented writer, and you'll find something."

"I like your faith in me."

She offers me a sympathetic look and stands, grabbing her coffee. "Well, I've got to get back before I end up next to you on that corner. You want to walk with me?"

I shake my head and lean back in my seat. "No, I think I'm gonna hang out here for a little bit. I've got nowhere to be."

She smirks at my joke and nods. "Dinner tonight?"

"Sure, that sounds good. Bring over some Chinese."

"You got it."

I stand and hug her before sinking back down into my chair and sighing. What the hell am I going to do now? It would have been nice to have a little time to plan my future before I quit my job but I can't regret what happened today. I'm a little angry with myself that it took me so damn long to stand up to him. That's not me, and I hate that I let myself get in that situation. When Mr. Carlyle ran the paper, he looked out for me. He saw my talent and he wanted to nurture it and help me grow as a writer. And under his guidance, I did. A lot of the writer I am now, I owe to him. When Mr. Klein bought the paper, that all went to hell.

He didn't have the passion for the written word that Mr. Carlyle did, and I have to wonder why he bought it in the first place. It didn't take long for all of us to see that our little paper would never be the same once he took over. Sighing, I take a sip of my coffee and look out to the street, watching all the other people bustling past the coffee shop on their way to work or school. What the hell am I going to do?

"Excuse me?"

I startle, and my head whips in the direction of the voice. A gorgeous blonde about my age with piercing green eyes smiles at me, motioning to the chair across from me.

"Mind if I sit?"

"Uh, no," I reply, looking around at all the empty tables around us. I didn't think it was possible but she smiles even brighter and slides into the chair across from me before taking a sip of her own coffee.

"I'm Mercedes Richmond," she says, holding her hand out, and I shake it, wondering what the hell is going on.

"Alison James."

"Oh, I know who you are."

My brows shoot up, and I glance around the coffee shop again before looking back to her. "Excuse me?"

"I'm sorry. That sounded a little creepy. What I meant is that I've been reading your work for a while, and I'm a fan."

I relax slightly and smile. "Oh. Well, thank you."

"I'm sorry to be so intrusive but I couldn't help overhearing the conversation you were having with your friend."

Crap. How much did she hear? Me telling a story about how I chewed out my boss is not exactly my finest moment.

"Yeah, I'm sorry if that bothered you. I was just venting, and I might have gotten a little carried away."

She smiles and shakes her head. "Oh, no. You misunderstood me. I kind of loved it, and I want to offer you a job."

I'm so shocked that I just sit here with a stupid expression on my face, blinking at her for a few seconds before saying, "What?"

She keeps smiling, and I can't help but think that she's got the most perfect smile I've ever seen. Her clothes are all name brand, too, and I wonder just what kind of job she wants to offer me.

"I run a blog called Champagne Dreaming, and I've been looking to add an advice columnist to my team. Like I said, I've followed your work for a while, and I love your writing style. Then, I heard your story, and well, I just had to jump on the opportunity."

I'm speechless.

On the one hand, I can't believe my luck but on the other hand, I'm skeptical. I mean, who gets offered a job in a coffee shop literally twenty minutes after they quit their old one. Her name sounds vaguely familiar but I haven't heard of her blog.

"I'm sorry. I'm just a little surprised."

"Oh," she says, rolling her eyes, "of course you are. I just totally sprang this on you. Let me tell you a little bit about me."

"Okay."

"You may have heard of my father, Charles Richmond."

My eyes widen, and I nod. Her father is one of the wealthiest men in the Baton Rouge area, and there were even rumors that he was looking at buying the paper when Mr. Carlyle put it up for sale.

"You might have heard rumors that he was trying to buy the paper you worked at."

Is she in my head?

I nod again, and she smiles.

"Yeah, those were true. He was buying it for me. Unfortunately, Mr. Klein started playing dirty, and my father does not like to do business that way. You were one of the big reasons that I wanted that paper. When the deal fell through, he gave me money to start something of my own, and I've created one of the top lifestyle blogs in the country."

"Wow, I'm honestly not sure what to say." My brain feels jumbled with all this new information and everything that happened earlier. I can barely form a response as my mind races, trying to process it all.

"I understand. It's a lot to take in one day. Just tell me that you'll think about working with me. I really believe that adding you to the team and adding in the advice column will make Champagne Dreaming a household name."

"I've honestly never thought about writing an advice column." I've always been a reporter, and even though I wanted to do something different with my column, this never occurred to me.

"There was this article you wrote about a year ago about a robbery but instead of focusing on the facts of the case, you talked about the victim. You wrote about how hard he had worked to build his business and how devastated he was walking into the building with you and seeing his dream torn apart. I knew, at that moment, that you would be perfect for this position."

I nod, remembering the article she's talking about. It was right when I started to feel drained from being a crime reporter, and I wanted to give the article a personal feel. "Thank you."

"You're welcome," she says, honesty radiating off her. "Listen, I've got to get going but please think about my offer. Take a couple days to check out the blog and make sure it's the right fit for you. I really hope we get to work together. This is what I'm able to offer you as a salary but if there is anything else you need, please call me and we can discuss it. I'm serious about getting you on my team."

She writes a number down and then hands me a card, and I take it, looking it over for a second before looking back up at her. The number she wrote down is more than I've ever made at the paper, and it's tempting to say yes right now. She flashes a smile and holds her hand out as she stands. We say good-bye, and when she leaves, I sink back into my chair and sigh, wondering if this is the right move for me or if I'm going to be looking for a job tomorrow.

A.M. Myers

Hopelessly Devoted

Chapter Six
Alison

Pulling up in front of my house, I throw the car in park and lean back against the seat, closing my eyes as I let out a heavy breath. Today has been a crazy day, and I'm completely drained. It's only one in the afternoon but I'm dying for a big glass of wine and my bed. It's five o'clock somewhere, right? Not like it matters since I don't have to be anywhere anytime in the near future. When I marched out of Mr. Klein's office this morning, I was so damn sure of myself but as I sat in that coffee shop, watching the various people walk by, I realized that I've got nothing. I have no job, and I have no plan. I open my eyes and turn to grab my bag out of the passenger seat, the business card from Mercedes in the cup holder grabbing my attention.

I pick it up and read over it before lifting my gaze to the street in front of me. There is a part of me that's screaming to accept this job but I have reservations, and to be honest, I'm not really sure why. I think it's mostly to do with the fact that I was offered this job out of the blue so quickly after quitting. My dad is a firefighter, and my mom teaches second grade. They taught me from a young age that I would have to work for everything I got. When most kids were just filling out applications for summer jobs and hoping for the best, I was calling and checking in with employers each day to see if they'd read over my application yet. If I had an interview, I prepared for hours the day before, and once I got the job, I did whatever was asked of me. So it's a little unsettling that I literally didn't do a single thing to pursue this job. Or maybe I'm just reeling from everything that happened today. I didn't even have time to process the fact that I quit before I was considering another job. And then there's this tiny little voice that is kind of excited about this prospect but I can't decide which feeling I should trust.

    Climbing out of the car, I shut the door behind me, and grab my box of stuff out of the back before starting up the front walk, smiling when I look up at my little house. It's my first house, and I've put so much work into it to make it my own. There is a mix of old and new that represents both sides of me. I found the columns that line the front porch in a salvage yard downtown and fixed them up. The black metal porch railing was new and plays off the white columns perfectly. The sweeping brick stairs are original to the house, and I'm lucky that they were in such good condition when I bought the place. Now, with all the work done, this truly is my little sanctuary.

    I'm jerked from my thoughts by a little tinkling sound, and before I can turn around to investigate, something slams into my back. I fall forward, my knee hitting the pavement hard as the box flies up in the air, all the knick-knacks from my desk scattering across the lawn. I cry out in pain, rolling to my side and hugging my injured knee to my body. I try to breathe through the pain as tears sting my eyes. After a moment, I try to move it. My mouth opens again as the pain shoots up my leg but no sound comes out, and I wonder if I'm going to have to call an ambulance.

That's exactly what I need today.

Something cold and wet pushes against my cheek, and I open my eyes, blinking in surprise when I come face to face with an adorable chocolate Lab. We just stare at one another for a moment before I burst out laughing, and the dog cocks his head to the side. Of course I would get rugby tackled by a dog. Could this day get any more bizarre? I push myself up into a sitting position, wincing at the pain in my body. Besides the pain in my knee, my entire body is starting to ache like I was in a car accident. The dog lets out a little whine, and I pat his head. He leans into my touch, and I can't help but smile.

"Well, hello there, puppy. You didn't need to tackle me for some attention."

He licks my face, and I laugh again as I scratch behind his ears. He lets me love on him for a second, his whole body leaning into mine like he can't get enough, and his exuberance lifts my mood.

"You're just a sweetheart, aren't you?" I ask, and he tilts his head up, his eyes drifting closed. I stop petting him to inspect my knee, and I swear I hear him huff in annoyance.

"Spoiled little pup," I mutter as I look down at my leg and wince. Blood runs down the front of my shin, and there's a pretty good gash in my knee but the tights I'm wearing are obstructing my view so I won't know just how bad until I get inside.

"Bear," someone yells, and I look to the dog at my side as he cowers beside me.

"Is that you?" I ask, and he peeks up at me, looking sheepish.

"Bear!"

"Over here," I yell out, hoping that whoever it is can hear me as I peek down at him again, petting his head softly. "Did you run away from your owner, big guy?"

At my sweet tone, his tail wags again, and I laugh.

"Jesus Christ," the same voice exclaims, and I shake my head at Bear before glancing up. My jaw pops open as I'm immediately captivated by the epitome of every bad boy fantasy I've ever had, running across my lawn, his long strides eating away the distance between us. The white t-shirt and dark jeans he's wearing mold to his body perfectly, giving me the most delicious tease of the muscles underneath.

"Shit. I'm so sorry. I need to fix that damn fence. Are you okay?" he asks, stopping in front of me and running his hand through his dark hair. His gaze is focused on my knee but I'm devouring every little inch of him that I can see like a starving woman. I'm suddenly aware of exactly how long it's been since the last time I had sex, down to the very second. My body is aching with need as I shamelessly eye fuck this stranger in front of me. He crouches down in front of me, and my gaze is drawn to the short beard lining his strong jaw. My fingers twitch with the desire to reach up and run my fingers across the coarse hair. And I can't stop myself from imagining what it would feel like scraping against my skin.

"Are you okay?" he asks again but all I can do is nod as he flicks his gray gaze up to my face and swallows me up whole. His eyes are gorgeous but it's the haunting sadness that holds me captive and draws me to him. It piques my curiosity, and I want to delve deeper, losing myself in this beautiful stranger.

My heart pounds in my chest, and I briefly wonder if he can hear it. Does he know what he's doing to me with just a simple look? Tattoos snake down his arms, all the way to the fingers that are delicately tracing around the torn skin on my knee. His touch ignites something in me, warmth flushing through my body, and I fight to keep my eyes open, savoring it. It's been a really long time since I felt like that when someone touched me, and I'm not ready to give it up quite yet.

"I need you to say something," he adds.

"Why?"

His eyes roam over my face for a moment before a reluctant smirk stretches across his. "Because I need to be sure you don't have a concussion."

"I didn't hit my head," I tell him, shaking my head, and he nods, losing his fight as he smiles at me. From my bleeding knee to the intense sexual attraction coursing through my body, there is absolutely nothing amusing about this moment but his smile lights up his face, and suddenly I don't care about anything else.

"This looks really bad," he says, the smile falling away as he looks back down to my knee, and I follow his gaze, wincing. It's already swelling, and I'm not even all that sure I can get into the house myself.

"It doesn't hurt that bad."

He arches a brow in challenge because we both know I'm lying my ass off, and when I try to move my leg in a stubborn attempt to support my claim, I hiss in pain. Goddamn, that hurts. He glares over at Bear, who happily wags his tail as he lies next to me in the grass.

"Shit, I'm really sorry. He's still a puppy, and I don't have him fully trained yet."

Peeking over at the eager dog who is now rolling around in my grass on his back, I smile and look back to him, reaching out and placing my hand on his arm, compelled to touch him for a reason that I really can't explain. "It's really okay. It was just an accident."

His gaze snaps to my hand on his arm before he meets my eyes again, the light gray darkening slightly, almost like a brewing storm as he looks over my face. Anger flashes in his eyes before it's quickly replaced by surprise and curiosity, and I wonder if he feels this, too. We're silent, just both looking at each other on my front lawn as the world continues around us. He leans in, and my heart jumps in my chest, my mind short-circuiting with the possibility of his lips pressing against mine. Just before he's about to close the gap between us, a car horn sounds followed by a bark from Bear, and he jerks back.

He blinks and blows out a breath as he drops his gaze to the ground, shaking his head and effectively pulling me out of my daze. When he looks back up at me again, I feel so incredibly stupid because there is nothing in his eyes. Did I just imagine all of that? No, there's no way. I don't know if I've ever felt a spark like that when I looked at someone, so I couldn't be imagining it, could I?

He looks up at my house before turning back to me. "You got a first aid kit in there?"

I nod, and he looks around at my stuff scattered all over the lawn. He stands, his hand falling away from my knee, and my entire body aches to reach out for him. I want him to touch me again. I can still feel his fingers on my skin, almost like he branded me. That couldn't have been fake, could it?

"Give me a second to get this stuff picked up, and then I'll help you inside."

"Oh, you don't have to do that," I say, wishing I could just go sit in my house and think for a couple of minutes without whatever the hell this is clogging my brain. He smirks at me, and my heart skips a beat.

"Yeah? You able to get up on your own?"

Scowling, I hold my hands out for him to help me up, and he grabs them, pulling me off the ground effortlessly. I try to stand but as soon as I try to put any weight on my leg, I'm falling again. He reaches out, catching me in his arms, and easily lifting me up before I can hurt myself further. He doesn't look away from me as he carries me over to the stairs and gently sets me at the top.

"Wait here and stop trying to be difficult."

Scoffing, I cross my arms over my chest and glare at him as he moves around my yard, picking up all the things from my desk. He's got a lot of nerve to call me freaking difficult after his dog just attacked me. Bear comes and lays down on the porch next to me, nudging me for more attention. I smirk and scratch behind his ears again, shaking my head.

"You moving or something?" he asks, stepping in front of me as he looks through my box.

"Or something."

His brow furrows as he meets my eyes again, and it's there this time. That undeniable spark that I felt the first time he looked at me. His brow arches in question, and I study him for a moment, feeling compelled to tell him the truth when normally I would just gloss over the details. With a heavy sigh, I give in. As I explain my shitty day to him, his eyes get wider and wider, and by the time I finish, he's shaking his head in disbelief.

"Shit."

"Yeah, it's been quite a day," I tell him before looking at the dog resting his head in my lap.

"Hell, now I feel even worse for Bear hurting you."

I look down and smile before shaking my head and looking at him. "Don't. It was just an accident. Like you said, he's still a puppy. Poor baby doesn't know any better yet."

He coughs out a laugh, and humor lights up his face, taking my breath away. Jesus, he's gorgeous when he smiles. "Oh, he knows better."

Silence falls over us once again but it's not uncomfortable, and I can't look away from the man in front of me. I feel this weird pull toward him that I just can't explain but I don't know a single thing about him.

"What's your name?" I blurt out, and one side of his mouth tips up.

"Why?"

"Because your dog mauled me, and you've already invited yourself inside my house. I think I should, at least, know your name."

"Storm," he says, and strangely, it fits.

"I'm Ali."

He nods and looks up at my front door, setting the box down on the porch next to me. "Let's get you inside and fix your knee."

When he scoops me up in his arms again, I wrap my arms around his neck and lean into him a little, unable to stop myself. He smells amazing, and I fight the urge to just take a deep breath. "You really don't have to do this," I tell him again, and he peeks over at me.

"You say that just to hear yourself talk, Darlin'? Cause you're not gonna convince me to just walk away and leave you bleeding. My mama raised me better than that."

"Well, thank you," I whisper, a blush creeping up my cheeks as he steps into my kitchen.

"What are you thanking me for? The dog attack or the aftercare?" Amusement lights up his gray eyes, and I'm totally enthralled as he holds me in his arms in the middle of my kitchen, both of us unable to look away from each other. What the hell is this? He seems to snap to his senses and sets me down on the counter before looking around.

"Where am I going to find that first aid kit?"

I point to the cupboard directly behind him. "Second shelf."

He grabs it and turns back to me, setting the kit on the counter next to me on one side before looking over at the sink on the other side. Without a word, he kneels in front of me and slips my shoe off my foot. I can't look away, curious and turned on as I wonder what the hell he's doing. He reaches into his pocket and pulls out a knife, flipping it open with ease, and I suck in a breath. If I were smart, I would be terrified right now. I would start screaming for help or kick my foot out and hope it catches him in the face so I can get away but he's rendered me completely fucking stupid.

No, instead I sit my ass on the counter and watch as he pulls my tights away from my leg and cuts them open all the way up, my skin sparking with the intense desire blanketing us. When he gets above my knee where the tights disappear under my skirt, I put my hand out to stop him, and he pulls the knife away.

"They're thigh highs," I mutter as I pull my skirt up slightly and pull the stocking off. I dangle it out in front of him but his gaze is glued to my bare leg. His tongue darts out, wetting his lips, and my eyes almost roll back in my head. Jesus, I think I could come just from watching him watch me. I clear my throat, and he looks up at me.

"Care to tell me why you murdered my tights?"

He smirks and stands, folding the knife, and tucking it back into his pocket as he points to the sink without answering my question. "Spin toward the sink and stick your leg in. I'll clean your wound."

"Okay," I say and do as he instructed, sticking my bare leg in the sink next to me, and folding the other one underneath me so it doesn't get wet.

"This is going to hurt a little bit," he warns, grabbing the sprayer, and turning the water on low. I nod.

"I'm okay."

He tests the water, making sure it's not too hot before he starts rinsing out the gash on my knee. It stings, and I suck in a breath before slowly blowing it out. As he cleans me up, he sends heated glances in my direction, sending my body into overdrive. Every little brush of his fingers is amplified, and when he finally turns off the water, my heart is pounding in my ears, and my breathing is choppy.

"Towels?" he asks, and I point to one of the drawers next to the sink, admiring the way the muscles in his shoulders bunch and flex as he leans down to grab one. After gently patting my knee dry, he tells me to turn back around so my legs are dangling off the counter. He pulls some gauze and tape out of the first aid kit, placing them on the counter next to me. Crouching down in front of me, he inspects my knee again. Gray eyes meet mine as he looks up at me and blows on my knee to make sure it's dry and goose bumps race across my skin. After a heated moment, he drops his gaze back to my knee.

"I don't think it needs stitches," he mutters, inspecting the wound now that it's clean, and I breathe a sigh of relief. The last thing I needed today was a hospital visit. "It's pretty swollen, though. You should stay off it for a couple days."

"I have crutches in that closet there." I point to the closet off the dining room, and he leaves me sitting on the counter to grab them. He gives them a nod of approval as he pulls them out and turns back to me.

"Why do you have crutches?"

"Broke my ankle a couple of years ago and just thought they'd be good to keep around."

He nods and comes back over to me, leaning down in front of me. He blows on my knee once more, and I'm convinced it's just to torture me as another shiver racks my body. He grabs the tape and starts tearing off pieces, laying them on the counter so he can grab them later. Grabbing some gauze off the counter, he presses it to my wound, making sure that the bleeding has stopped.

"Sorry," he mutters when I suck in a breath, and I nod, letting him know that I'm okay. He tosses the gauze aside and grabs another piece, applying first aid cream to one side, and my heart squeezes at the care he's showing me, a complete stranger. He lays the gauze over my knee and begins carefully taping it to my skin.

I'm enthralled as I watch him, unable to look away from his furrowed brow or the teeth sinking into his bottom lip as he works to get me all bandaged up. The thin scar running through his eyebrow is sexy as hell, and I'm dying to ask him how he got it. His little touches drive me crazy, and I can imagine him running one hand gently down my face while he lightly traces over my bottom lip with his thumb. Just picturing it in my head has me fighting back a moan. Finally, he stands and looks at me again, his gaze dark with the same desire that I feel coursing through my body with fervor. His tongue darts out, wetting his bottom lip, and all I can think about is leaning forward and kissing him.

"Let me have your phone," he says. It takes me a second to process what he said but when I do, I scowl at him.

"Huh?"

"Give me your phone." He doesn't give any explanation and yet, I hand over my phone without a second thought. He peeks up at me and smirks as I watch him type something in before he hands it back to me as his phone goes off in his pocket.

"My number is in there now. Call or text me if you need anything, okay?"

I slowly nod. "Um…okay."

"I'm serious. It's my fault that you're gonna be laid up for a few days so call me when you need absolutely anything. I live right next door so it's not a problem."

I nod, knowing damn well that I'm not going to do that. I'm perfectly capable of taking care of myself. Although, I can't say that I'm all that disappointed about having his number. How have I never noticed him before? Have I really been that closed off to the world? He takes a step toward me, and I suck in a quiet breath. He's so close now. I could just lean forward and press my lips against his. If I just wrapped my arms around his neck and pulled him into me, I could steal the kiss I've been daydreaming about for the last five minutes.

"Say it, Ali. Say you'll give me a call if you need anything." His voice is velvet smooth, and I feel a bit hypnotized as I stare up at him and nod.

"I'll call you if I need anything."

"Good," he whispers, leaning in instead of pulling away like I expected him to. Almost like he's having trouble fighting this, too. I know this is insane because I literally just met him but there's something about him that just gets to me. His eyes meet mine, and we freeze, his face hovering an inch above mine as his minty breath washes over me, and it's a struggle to keep my eyes open. I don't think I've ever wanted to kiss someone this badly in my entire life. I start to lean forward, and he follows suit, his lips barely brushing against mine as my body sparks to life from the simple touch.

"Ali!" Izzy's voice breaks through the sexual tension filling the room, and Storm pulls back sharply, like he's waking up from a dream, and just like before, his face shuts down. There is absolutely no emotion on his face when he looks up at me again, and it breaks my heart. No. I want the man that was just looking at me like I was his last supper back. I can't remember the last time I felt that desired in my entire life, and I hate that we were interrupted.

"Who in the name of sex are you?" Izzy asks after stepping into the kitchen, and I start laughing, unable to help myself as Storm's eyes widen. He drops his gaze to the floor and blows a breath out before running his hand through his hair and looking back up at me.

"I gotta go. You've got my number." Without waiting for a response, he stomps out of the room, and Bear follows behind him. The front door slams closed, and I look to Izzy, whose gaze is roaming all over the countertop. She walks over to me and picks up my shredded thigh high, holding it out in front of me.

"Oh, Lucy, you got some splainin' to do," she sings, and I start laughing again, falling back onto the counter with a sigh.

* * * *

"Food's here," Carly calls as she opens the front door and walks in. I wave at her from the couch, unable to get up with my bum knee. Before Izzy left, she made me tell her everything that happened with my neighbor and insisted that I elevate my knee. Carly's mouth pops open when she catches sight of my knee propped up on a couple pillows and the crutches leaning up against the couch next to me.

"Holy hell, your knee is the size of a softball!"

"Yeah, I know. I got mauled by the neighbor's Labrador."

She rushes over to the couch and throws the bag of food and her purse down on the coffee table before sitting next to me, trying to examine my knee.

"Shit, are you okay? We should call Izzy. Maybe she can get one of the lawyers in her office to sue the shit out of the guy."

"No, it was an accident. Bear's still a puppy, and he just wanted some attention. I'm sure I'll be fine in a couple of days."

She studies me for a second before smirking and reaching for the bag of food. "This wouldn't have anything to do with the man in your kitchen that Izzy described as 'hot as the devil himself', would it?"

I scoff, looking away, because truthfully, I haven't been able to stop thinking about Storm since he left my house earlier today. "No."

"Uh-huh," she hums, not buying an ounce of my shit. She hands me my box of food and a plastic fork before relaxing back into the couch with me.

"What are you looking at?" she asks, eyeing my computer screen.

"I got offered a job."

Her eyes widen for a second before a huge smile stretches across her face. "Seriously? When?"

"Literally two minutes after you left the coffee shop. She overheard us talking and offered me a position as an advice columnist."

"For what?" she asks around a bite of food.

"This blog called Champagne Dreaming. Mercedes is the daughter of Charles Richmond, and she runs it. I've been researching it all day." I start showing her stuff on the website as we eat, and by the time we're done, she's urging me to take the job.

"Seriously, you have to take it. It sounds amazing. Why wouldn't you?"

I shrug and look down at the computer screen. "I guess I've just never seen myself as an advice columnist."

"Listen, don't take this the wrong way, but I don't know that you've ever been classified as a reporter. Your articles always had this personal touch to them, and it's what makes you so good at your job. For what it's worth, I think you'd be amazing at this. Besides, didn't you say you want to do something new?"

I nod, thinking over everything she said. "What do you think about Mercedes?"

"Well, from what you've told me, I think she's kind of awesome. I mean, yeah, her dad gave her the money to start this business but she's turned it into something more. Look at this blog, it's incredible."

I know she's right about everything but I still feel hesitant. "Yeah, you're right."

Carly grabs my phone and shoves it into my hand. "Call her. Right now."

I sigh and look down at my phone before looking back up at my friend.

"Ali, I know it's scary to try something new, and I know you've always seen yourself as a reporter but maybe the universe has other plans for you. Besides, it's not like you're stuck here if you hate it. Just give it a try, it may be totally amazing."

I suck in a breath and dial Mercedes's number before I can talk myself out of it and put the phone to my ear. She answers quickly, and I smile, putting on my professional side.

"Hi, Mercedes. This is Alison James. I was just calling you about the job we talked about today."

"Oh my gosh, yes. Please tell me you decided to come work with me."

I look over at Carly, and an idea forms in my head, making me grin at her. She shoots me a confused look but I just grin wider. "I would love to work with you but I have one condition."

"Name it and it's yours."

"Do you have room on your staff for a friend of mine? Carly Mills, she's at the paper also."

Carly's mouth drops open, and she just stares at me, dumbfounded. She wants to get out of that place just as badly as I do, and if I can do that for her, I absolutely will.

"What does she write?"

"Mostly lifestyle pieces. She also did this big article about a year ago about corruption in the Port Allen Police Department."

"Holy shit, yes! I remember reading that. What was that girl's name? Emma something, right?"

"Yeah, Emma Harrington."

"That's right. That article was absolutely incredible, and we will make room for her."

"Perfect," I say, nodding at Carly as a smile curves my lips, and her eyes widen further.

"Why don't you both start on Monday?"

"That sounds great, Mercedes. Thank you so much." I quickly say good-bye, and when I hang up, Carly punches me in the arm.

"I can't believe you did that," she says, still looking shocked. "You could have lost the job trying to get me one."

I shake my head. "I have it on pretty good authority that she wanted me really bad, besides, don't act like you don't want to leave the paper, too. And now you can."

She finally smiles at me, shaking her head in disbelief. "Holy crap, I'm so excited. I'm gonna call Mr. Klein and tell him where to shove it."

I laugh as she jumps off the couch and marches off into the kitchen to quit her job. I'm happy that I could do this for her and even more happy that we'll still be working together. I take a sip of my wine and sigh. I guess here's to the universe stepping in and shaking up my world.

A.M. Myers

Chapter Seven
Storm

    I'm acting like a fucking chick. What kind of man stands at his kitchen window, desperate to get a glimpse of his insanely hot neighbor? And yet, here I am. My window looks directly into her living room and just behind that is her kitchen. My gaze keeps being pulled back to that spot where I bandaged her knee up today, remembering the way that I was drawn to her like she's a goddamn siren. No matter how much I tried to fight it, I was heading for disaster. The moment I looked at her, I wanted to bend her over the nearest surface and fuck her until I couldn't stand anymore, but it's more than that. I'm dying for just a flash of her face, just one second where I feel like I can breathe again. I want to drown in her blue eyes because it erases the pain that's constantly beating under my skin like a heartbeat.

    I shouldn't be doing this. A long time ago, I promised myself that I would never let anyone else get close to me. Resisting her is going to be a battle, and even after just meeting her a few hours ago, I fear it's a battle I'm going to lose. But I can't. It's better for everyone that I stay away from her. Even if her smile chases away demons that I thought would haunt me forever.

"Shit," I curse, pulling my phone out of my pocket and calling Streak, the club's tech guru. He's been with us for four years, and the guy can find anything about anyone.

"What's up, Brother?" he answers, and I only have a moment to remind myself that I shouldn't do this before I'm answering him.

"I need you to look into someone."

"Absolutely," he practically shouts into the phone, and I can hear the smile in his voice. He lives for this shit. "What do you know about 'em? And what do you want?"

"Her name is Ali, she's a reporter, and she lives next door to me. That's really all I know, and I want everything you can find."

The phone falls silent, and I pull it away to make sure he's still on the line. When I press it back to my ear, the only sound is the clicking of keys. "Is this, uh, personal?"

"Yeah."

"She important?" he asks, hesitantly.

"Just get me the information," I growl into the phone before hanging up on him. I swear to God, these fucking bikers gossip worse than old women but my life and my past have never been acceptable topics. Everyone knows that.

Hopelessly Devoted

Turning away from the window, I lean back on the counter and cross my arms over my chest, doing my best to resist the urge to go back over there. I could lie and say that I just wanted to check on her but the truth is, I need to see her. I just want this weight lifted off me, even if it is only temporary. I need to know if being around her makes the act of living a little easier to bear. It's so fucking selfish and fucked up, but I'm afraid that I'm already past the point of caring. My gaze lands on the nails in the wall where pictures once hung, and the pain is back in full force, throbbing throughout my entire body as I think about all the reasons why I'll never be truly happy again.

I don't need to go into the living room and pull the photos that used to adorn all the walls in this house out of boxes, because the face in them is already burned into my memory. I'll never forget. It will never get easier. This is my hell, and not even death will ease the torment – not like I deserve any better. I deserve every single ounce of pain that this world can dish onto my plate, and even when my life ends, it won't be enough. I took something so good and pure, so full of life and love, and in my own stupidity, I destroyed it. Maybe not directly, but through my inaction, I might as well have.

I wasn't always like this but after years in darkness, I adapted to survive. The only way to make it out of it at all was to twist and contort myself until I was just as bad as the thing that put me in there. To strip away pieces of my soul until I had nothing left. I feel nothing. Except the pain. After all this time, I am a monster and monsters belong in hell.

A girl like Ali deserves so much more than a man like me. I'm no good for anyone, especially her. But I don't know that I care. Or if I'm even able to stay away. She makes me feel something other than pain and misery for the first time in a long time, and I may already be addicted to that.

A car door slams outside, and I spin around, watching as an attractive woman walks up to Ali's house and goes inside. Sighing, I turn around and grab my phone off the counter, knowing that I won't go over there now. I quickly check the time and start heading for the door. I'm going to be late for church, and I'm sure Blaze will be pissed but I just couldn't walk away. Yanking open the front door, a large yellow envelope falls at my feet, and I look down, the hair on my neck raising as I slowly look up and scan the street in front of me. Everything looks normal, and I feel like I'm going a little crazy. I've been vigilant, watching for whoever has been following me but I never fucking see them.

Bear lets out a low growl behind me, sensing my unease and nudges against my leg as he peers out the door. I reach down and scoop up the envelope, slamming the door, and locking it before I grab the gun out of my waistband and set it on my dining room table. After sliding into the chair, I pull out the contents of the package and start flipping through this new batch of photos.

"Shit," I hiss when I get to the last ten or so. They are all of Ali today as I carried her up to her porch and helped her clean up her yard. What was this? Like, two hours ago…how the fuck did they get them so fast? The photos fall out of my hand, and I prop my elbows up on the table and rest my head against my fists, my knee bouncing under the table.

Fuck. What the hell was I thinking? It makes me so fucking uncomfortable to see the photos of her, knowing that I led whoever the fuck this is right to her. It may make me a shitty ass person but I should have just stayed away. She wouldn't even be on this person's radar if I had. Even thinking that though, makes it hard to breathe. I don't want to stay away from her. And then the guilt is back, reminding me of all the reasons that I should stay far, far away from her. It's like a war is raging inside me, each side pulling at me until I'm afraid that I'll tear right down the middle.

Another photo catches my eye underneath all the others, and I pull it out, my heart seizing in my chest. It's a photo of Ali petting Bear on the porch, and there's a note on this one. When I read it, I slam my fist down onto the table, my blood running cold.

She's almost as gorgeous as our girl.

Rage that I've kept buried so long bubbles out of me, and the face that I was trying so hard to forget is front and center in my mind. Pain hits me. A stab of white-hot agony smacks right in my chest, and it's just as potent as the day I lost everything. I lay my forehead on the table, closing my eyes as I try to just fucking breathe without a wave of pain rocking me, but the longer I sit, the angrier I get. My fist starts pounding against the table as I think about that piece of shit sending me this photo. He won. He doesn't get to taunt me with that fact for the rest of my life. Not like I need the reminder anyway. Each time I close my eyes, it's all I can fucking see.

I look up and focus on the photo again, rereading the words over and over, the anger building higher and higher until it feels like my body is going to come apart at the seams. Reaching under the table, I flip it and jump out of my chair, screaming out into the empty house in a desperate attempt to release this anger before it kills me. Photos flutter through the air as I march to the door and press my forehead to it as I pound my fist against the wood, screaming again in agony. The girl I love is gone, and it's all my fucking fault. This pain, the all consuming, eat away at your soul, rip me apart because it would feel better than this, anguish is all that I deserve. If I could go back in time and fix things, I would, but life is never that kind.

Spinning, I pick up a chair and throw it against the wall. Anything to release this anger because I feel like it's burning me alive, eating away at my insides. It shatters and knocks a box down off a shelf. Picture frames scatter across the hardwood floors, and I'm face to face with her once again. I fall to my knees and place my hand over my chest as I struggle to draw air into my lungs. Each breath stabbing my insides, and if I close my eyes, I can picture the day I met her perfectly in my head. Her smiling face taunts me, pulling me deeper into that darkness, and any light that Ali gave me today is gone. Once again, I'm at the bottom of the pit, and there is no escape.

Hopelessly Devoted

* * * *

Blaze:
Where the fuck are you?

Me:
On my way.

    I shove my phone back into my pocket and drop my head, unable to look at her face any longer. I have no idea how long I've been sitting here but I'm sure that I missed church and Blaze is pissed. I can't seem to give a shit right now though. Bear whines from his place next to me, and I run my hand through his fur. When Emma handed me this little ball of fur that she rescued from a shelter, I thought she was crazy, but now I've kind of gotten used to him. In fact, this house wouldn't be the same without his crazy antics.
    Sighing, I get up off the floor and quickly pick up all the frames, doing my best to avoid looking at them. I can't stand to look at her, and I can't stand to get rid of these photos either. My eyes close, and I breathe out slowly, shoving all this shit down where it belongs again as I return the box to the shelf. I'm the VP of this club, and all these guys count on me. I can't go losing my shit on them.
    When I feel under control again, I open my eyes and march over to the upturned table to find the photo. I

fold it and shove it into the pocket of my hoodie as I head outside and scan the street. I don't see anything out of place but I know he's got someone watching me somewhere. At least now we know the girls aren't in any danger. I jump on my bike and fire it up before backing out of the driveway, taking off down my street, loving the feeling of weightlessness as I ride to the clubhouse.

Everyone's bikes are still lined up outside when I pull up, and I wonder for a second why they all didn't bail out after church. Then again, there's a good chance most of them were already drunk before church. I park my bike and climb off, stomping up to the front door and flinging it open. That photo is burning a hole under my cut, and I know I gotta tell Blaze what's going on. Everyone is gathered around the bar, laughing, and they all freeze as I walk in. I give them a quick nod.

"Blaze is lookin' for you," Chance says, tilting his head to the side to indicate that he's in his office, and I nod.

"You all right, Storm?" Streak asks, and I nod again, starting off toward the office.

"Fucking peachy."

I stop in front of the office and knock on the door before opening it and stepping inside, shutting the door behind me. Blaze looks up from the papers in front of him and arches a brow.

"I know who's following me," I snap, tossing the photo down on his desk. He picks it up and reads over the message, a grim expression falling over his face. He lays the photo down and glances up at me.

"I guess I don't have to ask how you are."

"I'm great," I bite out, the anger building inside me again.

"Who's the girl?" he asks, pointing to the photo on his desk.

"My neighbor."

He studies me for a moment and reaches out for the glass of bourbon on his desk, taking a sip. "She important?"

I shrug. I don't know what the fuck she is. "No."

"You know, it's okay to move on with your life."

I scoff and look away from him. That'll never fucking happen.

"She's gone, and you torturing yourself isn't gonna do a single fucking thing to change that. She would hate that you're doing this to yourself."

I turn my gaze back to him, letting him see how dead serious I am when I say, "This conversation is over."

He sighs and nods, taking another sip of his bourbon as he stares down at the photo. "Why now?"

I just shrug, and he slams his glass back down on the desk. "Come the fuck on. You don't expect me to believe that, do you?"

"He may be out for revenge."

"Revenge for what?" he asks.

I shrug again, and he watches me for a second before his eyes widen and he stands up. "Jesus Christ. What the fuck did you do? I explicitly told you to leave him alone."

"I did what you and every other guy in this building would have done. Don't act like you wouldn't have either, Prez. I was never going to let him get away with what he did."

He shakes his head and leans forward, planting his hands on the desk in front of him. He may not like it but he knows I'm right. When Emma was in trouble last year, there isn't a thing Blaze wouldn't have done to protect her.

"You had any other communication with him?"

"Nope. I was kind of hoping he was dead."

He stands and nods, pointing to the door behind me. "Time for church. I'll deal with you later. I'm putting you back on runs but don't go doing anything until we figure this shit out."

"Not likely," I mutter to myself, too quiet for him to hear before I spin and march out of the office, ignoring everyone else as I head into the room where we have church and sit in my chair, directly to the left of Blaze's seat at the head of the table. Everyone else files in, casting questioning glances in my direction but I ignore them, wanting to get out of here. Chance walks in and arches a brow in question as he looks at me, and I just shake my head. Everyone in this room knows the shit I went through and would sympathize but I can't talk about it right now. It's still too fucking raw.

"Sit down," Blaze barks, marching into the room and taking his spot at the table. We all settle into our chairs, and he looks down at the papers in front of him for a moment. "All right, we got three jobs this week. All transfers but don't go thinkin' that it's gonna be easy. I don't need to remind you about the last one."

He looks around the table to each of us, and a few guys drop their gaze and shake their heads. I'm not sure I'll ever get the sight of that poor woman passed out on the floor out of my mind, but she's safe now and that's all that matters.

"First up, we have Jenny. She first came to us about a month ago but backed out. Her old man is a lawyer so no doubt he's got the resources to have eyes on her at all times, but as of now, we don't know if he does or not. He may have gotten comfortable and thinks she'll never leave. Let's hope for that. We got a burner phone to her, and she's gonna send us a text on the day when she's ready to go so ya'll need to be ready to go at any point Tuesday."

Blaze looks up, and everyone nods in agreement.

"Is it just her, Prez?" Smith, our sergeant at arms, asks, and Blaze nods.

"Yeah, but she just found out she's pregnant so use extreme caution."

"Understood," he replies. He doesn't have to break down how dangerous this situation is for her. If her man got tipped off somehow and went after her, it wouldn't just be her life in danger.

"Good. Wednesday at noon, we got Laura and her two kids. You'll grab Laura at the house and take her to the school to get her kids. Her husband is heading out of town on a business trip the day before so you shouldn't have any issues but as always, keep your eyes open. And tomorrow, we got Sheila and her daughter, Kaley. The husband isn't hitting Sheila but the daughter's doctor noticed signs of sexual assault, and she put a camera in her room. The dad's been sneakin' in and abusing her."

Several growls ring out in the room, and Kodiak slams his fist down on the table. Blaze just holds up his hand and waits.

"I know all of you would love to dump this bastard in a hole somewhere but it isn't the priority. Now, Sheila's got a sister in Florida who's coming up to meet them but we gotta get her in a hotel until then. We can't leave that little girl in that house any longer."

"Why are we waitin' till tomorrow, then?" Fuzz asks, looking downright murderous.

"Husband is off work today but goes in for a twenty-four hour shift at the firehouse tonight so she'll be safe until tomorrow."

Fuzz is silent for a moment but finally nods. Blaze passes out assignments but I tune it out, ready to get out of here. I need time. Time to get my shit together and time to plan my attack because there is no way in hell I am going to let this shit continue. The past may haunt me but he doesn't get to, and I will do whatever it takes to end this.

Chapter Eight
Alison

"Go find a table, and we'll get your drink, Hon," Carly says, motioning to the various tables littered throughout the club, and I nod, hoping I can find one nearby so I don't have to maneuver through crowds of people on these crutches. The swelling in my knee was down today but I still couldn't put much weight on my leg. I'm just hoping that I can walk by Monday morning because I don't want to start my new job like this.

Thankfully, a table opens up close to the bar, and I hobble over to it as fast as I can, throwing myself into a chair and letting out a sigh. Looking down at my knee, I can't help but smile when I think about Storm carrying me into my house and bandaging me up. I was so tempted to text him last night and this morning but I had no idea what to say. I guess I could pretend like I needed something but I really didn't.

Oh, God, what am I thinking?

I don't date. But no matter how many times I remind myself of that, I can't help but think of Storm anytime I have a spare moment. Maybe I need to get laid. Then, I wouldn't have lost my shit at the first handsome man I've seen in awhile.

"A cosmo for the lady," Izzy says, setting my drink down in front of me, and I offer her an appreciative smile before taking a sip and looking around the club. The music pumps through the club, and couples grind on the dance floor as I wrinkle my nose.

"Remind me why we came here?" I ask, and Izzy shakes her head.

"Uh, 'cause we're celebrating the fact that you two got an amazing job."

"We could have just ordered pizza and watched movies at my house."

Her eyes widen, and her jaw drops for a second before she sighs and rolls her eyes. "Oh my Jesus." She drops her head to the table with a thud, and I laugh at her while Carly rolls her eyes with a smirk on her face. Izzy lifts her head again and points a finger at me.

"No. We need girl time so we can talk about what happened with your hot as shit neighbor."

I shake my head, my gaze roaming around the club. "I already told you what happened."

"I think you're keeping things from me. I almost had an orgasm from just walking into that kitchen so there's no way nothing happened," she protests, taking a sip of her drink.

"Listen real carefully," I tell her, and she leans in, "absolutely nothing happened. Nada. Zip. Zilch. Got it?"

She studies me for a moment before a smile slowly creeps across her face. "Oh, man, if that's true, when you two finally bang, it's going to be…" Her voice trails off as she makes an exploding motion with her hands, and I laugh, Carly joining in.

"Bang? Seriously? What are you, a dude? And who says we're going to have sex?"

"Oh, Honey, I saw you two together. That man's gonna be getting it in before the week's over."

I snort and shake my head. "Thanks for your vote of confidence."

"You can deny all you want but the chemistry was literally off the charts. I've never felt anything like it."

I hold my hands up in surrender, needing a distraction from the reminder of what it felt like to be around him. "All right, enough about me. What about you, Iz? Got a new flavor of the week?"

"Yeah," she says, scowling into her drink, "but I think it's time to end it."

"How long did this one last?" Carly asks, a knowing smile on her face.

"Two days."

I choke on my drink as laughter bubbles out of me, and when I'm finally done coughing, I grin at her. "That a new record?"

"Yes. I need to stop being so interesting and good in bed, and maybe they'll last a little longer. Two freaking days of mind blowing sex and this guy is telling me that he's falling in love with me."

"Always so humble," Carly mutters, and Izzy flashes her a grin. I smile and look over to the dance floor, my face falling when I make eye contact with Troy and he waves at me. He starts moving closer, and I turn back to the girls.

"Shit," I hiss, and they both look at me with concern. "Troy is here, and he's coming over."

"Troy?" Izzy asks, and Carly fights back a smile.

"Troy from date number one?" she asks, and I nod, wishing a hole would open up and swallow me. Izzy starts smirking, and I glare at both of them.

"This is not funny," I hiss, and they laugh.

"Hey, Ali!" Troy says, stepping up beside me, and I plaster on a smile as I turn to him.

"Troy! Hey, how are you?"

He grins and throws an arm over my shoulders that I immediately want to throw off. "Real good now that you're here."

Oh, Jesus Christ, shoot me now.

"Shit, what did you do to your knee?" he asks, pointing down to my injured leg.

"Got tackled by a dog."

"No shit?" he asks, and I'm not really sure how to respond.

"Yep. Pretty crazy." I look to Izzy or Carly for help. Izzy is sitting in her chair with her chin propped up in her hand as she watches us. She catches my eye and bats her eyelashes at me.

I swear to God, I'm going to kill her.

Troy maneuvers himself between me and the table so I have no choice but to look up at him as he grins down at me. "So, what do you say you and me get out of here? We can pick up where our last date left off."

His gaze drops down my body, letting me know exactly what he means by that, and I resist the urge to roll my eyes.

"Sorry, she can't," Izzy cuts in, and I rethink killing her. "It's girls' night. No sausage allowed."

Carly's hand flies to her mouth, and she looks away quickly to hide her laughter. I shrug up at Troy, fighting off a smile of my own. "Sorry, you heard her."

"Oh, come on. I'm sure we can make an exception to the rule." He winks, and I want to gag.

"Dude, is there something you're not getting about no sausage allowed? Unless you've got a secret in those jeans, you're not welcome."

He steps to the side so he can glance over at her and smirk. "Oh, I've got something for you."

She rolls her eyes and nods. "Sure ya do, cowboy. Is it gonna be one of those things where I have to guess if it's a tiny dick or a huge clit?"

I spray my drink across the table, and Carly throws her head back in laughter, unable to stop herself. All the while, Izzy just sits in her chair with a proud smirk on her face.

"Why don't you come find out just how wrong you are," he taunts, grabbing the front of his jeans, and once again, I want to gag.

"Aw, that's cute but no. If I wanted to suck on a Jolly Rancher, I'd go to the convenience store across the street."

"What the fuck?" he hisses, his shoulders tensing up as he takes a step back.

"It was great chatting with you Tony but we're done here," she says, waving at him, and his face turns the color of a tomato.

"It's Troy," he growls, and she nods, taking a sip of her drink and looking out at the crowd.

"Uh-huh. Buh-bye now."

He stands there awkwardly, unsure of what to say or do for a moment before he growls and spins, stalking back into the crowd. He slips behind this tiny little thing who couldn't be more than nineteen and makes eye contact with me, grinding his hips against her ass.

"Dude is delusional," Izzy says, and when I look at her, she's got her head cocked to the side as she watches the show he's putting on. "Is that supposed to entice you? He looks like he's having a seizure."

I laugh, and she takes a sip of her drink, turning to look at me with a sympathetic expression on her face. "This guy's got a tiny Johnson, and he has no idea what to do with it. If there's one thing I can't stand, it's a man that doesn't know how to use his own cock."

"Oh my god," I gasp through my laughter but she doesn't stop there.

"Oh, what do you want to bet he's one of those guys that just flops around on top of you, moaning to some old classic rock song while you pray for a sinkhole to open up under the bed."

Tears streak down my cheeks as I struggle to breathe.

"You're a menace," Carly tells her, and she gasps, slapping her hand over her heart in mock horror.

"I'm not the one who marched over here and tried to piss all over poor Ali like I owned her."

"Yeah, Car, he kind of deserved what he got," I add.

She finishes off her drink, fighting back a smile. "I mean, I'm not saying you're wrong but that was savage, Iz."

Izzy shrugs. "Don't fuck with my girls and I'll be the sweetest bitch around."

"Okay, so now that I've had a drink and put up with Troy, can we go back to my place and watch movies?" I ask, and Izzy nods, grabbing her bag off the table.

"Yeah, let's get the hell out of here before I have to put someone else in their place," she teases, and I laugh as we gather up our things and head out to relax at my house.

* * * *

My knee aches as Carly and I walk up to the front doors of our new office building but I'm happy to be starting this job without the crutches. I'll probably be laid up on the couch tonight but it's worth it.

"Nervous?" I ask, looking over at Carly, who is beaming.

"Hell, no. I'm so excited that I never have to go to that paper again that there's no room for anything else."

I nod in agreement. Since quitting my job only three days ago, I've had this weight lifted off of me, and I'm thrilled to get started on something new. We open the door and walk into a clean, modern lobby that feels comfortable and stylish. The receptionist looks up and smiles but before she can say anything, Mercedes is rounding the corner and coming toward us.

"Ali," she exclaims, taking me by surprise when she pulls me in for a hug. "I'm so glad you're here."

When she releases me, she turns to Carly and beams. "And you must be Carly, it's so great to meet you. I spent the weekend reading some of your past articles, and I'm so happy to have you on the team."

Carly blushes and holds out her hand. "Well, thank you. I'm excited to be here."

"I have to tell you, the article about the crooked cops was amazing. I was riveted."

She lets out a nervous laugh, and I smile. Carly is an amazing writer but she hasn't gotten the recognition she deserves over at the paper. I'm so glad that I had the idea to bring her along.

"Gosh, you're making me blush," she jokes.

"I did have a question, though," Mercedes adds, and Carly nods. "Whatever happened with all that? I looked for hours for a follow-up article but I didn't see one."

"Oh, I'm not really sure. Our boss, Mr. Klein, didn't even want me to publish the first one but I've got a few friends over there, and they helped me sneak it past him. He was furious when it came out and wouldn't even hear me out on a follow-up article."

Mercedes rolls her eyes and sighs. "That's ridiculous."

"Hence, why we're here," Carly adds, looking over to me, and I smile at her.

"Right, of course. Well, follow me and I'll give you a quick tour of the office." She waves her arm for us to follow behind her, and we make our way down a hallway that branches out into a large open room with private offices lining both sides of it.

"This is our conference room of sorts. We meet in here once a week to talk about articles coming up and the schedule. We usually rotate pieces so there is something new on the blog for fans each day, but Ali, your column would be twice a week. We've already got so much interest in an advice column, and I can't wait to get the first article out."

Both Carly and I nod as she explains everything, and the longer she goes on, the more excited I get. I already feel inspired to write, and I'm anxious to get settled in my office and get to work.

Mercedes points to one of two doors at the front of the room and says, "That office is mine, and Ali, yours is the one right next to me."

My eyes widen, and I wonder how I got the office right next to the boss, and I catch Mercedes smiling at me out of the corner of my eye. "The advice column is kind of like a new branch of the blog so essentially, we would be partners."

"Wow, I wasn't expecting that."

She smiles at my response. "Go ahead and check it out while I show Carly to her office and then we can talk some more."

I agree and head toward my new office while Mercedes takes Carly into one of the offices on my left. A smile spreads across my face as soon as I walk in the door. It feels right, like I'm supposed to be here. The walls are purple but the rest of the furniture throws off a somewhat masculine vibe that balances the space. There is a large glass desk in front of a wall of windows that looks out into the city I love. In front of the desk are two pristine white lounge chairs that look like you just sink into them and never come out again.

"Like it?" Mercedes asks, stepping into the office behind me, and I turn to face her, grinning.

"Yeah, I love it."

"There was this study that said purple promotes creativity but you're welcome to change it if you would prefer something else."

I shake my head. "No, I really do love it."

"Good, sit down and let's chat then." I move behind the desk and sit in the office chair while Mercedes sits in one of the lounge chairs across from me.

"So, like I said, we've had a ton of interest in the column already, and I'll have one of the interns bring you the letters. You can go through and pick a couple that you want to answer first. I'd really love to do one a day during launch week just to kick things off right."

I nod, looking down at the desk calendar laid out in front of me. "And when were you thinking launch week would be?"

"Uh, well, kind of this week. Do you think you can write a response a day?"

"Okay," I laugh, looking down at the calendar again. "Yeah, I think I can manage that."

She claps her hands together and smiles. "Perfect. I'll have those letters here soon."

"Thanks, Mercedes," I say, and she smiles as she stands and leaves my office. I take a deep breath and lean back in my chair, looking around my office and soaking up this feeling of happiness that I'm unaccustomed to feeling at work. My phone buzzes on the desk, and I scoop it up.

Storm:
How you feelin'?

I bite down on my lip as I try to fight back a smile. It's just a simple text but it makes me practically giddy.

Me:
I'm good.

I set my phone on the desk, staring at it intently and willing it to buzz again. When it does, I jump and snatch it up.

Storm:
You sure? You need anything?

Me:
No, I'm all right. Thank you, though.

I'm grinning like a thirteen-year-old girl with her first crush, and I can't even tell you what it is about Storm that makes me act like this.

Storm:
What about some company?
Bear and I could come over.

I stare at his text, pursing my lips as I read it again and again. I can't deny that he makes me feel something I haven't felt in a long time. And yet it's different with him in a way I can't explain. It scares the hell out of me though, and I know I should stay away for my own well-being. My whole no-dating rule flew right out the window the first time he looked at me, and I'm desperately trying to hold on to it. My phone buzzes again, and I glance down.

Storm:
I would promise that we don't bite but
you already know how well trained Bear is.

I giggle and think about just how much I would enjoy Storm sinking his teeth into my skin. No, Ali!

Thinking things like that will definitely not help my situation. Blushing, I turn back to my phone and blow out a breath, a little disappointed that I'm not home.

Me:
I wish I was home but I started my new job today. Sorry.

"Miss James," someone calls, and I look up. A college-aged guy with curly brown hair is standing in the doorway to my office with a big box in his hands.

"Are those the letters?" I ask, my eyes wide, and he nods, stepping into the office and bringing them over to my desk. Holy crap. Mercedes wasn't kidding when she said there was interest in the advice column.

"Thank you."

He nods in response and turns to leave. As he walks out of the office, I grab the box and move it to the floor with a thud. I run my hands over the letters on the top, wondering how the hell I'm going to pick from all these. My phone buzzes again, and I look away from the box, sighing.

Storm:
No worries. Some other time, then.

That goofy grin is back on my face, and I bury my head in my hands, trying to think through this crazy giddiness fogging my mind. Am I really doing this? No, I can't.

Me:
Yeah, maybe.

As soon as I press send, my stomach knots but I set my phone down on the desk and reach for the first letter in the box to distract me. Enough thinking about my stupid hot neighbor. Hopefully, work will distract me enough to get back on track.

Chapter Nine
Alison

Stepping into the foyer, I close the door behind me and lean back against it as I reach down and slip my heels off, letting out a sigh of relief. As I drop each heel to the hardwood floor, I wiggle my toes and close my eyes. My feet ache, and my knee is killing me but I'm riding a high from my first day at the blog. It's been so long since I felt this excited or inspired by my work, and I already can't wait to go back tomorrow and do it all over again. Most of my morning was spent going through letters, trying to find the perfect one to respond to before I went to Mercedes and asked if I could publish the article I wrote for Mr. Klein as my introduction for the blog.

I wanted to let the readers know who I was and despite the terrible situation, I really did like the article I wrote. She was thrilled with the idea and said it was the perfect thing for my first piece. I had to tweak it some, adding in the backstory as to why the article got written in the first place and then how I ended up at the blog, but I think it only made it better. I handed it off to Mercedes as everyone headed out for lunch, and by the time we got back it was up on the blog.

I'm terrified to hear the response to it tomorrow but I'm happy. Like deep down in my soul happy for the first time in a long time, and it wasn't until I was standing in my new office moments after my first column went live that I realized just how unhappy I had been. Mr. Carlyle retired, handing the reins over to Mr. Klein right around the time that Adam cheated on me, and it all took a toll on me. While I focused on work to avoid my pain, all the color drained out of my world. I didn't notice that my life had been diminished to lifeless shades of gray, and I was just going through the motions. Until Storm lit up my sky.

He spent all day texting me, and by the time I left work, I was actually considering giving this a shot. With each new message, I would smile and my heart would warm a little more, giving me hope that this could really be something. I've never felt anything like what I feel when I'm in Storm's presence. Sure, I had chemistry with Adam but not like this. It's different. It feels deeper, more meaningful, and it sounds ridiculous since I literally just met him but I feel like he could be the one.

That still scares the shit out of me but after the rush I got today, I promised myself that I'd do things differently. I'll soak up the small moments and find happiness in the little things. I'll stop hiding from the world and closing myself off from the possibility of love. I may be slightly jaded and that's not going to change, but despite that, I do want to share my life with someone. My phone buzzes in my purse, and I grab it, my heart skipping a beat when I think about it being from Storm. When I manage to wrestle it out of my bag, my face lights up.

Storm:
Hi

I giggle and lean back against the door again with a sigh. It's absolutely ridiculous that a single text from him, one simple word, is enough to have me acting like my head is in the clouds. I don't know if it's my earlier resolve to try again or if it's just him but I'm not fighting this anymore. I can't. My phone buzzes again, and I look down.

Storm:
Darlin', you want to let me in?

I look over my shoulder to the door behind me before looking back at my phone and standing up straight. Whipping around, I yank the door open and suck in a breath. There he is, standing on my front porch in a sexy leather jacket and jeans with a fast food bag in his hand.

"Hi," I whisper, butterflies dancing around in my stomach, and when a smile slowly stretches across his face, he steals my breath.

"Hey," he replies, taking a step into the foyer and closing the door behind him.

"What are you doing?"

"Well, we said later," he explains, shrugging like it should be obvious.

I nod. "Yes, we did."

His eyes dance with humor and something more, and as he looks down at me, the temperature in the room cranks up a few degrees. "And as far as I can tell, it's technically later."

"Technically."

He takes another step toward me but this time I don't move so we're only a whisper away from touching. My breathing quickens as I meet his eyes, and my lips part. "That still doesn't answer my question."

"About what I'm doing here?" he asks, his voice lower and huskier than just moments before.

I lick my lips and nod. "Yes."

His gaze darts to my mouth, so intense that I can feel it rocking through my body. He looks at me like he wants to devour me, and I have absolutely no objections to that. Everything about him seems intense from the heartache in his gray gaze to the "don't mess with me" aura around him, and I can't help but imagine how incredibly good it would feel if he focused that intensity on my body. Just the mental image is enough to force a shiver down my spine.

"I really want to kiss you," he whispers, moving a fraction of an inch closer like he can't stop himself.

"I'm okay with that." I rise up on my tippy toes just to get a little bit closer to him, and his eyes lock onto mine and we both freeze. Why the hell do we always get stuck in this suspended almost kiss position? It's making me crazy. In the past three days, I've imagined kissing him more times than I can even count.

I've spent hours wondering if he would be soft and gentle or if he would own my mouth with that same passion that lights up his eyes occasionally. He sighs, turning his head away from me, and I blink, taking a step back as I'm ripped from my fantasy.

"Fuck it," he growls, using his free hand to grab my shirt and pull me into him. The bag of food falls to the floor, and his hand dives into my hair as he slams his lips down on mine. My arms go around his neck as his other hand finds the small of my back and pushes me into his body. A low groan rises up from his throat when I nip at his lips and suddenly, we're moving. He spins us around, and my back is shoved up against a wall as he pushes against me, rubbing his hard cock against my hip.

The hand on my back creeps down, grabbing onto my ass, and I gasp, granting him entrance into my mouth, and he takes full advantage, his tongue plunging inside and tangling with my own. I can't think. I can't breathe. All I can do is hold on for dear life as he completely knocks me off my feet with a kiss. I spent so much time imagining this but it's better than I could ever dream up. I slip my hands under his leather jacket, and he rips his mouth away as he groans and gently grabs my wrists.

"I really didn't come here for this," he whispers against my lips, his chest heaving with labored breaths.

My fingers dig into his chest. "You don't hear me complaining."

He sighs, like he's in pain, before pulling back and meeting my eyes. "I should feed you."

He looks over his shoulder to where he dropped the food. "Oh, shit."

I peek over and immediately start laughing. The bag is crushed, and food is spilled out across the floor. We must have kicked it or something when he was moving me to the wall. He focuses back on me as I giggle, his eyes boring into me as my laughter slowly dies. God, I want to kiss him again but after he pulled away, I'm not sure that's what he wants.

"How does pizza sound?" I ask instead.

"Fine but I'm paying."

"Uh, no."

He levels a glare at me, almost like he's daring me to defy him. "This was supposed to be an apology so I'm buying."

Feeling brave, I lean up and kiss his cheek. "You really don't have to do that."

Questions spark in his eyes as he scans my face, and all I can think about is kissing him again. Even when I tell myself to think of something else, it always comes back to his full lips.

"Of course I do. I still feel really bad about Bear hurting you so I'm buying."

"Storm," I whisper, shaking my head, "you don't need to apologize anymore for Bear. It was an accident. And you certainly don't need to buy dinner for me as a peace offering."

"Sweetheart," he drawls, one corner of his mouth pulling up in an easy grin and sending tingles across my skin, "it's not often I'm accused of being a gentleman so you might want to take advantage of my offer."

I sigh, and my stomach chooses this exact moment to growl. When I peek up at him to see if he heard it, his victorious grin tells me all I need to know. "Well, all right then."

He orders me to sit on the couch while he calls to order some pizza, and when he's done, he sits down beside me, pulling my feet into his lap, and massaging them as we talk.

"How was your first day?" he asks, and I beam.

"Amazing," I say before launching into a detailed description of my day. I tell him everything, excited to share my happiness with someone but about halfway through my story, I realize I'm rambling and stop. "I'm sorry. I'm sure it's kind of boring."

He shakes his head and reaches out, gently brushing his thumb over my cheek. "No. Please keep going."

I study him for a moment but when I don't see anything but sincerity, I decide to finish my story. I explain about the article, and then that leads to me having to explain about the three dates. He watches me as I talk, and I can tell that he's really listening. He really cares about how my day was, and my heart warms at the gesture.

"And that was the day we met?" he asks, and I nod. "Shit. What a day."

I laugh, nodding my head. "Yeah, it was certainly interesting."

"Well, I'm sorry again for Bear."

I give him a look, and he holds his hands up in surrender.

"So, you've never told me what you do," I point out, and he nods, looking down at the foot he's massaging.

"You ever heard of the Bayou Devils?" he asks, and when I shake my head, he sighs.

"So, it's an MC…"

"An MC?" I ask, cutting him off.

"Yeah, a motorcycle club. A lot of clubs are involved in criminal activity, and the Devils used to be before I joined but shit started going down and our president, Blaze, decided to make some changes."

"Do you even realize that you do that?" I ask, and his brow creases.

"What?"

Smirking, I shake my head. "You respond to my questions but you never really answer them."

"I don't do that," he says, a stubborn expression crossing his face that does all sorts of things to my insides.

"Yes, you do. I asked you what you do and you told me you're in an MC but I still don't really know what you do all day. Like, how do you make money to buy things like apology pizza?"

He snorts, fighting back a smile as he peeks up at me. "The club has several businesses that we run. When Blaze decided to go legitimate, we needed a way to make money. He already had the motorcycle shop but then he decided to open a P.I. business and a bar as well."

"And you just work at all of them?"

"Yep," he says, nodding, "We all take turns working in each place."

"What made Blaze decide to turn things around?" I ask, wanting to soak up as much knowledge as I can. The doorbell rings, and he moves my feet before jumping up.

"One second." He goes to the door and comes back a few seconds later with our food, setting it on the coffee table, and handing me a slice. He grabs one for himself before sitting back down again.

"About six years ago, a lot of shit went down, and it was just too much for all of them. Blaze had lost touch with his son, and he'd been shot during a run. One of the other guys went to prison, and he's still there. Like everything just came to a head, and Blaze couldn't do it anymore."

I nod, studying him as he tells the story. "Why did you join?"

He shrugs and looks away. "Blaze got involved in helping women escape abusive relationships, and I liked what they were doing. I didn't have much else at that point in my life. They became my family."

My heart hurts as I think about him all alone in the world. "You don't have any family?"

He turns back to me, giving me a soft smile that makes me sigh. "No, I've got my mom and dad but they're separated, and they never had any more kids so it was kind of lonely."

"I'm an only child, too, so I get it. Did you grow up around here?"

He nods. "Yeah, born and raised. I left for a little bit after high school but then I came back. This was home, you know?"

"I grew up in Texas, and I don't know if I would go back now. I came out here for school because I wanted to be on my own but I fell in love with it."

He smiles. "I'm kind of glad that you did."

I blush and look away from him, my heart racing. God, this is exciting and terrifying all rolled into one, and I don't know what feeling to latch on to. Maybe I should just go with it and enjoy the ride. "Me, too," I whisper.

Storm reaches out, gently tapping under my chin with his fingers, and I look over at him. "Tell me more."

It's not a question but even that doesn't bother me. I like that he wants to know more about me. "What do you want to know?"

"Everything."

"Well, that's a super vague request. Can you narrow it down for me?"

He laughs and takes a bite of his pizza as he thinks. The scar in his eyebrow catches my eye, and I reach toward him, trailing my finger over it.

"How did you get this?"

He watches me for a second. "Got in a fight."

I finish my pizza and toss the crust down on the open pizza box before pulling my knees to my chest and looking at him. He glances over at me out of the corner of his eye and grins.

"I've been meaning to ask you, your friend the other day, the one that walked in on us in the kitchen..." he prompts.

"Izzy?"

"Yeah. She always that forward?"

I laugh and nod. "Um, yes."

"Great," he mumbles, and he seems upset by that fact.

"Did it bother you?" I ask, and he sighs, turning to look at me. He just watches me for a couple moments before shaking his head.

"No, it didn't."

An awkward silence falls over us, and he grabs another slice of pizza, asking me if I want one. I shake my head, and as he starts eating, I sigh.

"Okay, your turn. Tell me something about you."

He smirks. "That's a super vague request. Narrow it down."

"Smartass," I laugh, shoving him, and he quirks a brow in my direction, his smile turning predatory as he lunges at me. I squeal and try to get away but he scoops me up before I even make it off the couch, taking us down to the floor as he lies on top of me.

The air punches out of my lungs as I stare up at him, the warmth of his body blanketing me, and his breath fanning across my face. He holds my gaze, both of us suspended in this ridiculous "will we or won't we" thing that we keep doing. Slowly, without taking my eyes off him, I lean up and press my lips to his. When he doesn't pull away, I press my palm to his cheek, and he sighs, kissing me back just as softly.

I fall into him. It's the kind of kiss that can last all night – slow, sweet, but still hot as he nips at my bottom lip, earning a breathy moan from me. My legs wrap around his waist, and he groans as he slips a hand behind my head, pulling me closer this time instead of pushing me away. His tongue teases mine as he grips my hip and moans.

His phone starts ringing, and he pulls away, breathing heavily as he stares down at me, thunder building in his eyes. The phone stops ringing, and he sighs, climbing off me and sitting on the floor as he pulls it out and checks his messages.

"I've got to go," he says when he pulls the phone away. He stands and holds his hand out to me to help me up. My heart hurts when I look up at him because he's different than he was just a moment ago, and I have no idea what sparked the change. His fingers slip through my hair, and he presses his lips to my forehead before whispering "good-bye" and walking out of my house.

I stare at the door, my chest aching, and wonder if I made a big mistake here.

* * * *

Walking into my office, I set my bag down on one of the chairs across from my desk and strut over to my chair. I was so pumped walking into work today, and I can't wait to get started. Once the first article went live yesterday, I went through the box of letters again and found the perfect one to do today. I've already got most of the response formulated in my head. I just need to get it down on paper.

Sitting down in the chair, I think about Storm and can't stop the wide smile from stretching across my face before it falls. I don't know what happened between us last night, and I absolutely hate the way it hurts right now.

"Ali, come here, please," Mercedes calls from her office, and I grab my coffee before standing and walking over. When I walk in, her face is buried in her computer. I sit down in one of the chairs and smile at her but she just looks at me with a somber expression on her face. Oh, shit, what happened?

"What's wrong?" I ask, and she looks down, shaking her head. My stomach knots, and I wonder if it's something to do with yesterday's article. What if people hated it and she's going to fire me? When she looks up again, she's beaming, and I get whiplash from her sudden mood change. I just stare at her with wide eyes for a second, trying to figure out what the hell is going on.

"Seriously, what?" I ask, really starting to freak out.

"You went viral."

I blink at her in shock and then do it again, unsure of what to say. I went viral... what the hell does that even mean?

"What?"

"Ali, the article. People freaking loved it, and you went viral. Three point five million shares overnight."

I stand up and walk around behind her, looking at her computer screen. "Shut up," I whisper, more to myself when I see the number she just quoted staring back at me. I go back to the chair, walking like a zombie as I try to process what's happening right now.

"They loved it?" I ask, plopping down into the chair again. Mercedes nods enthusiastically, looking a bit like a bobble head, and I take a sip of my coffee.

"Yes, everyone is talking about you this morning. Everyone loved it." She pauses and makes a face. "Well, not everyone. I've gotten two calls from Klein this morning, threatening to sue but that's just icing on a very tasty cake."

I laugh. "You like getting sued?"

"No," she scoffs. "He's got nothing, and I already called my dad and had him get the lawyer on it. He can't touch us which is just going to piss him off more."

She rubs her hands together like an evil villain, and I laugh again, all of this starting to sink in a little bit.

"I can't believe this," I tell her, and she scoffs again.

"I can. I knew you would be great. It's why I jumped on the chance to hire you."

I nod, my mind working overtime right now as I try to understand what all this means for my life. "Is this going to be bad for the advice column? It wasn't exactly an advice piece I wrote."

"I don't think so but I wanted to talk to you about that."

I take a deep breath and nod my head, readying myself for whatever she's going to throw at me. She has a smirk on her face that worries me a little. "Okay, shoot."

"So, I think we've got people's attention, and that's great, but now we've got to capitalize on it."

"And how do you want to do that?" I ask, warily, not sure that I like where this is going.

"Hear me out here. I want to set up a photo shoot for some ads and get you some radio interviews. Maybe even some local TV shows."

I start shaking my head immediately. There is no way I'm agreeing to this.

"Come on, Ali. Please? We need this if we're going to make your column a success; otherwise, people are going to forget about you as soon as something else goes viral."

I sigh and take another sip of my coffee. I know she's right but I don't like it. "All right, if I agree to the photo shoot and radio interviews, will you drop the TV appearances?"

"Deal," she practically shouts, sticking her hand out for me to shake. I laugh and do it as I shake my head, my stomach sinking.

"Why do I feel like I just made a deal with the devil?" I ask, and she grins, winking at me.

"Don't worry about a thing, Ali. You're on my team now, and I promise that we'll take care of you, okay? You'll see; this is going to be amazing."

"If you say so."

She shoots me a look, and I hold my hands up in apology.

"I'll have the shoot and interviews set up and sent over to you later today, okay?"

"Sure, sounds good."

"At least try and sound excited about this," she says, and I give her a very unenthusiastic smile. She laughs loudly as I stand and go back to my office, still trying to process all this. This is not where I saw this going but the only thing I can do is hang on tight and hope it all works out.

Chapter Ten
Storm

Me:
Free tonight?

Sighing, I shove my phone back in my pocket and scan the road in front of where we're parked, looking for any sign of danger as I try to forget how badly I want to see Ali again. What I'm feeling when it comes to Ali can't even be described as want anymore. It's need. I've taken a sharp left into obsession when it comes to my gorgeous neighbor, and I want to spend every second of every day with her. I can't even bring myself to care. Call me crazy but I enjoy not feeling like I'm suffocating every second of the day too much to care that she's consuming me in a whole new way. I like the way that my heart feels light for the first time in six years instead of weighed down with pain. But then the guilt takes over and makes me sick to my stomach. I shouldn't want her this much. I shouldn't pursue her.

I've managed to not go back over there since the night I surprised her with dinner but we've also been texting back and forth everyday. That first day I met her, the attraction was instant. I'd have loved nothing more than to pin her to the bed underneath me and sink into her again and again until I fucked her out of my system, but by the time I left after bandaging up her knee, it was different. Something about her got to me, and even if I don't know what I'm doing, I can't stay away. It's almost like the moment we met, this string was tied between us, and no matter how far I try to run from the shit I'm feeling, the shit that I never expected to feel again, the harder she pulls me back. And I don't know how long I'll be able to keep resisting her. My phone buzzes, and I pull it out of my pocket.

Ali:
Not sure yet. Crazy day.

My smile transforms, and I scowl down at the phone, worry coursing through me. I want to know about anything that erases her beautiful smile and take it out so it never bothers her again. Jesus. What is happening to me? I haven't felt like this in so long. And I was convinced that I never would again. But Ali knocked me flat on my ass.

"You all right?" Chance asks from the other side of the cab, and I nod.

"Yep. All good."

Hopelessly Devoted

Me:
You okay?

Tucking my phone away, I look up and scan the street again. Everything looks normal. A few cars are parked along the tree-lined street but they are all empty, and as far as we can tell, he doesn't have eyes on her.

"What's her name again?" Chance asks from the passenger seat of the truck.

"Jenny."

He nods, doing another scan of the street. "And when are we supposed to get her?"

"Jesus, dude. Did you not read the sheet at all?"

"Just remind me."

I sigh and look up at her front door. "She'll text when she's ready to go. Kodiak is at the boyfriend's office, and he'll let us know if he leaves."

He nods and stares straight ahead as my phone buzzes in my pocket.

Ali:
How about I buy dinner this time?

I grin and shake my head, quickly typing out a message back to her.

Me:
That's not happenin'.

Ali:
Why the hell not? This still isn't about Bear, is it?

Me:
Naw, Sweetheart, it's not about that.

Like it was ever really about Bear. He just serves as a perfect excuse to go over and see her. I wish she hadn't gotten hurt but I can't deny that I love the outcome.

Ali:
Why not?

Me:
**Baby, this whole independent woman thing you're doing is really sexy but there is no way in hell
that I'm letting you pay for dinner.**

"Dude, you got it bad," Chance says, and when I look up at him, he's smirking at me.

"What?"

He makes a circle around his face. "It's all over your face. You've practically got hearts popping out of your eyes."

"Shut up," I snap. I'm not ready to talk about this yet. I need time to figure out what the hell is going on between us and to end the shit from my past that's coming back to haunt me. I switch over to my texts with Streak and type out a quick message to him.

**Me:
Need you to look into someone.
Ian Blackwell.
Find everything.**

"Who is she?" Chance asks, glancing away from the road to look at me. I almost tell him that she's no one but I can't even force the words out of my mouth. There's no scenario where Ali is no one to me.

"My neighbor."

He laughs and nods. "I would ask if it's serious but I can tell by the expression on your face that it probably is."

"Man, I don't know what the fuck is going on," I admit. I was born and raised here in Baton Rouge, and Chance moved here in the third grade. We've been best friends since the day we met. He's been like a brother to me, staying by my side through all the dark shit I've been through and always having my back. So he already knows what I'm going through right now. He knows how hard I'm fighting this and how badly I'm losing that fight.

"Yeah, you do. It may have been awhile since you felt like this but you know what it is."

I look up at the house that we're guarding as I ignore his comment. It's wrong to feel this way about someone else after everything I've done but I'm too goddamn selfish to leave her alone.

"Brother, I know better than anyone the way you've been torturing yourself for the past six years but it's okay to like her. Hell, it's even okay to love her.

And don't bother denying it. I can tell you're crazy about this girl even if you won't admit it."

"I just met her," I grumble, like that's a good reason why everything he's saying is complete shit.

"So what? Three weeks after you met Fi, you were begging her to move in with you. You've never half-assed anything in your life, why would you with love?"

"Stop saying that fucking word."

"What?" He laughs. "Love?"

"Yes. I'm not fucking in love with her. Maybe, fucking, maybe I like her but that's it."

He laughs again and shakes his head. "Denial… it's not just a river in Egypt."

"Shut the fuck up, Brother," I growl but he just shakes his head at me.

"Man, it's okay to like her."

I'm about to tell him to shut it again when my phone buzzes and instead, I pull it out and ignore him.

Unknown:
I'm ready.

I point to the house, indicating to Chance that it's time. After yanking open the door, I slam it shut and stomp up the steps, ready to do what we came here to do. Stopping about halfway up, I look back just as Chance steps out of the truck.

"You coming or you want to stay here and talk about your feelings like a fucking girl?"

"I'm right behind you, asshole," he shoots back with no venom in his voice. I push back everything he said, needing to focus on the task at hand. We scan the street, looking for anything out of order. This has to go perfectly, and we can't afford to be caught up in other shit when our job is this important. When we reach the door, I knock softly and Chance keeps a watch behind me.

"Who is it?" a hesitant voice calls from the inside.

"Storm and Chance, Darlin'."

The door flies open, and I bite out a curse at the fresh bruise under her eye. I slowly reach out so I don't scare her and brush my thumb over it. "What happened?"

Her shaking hand comes up to her face, and she lightly touches her fingers over the bruise, shaking her head. "It was nothing."

I nod. We've been doing this long enough that we know it will take some time for her to process all the shit he did to her. I spent a lot of time talking to Emma about her mental state after everything she went through so I could better understand what these women are thinking when we rescue them. It was a fucking difficult conversation to get through but now I'm glad that I did.

"You got a bag ready, Sweets?" Chance asks, offering her a kind smile that makes some of the tension leave her shoulders.

"Yeah. I'll be right back."

She bustles off into the house, leaving the door open a crack, and I glance around the neighborhood again. "What does the boyfriend drive?" I ask.

"Dark blue Lexus," Chance says and rattles off the license plate number as I scan the road. It's a quiet little street, and nothing seems out of place. We scoped the house out for the last three days, getting to know the area so we would recognize something out of the ordinary. My phone buzzes, and I pull it out while trying to keep an eye on the road.

Streak:
On it.

I tuck the phone back into my pocket with a sigh. I feel better knowing that I'm moving forward and doing something to end this. This fucker doesn't get to mess with my life anymore, and I'll do whatever I have to do to keep him away from Ali.

"We're good," I say, turning back to the door just as Jenny comes back with her suitcase. She offers us a weak smile, and my stomach twists as I think about all she's been through.

She came to us about a month ago after a particularly bad fight with her boyfriend. Most of her face was bruised along with several splotches down her arms. She walked to the clubhouse from the house she shares with him when he left for work and asked us for help. We tried to get her out shortly after that but when we showed up, she backed out. These women are terrified, and it happens a lot so we left a phone with her and told her to call us whenever she was ready.

"You ready to do this?" I ask her, and she nods, standing up a little taller and, as always, I'm amazed by the strength these women show. She steps out onto the porch and closes the door behind her, not bothering to lock it. Chance steps out in front of her, and I follow behind as we walk over to the truck. She glances around nervously in each direction again and again like her man is going to come storming the castle any second.

"We've got a guy watching him at his office, Darlin'," I tell her, and she peeks back at me. "You're safe."

She lets out a long breath and nods. "Thank you."

My phone buzzes, and I pull it out.

Kodiak:
He just left the office. Following.

I glance up, and Chance looks over his shoulder at me, letting me know he got the same message, and Jenny picks up on it immediately.

"What? What's going on?" The pure terror in her voice nearly kills me but we won't let anything happen to her.

"Jenny, focus for me, okay?" I ask, and she nods.

"Your old man just left his office but we've got a guy following him, and we'll be long gone by the time he gets here if this is where he's going," I assure her, and she nods, her gaze nervously flicking from our faces to the road in front of us.

"All right, let's get in the truck. We got places to be," Chance says and helps her in the truck. She slides to the middle seat as I climb behind the wheel, and Chance climbs in on the other side. Just as I'm about to pull away, my phone buzzes again.

Kodiak:
He's going to the house. 5 mins out.

I shove my phone back in my pocket and start the truck, pulling away from the curb and taking off down the street. I drive a little faster than usual, wanting to get as much distance between her and her man as I can. I look over, and she has tears streaming down her face as she rubs her stomach with her hand.

"Hey, whoa, are you okay?" I ask, and Chance rubs her shoulder. She sobs harder, and I contemplate pulling over for a second.

"Thank you," she gasps just as I'm looking for a spot to stop, and I look over at her again. "You saved our lives."

I look back to the road, my eyes burning, but I force it back down as I head toward Emma and Nix's house. After everything Emma went through, she wanted to help us with what we do. Obviously, we couldn't let her do any of the rescue part, and Nix would skin our hides if we even thought about it, but Blaze loved the idea of bringing girls there every so often while we found other accommodations for them. It's safe, and they get to see a success story. It gives them hope and makes them strong enough to keep going when they feel like giving up and going back to the devil they know.

When we pull up to the house, Nix steps out, his arms crossed over his chest. Jenny looks over to us, a little nervous.

"That's Nix, he's Blaze's son. His wife, Emma, was in the same situation as you not so long ago. You're safe here. I promise," I tell her, and she nods, looking back to the house just as Emma steps out. I climb out while Chance helps Jenny and brings her around to my side.

"Hey, little mama," I say, and she smiles at me as she walks over and wraps her arms around my middle. "How are those babies doing?"

"Sleeping, finally."

"Aren't you supposed to nap when they do?"

She scoffs and rolls her eyes. "You know, I would if I didn't have a constant rotation of bikers coming through here."

"You want us to stop comin'?" I ask, already knowing the answer. Emma loves having all of us around even if she likes to give us a hard time.

"Don't you dare."

"Em, this is Jenny," Chance says, and Jenny shakes like a leaf in front of her.

"Hey, Sweetie, I'm Emma. It's really nice to meet you."

Jenny just nods, quiet as she looks around at all of us. Emma steps up to her and places her hands on her arms. "You see the man over there?" Emma asks, pointing to Nix, and Jenny nods.

"That is the most amazing man on the planet, and you already know that these guys are pretty great, too. No one is going to hurt you ever again. You're safe here. You hear me?" Emma asks, looking her right in the eye, and after a few silent moments, she nods and starts crying again.

"Hey, it's gonna be okay," Emma coos, hugging her tight for a moment before she grabs her shoulders and pushes her away a little. She looks her in the eye and smiles. "You've got this, Honey. You're going to be okay. Say it with me."

I watch in awe as it's almost like Emma transfers some of her strength into Jenny. She stands up taller, and after a moment, nods.

"I'm going to be okay," she whispers, her voice so weak that I almost don't hear her, and Emma beams.

"Damn right, you are. Now, are you hungry?"

Jenny nods and Emma hooks an arm around her shoulder and takes her bag from her hand and sets it down in the grass next to Chance, winking at him. He laughs as she escorts Jenny into her house, and I turn to Nix.

"What the hell was that? Nix gets most amazing man on the planet and all I get is pretty great," Chance protests, and we laugh.

"Perks of the job," Nix says, watching his wife disappear into the house with a grin on his face before turning back to us.

"Her boyfriend was on his way to the house when we bailed so no doubt he already knows she's gone. We'll keep her here for a little bit until we can find a safe place to send her. Oh, and she's pregnant, and I'm not sure that she's seen a doctor yet."

He nods. "I'll let Emma know."

"All right. I'm sure Blaze will call later to check in."

After we say good-bye, Chance and I jump back in the truck and head for the clubhouse. I'm ready to drop his ass off and go see Ali again. My phone buzzes, and I grab it.

Ali:
I guess I'll just have to think of a way to thank you ;)

I can't fight back the smile as my cock twitches in my jeans. God, I'm dying to get that woman underneath me, and I'm not gonna last much longer. It probably doesn't help that I jerk off to one of the pictures of her that Streak sent over.

"Oh, Dude, you're so screwed," Chance laughs, and I shake my head as I shove my phone back in my pocket. I shoot him a glare and pick up the speed, impatient to get to my girl.

Chapter Eleven
Alison

"Hi," I say, grinning as I swing the door open. He grins back and holds up a fast food bag that makes me frown. "Hey, I was going to buy this time."

"No, you weren't." He steps into the foyer with Bear on his heels, and I close the door behind them before turning to face him.

"Yes, I was. We talked about this."

He grins and leans back against the wall, gazing down at me in amusement. "You talked about it, and I said no. Besides, this is a make-up dinner for the bag of food we stepped on."

"Then what was the pizza?"

He shrugs. "My apology for Bear."

"You seem to have a lot of excuses."

He pushes off the wall and steps closer to me, one arm snaking around my waist as he pulls me into his body. "You could just stop fighting me."

"You could just let me buy," I whisper as I savor the feeling of being pressed up against him. I love the way his arm wraps around my waist and the way he pulls me into him like I belong there. My eyes close, and I press my hand to his chest, just feeling him.

"No."

My eyes pop open, and I glare up at him. "What do you mean, no?"

"It's a pretty universal word, Sweetheart," he says, his voice dropping lower as he leans in closer. My breath catches, and my eyes stay locked on his as he moves toward me. "It's got two letters – N and O. It means over my dead fucking body."

I let out a huff and push him away from me as he laughs.

"Fucking Neanderthal," I grumble, and his laughter stops immediately. He sets the bag of food down on the entry table, and his eyes take on a predatory quality that has me taking a step back and holding up my hand.

"Oh, no," I tell him, and he just grins in response, taking a deliberate step toward me, and I back up again. He lunges, and I scream as I take off running down the hallway. I turn the corner and sigh when I see the light from the kitchen at the end of the hallway. If I can make it there, I have many more options for escape.

His arms wrap around my waist, and I scream again as he hoists me in the air and spins me in his arms so I'm facing him before pinning me to the wall. His heavy breaths hit my face and I meet his eyes in the dark hallway, gasping at the desire that rushes over me from just one look.

"What was that you said, Baby?"

"Nothing," I whisper, unable to pull my eyes away. His gray gaze hypnotizes me, and I'd do anything he told me to right now.

"Nothing?" he asks again, and I shake my head, biting down on my lip. His gaze drops to my mouth, and he reaches out, tugging my lip free with his thumb before he lightly brushes it over the spot where my teeth were. My whole body quivers in response, and I let out a soft moan.

He attacks my mouth. His hand slides into my hair, and he holds me close as his lips devour me with a need that rocks me to my core. It's validation. I'm not the only one feeling all these crazy things, and there is definitely something between us, no matter how hard we both fight it. He pulls away, and I gasp for breath, seeking out his eyes again. He stares back at me and shakes his head.

"Why do I always end up back here with you?" he asks, almost like he's not expecting an answer from me. I open my mouth to say something but Bear barks, and he kisses me again before letting me down without another word.

"Let's go get that food."

He turns and takes off down the hallway, and I sigh as I follow behind him. Grabbing the bag of food, he turns to me and holds it up. "Where do you want to eat?"

I point to the dining room table at the end of the hall, and he nods, stomping toward the kitchen as I follow behind once again. I watch him closely, trying to figure out what it is that causes his sudden changes of mood but I can't for the life of me, see anything.

When the food is laid out on the table, I sit down and pull my knee up to my chest as I grab a few fries and stuff them in my mouth. He smirks, watching me as he sits down with a couple of beers and hands one to me before take a sip of his own. "So, you gonna tell me about this crazy day?"

"Oh, Man," I sigh, having completely forgotten about that. "Well, my first article apparently went viral."

"What? The one you told me about the other day? About those terrible dates?"

I nod, grabbing a few more fries. "Yep, that's the one."

"Is that a bad thing?" he asks, studying me, and once again I feel warm all over that he's actually listening to me and interested in what I have to say. He's so damn confusing.

"I don't know. I guess, technically, it's not a bad thing for the blog, and Mercedes is already trying to capitalize on it but it's weird for me. I mean, three point five million people and counting have read my words."

He nods as he finishes chewing a bite of his burger. "How is this Mercedes person capitalizing on it?"

"Mercedes is my boss, and she wants me to do a photo shoot and radio interviews. She tried to get me to do TV appearances but I put my foot down on that."

He smirks, and Bear lies down at my feet. "That was your limit, huh?"

"It was. I'm nervous enough about the radio interview. I don't need to be freaking out about being on TV."

"You shouldn't be nervous. I'm sure you'll do great."

Warmth spreads through me, and I smile. "Well, thank you but enough about my day. How was yours?"

Sighing, he folds a couple fries in half and shoves them in his mouth, taking a sip of beer before he answers me. "It was a rough one."

"Tell me about it?" I ask, finishing up my food and resting my chin on my knee.

"We had a transfer today…"

"What's that?" I ask, shooting him an apologetic look as I cut him off.

"It's when we get a battered woman out of her home and take her somewhere safe."

I nod. "Okay, continue."

"Anyway, it's a complicated process, and there are lots of moving parts. We usually have someone watching the piece of shit that she's running from just in case he decides to come home and we need to get her out of there faster, and we've got a safe house to take them to."

"Is that why it's rough?"

He shakes his head. "No. Today, the girl we picked up, she's pregnant, and she started crying in the car, thanking us for saving their lives, and it just hit me. It does that. Sometimes I forget what we're really doing. I get used to the routine and forget that these women's lives depend on us."

"I think you're kind of amazing," I whisper. "The fact that you don't see what you're doing as amazing makes you even more amazing. What made you get involved with this?"

His eyes darken, and he looks away from me. "Personal experience."

"I'm sorry. You don't have to…"

His chair slides back, scraping against the floor, cutting me off, and I look up at him. He doesn't even look at me. "I should get going."

Without even a glance in my direction, he stomps out of my house with Bear on his heels, and I wonder what the hell I said this time to upset him.

* * * *

I suck in a nervous breath as I climb out of my car and lock it before walking toward the warehouse that Mercedes directed me to. What is with people sending me to places that look like a possible murder scene lately? Maybe I need to rethink the company I keep. My stomach rolls as I think about what's waiting for me on the other side of the rolling barn door. I stop and lean up against the building, taking a couple of deep breaths, still trying to let this sink in. It's surreal that millions of people know my name and read my article. I'm not sure that I like it.

Mercedes wanted to strike fast, and it's still only been two days since I found out about the article going viral. I feel like I haven't really gotten a chance to stop and consider all the ways my life is going to change in the very near future. Mercedes is determined to make me into a mini star and make the blog even more successful than it already is, and I want that, too, but I'm just not sure I'm ready for anything that comes with that. My phone rings, and I pull it out of my bag, smiling at the caller ID.

"Hey, Gorgeous," he says as soon as I answer, his deep raspy voice coating me like caramel.

"Hi," I sigh. Two nights ago, he walked away but he came back last night, and it was like nothing happened. He was sweet and charming, and we had a great time. I could over analyze this but I've just decided to go with it.

"Is that how you're going to greet me every time?"

"Maybe. Are you complaining?"

He laughs, and I can just picture the way his face lights up when he smiles. "No. You may not like what it's doing to my ego though. Where are you?"

I look over my shoulder at the door and scowl. "This photo shoot. I'm not sure that I'm ready."

"Why not?"

"I don't know. It still just seems so surreal, and I hate being the center of attention. This photographer is supposed to be one of the best though."

"Who is it?" he asks.

"Fernando something. I don't know. He's friends with Mercedes, and he made room in his schedule for her."

He doesn't respond, and I'm just about to ask him if he's okay when someone taps me on the shoulder.

"Are you Miss James?" the woman asks, and I nod. "We're ready for you."

I nod and motion for her to give me a minute before turning away again. "Hey, so I guess I gotta go but I'll see you later?"

"Yeah, Baby. I'll stop by."

A grin stretches across my face when he calls me baby, and a blush rises to my cheeks. "Okay. See you later, then."

We hang up, and I turn back around, smiling. "Sorry about that."

She grins and shakes her head, directing me to follow her. "Don't even worry about it. You've got that new relationship glow. I'm a little envious."

"Well, thank you."

"You're welcome. I'm Candace, Nando's assistant, so I'll be glued to your side all day. First off we need to get you to hair and make-up, and then we'll pop over to wardrobe. Sound good?"

I nod dumbly. "Sure."

She laughs and stops walking to place a hand on my shoulder. "I know it's kind of overwhelming but just try to relax. Nando really is the best, and he'll capture who you are if you let him."

"I'll give it a try."

She puts her hand on the side of her mouth like she's about to tell me a big secret and whispers, "And we also have some champagne in the back if that'll help."

I laugh again, feeling more at ease already. "A glass might be good."

"Perfect. I'll have someone fetch it for you."

I nod, and she makes small talk as we walk to hair and make-up. When we get to the room, she directs me to sit in the chair in front of the mirrors just as another woman walks into the room. She's a little older than me, and her dark hair is piled on top of her head.

"Hi, Sweetie, I'm Bailey, and don't let this unkempt hair deter you from trusting me with your beautiful locks."

I laugh and nod. "All right, I won't. I'm Ali, nice to meet you."

"Lovely to meet you, too. Now, has anyone gone over the two concepts we're working on today?" she asks, and I shake my head. Candace looks up from her phone.

"Oh, my bad. Forgot all about that part. Okay, so look one, we want something down to earth. You know, your best friend, the person you can tell your deepest darkest secrets to. They're going to dress you in a sweater and jeans, I think, and have you posing on a couch. Super relatable. But it's still a little sexy."

"Okay," I agree, nodding. I can do relatable.

"The second look is a little sexier. You in a pencil skirt and button up shirt posing on or behind a desk. Still try and look like people can tell you their secrets but just do it in a sexy way. Maybe with some glasses, too. Let me text Nando and see what he thinks."

She starts typing away on her phone, and I'm tired from just being around her. She moves in hyper speed, and I can't imagine doing that all day.

"Nando likes the glasses," she says, hopping up from the couch. "Let me go look in wardrobe and see if we've got something that'll work."

She practically bounces out of the room, and I turn to Bailey as she starts parting my hair. "What if they don't have any that will work?"

She shrugs. "They get new ones delivered. Nando is a stickler for details, and if it's in his mind you're wearing glasses, then he'll make it happen."

I try to breathe as she starts on my hair but it's difficult. This is all so crazy, and it's hard to imagine a photo of me being up on billboards and all over the Internet soon. I guess I should get used to the idea though. If Mercedes's plan works, a lot of people will know who I am and read my advice.

I would be so much more comfortable if it was just people reading my words. That, I can handle but people seeing my face and now Mercedes is talking about doing a few appearances if things take off. It's all so much, and I think she's getting way ahead of herself. I mean, I'm an advice columnist in Baton Rouge, Louisiana, for Christ's sake, not some big movie star. Maybe nothing will come of it. Maybe we'll do all this and no one will really care. Honestly, now that I think about it, I don't know which one is worse.

"Good news! We've got the perfect black rimmed glasses over in wardrobe," Candace exclaims, bouncing back into the room, and I smile at her. She plops back down on the couch and goes back to texting as Bailey continues on my hair, curling it.

I lean back in my chair and just try to relax as she works on me, and before I know it, Candace is handing me a glass of champagne and guiding me to wardrobe. I down the last of the alcohol just before the woman in wardrobe shoves me behind a partition and hands me a gorgeous white sweater that doesn't even reach my belly button and a pair of jeans.

"How are your toes?" a woman asks, peeking her head around the partition without waiting for my answer.

"Can we get polish in here?" she yells out into the room, and everyone starts scurrying around, rushing to get me all put together before I have to go out there. Someone comes back with red nail polish and rolls up my jeans as she kneels in front of me and starts painting my toes. Everything happens in a blur, and then I'm being shoved out into the main room where the sets are built side by side with a wall separating them.

"Ah, here she is. I'm Fernando, Gorgeous. So nice to meet you," the small man who just introduced himself says as he rushes over to me and grabs my hand, leaning down to kiss it. A growl sounds from the back of the warehouse and everyone turns to look as Storm steps out of the shadows.

"Do not kiss her fucking hand," he snaps, shooting a glare at Fernando, who is still holding my hand in his. He drops it and looks over to me.

"Who is this, love?"

"Uh…" I say, unsure of what to call him.

"Her man," Storm answers for me, and I turn to look at him with wide eyes, a slow smile stretching across my face.

"We don't allow boyfriends," Fernando says, huffing in annoyance, and Storm doesn't even glance over at him.

"I'm not leaving."

Fernando throws his hands up in the air and looks around him for some support but no one says anything. Storm is huge, and there is no one in this warehouse who would even dream of taking him on.

"Fine," Fernando says, doing his best to level an intimidating glare at Storm but he's not even fazed. "But do not get in the way."

"What are you doing here?" I whisper as he steps in front of me. His gaze lingers on my face before dropping down to the hint of cleavage that the sweater shows off. He licks his lips, and I instinctively move closer to him. "Just wanted to see you, Darlin'."

"I'm glad you did," I tell him, forgetting about all the other people in this room as I stare up at him. His eyes heat as they roam my face, and he reaches out for me. Candace slaps his hand hard, and he turns a glare to her that would scare most men.

"No touching. She's perfect, and you'll mess her up."

He clears his throat, a pained expression taking over his face for a second before he pushes it away. He may not be able to touch me but I sure as hell can touch him. I reach out and lay my hand on his arm, letting him know that I'm here for him. His gaze snaps to mine. The fire dancing there is hot enough to consume me.

"I'll wait for you here," he says, and I nod before blowing him a kiss. He grins as I start walking backward, not wanting to pull my gaze away just yet.

"Hey, how did you know where I was?" I ask, still backing away from him, and he shrugs.

"I've got a guy."

I laugh and stop, shaking my head at him. "You know that makes you sound like a stalker, right?"

He grins and tips his chin to the scene behind me, telling me to get to work. I wink and spin around, following Candace over to the set where a black leather couch is set up against a brick wall backdrop. The entire set looks like a stylish but homey living room, and I get a little rush of excitement for the first time since this whole thing started.

"Okay, Gorgeous," Fernando says, wrapping an arm around my shoulders as he points to the set in front of us. Storm growls again from the back, and Fernando rolls his eyes. "For this first one, I want you to be everyone's best friend, someone they can confide in. We'll start with you on the couch and see where it goes from there. Sometimes my best ideas come to me when I start shooting."

"Sounds good."

"Now, Darling, I want you to sit on that couch in the corner and curl your legs underneath you. Look sweet but still a little sexy for me, yes?"

Another growl sounds from the back of the warehouse, and I bite down on my lip in an attempt to stifle my laughter. Fernando sighs and flicks an annoyed glance over his shoulder. "And please remind your man that he is not a jungle cat."

The laughter spills out of me, and I meet Storm's eye as he shakes his head, a smirk on his face. His gaze is intense, staring at me like I'm the only woman in the room. I know I'm the one under these lights but Candace is right next to him, and she's gorgeous, but still, he only has eyes for me.

As the make-up artist rushes out to touch up my face, I keep my eyes trained on him, the unmistakable spark between us making my body all tingly as I wait for the photos to start. God, how is he doing this to me? How is one look enough to make me want to strip naked in front of him?

"Okay, here we go," Fernando calls, and I divert my attention to him just as he starts snapping the camera like crazy, calling out instructions to me. I'm constantly moving, putting my hand in my hair, taking it out again, smiling, pouting, looking understanding. Again and again the shutter snaps, taking photo after photo, and I wonder just how many he needs.

I can feel Storm's eyes on me through the whole process, and every time I peek over at him, his gaze is locked on me. The hunger in his eyes is driving me wild, and a blush creeps up to my cheeks. I turn back to Fernando, my pulse beating between my thighs.

"Yes, just like that, Darling. You look incredible," Fernando calls, and I turn my gaze back to Storm. I want him to see me like this. I feel sexy, and it's all because of him. He's the one evoking these reactions in my body, and I want him to know it. When my eyes meet his, he licks his lips, taking a step forward before he can stop himself. He drops his gaze, and I look back to Fernando.

"Okay, that's all for this set. Go get changed, love, and we'll start on the next set."

I nod and climb off the couch. Seeking out Storm in the crowd of people standing around watching the shoot, I finally find him off to the side and go over to him, ignoring Candace calling my name.

"Hey," I whisper, my chest swelling as I quietly gasp for air.

"Fucking gorgeous," he says, almost to himself as his gaze drops down my body.

"I have to go change, okay?"

"Yeah, I'll be here."

I nod and sneak in one last glance before I follow Candace to hair and make-up, where they quickly change me into the second outfit and pile my hair into a bun. They give me a few moments to myself to relax but before I can even sit down, there's a knock at the door. I open it and smile when Storm immediately steps into my space and hooks his hand around the back of my neck.

"Hey, stranger," I say, looking up at him, and he doesn't respond, his gaze solely focused on my red painted lips. He doesn't waste a second dipping down and claiming my mouth in a kiss that makes me want to lock the door and tell them all to go to hell. How long is he going to make me wait? I want him.

"Shit," he mutters when he pulls back and looks down at my face. I start laughing at the red lipstick smeared around his mouth and start wiping it away with my thumb.

"You're going to send poor Fernando into a tizzy," I tell him, and he glares over my head.

"Fuck him. He needs to keep his goddamn hands off you."

"Oh, yeah, tough guy? Why's that?"

"Because," he replies, and I just stare up at him, willing him to say the words. I want to hear him say that I'm his, that the thought of any other man touching me kills him.

"Because?" I finally break and ask him.

"Because I don't like it."

It's not exactly what I was hoping for but I'll take it. I finish wiping the make-up off his face and lean up on my tiptoes, planting one more quick kiss on his lips.

"Well, you shouldn't worry because I was too preoccupied by this other guy to even notice that he was touching me," I tease, running my hand up the open zipper of his leather jacket.

"Yeah? Sounds like a lucky bastard."

I shrug, and he grins at the face I make. "I can't disagree with you."

"Two minutes," someone calls and knocks on the door, opening it without waiting for a response. Candace takes one look at me and rolls her eyes.

"We need make-up in here again!" she yells down the hall.

"You should probably go," I say with a sigh and he nods.

"That's actually why I came in here. I just got a call from Blaze and I gotta run."

I frown, too disappointed to even try and hide it. "Okay. Dinner tonight?"

"I'm not sure. This might be an all nighter."

I nod and hate how easily he can get to me. My mood immediately picked up when he showed up here, and it's plummeting again now that he's leaving. "Okay."

His hand slides in my hair, and he pulls me forward, planting his lips on my forehead. "I'll text you later, Baby. I gotta go."

People start filing into the room, and I nod, peeking up at him as he releases me. He slips out as they start fixing my make-up again, and I sigh, pushing away my disappointment so I can finish this shoot. With any luck, I'll see him again later tonight.

Chapter Twelve
Alison

The nerves hit full force as I step out of my car and shut the door behind me. My stomach twists, and each breath I pull into my lungs echoes in my ear as my heels click against the concrete. The building that houses the radio station looms in front of me, and I stop for a moment, taking a deep breath. I've been a reporter for years but the thought of going in there and being on the radio makes my entire body tremble. I'm much more happy tucked away in an office somewhere, writing to everyone.

"Ali," a familiar voice calls, and I turn, catching sight of Mercedes striding across the lot like she owns it. Who knows, she just might. I smile at her when she reaches me and wraps me in a hug.

"Hey, what are you doing here?"

She shrugs and checks her phone. She's constantly glued to that thing. "Here for support."

"Oh, you didn't have to do that," I say, even though I'm honestly touched. It's nice having your boss in your corner. She glances up from the screen and locks her eyes on mine.

"You seemed nervous about all this, and I told you, I've got your back. I'm not Klein."

"Well, thank you."

She tucks her phone back into her bag and smiles brightly at me. "No need to thank me. We ready to do this?"

I look up at the building again and suck in a nervous breath before nodding. With Mercedes at my side, I do feel a little more comfortable walking into the bland reception area. From the muted gray carpet to the white walls, everything about this place is boring. Then again, I suppose they don't really need to look good. It is radio, after all.

"Can I help you?" an older receptionist asks from behind the desk, and Mercedes takes control of the situation, walking over to her and hoisting her large bag up on the counter.

"Yes. I'm Mercedes Richmond, and this is Alison James. She's doing an interview here today."

"Yes, of course. Follow me, please." She rises from her seat and starts off down the hallway to her left as we follow behind her. We pass a few empty offices, and when we reach the back, she stops and waves to a man behind a glass wall. He gives her a thumbs-up, and she turns back to us with a professional smile.

"Just wait here. He'll be out in a moment." She hurries off the way we came, and Mercedes grabs my arm, giving it a little squeeze.

"How you feeling?"

I nod, looking over the sound booth. "I'm okay, I think."

"Just be yourself, Ali. It's why I hired you and why people loved your article. Don't forget that."

I nod, smiling at her. Having her here really does help me feel better. "Wow, you give good pep talks."

Before she can say anything else, the sound booth door opens, and a man who looks like the real life Shaggy from the Scooby-Doo cartoons pokes his head out. Long messy blond hair falls into his face, and his plaid shirt looks like it's two sizes too big for his tall, lanky body.

"Alison?" he asks, looking between Mercedes and I. I raise my hand as she pushes me forward, still not looking up from her phone and I roll my eyes. He motions for me to follow him, and I start walking toward the door but he looks behind me to Mercedes.

"You'll need to stay out here. There is a pair of headphones and a chair over there for you." He points to a small desk that's pushed up against the glass with a set of headphones laying on top. She finally looks up from her phone and nods, dragging the chair from the wall over to the desk as she plops her purse down and sets up shop.

He turns back to the booth and I follow him inside. "We don't have a lot of time but I'm Sam. It's nice to meet you."

"Nice to meet you, too, Sam," I say, offering him a polite smile.

"Just go ahead and have a seat over there and put those headphones on. I'll introduce you, and then we'll get started. Sound good?"

"That sounds great." I take a deep breath as I move around the round desk and sit at the microphone next to his. He throws the headphones on his head and turns his chair to face me. Just as he starts counting down from five, I put the headphones on and set my bag down on the floor next to me, trying not to freak out that I'm about to go on the air.

"Welcome back," he booms into the microphone as soon as he gets to one, his entire face coming alive as he speaks to his listeners. It's easy to see why he does this. If you saw a side-by-side comparison of the man who greeted me outside this booth and the man I'm sitting next to right now, you'd never believe they were the same person. "I've got something exciting for you all today! Viral star, Alison James, is here!"

It feels weird to hear him call me a viral star but I guess that's what I am now. But that doesn't mean I like it.

"Now, you all may remember the article Alison wrote a few days ago about her horrible online dating experiences. She's also the new advice columnist over at Champagne Dreaming, a blog run by Mercedes Richmond, daughter of billionaire Charles Richmond. Thanks for being here today, Alison."

I startle and lean into the microphone. "Thanks for having me."

"Oh, we're glad to have you, and can I just say from guys everywhere, we're sorry about those dates."

I laugh. "Well, thank you but there's no need. They are done and over with, and I'm happy to put them in my past."

"So, I kind of have to ask the obvious question here, are you single? Did anything come of those dates?"

I open my mouth and close it again, not sure what to say. Are Storm and I dating? He's always around but it's not like we've talked about it. And yeah, I really like him a lot but still, we just met.

"Oh, boy, I'm judging by the look on your face that there might just be someone in your life."

I laugh and tuck my hair behind my ear, trying to keep the blush from rising to my cheeks. "Well, it's new so I'm not really sure what we are yet but I did meet someone."

"And am I safe in assuming that it's not one of the guys from the article?"

I decide to let as little information slip as possible and look up at him as I pretend to zip my lips. "I'm afraid that that's all the information you're going to get from me."

"Oh, what a tease," he says, laughing, and I join in. I peek out at Mercedes, and she grins at me.

"All right, well, let's get down to the real reason why you're here, shall we?"

I nod. "Let's do it."

"You heard her, folks. When we get back, Ali's going to be taking your calls and dishing out advice so stay tuned."

Music starts playing over the headphones, and the guy across from me pulls his off, and I follow suit. "How was that? Not so bad?"

"No, that was fun. I definitely feel less nervous now," I tell him, and he smiles.

"Good. No need to be nervous. You ever done promo like this before?"

I laugh and shake my head. Before this, I worked at a small paper. I've never been interviewed like this in my life. "No."

He grins and nods, taking a sip of the soda next to him. "Yeah, most people haven't."

"How did you get started?"

"Did it in college and never stopped doing it, I guess. They say I have a face for radio."

Thank god, he laughs because I can't help but join in with him. He looks over at something and sits up in his chair again.

"Here we go," he says as he starts counting down on his fingers again, and I slip my headphones on.

"And we're back with Alison James. She's gonna be dishing out advice for you all so let's take our first caller. Caller one, you're on the air. What's your name?"

"Hannah." The timid voice comes over the headphones, and I smile.

"Hi, Hannah."

Sam smiles at me. "Thanks for calling, Hannah. You got a question for Ali?"

"Yeah, I do."

"Let's hear it," I prompt, and even through the headphones, I can hear her take a deep breath.

"So, there is this guy that I've had a crush on forever, and sometimes he seems like he's into me, too, and then other times it's like I don't exist. When things are good, they are so good but I have no idea what he really wants from me. What should I do?"

"Well, Hannah, this one is kind of easy, and let me start off by saying that boys are stupid, sometimes. No offense, Sam."

He holds his hands up, grinning. "I'm right there with 'ya. We're idiots, Hannah."

She giggles, and I can feel some of her tension melt away.

"The real question you need to consider, Hannah, is if you can live with regret. You basically have two options. You can ignore this and spend the rest of your life wondering what would have happened if you'd had the balls to act or you can make the leap and hope it works out."

"But… what if he doesn't like me?"

"Tell me something, Hannah. Why would you want to spend your life pining after a guy who doesn't realize what a babe you are?"

She giggles again, and I smile as I look out at Mercedes, who is practically bouncing in her seat.

"Well, when you put it that way," Hannah says and laughs again.

"Listen, either way, it's good for you. Either you get the guy you like or you can stop wasting your time wondering if there is anything between you. And if he doesn't want you, there are plenty of other guys who will."

"It's just that he's been a part of my life for so long. We've been friends since we were kids. I don't want to lose him."

"Whoever said you had to cut him out of your life completely? You can let go of this crush without letting go of him. But, Hannah, you deserve to be happy, and it sounds like you're kind of miserable right now."

"Well, yeah. He's got this on again off again thing with someone but he always comes to me when he needs anything."

"Ouch," Sam cuts in, "I hate to say it but it sounds like you've been friend zoned hard, Hannah."

"I agree. But I'm curious why you would want a relationship with a guy who clearly doesn't appreciate you. I'm a big believer in fate, Hannah, and I think if you let this guy go and just be his friend, you're going to meet someone who will really sweep you off your feet."

"Damn. Mic drop," Sam calls out into the room, and both Hannah and I laugh. "Thanks so much for your call, Hannah. Let's take one more before we go to break. You're on the air, caller. Who am I talking to?"

"I'd rather not say my name," a deep voice says, and Sam looks to me for confirmation. I shrug.

"Okay, that's fine. You got a question for Ali today?"

"Uh, no, not really. I just wanted to talk to her and tell her that I'm a huge fan."

"Well, thank you. I appreciate that," I say into the microphone.

"Hi, Ali. It's so nice to be talking to you," the caller says, his voice getting softer when he speaks to me, and I look up at Sam, who smirks at me.

"You, too."

"Seems someone's got a little crush on Ali. Eh, caller?" Sam asks.

"No, I just wanted to tell her I'm looking forward to reading the new column," he says, and you can hear how uncomfortable he is.

"Thank you so much. I hope you're going to like it."

"Oh, I'm sure that I will. Everything you write is so good, and you're so talented."

"Well, thank you for saying that."

"Of course. You should hear how great you are everyday and so beautiful, too. I love that picture of you they put next to your articles. I've read everything you've ever written."

"Thank you," I mumble, really not liking the icky feeling that's washing over me right now.

"Anytime, Gorgeous. I'm just a huge fan, and I can't believe I'm actually talking to you right now."

I look over to Sam, desperate for him to do something and he nods, leaning in toward the mic.

"We've got to take a break, folks, but we'll be back with Ali in a few."

Sam starts up the next song and pulls his headphones off at the same time that I do. I toss them on the counter in front of me and sigh. He looks over at me and shakes his head.

"Man, that was…" Sam starts to say, his voice trailing off when he can't find the right word.

"Uncomfortable?" I ask, and he laughs.

"Yeah, that's one way to describe it." He stands from his chair and stretches. "Let's go grab a soda. We've got a little time before we go on again."

We step out of the booth, and Mercedes squeals as she rushes over to me. "My god, Ali. That was great."

"Yeah, except for that last call."

She shrugs. "Brush it off, buttercup. You've got another forty-five minutes of this to go."

I nod and follow Sam to the break room where he grabs a soda for himself before grabbing another one for me. We walk back to the sound booth and settle back into our seats just as time is running out. I slip my headphones on, and Sam points to me.

"That was *I Can't Go On Without You* by Kaleo, and I'm back with Alison James, taking your calls. What's your name, caller?" Sam asks into the microphone.

"Karen."

"Hi, Karen," I say.

"You got a question for Ali today?" Sam asks, leaning back in his chair as he pulls the microphone closer.

"Yes. So, recently, my husband has been acting strange. He comes home late, and he's not interested in sex anymore. Do you think he's cheating on me?"

"That's a tough one, Karen. You say he's been working late; have you asked him about what's going on at work?"

"Well, no."

"Have you tried to do something nice for him? Maybe set the mood a little so he'll be in the mood for sex?"

"No," she answers, and I nod even though she can't see me.

"Have you tried to get him to open up at all about what's going on?"

"Yes, once. But he wouldn't talk to me at all," she says, sounding distraught and I feel for her.

"Okay, we've got a couple of scenarios here. Either, one, he's cheating on you, or he really is working a lot and he's stressed out. Have you guys had infidelity issues in the past?"

"We've been together since college, and he did cheat on me once when we were still in school but we've been solid ever since then."

"Here's what I think you should do. While he's at work, go get your hair done, your nails done, get a wax. Then come home, get all dressed up and cook him a nice meal. After that, just jump his bones. As I mentioned earlier, Karen, guys are kind of stupid sometimes, and you need to take the reins."

"What if he's still not interested?" she asks, her voice so timid that it breaks my heart. Her fear for her marriage is coming through her voice loud and clear.

"If he doesn't want to have sex with you after all that, you turn into the FBI, Karen. You search his car, his email, his phone - everywhere. You figure out what the hell is going on with that man, and if you find out he is cheating, leave his ass. Life's too short."

"I take it you believe once a cheater, always a cheater, eh?" Sam asks, looking uncomfortable, and I'm willing to bet a million dollars that he cheated on a girl at some point in his life.

"No, not always. If it's a one-time mistake and the guy goes to his girl and confesses then no, I don't think he would do it again but when you've got someone that's carrying on a relationship with a whole other person, you've got to think about cutting your losses."

"That's kind of harsh, don't you think?" Sam asks, and I look over at him with a raised brow.

"Why? He made vows to this woman, and if he broke them, why the hell should she just bend over and take it? Why should she devalue herself to accommodate whatever is wrong with his tiny ego? If he's cheating, and that's still a big if, he knew the consequences. He knew when he started this that it could end his marriage. Or he thought she'd never leave which is honestly, worse."

"Thank you, Ali," Karen says, cutting through our argument, and I turn my attention back to her.

"Sorry we got a little carried away there, Karen."

"No, thank you. It was exactly what I needed to hear. I'm going to try your advice and seduce my husband."

I laugh. "Good. I'd love to hear how it all turns out, okay? You can find my email address on the blog."

"Absolutely. Thank you so much."

"Thanks for calling in, Karen. We'll take a quick break and be back to answer more questions,"

Sam says before tossing his headphones off. The awkwardness descends on us, and I slip mine off, looking over at him.

"Sorry about that. It's kind of a hot button issue for me."

He's quiet for a second before shaking his head. "No, it's okay. It's obviously something that bothers me, too. Just for a completely different reason but I can't say that you were wrong in anything you said."

"Well, thank you for that."

He nods, and my phone buzzes on the desk next to me. I grab it, a smile pulling at my lips as soon as I look at the screen.

Storm:
I want to see you tonight.

I set my phone down, ready to get this all over with so I can rush back home and see him. If we keep going the way we're going, I'm going to fall for him. It's inevitable.

A.M. Myers

Chapter Thirteen
Alison

Glancing in the mirror one last time, I run my fingers through my hair and wipe under my eye to brush off any excess powder before grabbing my bag and turning toward the door. I pull it open and stop short when I almost crash into Storm, standing on the other side. It's been a few days since I've seen him, and I missed him. I'm sure that it sounds stupid since I literally just met him but I missed not seeing him. Texting him just wasn't cutting it for me.

"Hi," I say, taking my time looking over him. I like him, and I don't care about hiding it anymore. I don't care about what I should or shouldn't say. Not like it matters. I'm probably shit at keeping the fact that he gets to me a secret.

"Hey, I brought you something." He holds up a small brown paper bag, and I smile.

"I get the distinct feeling that it's some kind of food."

He frowns and crosses his arms over his chest. "You saying I'm predictable?"

"If it walks like a duck..." I reply, letting my voice trail off as I shrug, and he scowls down at me. "Or maybe, you just have some odd fetish where you like to watch me eat. So...which is it?"

A deep growl rumbles in his chest as he leans down and latches on to my waist, lifting me up in the air so I'm eye to eye with him. "Or maybe I just like taking care of you."

I melt. It's a damn good thing that he's holding me otherwise I'd be a puddle on the floor. "Well, I like that answer but I don't have time for breakfast."

"Make time," he demands, walking into the house and shutting the door behind him before carrying me into the kitchen and setting me down on the counter in the exact same spot that he bandaged my knee.

"Seriously, Storm. I'm going to be late if I stay and have breakfast with you."

He grabs the pot of coffee I made a little bit earlier and pours a cup. "Cream or sugar?" he asks.

"Are you listening to me? I really have to go."

"Cream or sugar?" he asks again, and I sigh, nodding my head as I point to the fridge.

"Two creams. They're in the fridge, second shelf."

He opens the fridge and grabs the little individual cream cups and pours them in the mug before bringing it over to me.

"Storm, I have to go now," I say again, glancing up at the clock on the wall.

"Baby, shut up and eat breakfast with me. I'll get you there on time."

My brow quirks, and I shoot him a look. "And how are you going to do that? Traffic is terrible in the morning."

"Not on a bike." He holds a pastry in front of my face. "Now, eat."

I bite into it, not taking my eyes off him. His eyes are warm like a crackling fire as he watches me eat, a smile lighting up his face. He pulls the pastry away and leans in, licking a drop of frosting off my lip, and I barely hold in a moan.

"I fucking missed you," he mumbles like he can't quite believe it himself, and I lean into him, kissing his cheek just below his ear.

"I missed you, too," I whisper, surprised that I admitted it out loud. He pulls back and searches my eyes, seeking an answer to some unspoken question. After a moment, he leans in and presses his lips to mine with a hunger that makes my entire body ache with need. He pulls away and shakes his head, turning away for a second.

"Here, finish this, and I'll get you to work." He hands me the pastry, and I take a few more bites before setting it down on the counter and drinking some more coffee. He turns back to me, and I set the mug down before jumping off the counter and grabbing my bag.

"Okay, let's go."

"Shit. I'm really sorry but I just got a text from the guys, and I gotta go. Tell your boss it was all my fault, all right?" He leaves without another word, and I just stand in my kitchen for a moment, trying to catch up to what the hell just happened. Just when I think there might be something here, he disappears and I can't help but wonder if he's making up all these excuses to avoid me.

Shaking my head, I walk out to my car, and just as I'm opening the door, he drives past me on his bike. I watch him until he turns the corner and sigh as I slide behind the wheel. I don't want to push but I need to know what the hell this is and soon.

I start the car and head toward work, doing my best to rush, but as predicted, the traffic is terrible. Luckily, I'm only five minutes late when I walk in, and Mercedes smiles at me.

"Sorry I'm late," I say, and she laughs.

"Five minutes? Please, I'm five minutes late all the time. No biggie. Meet me in my office in ten though. There are some things that we need to go over."

"Okay."

"Oh, and if you're late 'cause you were totally having sex with that hot as sin man that came in asking for you the other day, then I fully endorse you not coming in on time."

I scowl. "Wait. What guy?"

"I don't know. He showed up the day of your photo shoot, asking for you."

Is that how Storm found out where I was? "Did you tell him where to find me?"

"No way in hell, girlfriend," she says, shaking her head. "I've watched way too many Criminal Minds episodes to fall for that shit. Come see me in a few," she calls as she walks off.

I nod and rush off to my office, ready to lose myself in work so I don't have to think about what the hell happened this morning. Carly is ducking into her office as I walk by, and she waves at me. I force a smile to my face and wave but she spins around and starts following me.

"I know that look. Spill," she says as I sink into my chair, and I sigh. I bury my face in my hands and shake my head.

"I honestly don't even know."

"Don't know what?"

I peek up at her and she sits down in one of the chairs across from me. "Storm."

"What about him?" she asks, looking concerned, and I lift my head, letting my arms fall to the desk.

"I have no idea what's going on with him. One minute he's all over me, and the next he's backing away. I was already scared to even try again after everything with Adam, and now this is just making it worse."

"Have you tried talking to him about it?"

"No, we never talk about stuff like that. I mean, I can tell you his favorite color or stories from when he was a kid but I have no idea what he wants from me. Like, this morning, he showed up with breakfast, and he was being so sweet then he just shut down and walked out."

A worried expression crosses her face, and she leans back, folding her arms over her chest. "Maybe you should just back off."

"I don't know, Carly. I've never felt a connection like this to someone."

"Is it worth all this though?"

I look up at the clock and sigh, standing to go over to Mercedes's office. "I guess that's what I have to figure out. Mercedes wants to see me so we'll talk more later."

She nods and stands, giving me a quick hug. "Sure. Come find me later."

After I agree, she leaves, and I walk over to Mercedes's office, pushing all the stuff with Storm down so I can focus on work. Sucking in a breath, I stand up straighter and knock on Mercedes's door. She glances up and smiles.

"Come in. I've got so much to show you."

As I step into her office and sit across from her, she spins in her chair and grabs a few things from the table behind her before laying them in front of me. They are the photos from the shoot, and even I have to admit they look incredible.

"Wow," I mutter, spreading them out across the desk so I can look at all of them.

"Right? They're incredible. I don't know who you were channeling there but it's perfect. You look sexy and alluring but approachable. Every girl in this city will want to be you and the guys will want to be with you."

I laugh and push them away. "Well, I'm not sure if that was the point of the shoot."

"Oh, but it was. We've gotten so many letters since these went live yesterday morning. Everyone wants to hear your advice, and I'd bet good money that after the radio show yesterday, we'll get even more today. I might have to get another intern just to handle it all."

I laugh again and shake my head. "I'm glad you're happy with it."

She stops and scowls as she studies me. "What's wrong?"

"Nothing. Just personal stuff."

"Is it a guy?"

I laugh. "What makes you think it's a guy?"

"Oh, Honey, it's always a guy," she says, waving her hand through the air as she turns back to look at her computer. I laugh again, feeling better already.

"Whatever. I'm sure I'll figure it out soon."

"Are you sure? You can talk to me if you want."

I shake my head and stand. "No, really. It's okay. I need to go read through a bunch of letters apparently."

"Oh, yeah you do."

I wave good-bye and head back to my office where two large boxes of letters are already waiting for me. Jesus. I don't know what Mercedes did but, apparently, she's a marketing genius. I grab the first letter off the top and open it as I walk over to my desk and sink into my chair.

Dear Alison,
I'm sure you don't remember me but we spoke on the radio show yesterday. I wasn't comfortable giving my name on there but I just wanted to take a moment to tell you how much it meant to me. You were so incredibly sweet, and I think everything about you is

amazing. You're so talented and kind. The new ads of you look incredible also. You are gorgeous, and any guy would be lucky as hell to have you. I really mean that. You're a treasure. I won't take up any more of your time since I'm really looking forward to reading anything and everything that you write. Actually, now that I think about it, I do have a question for you. What would a guy have to do to win the heart of a woman who probably wouldn't even give him a second glance on the street?

Your biggest fan,
Chris

"Hey, Ali," Carly says, laying her hand on my shoulder, and I jump, my heart pounding in my chest. I look up at her with wide eyes as I try to catch my breath, and a worried expression crosses her face. "What's wrong?"

"God, Carly, you scared the shit out of me."

"I'm sorry. I thought you saw me walk in."

I shake my head and hold up the letter. "No, I was reading this and freaking out a little."

She grabs the letter from me and begins reading through it before glancing up at me again. "Why did this freak you out?"

"I don't know. I mean, I talked to the guy yesterday at the radio show and felt a little weird there, too."

She looks down and reads it again. When she's done, she tosses it down on the desk. "It seems innocent enough to me. Your column went viral, Ali. You're bound to have a couple of letters like these come in."

I nod and shake off the lingering fear before smiling at my own ridiculousness. "You're right. I'm making way too big of a deal about this."

"You've got fans now, girl. Remember us little people when you become a big superstar," she teases, and I wrinkle my nose up at her.

"Yeah, right. Did you come in here just to harass me?"

"Oh, no, actually. I wanted to talk about your sexy neighbor some more."

I point to the chair across from me, and she slips around my desk and plops down in the seat. I begin telling her everything – hoping that she can help me figure out what to do about Storm and whatever this is between us.

Chapter Fourteen
Chris

4:35 p.m.
She's usually out here by now.
Where is she?
I check my watch again and make sure I got the time right because she's always out of the office by four-thirty at the latest.
4:36 p.m.
I scan the street around the entrance to the building where she works, making sure that I didn't miss her before laughing at my own stupidity. I would never miss her. Never. My knee bounces, and I check my watch again, sighing loudly when I realize that the minute hand hasn't moved at all. I feel like I'm suffocating, a burning sensation burrowing into my chest, and I know it won't ease up until I see her again. Glancing over in the passenger seat, I run my fingers over the picture of her that I always keep with me but it's not enough.
Where the hell is she?

This situation kills me. I know why she wanted to keep our relationship private for a little while with her new job, but right now, I despise the fact that I can't march over there and find her. My fingers tap against the steering wheel, and I look back to her building. I wish I wasn't so far away but my usual spot right in front of the doors was taken today so I had to park all the way across the street. It pains me to be this far away from her. I need just one little peek to get me through the rest of my day until I can be with her again.

I shouldn't have let her talk me into this. When she suggested that we not tell anyone about us, I should have put my foot down and told her no way in hell, but God, I love her, and I just couldn't say no. I would cut off my right arm if that's what she asked me to do or she gave any indication that it would make her happy. I live to see her smile.

4:40 p.m.

Jesus Christ, where is she?

What if she's hurt?

What if she's in danger?

Panic claws at me as that possibility twists in my mind, and anger bubbles down deep inside me. The thought of someone putting their hands on her makes me fucking homicidal. She's my goddamn world, and I would die before I'd ever allow someone to take her from me or tarnish her beauty. I'll tear this entire goddamn city apart to find her. There isn't anywhere that they can hide her, nowhere that they'll be able to keep her from me.

She's mine.

MINE.

Hopelessly Devoted

The moment we met, her soul was marked, and she'll never be free of me again. I dare someone to try and steal her away from me. I'll destroy them.

Just as I'm reaching for the door handle, ready to say screw it to her request to keep our relationship private, a flash of blonde hair catches my eye across the street. There she is. My angel. Air rushes into my lungs, unhindered by my need no longer, and I smile as she stops in front of her building and digs through her purse.

She's absolute perfection – everything I've ever wanted, and I knew it from the moment I laid eyes on her. I'll never get tired of running my hands down her generous curves or pressing my lips to hers. There isn't a single flaw on my woman, and I can't wait until I can finally show her off in front of everyone. Someday, she'll walk down the aisle to me in a white dress, and everyone will know that she's mine.

Mine.

The word rings through my head as I watch her pull her phone out of her bag and smile down at the screen. I run my fingers down the window, wishing I could just touch her for a second before I have to go back to work. Someone bumps into her, and she stumbles forward a little. My body lurches forward, and my hand is already on the door handle, one hundred percent ready to march across the street and bury this fucker for even thinking about touching what's mine. I'll teach him a lesson he'll never forget.

She stands up straight and runs her hands down her skirt, smoothing it as she smiles up at the man and seeing her at ease is the only thing that keeps me in the car, keeping my promise to her. If she had been upset, I'd be burying a body instead of going back to finish my shift. She slips the phone into the front pocket of her purse and lays her hand on the man's arm, and I see red. Oh, fuck no. We're going to have a conversation later about her touching other men. Not gonna fucking happen.

I grind my teeth as the man walks off, and Ali turns toward the parking garage, smiling at everyone as she passes them. She looks like she had a good day at work, and that makes me breathe a little easier. I wonder if she got my letter today. Maybe it was stupid but I just thought it would be a fun little game since I can't really talk to her during the day. That way, she'll know that I'm thinking about her.

She disappears into the parking garage but I stay rooted in my spot to make sure she gets out of there okay. A few minutes later, her car pulls out, and I glance at my watch, cursing the fact that I don't have enough time to follow her home to make sure she's safe. Taking a deep breath, I remind myself that I'll be seeing her soon enough as she disappears in my rearview mirror.

Chapter Fifteen
Alison

As I pull up in front of my house, I throw the car in park and lean back in the seat, unable to stop the smile from spreading across my face. I'm totally in love with my new job, and not even Storm's weirdness this morning or the letter I got today can dampen my mood. Just the thought of him pulls my gaze over to his house. His bike is parked out front, and I really want to see him again but nerves twist in my stomach, and I turn toward the house instead. I still don't know what the deal is between us, and I know I won't figure it out until he decides to talk to me – if he ever does. Maybe I read into this too much and mistook the constant texting for more than it was. No, that's not possible. I've seen the way he looks at me and the way he can't seem to stay away. A woman knows when a man wants her. But something is making him pull away.

Someone screams across the street, and I turn just as two little boys run through the front yard, shooting toy guns at each other and I smile. The streetlights are just coming on, and they cast a warm glow over the darkening neighborhood, giving it a cozy feel. Turning back to the house, I decide to just let this go tonight. I told myself I wasn't going to overanalyze this but it's all I've done. All I want to worry about tonight is a comfy pair of sweats and a glass of wine while I lose myself in some mindless television. I pull my keys out of my bag and unlock the door, setting my bag down on the entry table as I flick the light switch up.

Nothing happens.

Shit.

I peer into the pitch-black house but what I'm looking for, I have no idea. The fuse box is in the utility closet in the hall but I hate the dark. Even when I go to bed at night, I usually leave a small light on somewhere so it's not completely dark if I wake up in the middle of the night. As I stare into the house, an uneasy feeling washes over me, and I take a step back. It's probably just an outage, maybe someone hit a pole or something but my stomach knots when I turn and see every other house on the block with their lights blazing. God, I'm being ridiculous.

Taking another step back onto the porch, I sigh and weigh my options. I could go into the dark and make my way to the creepy utility closet or I could text Storm. As much as I don't want to see him right now, I want to stumble around my house in the dark even less. I lean in and grab my phone from the bag before stepping back out onto the porch.

Me:
I need your help.

    I stare down at my phone and wait for his reply, growing impatient with how long it's taking him to get back to me. Figures the one time I actually need his help, he's not around. I gasp and whirl around when someone stomps up the steps behind me, and there he is. He rushes over to me and puts his hands on my face while his eyes roam all over my body.
    "Are you okay? What's up?"
    "Jesus, Storm. You scared the hell out of me. Did you run all the way here?"
    "Yeah, you said you needed me."
    I sigh and shake my head. This man is so goddamn confusing. "It wasn't like an emergency. I just need help with my lights."
    "Your lights?" he asks, and I point to the dark house behind us.
    "I came home and the lights won't turn on. The fuse box is in the closet in the hall but I hate the dark."
    He pulls his gaze away from the open doorway to look down at me, and he grins, his eyes sparkling with amusement. Damn him for being so hot when he smiles. "You afraid of the dark, Baby?"
    "Stop calling me that," I snap. I love hearing him say it but I hate that it only confuses me more, and I don't want to hear it unless he really means it.
    "What? Baby?"
    "Yes."
    His brow furrows, and he studies me for a moment. "Why?"

"Because that is reserved for boyfriends," I say, looking him right in the eye and squaring my shoulders.

"And I'm not your boyfriend?"

I shrug. "I don't know, Storm. Are you?"

His stare is intense, kicking up butterflies in my belly and pouring warm honey over me all at the same time. My body aches to lean in to him, steal a touch, but I stay rooted in my spot, demanding answers. Finally, he sighs and looks back to the house.

"Fuse box is in the hallway, you said?" he asks, and my heart sinks to my feet. I nod, and he pulls his phone out, bringing up a flashlight app as he disappears into the house. Tears sting my eyes. I step into the foyer, and try to get myself under control. I'm such a stupid girl.

How much of the past week has even been real? Have I been imagining this thing between us? That spark I felt when I met him, was it completely one-sided? The light over my head flicks on, and I quickly wipe away any tears that may have escaped while he stomps back over to me. He steps around the corner, and I force a smile to my face.

"Thank you so much, and I'm sorry for bothering you."

He stops in front of me, close enough that I could just reach out and grab him but my hands stay firm at my sides. My eyes burn with unshed tears, and I need him to leave.

"It's not a bother, Sweetheart," he says softly, and I turn away from him, surprised by the ache in my chest.

"Alison, look at me." His voice is firm but I don't want him to see how upset I am right now. I keep my gaze on the hardwood floor and hope that he'll give up soon and just leave. I should know better though. He nudges under my chin with his fingers, and when I still don't obey his command, he presses his hand to my face and guides my eyes back to his. I glare up at him, and he drops his hand.

"Fuck this," he growls, grabbing my face again and pulling me into his body. I gasp just as he slams his mouth on mine and he uses it to his advantage, his tongue slipping past my lips and teasing me. I whimper and melt into him, gripping his shirt in my hands as I try to hold on to something – my sanity, this moment, him – I'm not sure.

Reality crashes down on me, and I rip my lips away, pushing against his massive chest. "Stop."

"No," he rasps, coming back toward me, "I don't want to stop. Ever."

I push on his chest again but he's not deterred, leaning in to kiss my neck instead. "Look, Storm. I'm not really into being strung along while you figure out your commitment issues."

He pulls back and levels a glare at me. It's full of fire but there is no anger. Only the same intense need that I feel blazing a path through my body right now. "I don't have fucking commitment issues. I'm yours, and you are mine. End of fucking story."

"Oh, yeah?" I whisper, a reluctant smile tugging at the corner of my lips but a sliver of doubt remains.

He leans in, his breath wafting over my face as he keeps his eyes locked with mine. "Mine."

I nod and slide my hand up his cheek, his beard tickling my skin. "Yours."

A thrill runs through me as I give in to him. I haven't been someone's girl in a long time, and a mix of excitement and fear pulses through my bloodstream at the thought of being his. I like it – the way it sounds and the way it feels. He turns into my touch and nips at my palm before kissing over the same spot but I'm too turned on to smile at the gesture.

His fingers curl around my wrist, and he moves my hand down his body, going slowly so my fingers can trail over his large chest and the defined ridges on his stomach. I suck in a breath when he keeps going, guiding my hand down further until I'm rubbing his cock over his jeans. He lets out a quiet groan, and his eyes close as his head drops back. My other hand slips up under his shirt, and I take my time exploring him. He's ridiculously fit, and I wonder what he does to keep his body looking and feeling like this.

He groans again, and his head falls forward to look at me as he pushes my hands away from his body and pushes me up against the wall while kicking the front door closed. Jeez, I hadn't even realized that it was still open. That's what he does to me. Claiming my lips again, he shoves one hand into my hair while the other grips my hip, pulling me into him like he can't get me close enough. I throw my hands over his shoulders and grind against him, earning me another groan.

"This is in the way," he growls, releasing me and grabbing the sides of my pencil skirt before yanking it up to my waist. A breathy moan slips out of my mouth, and my eyes drift closed as he shoves his thigh between my legs. Oh, God, yes. He grabs my hips and rubs me on his leg, giving me exactly what I need as his hands then slip under my shirt. His touch sears my skin, and I rub against him, pressure building in my belly as I grip his t-shirt in my fists.

"You're the sexiest fucking thing I've ever seen," he murmurs, and I lose it, an orgasm rocks through my body and surprises the hell out of me. I gasp and ride it out, my body shaking in his arms as the pulses of my release seem to never end. When I can finally open my eyes again, I lean back against the wall with a sigh and look up at him.

"Oh my god," I whisper, and he grins – a sexy, terrifying little grin.

"Sweetheart, I haven't even started yet."

I raise my hands above my head and raise my brow at him in challenge. I don't know why I decided it would be a good idea to poke the bear right now but my heart is racing at the possibilities. "Show me what you've got, then."

His eyes trail down my body, and he smirks at me when he meets my eyes again, pressing up against me. "In an hour or so when your legs are shaking, your heart is pounding, and your body feels like I've wrung every last drop of pleasure out of you as I demand another orgasm, just remember that you asked for this."

All the air punches out of my lungs as my hips buck against him of their own accord, my mind racing with images of that vivid scene he just painted for me. A thrill races through my body, desire pooling between my legs, and my skin tingling with a need stronger than I've ever felt before. I thought I knew what chemistry felt like, thought I knew what it was like to feel desire, but none of it comes close to this. With just his words, he could make me lose myself as if he'd been expertly touching my most sensitive areas.

Reaching out, I fist his t-shirt in my hands and pull him to me, planting my lips on his. He smiles against my kiss for a moment before my need consumes him, too. His hand slides into my hair, and he cradles the back of my head as he takes control of the kiss, commanding my body like a puppet master. Thick arms wrap around my waist, and he pulls me away from the wall into his body, and I sigh. I may never get tired of the way it feels to be pressed up against him, his hard to my soft. We mold together like that's what we were made to do.

He starts walking us down the hallway without pulling away from me, and his hands slip under my shirt. We separate only long enough for him to rip the shirt over my head. Reaching behind my back, I fumble with the zipper of my skirt for a moment before I get it down and shove the skirt down my legs. I kick it away and push his back up against a wall as I reach for his shirt.

I pull away, and he reaches behind his back, pulling the shirt over his head and his body comes into view. I bite down on my bottom lip as I do my own little exploration of him. A giant black and gray eagle covers his chest, and he's got a full sleeve of tattoos down each arm, starting at his shoulders. He grabs my hips and pulls me back into him, his desperation matching my own. His hard cock digs into my hip, and I moan as I reach between us and unbutton his jeans.

Groaning, he grabs a chunk of my hair and pulls my head back as he leans in and starts kissing down my neck. Goose bumps rush over my skin, and I pull the zipper of his jeans down before shoving them down his legs.

His cock springs free between us at the same moment that I realize he's going commando, and it pulls another moan out of me. My fingers dig into his stomach, and he rips his mouth away from me to groan in my ear. He releases my hair and reaches down, hooking his hands under my thighs before lifting me effortlessly into his arms. Reaching behind my back, he unhooks my bra and pulls it away from me, tossing it on the floor behind him as he marches toward my bedroom.

Leaning in, I throw my arms over his shoulder as I kiss him again, hoping that this never ends. I think I'm addicted to his lips, and I could spend forever kissing him. My back hits another wall, and his hand cradles the back of my head so I don't get hurt, and I only like him more for it. Even through the haze of his desire, he thought of me. I rip my lips away and turn my head as he starts biting my neck.

We're right next to the door to my bedroom so I reach out and turn the handle, pushing the door open. "Storm," I complain, wiggling in his arms.

"What, Baby? I want to hear you say it," he rasps against my skin, his voice deeper than before. I shiver and try to work my hips against him but he's got a firm hold on me.

"I want you inside me," I moan, my body in a constant state of desperation as I hover over an orgasm that I just can't quite reach. His only response is to pull away from the wall and carry me into the bedroom. He tosses me, and I land on the bed with a bounce. I don't even have time to orient myself before he's kneeling next to the bed and pulling my legs apart. His teeth nip at the sensitive skin inside my thigh before he soothes the sting with his tongue, and my hips rise off the bed, begging him for everything that I no longer have the mental capacity to say.

He kisses a path up my thigh, stopping right before where I really want him, and the only thing I can do is growl out into the room as I slam my fists down into the bed. He laughs, and when I prop myself up on my elbows and peek down at him, his sexy little grin steals my breath. He holds my gaze as he reaches up and trails a finger over my panties, and I moan, my head dropping back.

He hooks his fingers in my panties and pulls them down my legs. I can't resist looking down at him again. His gaze is focused between my thighs, and he licks his lips as my pussy comes into view. Storm looks like a starving man, and I can't wait to be his next meal. He flicks his eyes up to me, and I swear, his gaze could melt me on the spot. Pure fire lights up his gray eyes, sending warmth rushing over my entire body.

He slowly pushes my legs apart and flattens his palm to the inside of my thigh just above my knee before he starts sliding it up. With his other hand, he presses his thumb to my clit, and I fall back to the bed, my hips lifting off the bed for more. He rubs tiny little circles against the sensitive nub, and I moan, needing more.

"Storm, please," I beg.

"Logan," he replies, and I prop myself up on my elbows again to look at him.

"What?"

"My real name is Logan. I want you to call me Logan. Storm is my road name."

I nod, testing out the way it sounds in my head and I like it. "Okay."

Without another word, he flicks his thumb against my clit again. and I fall back with a loud moan as he starts kissing up my thigh. My hands fist the sheet beneath me and I moan again as his mouth closes over my pussy, and he flicks his tongue against my clit.

My hips lift into him, and he grabs the tops of my thighs to hold me still as he laps at me. He switches from sucking on my nub to plunging his tongue inside me, and I think that I'm about to lose my mind. Every thought in my head is just complete gibberish as my body builds toward another orgasm. His fingers dig into my legs, and he sucks on my clit again, sending me barreling over the edge as I cry out into the room.

When my release subsides, I sigh and relax back into the mattress as his grip on my legs eases, and he brings me back down with gentle kisses against my flesh. After a couple seconds, he pulls away and stands, wrapping his fingers around his cock as he stares down at me. I watch him work himself for a moment before I sit up and scoot to the edge of the bed. Pushing his hand away, I wrap my fingers around his length, and he groans but keeps his eyes firmly locked on me.

Leaning forward, I open my mouth and lick around the head of his cock before sucking him into my mouth. His hand slides into my hair, and he groans. "Fuck yes, Ali. Just like that, Baby."

I hollow my cheeks and take him all the way to the back of my throat, focusing on not gagging as I hold him there for a moment before pulling back. I release him with a pop and stroke him a few times before sucking his length back into my mouth. I don't go all the way this time, leaving a little room to extend my tongue and lick the underside of his shaft near his balls. His grip tightens, and he groans louder.

Gently, he pulls my hand away from him and releases my hair as he shoves me back onto the bed. "Scoot back."

I crawl backward on the bed until I'm right in the middle, and he plants a knee between my thighs as he positions himself over me. He looks down between us and mutters a curse.

"Shit. I need a condom. Where are my pants?"

I start laughing and point to the bedroom door. "Out in the hallway."

He looks over his shoulder before pinning me to the bed with his stare. Leaning down, he plants a hard quick kiss on my lips and mutters, "Don't you move an inch."

I watch him run out the door, and the seconds feel like hours as I wait for him. It's impossible that I've already had two orgasms, and I still want more and yet, here I am – spread out on my bed and aching for him. He struts back into the room as he's rolling the condom on, and I bite down on my lip as I wait for him.

When he gets it on, he climbs back over me and locks his hands over my wrists, pinning me down to the bed. He leans down and takes my lips again. Moaning, I wrap my legs around his waist and lift off the bed. His teeth nip at my lip, and I gasp as I fall back to the mattress and look up at him.

"You think you're ready for me?" he asks, his eyes teasing me, and I nod.

"Yes."

He looks down between us and cocks his head to the side as he looks back up at me. "I don't know. I think you need more."

Shaking my head, I try to free one of my hands but he tightens his grip. My core clenches, and I want to cry. I don't need more. What I need is for him to fuck me until I can't walk anymore. He transfers both of my wrists to one hand as he grabs his cock and rubs the tip against my clit.

"Logan, please," I cry, squirming underneath him, and he grins up at me.

"That's what I wanted to hear," he shoots back before plunging into me, and I cry out again, this time in relief. Oh, yes. This is exactly what I needed. His cock is stretching me wide, and it feels incredible. I squirm again, trying to get him to move. He grabs my hip with his free hand and takes my lips again in a bruising kiss as he pulls out and plunges back in.

A moan bubbles up from the back of my throat as his tongue pushes past my lips, imitating the same movement as his hips as he drives into me again and again. He starts kissing down my neck, and my teeth sink into his shoulder, earning me a long loud groan as his thrusts gain speed.

"Do it again," he commands, and I do. He groans into my neck as he releases my hands and plants his fist into the bed by my head. My fingers dig into his shoulders and pull back to press his lips to mine again. Just as I start to feel the climax building deep in my belly, he slows his movement, pulling out and slowly pushing back in. It keeps me suspended, holding me in bliss but not allowing me to reach release.

"Logan," I moan, dying to chase my orgasm and feel it crashing over me. "I need to come. Please."

"Ask me," he whispers in my ear. "Ask me to make you come and maybe I will."

"Please, make me come, Logan," I beg, and he smiles against my skin.

"No."

I yell in frustration, and he pulls back to look at me. "I don't think you want it bad enough yet."

"Then you must not be very perceptive," I shoot back, and he laughs, still lazily thrusting into me.

"No, I am." He grips my hip again, and his next thrust is hard and fast. My eyes shoot open as he pounds away, driving me to the brink faster than before. My body is torpedoing to my release, and I just need a little bit more. I grip the sheets, my eyes rolling back as I grow closer and closer to an intense orgasm. Right as I'm about to go crashing over the edge, he stops completely, and I scream.

Opening my eyes, I glare at him as he laughs and starts idly pushing into me again. "I hate you," I spit at him, my entire body aching violently for the release he just robbed me of.

"No, you don't, Sweetheart. And you're going to love the shit out of me when I finally decide to let you come."

Finally?

I whimper at the thought of waiting any longer for what I want. He smiles and leans down, kissing me gently to match the way his cock is sinking into me.

"Please," I whisper against his lips, and he leans back just enough to look into my eyes as he pulls back and slams into me. I jolt on the bed as my eyes flutter closed, and I moan, but then he's still again. When I open my eyes, I practically moan from just the look he's giving me. He's the hungry lion, and I'm the gazelle and he's so enjoying his little game. I dig my fingers into his arms and give him a pleading look.

He reaches between us and starts circling my clit with his thumb again, and I moan, my hips lifting for more. He performs the same torture there – rubbing me until I'm about to come and then stopping or slowing down enough that I can't reach release. Random whining and begging noises spill out of my mouth, and I'm not sure that I can even speak anymore. Everything in my body is screaming for the climax that I'm being denied.

"Now, you're ready," he finally says, and if I could speak or move, I would start shouting my thanks. He pulls his hand away and grabs my hip in one hand as the other presses into the bed next to me. Pulling back slightly, he surges forward, thrusting his cock into me again and again. My orgasm races to the surface, and my entire body is tense – a mixture of fear and anticipation – as I wait for the crash and half expect him to deny me again. Logan releases my hip and reaches up to tug on my nipple, and it sends me careening over the edge. My entire body locks up, and I throw my head back against the mattress, my mouth wide open but no sound coming out as my pussy clenches down on him in waves.

He groans and grabs my hip again as he chases his own release, relentlessly driving into me as I lay here, spent. After a few more thrusts, he tenses, and a long, low groan rumbles up from his chest. He's still for a moment and then he lets out a breath and collapses at my side. We just lay in silence for a while; both of us sweaty and breathing hard as we try to drift back to earth.

"Oh my god," I finally whisper when I feel like I've come back to my body. Everything is tingling and sore but in the best possible way. I turn to the side and peek over at him. He grins at me, and I can't help but smile back. My heart pounds for a completely different reason as we just stare at each other. It's like he's seeing right through me, all the years of my life, the pain and happiness all on display for him.

He smiles wider and rolls over, throwing his leg over mine as he kisses me softly, and he owns me. He pulls back and glances over at his watch before his grin takes on the predatory quality he's been sporting since he got here.

"It's only been thirty minutes," he prompts, and I scowl up at him, trying to figure out what he's talking about. He runs his finger down my side, over my breast, and trails it down my stomach. "I remember promising you an hour."

Chapter Sixteen
Storm

"You ready to do this?" I ask Chance as he rounds the truck, and he nods, his expression grim. We both know that the situation we're about to go into is volatile. Two days ago, we got a call from a woman named Dina who was in the hospital after her husband had beat the shit out of her. One of the nurses gave her our number and even offered to hide her until we could make arrangements for her. But the husband has been sniffing around, and he has enough money that he'll find her sooner or later. We want to get her out of here before that happens.

"Kodiak and Fuzz are ready at the hotel."

I nod and climb into the truck, firing it up, and tossing my phone in the cup holder so I'll hear it if it goes off. Dina's parents live up in Maryland, and they are coming down to get her but they can't get here until Wednesday so she'll have to hang out in the hotel until then. We could leave her where she is for the next three days but the husband is getting a little too close, and

Blaze decided we needed to move now. There is such a delicate balance to these situations – when it's safe to move someone and when it's not – and I'm kind of glad that it's not on me to make the call. My phone buzzes, and I grab it.

Ali:
Am I going to see you tonight?

Sighing, I toss it back down and focus on the road. There are so many fucking reasons why I should stay far away from that woman but I can't do it. I always end up back on her fucking doorstep in the end. I could be putting her in danger but not even that deters me. I'll do whatever I have to do to protect her, except stay away. I can't anymore. Every night since I met her, I've lain in my bed and thought of her, wondering what she'd feel like pressed up against me and now that I know, I'm fucking toast. My phone buzzes again.

Streak:
I've got something you're going to want to see.

Me:
I'll swing by later.

My grip on the steering wheel tightens as I think about everything I always keep buried but there is a sense of relief under all the pain, and I'm ready to end this, end him, and put all this pain in my past. For the first time in six years, I see a future in front of me, and I want it more than anything.

"You all right, man?" Chance asks, and I glance over at him before turning back to the road.

"It's Ian," I finally admit, his name tasting like acid on my tongue. He straightens up in his seat, staring at me.

"What about him?"

"He started sending me shit, pictures, mostly. He's had someone following me."

"Fuck," he mutters, his tone reflecting the gravity of the situation. He was right there with me when I lost everything, and he knows about the pain I've lived with for the past six years – the depths of utter agony that I've been pulled into. "You got a plan?"

I nod.

"What is it?"

I glance over at him and shake my head "Don't worry about it."

"No, fuck that, Brother. I'm not going to let you handle this by yourself. Tell me what you're thinkin' and let's end this fucker."

"I said I got this," I grit out through clenched teeth. I appreciate the sentiment but this is something that I need to do.

"And I said, fuck that. You're the closest thing I've got to family and I'm not gonna let you do this alone."

"What the fuck is he gonna do? He's behind bars."

He stands two fingers to his forehead and twists them. "He's gonna fuck with your mind. He's gonna make you dredge up pain that you thought was behind you because that's what he does. He's evil incarnate and a master manipulator, and you're stupid as shit if you go into this without admitting that."

"Noted," I snap just as we pull up to the house, and he shakes his head.

"I'm not fucking dropping this."

I sigh and nod. Chance only has my best interests at heart, I know that, but letting someone see just how fucking broken I still am after all these years isn't easy. Except, I don't feel all that broken since I met Ali. "I didn't expect you to."

My phone buzzes again, and I grab it, glancing up at the house.

Dina:
I'm ready.

I glance up at the little yellow house, and the curtains in the front window move back into place. I reach for the keys before deciding to leave it running. I've got a bad feeling today, and I don't want to get stuck here.

"Let's do this," I say, and we both climb out. Chance scans the street as we walk up the steps. The front door opens, and Dina steps out with a suitcase in her hand and a tentative smile on her face.

"You ready to get out of here, Sweets?" Chance asks, and she nods as she looks down the street.

"You know where Mitch is, Dina?" I ask, and she looks back to me, shaking her head. We usually like to have eyes on the husbands just so we have a warning if he's headed for us but Dina's husband is a hard guy to track down. His hours are erratic, and we couldn't ask around too much without word getting back to him.

"What do you say we get you out of here then?" Chance asks her, and she nods, taking a couple steps toward him. I nod at the woman standing in the doorway who gave Dina our number and gave her shelter.

"Thanks for what you did."

She shakes her head. "No need. I was happy to help her."

I nod and hold my hand out to her. She takes it, and I slip the hundred dollar bill into her palm. "For your trouble."

She looks down at it as Chance starts leading Dina to the truck and shakes her head before trying to hand it back to me. "Oh, I couldn't take this."

A car squeals around the corner, and I glance behind me, cursing when I see the blue Mustang we were supposed to watch out for. "Get back inside and lock your doors," I tell her.

Her eyes widen, and she disappears into the house, slamming the door, and locking it behind her. I turn to Chance. "Get her in the truck!"

He looks up and I hear him curse before he runs to the truck and opens the door for her. She climbs in and locks it, glancing out the back window nervously as the Mustang skids to a stop, and Mitch jumps out, not even bothering to close his door.

"Dina!" he bellows into the quiet neighborhood and tears start falling down her face as she shakes in the passenger seat.

"Get back in your car and leave," I tell him calmly but inside I'm raging. Fuck this piece of shit, thinking he can show up here and take Dina back by force. I'll end that little illusion right now.

"Fuck you," he spits, trying to move around Chance to get to Dina. I move in front of the truck door and let my arms hang loose at my sides.

"Last chance. Get in your car and never come near this woman again."

"You don't get to take her from me. I'll kill every last one of you fuckers if you don't give her to me."

I shake my head. "That's never going to happen. You lost her, that's what happens when you knock a girl around to make yourself feel better. You're a fucking coward, and no woman wants a coward."

His face turns red in his rage but he turns to Dina and softens his gaze. Even I have to admit that he's a pretty damn good actor but Dina's still got bruises around her neck where he tried to choke her the last time they were in a room together. "Dina, Baby, please don't do this to me. I love you; you know that I do. I'm sorry, Sweetheart. Come home with me, and we can fix all this."

For a moment, I think she's going to break. She looks back at him with tears in her eyes, and it's obvious that she's struggling. What the hell am I supposed to do if she decides to go back to him? After a couple of seconds, she takes a deep breath and turns away from him, hardening her face, and all hell breaks loose. Mitch bellows as he runs at Chance and punches him in the face before Chance can react. As he falls from the blow, his head smashes into the side of the truck, and he slumps to the ground, not moving. I don't have time to check on him as Mitch keeps coming for me, his gaze homicidal.

He slams into me, and we fall to the ground. Mitch manages to get a couple of good punches in before I'm able to roll him to his back. Laying my fist into his face again and again, I think about how many times he's probably done this shit to poor Dina and any woman unlucky enough to come before her, and it fuels me on. I want to make sure that he's never a problem for any woman ever again.

Mitch lands a punch to my throat, and it knocks the wind out of me long enough that he rolls us again and starts returning the beating I just laid down on him. I know my face is probably already swollen and bruised but the adrenaline keeps me going, trying to get him off me. His fist comes flying at my face again, and I turn my head, causing him to punch the ground right by my head instead, and in the next moment, a booted foot is kicking him off me.

"Piece of shit," Chance growls, gently touching the side of his head as he stares down at Mitch in disgust as he lands half on the concrete steps. Mitch rolls around on the grass, shouting that Chance broke his ribs.

"Serves you right, fucker." He laughs but there is no humor in his tone. He walks over to me and holds out a hand to help me up. My head spins when I'm back on my feet, and Chance slaps a hand on my shoulder to steady me.

"You okay?"

I nod. "Yeah, I'm good but we should split."

"I called Smith. He's coming to sit with our friend here until we get her somewhere safe."

"You can't hide her from me," Mitch snarls, spitting blood out on the ground. "I'll always find her."

Chance crouches down and gets right in his face, pulling a gun out from his waistband and pointing it between Mitch's eyes. Mitch freezes, and his eyes widen in fear. "You're making the bullet I'm dying to put in your brain look better and better. If I were you, I'd shut the fuck up. Unless, of course, you'd like to splatter this nice woman's house with pink mist."

"Jesus Christ, Chance. Put it away," I growl, looking around at the houses on either side of us. This is not the kind of neighborhood where nobody bats an eye when you pull a gun out and I'm sure the fight drew some attention.

Chance stands and tucks the gun back in his waistband just as Smith pulls up on his motorcycle, nodding at us. "I got this. Get her out of here, yeah?"

I nod, and Chance stalks off to the truck without another word. I can't say that I blame him. This is personal for all of us in a way, and I'd love to find an old back road and bury this waste of space somewhere even the gators won't find him. It's a fine line I walk between being the man that I know I should be and turning into the monster that years of darkness contorted me into. But maybe with Ali in my life, I stand a fighting chance.

* * * *

"What is it that you wanted to show me?" I ask Streak, the bottle of Jack firmly in my grasp as he walks past me. He stops and looks at me with a grimace on his face.

"You look like shit."

I take a swig of alcohol and grit my teeth. "You got something to show me or not?"

He holds his hands up in surrender and points to the little office where he works most of the time. "Follow me."

I follow him back to his office and he shuts the door, sitting down in his office chair, and I throw my body down on the couch we put in here since he'll go days without sleeping sometimes. He powers up the computers and turns to me.

"So, the guy you told me to keep an eye on," he starts, and I nod. "He's been a model prisoner, and I can't find a single thing on him no matter how hard I dig."

"You already told me this shit," I snap, irritated that he can't find the proof to back up what I already know.

"Well, then I got to thinking that if he was smart, he would stay far away from all of this so I looked into his family. Did you know he's got a twin brother?"

I sit up and blink at him, trying to figure out if I heard him right. A twin brother? I search my memory but I can't ever recall Fi telling me about a twin. "No, I didn't."

"Not surprising. It seems he's a bit of a black sheep. The family keeps him out of the limelight and that means, he doesn't get to share in the family money."

"Where the fuck are you going with this, Streak?"

"Recently, withdrawals of two thousand dollars have been coming out of Ian's account every week and going into the brother's account. And I can't find a record of the brother working anywhere."

I run my hand over my face, trying to process what he's telling me. "So, you think the brother is being paid to follow me? For what reason?"

Streak shrugs. "Just to mess with you. I mean, based on everything I've found out about this son of a bitch, that's his MO, right?"

"Yeah, that sounds like him."

"Look, man, I could be wrong but the brother barely has a criminal past. A couple of drug charges for weed and an assault charge for a bar fight, but he certainly doesn't seem like a criminal mastermind."

I take another swig of Jack and stand, stumbling a little. "Yeah, I hear you. I'm goin' home."

He nods and turns back to the computers. "Get a ride."

"I will, Mom," I sneer, and he laughs.

"Asshole."

Hopelessly Devoted

Chapter Seventeen
Chris

It's cold out tonight. My breath fogs up the window as I lean in, unable to stop myself from trying to get closer to her. I hate that there's anything between us. Pulling my glove off, I press my hand to the window, imagining that it's her warm soft skin against my palm instead of this cold hard glass. If I close my eyes right now, I could imagine what it feels like to run my hand down her body, let it graze over the curve of her hips as I pour my love into her. The noises she would make as I pull pleasure from her body fill my ears, and I groan softly, the wind masking my sound of torment. She could have absolutely anything her heart desired. All she would have to do is ask, and I would do whatever it took to give it to her. Someday, I will build heaven for my angel and count my blessings everyday that she lets me stay there with her.

Weekends are so hard. Our schedules don't match up, and I don't get to see her as much as I would like, but tomorrow she'll be back to work, and I'll be able to steal glances at her throughout the day. It's the only thing that keeps me going through the long days when she's absent from my life. I just keep pushing forward until I can see her gorgeous face again. God, she is perfect. Even lying in bed, sound asleep with her hair all over the place, she's the most beautiful thing I've ever seen, and my heart belongs to her.

Rubbing my finger over the glass, I pretend it's her face I'm stroking, and my body aches to be near her again. A pang hits my chest, and I know just standing at this window won't be enough tonight. It's been too long, and I need her – even if it's just a few stolen moments in the night. Leaning in, I press my lips to the glass, keeping my eyes open so I don't lose even a second of my time with her, and my breath clouds my view.

Pulling away, I drop my hand and take one last look at her before creeping along the back of the house, my heart pounding with the knowledge that she'll be back within reach in only a few moments. Butterflies fill my stomach, and an excited smile stretches across my face as I reach the French doors that lead into the kitchen and jiggle the handle. They're locked but I've done this enough times that it's not a problem. After a couple of seconds, it pops open, and I gently swing the door open, making sure to stop it before it gets to the part that squeaks. Stepping into the house hesitantly, I do my best not to wake her. She's got work tomorrow, and I don't want to make her too tired during the day.

Gently closing the door behind me, I walk into the kitchen and run my hand along the granite countertop of the island. Her wine glass from dinner is sitting by the sink, unwashed, and I pick it up, licking along the rim, dying to get just a quick taste of her. Closing my eyes, I take a deep breath, breathing in her mango scent. She's all over this house, in every place I look, and I can't wait for the day when this is *our home*. I pull one of the barstools out and sit down, imagining our kids running down the hall, laughing as they play. Two little girls that look just like their radiant mother giggling as they whisper secrets back and forth in the living room and my sweet Ali in the kitchen making us Christmas dinner. I can see it all with her here, and I'm eager to see all my dreams come to life.

Sighing, I stand and tuck the stool back in before going to her. I stop at the doorway to her bedroom and just look down at her as she sleeps. She's turned toward the window and the urge to crawl in behind her is just too strong to ignore. I have to feel her. Slipping off my boots, I climb into bed, staying above the covers so I don't disturb her and I wrap my arm around her waist and bury my nose in her hair. The smell of mangoes fills my nose, and I sigh, everything in my world righting itself now that she's in my arms. She wiggles in my grasp, cuddling closer to me, and a wide grin stretches across my face.

"Hey, Baby," I whisper, still doing my best not to wake her but unable to keep quiet. "I've missed you so much."

She hums in her sleep, and my heart swells. Her body recognizes me even when she's not conscious. That's how strong our connection is, and I knew it from the moment I laid eyes on her. The very second her blue eyes met mine, she belonged to me. Reaching up, I brush the hair out of her face, losing myself a little as I watch her sleep. Her eyelids flutter, and I hope that she's dreaming about me. No, I hope she's dreaming about us – about everything we're going to have together. So very soon.

"It's torture to stay away from you, Sweet Girl," I whisper, lightly trailing the back of my finger down her cheek. "I hate that you're making me do this."

She shifts in my grasp, and her lips part slightly. I freeze, squeezing my eyes shut because I'll be so angry with myself if I keep her from sleep, and when I open them again, she's peaceful. Sighing, I know I have to go but leaving her is getting harder and harder each time. Climbing out of bed, I leave my boots by the door as I walk across her room so I don't wake her. Her jewelry catches my eye, and I run my hand over the neat line of necklaces, picturing them hanging around the curve of her neck. Peeking back at her, my cock aches inside my jeans, and I let out a quiet groan and readjust it.

Goddamn it, I don't have time for this.

I fight with myself for a few moments before pulling out my phone and snapping a couple of pictures of her that I can take with me. A smile forms on my face, and I sit down on the floor next to her bed, moving into the picture with her. I snap a couple before hopping up and looking through them. God, she's fucking gorgeous. Too gorgeous for a guy like me but not like I'm ever going to complain. The time in the corner of the screen catches my eye, and I curse. I hate to leave her but I really do have to go soon.

Hopelessly Devoted

    Staring down at her, my cock springs to life, pressing against my zipper and I hiss. I'm never going to be able to leave without dealing with this. I tuck my phone back into my pocket and unbuckle my belt. After shoving my pants down enough to free my dick, I sit in the chair in the corner of her room and watch her as I slowly stroke it. Closing my eyes, I imagine her on her knees in front of me, peeking up at me as she wraps her lips around my length.

    Groaning softly, I imagine her sinking down, peeking up at me again when it hits the back of her throat and my strokes get harder and faster. Her hands splay out on my thighs, and she bobs on my cock, massaging it with her tongue, and my hips buck in the chair. She stands, smiling down at me as she strips, her perfect body coming into view and making my mouth water. Climbing on top of me, her hot little cunt hovers over my cock, and she sinks down, sighing in satisfaction.

    A choked groan spills out of my mouth as I reach down next to me and grab a towel from the shelf next to the chair and come into it, breathing hard. I open my eyes, and Ali shifts under the covers, sighing in her sleep, and I know my time is up. After cleaning myself up, I stand and tuck my cock back into my jeans. As I pass by the bathroom, I notice a pair of pink lace panties that missed the hamper, and I can't stop myself from grabbing them and bringing them to my nose. Her scent assaults me, and I barely hold in the groan threatening to burst free. Tucking the panties into my pocket, I grab my boots and pause at the door, taking one last look at my gorgeous girl. I blow her a kiss and promise her that I'll be back soon.

I won't be able to go long without needing to see her again.

Hopelessly Devoted

Chapter Eighteen
Alison

Sighing, I toss the letters down on my desk and spread them out with my fingers, trying to decide which one I should respond to this week. I've been replying to two letters in each article and most of the letters we get in are about the sender's love life so I like to find something different to accompany it. But I'm just not finding much this week that isn't about love. I could also be distracted by the fact that I haven't seen Logan since the night we had sex. He stayed the night with me, and then in the morning, left saying he had work to do with the club. He's been texting occasionally but I can't help but wonder if he just uses the club as an excuse to avoid this connection we have.

It's not something that I'm all that comfortable with but maybe I should just trust him until he gives me a reason not to. I compare him to Adam and I know that's not fair but I'm not sure that I can help it. Before Adam hurt me, I was naïve. I trusted blindly and I loved recklessly, with no reservations, and no matter how much I heal from what he did, I think there will always be a little voice in my head saying "what if". I'm not sure that I'm even capable of that blind trust anymore. Not when someone who was entrusted with its care has shattered my heart.

I don't want to be like this. If I could go back and never meet Adam, I would. Even if it was just to erase this fear that runs through me when I think about letting Logan in. My phone rings, his name popping up on the screen, and I smile at the photo I took of him the other night as we laid in bed. His dark hair is falling in his face, and he has a relaxed smile as he stares back at me, and my heart warms.

"Hey, you," I answer, unable to wipe the smile from my face. I hope he's free tonight. I'm dying to see him.

"Thought you weren't into playing games," he responds, his voice tight, and the smile drains off my face as I stare out the window behind my desk.

"What are you talking about?"

"The other night when I said I was yours, was there something unclear about that? Because I assumed that you understood that this is exclusive but if you'd rather go fuck around, please just let me know right now so I don't waste anymore of my goddamn time."

I spin around to my desk and flatten my palm against it as I take a deep breath. "Logan, I have no idea what you're talking about."

"I'm talking about the other guy or guys that you're opening your legs for," he snaps, and I suck in a breath, my chest aching at the tone of his voice. He sounds so angry, hateful almost.

"I'm not sleeping with anyone else. You're the first guy I've been with in two years. And if you want our relationship or whatever this is to be clear, maybe you should have a fucking conversation with me."

Carly walks in at the end of my rant, her brows raised, and I shake my head as I close my eyes and take a deep breath, trying like hell to not overreact.

"We did have a conversation. Remember, I said you were mine and I was yours right before I fucked you for an hour straight."

"Yeah and then you disappeared for two days with barely any contact. So excuse me if I'm a little confused about how into this you really are."

The phone call has gotten way off track, and I don't even really know what started it anymore. Everything that I've been keeping inside for the past two weeks is just bubbling out of me. Has it really only been that long since I met Logan? It feels like forever.

"Oh, I see, so that's your excuse for you going out and banging the first guy you could get your hands on? You thought you'd show me?"

I suck in a breath, and the line falls silent. I seriously consider just hanging up on his stupid ass and writing this whole thing off but then I think about how it feels when I'm with him, and I can't bring myself to pull the phone away from my ear.

"Why would you say that to me?" I ask, my voice a whisper, thick with hurt.

"Because of the guy I just saw strolling out of your fucking house like he just had the best night of his life."

Everything moves in slow motion. I stare at Carly with wide eyes, and the only thing I can hear is my heartbeat, pounding relentlessly in my ears as what he says sinks in.

"Logan," I whisper.

"What?"

"Call the police, please."

He's quiet for a moment before asking, "Why?"

I lock eyes with Carly, and I can only imagine what my face must look like right now. It feels like my whole world is falling down around me. "I'm not sleeping with anyone else so there shouldn't be anyone in my house."

My statement is met with silence for a moment before he mutters a curse. "Shit. Ali, I'm so sorry…"

"I'm hanging up now, and I'll be there in fifteen minutes." I don't want to hear his apology right now. There is too much for my mind to process and what he said is on the very bottom of the list.

"Sure, Sweetheart. I'll be here."

I hang up the phone and drop my head to my desk, panic washing over me as I imagine someone in my home, my little oasis.

"Ali, what's going on?" Carly asks, and I look up at her, tears welling up in my eyes.

"Logan saw someone leaving my house just now. They… they broke in."

She gasps quietly and just watches me for a moment before nodding and walking around behind my desk. Grabbing my bag off the floor, she urges me to stand and starts leading me out of the office, where we run into Mercedes. I can hear Carly explaining the situation to her but it's muffled, almost like I'm underwater, then we're moving again.

I don't really remember the walk to the parking garage or getting in Carly's car but the next thing I know, we're almost to my house, and my heart kicks in my chest. A slimy feeling washes over me as I think about someone going through all my things. Why would someone even break into my house? It's not like I have anything super valuable. It just doesn't make sense to me.

By the time we pull up in front of my house and see the line of bikes out front, my whole body is shaking and I'm on the verge of tears. My stomach rolls and my heart pounds as I walk up the front steps with Carly's arm guiding me, a million different scenarios running through my mind about what's waiting for me on the other side of the door.

"You think it's got something to do with the pictures?" a gruff voice asks just as we step through the door, and everyone turns to look at us. My house is full of large men decked out in leather vests and tattoos. I freeze, eyeing each one of them up until Logan steps through the crowd. I let out a sigh of relief, and he marches over to me with determination on his face along with a few fresh bruises. Where the hell did those come from? He slides his hand into my hair and presses his forehead to mine as my eyes drift closed.

"You okay?" he asks, and I shake my head. My house looks exactly the way I left it this morning, except it's tainted now. Almost like the man who broke in here is still lurking in the corner waiting to strike.

"I'm sorry for that call, Baby," he whispers, so low only I can hear, and I shake my head again.

"Not now," I whisper back. I'm not ready to talk about all that. I need to compartmentalize and deal with one thing at a time. First up is my house.

"I fucked up, okay? I didn't mean what I said."

Okay, apparently, we're talking about this now. I peek out of the corner of my eye to see if they are all watching us but they've all backed away, giving us a little privacy, and Carly is nowhere in sight.

"Please say something," he pleads, and I sigh, looking back into his gray eyes. I don't want to tell him that there is a part of me that kind of liked his possessive side. At the very least, it lets me know that he's feeling this, too.

"I'm not sure what you want me to say."

His grip in my hair tightens, and a feeling of calm washes over me. I like it when he holds onto me, like maybe he really doesn't want to let me go. "I didn't mean it, Ali. I fucking swear to you that I didn't."

"Maybe, but when you saw that man leaving my house, it was still your first reaction so a small part of you is still looking for an out. Either you want to be with me or you don't. It's pretty simple."

"Excuse me, Miss James?" someone says, and Logan steps back, releasing me. "I'm Detective Rodriguez. Do you mind if I ask you a few questions?"

I force a smile to my face and shake my head as Logan hovers behind me. "No, of course not."

"Great. First off, let me just say that I'm sorry this happened to you," he replies, pulling a notepad out of his suit jacket and I nod.

"Thank you."

"Now, what time did you leave this morning?"

I sigh and start answering all his questions. He asks about my daily routine, seeing anything weird lately, and if I can think of anyone that would do this but all my answers sound the same because I have no clue why this happened. Still, as I stand in my home, I have no idea why anyone would break in.

"All right, Miss James, I'll need you to walk through the house and see if anything is missing."

I nod, crossing my arms over my chest as a chill rushes through me. "Sure."

I start walking through my house, room-by-room, looking for anything that's out of place. It's hard to focus, and it's like I've never really looked at my house before because I can't, for the life of me, remember where things were. When I walk into the bedroom, I gasp, and Logan is at my side in an instant. My panty drawer is wide open, and my bed is messed up.

"The dresser drawer wasn't open when I left this morning, and my bed was made," I say and look over as Detective Rodriguez nods and scribbles something in his notepad. "What does that mean?"

He sighs and looks up at me. "It's hard to say. Could be nothing, just some random guy who gets his rocks off by breaking in and doing shit like this."

"Or?"

"Let's just wait and see what else we find."

"Storm," one of the guys from the living room says, poking his head in the door, "need to speak with you."

Logan looks to me, and I nod before turning back to my room, my stomach rolling in disgust. Detective Rodriguez leads me to the kitchen, and I start looking through everything, trying to take my mind off what I witnessed in my bedroom.

When we get back to the living room, I sigh. "I don't think anything is missing."

"Are you sure?" Detective Rodriguez asks.

"I think so. I don't know. I can't seem to remember what my house looked like."

He nods, putting a comforting hand on my shoulder. "That's normal. Just take my card and call me if over the next few days, there are some things that you notice are missing."

He hands me a card, and I nod before shoving it in my pocket as he leaves. I look around my living room, feeling like the walls have eyes and they're closing in on me. My phone buzzes, and I take one last look around before pulling it out.

Carly:
Hey, taking Chance to bring your car back. Call if you need anything.

Sighing, I slip the phone back into my pocket without replying and go out to the front porch where all the guys were talking to find Logan.

"Hey, Darlin'. I know we didn't get a proper introduction earlier. I'm Blaze," one of them says as he rocks back and forth in my rocking chair. I smile, recognizing his name

"It's nice to meet you, Blaze. Where's Logan?" I ask, scanning the empty porch. All but one of the bikes are gone, too. He shoves off the arms of the chair and stands.

"He left."

My face falls, and I feel like crying all over again. He just left me here without a word? "Oh."

"Don't give up on him."

I peek up at him; his kind brown eyes a stark contrast from his dark hair and menacing stature. "Why's that?"

"He's been through a heap of shit that most people couldn't even imagine but the way he was with you today…it's been a long fucking time since I've seen him like that."

I nod. In some ways, I already knew that Logan had been through things in his life, that he harbored more than a lifetime's worth of pain. "I can take the heap of shit but he needs to decide if he wants this or not."

Blaze laughs and shakes his head. "Oh, Darlin'. He wants it but he's as stubborn as they come so it might take a little bit of time."

Sighing, I let my gaze drift over to Logan's house.

"You okay? I could hang around for a bit if you're not ready to be alone," Blaze offers, and I look back into my house, wondering if I'll really be okay alone, before turning back to him.

"Thank you for the offer but I'll be okay."

"You sure?"

"Yeah." I nod, and he hands me a piece of paper with a phone number written on it.

"That's my number. Call if you need absolutely anything, ya hear?"

I thank him, and he offers me an easy smile before he walks down to his bike, scanning the street in front of him, and I turn back to my house, taking a deep breath as I step over the threshold.

* * * *

"Ali," Izzy calls into the house as the front door opens but I don't say a word, curled up on the couch in the back living room, staring at the wall. I didn't go to work today, and I figured that they would be over at some point. It's a good thing they both have a key because I haven't unlocked a single door since everyone left yesterday.

"There you are," Izzy says, walking into the kitchen and setting her stuff down on the counter. I flick my gaze over in her direction before focusing back on the wall.

"In here, Carly," she calls over her shoulder as the front door opens again.

"Hey, Hon. How are you doing?"

I sigh and climb off the couch, walking to the kitchen where Carly is setting bags of food down on the counter. My stomach rumbles, and I realize I haven't eaten all day.

"Did you sleep on the couch, Ali?" Izzy asks, and I nod.

"Yeah."

"Why?"

I look over at my bedroom door and sigh again as I motion for them to follow me. When I reach the door, I grab the handle and stop, taking a deep breath before pushing it open. Standing back, I let them walk in, and they look around in confusion.

"What are we supposed to be seeing here, Ali?" Izzy asks, and I point to the dresser and my bed.

"When I left yesterday morning, the drawer was closed and my bed was made."

"Oh," Carly breathes.

Izzy looks at me with worry in her eyes. "What did the police say?"

"Not much. I'm not even sure if anything is missing but I just couldn't sleep in here last night. It felt like someone was watching me." That's the understatement of the year. Even out in the living room, it felt like someone's gaze was on me, creeping over my skin like a thousand tiny bugs, and I was on the verge of tears as the night stretched on.

"Why don't you come stay with me?" Carly suggests, and I shake my head.

"No, I don't want to leave."

Izzy and Carly share a look before focusing back on me. "What about Storm? Could he stay with you?"

"Logan."

"Huh?" Izzy asks, scrunching her nose up in confusion.

"His name is Logan. Storm is just a nickname."

She nods, flicking a look at Carly again before her eyes meet mine. "Could he come stay with you?"

"I'm gonna go with no since he left without even saying good-bye to me yesterday, and I haven't heard from him since."

Carly sighs and gently pushes me out of my room, toward the kitchen, and I plop down on one of the barstools, pulling my knees up to my chest. They both start pulling food out of bags, and I just stare at the pattern of the granite, their eyes boring into me.

"Are you okay, Hon?" Carly asks, and I shrug, looking up at her.

"I just feel…numb. Like I can't quite believe that some stranger was looting through my most personal things but at night every little sound and every little shadow makes me jump, and I wonder if they came back."

"Oh, Sweetie," Izzy says, and when I glance over at her, she has tears in her eyes. "Come stay with me tonight. At least get one good night's sleep, okay?"

I sigh and nod, giving in because I don't have the energy to fight her on it, and I really could use some sleep. After we eat, Izzy goes into my bedroom and packs a few things for me, and as we walk out to her car, I glance over at Logan's house, wondering if he's missing me just as much as I'm missing him right now.

Hopelessly Devoted

Chapter Nineteen
Alison

"You sure you're okay?" Izzy asks from behind the wheel, and I turn to look at her, sighing as I nod.

"Yeah, I'm okay. Thank you for letting me crash at your place last night. Sleep definitely helped."

She smiles. "Don't mention it. You're my bestie and there isn't anything I wouldn't do for you."

I reach over the center console and hug her, thankful to have two really great friends in my life. When I pull away, she slumps back in her seat and looks in the rearview mirror.

"Any idea what you're going to do about that?"

I peek over my shoulder just as Logan pulls out of his driveway on his bike and speeds past us. Sighing, I shrug. "No. I mean, what can I do if he doesn't want this? I think I got way too ahead of myself and read into things that weren't really there."

"Not according to Carly. She saw the way he was with you yesterday."

"Then why have I still not heard from him?"

She scoffs, crossing her arms over her chest as she looks out at the road. "'Cause men are fucking idiots. It's a flaw in the grand design."

"What is?"

"Giving something two brains. It's bound to confuse the poor creature."

A giggle bursts out of my mouth, and she flashes me a sly grin before turning back to the road.

"You might be on to something there," I tell her, and she nods.

"I know I am."

"All right, well, I'll talk to you tomorrow."

She uncrosses her arms and turns in the seat to face me. "You going to work tomorrow?"

"Yeah. Can't hide out here forever."

She gives me a sympathetic look and a hug before I climb out of the car and walk up the sidewalk. Izzy waits on the curb until I unlock the door and step inside. I turn around and wave to her, and she waves back before pulling away. Shutting the door behind me, the quiet closes in on me, and I take a deep breath, reminding myself that I'm okay, before setting my bag down and walking to the kitchen.

Izzy and I spent the day watching romantic comedies and eating junk food so I'm not all that hungry even though I missed dinnertime. I stare at the contents of my fridge for a moment before grabbing the bottle of wine and a glass from the cupboard. Just as I'm shoving the cork back into the bottle, my phone rings and I jump. My mom's picture pops up on the screen of my phone, and I shake my head, scooping it up and pressing the green phone icon.

"Hey, Mom."

"There's my girl. How are you, Sweetie?"

I grab my glass of wine and sit down on one of the barstools, folding my legs underneath me. "I'm good, Mom. How's everything back there?"

"Oh, same as always. Your father has decided that he's going to build us rocking chairs but you know your father, they'll never get finished. I may just steal his truck and sneak over to Cracker Barrel to buy a couple."

I laugh and take a sip of my wine. "That sounds like a good plan, Mom."

"Doesn't it? How's work?"

I realize that I forgot to tell her about that whole situation, and I gasp. "Oh, gosh, Mom. I totally forgot to fill you in on all that."

I start telling her the whole story, starting at Mr. Klein putting me up against Chelsea to Mercedes cornering me in the coffee shop.

"Hold on a minute, isn't Chelsea the little hussy that rubbed her tits on your father's arm when we were there visiting you?"

I laugh and nod even though she can't see me. "Yep, that's her."

She laughs as I tell her all about the final confrontation with Klein and Chelsea in his office. I don't spare any details. My mom and I have always been close, and she'd never judge me for the choices I made.

"You should ask Izzy to slap a lawsuit against that man for what he did to you," she says when I finish, and I chuckle.

"No, there's no point. Besides, I'm probably doing better than he is now. The paper wasn't doing well when Carly and I left."

She squeals, and I pull the phone away from my ear for a second to save my eardrums. "I almost forgot. Tell me all about this new job."

I start telling her about how Mercedes approached me that day and about my new job. When I get to the part about my article going viral, the line goes quiet.

"Good Lord, I forget to call you for a few weekends and you've got a whole new life, don't you?" she asks, and I laugh.

"I suppose I do."

"Anything else new? Got a new man in your life?" I pause, unsure of what to tell her, and she picks up on it immediately. "Spill, young lady."

Sighing, I start to tell her about Logan and how we met. I spill my guts, explaining how weird it's been and how unsure I am about what's going on between us, and when I'm finished, she's quiet again.

"Mom? You still there?"

"Yeah, I'm here, Honey. I'm just thinking."

I chew on my bottom lip for a moment as I wait for her but my impatience gets the best of me. "Penny for your thoughts?"

"Well... I guess I'm a little surprised because it's been so long since you felt anything for a guy but also, the way you talk about him – it's like you're in love with him. You never talked like this about a guy. Not even Adam."

I scoff, almost falling off my stool. "Don't be ridiculous. I don't love Logan. I mean, I barely know him."

"So? Your dad and I were only dating for six months when we ran off to get married. When you know, you know, Ali, and time doesn't matter. Not really."

I'm about to respond when something bangs against the back of the house, and my heart kicks in my chest.

"Hang on, Mom," I whisper, setting the phone down as the fear runs rampant through my body. All I can picture in my mind is the faceless person lurking around my home, waiting to burst in. Grabbing a knife from the butcher block with a shaky hand, I slide off the barstool and creep toward the French doors in the back of the house.

Since the break-in, I've had the blinds drawn, and it hinders my view of the backyard, only increasing my fear as I draw closer and closer. My heart pounds in my ears, and my breath is choppy as I reach for the door handle, the knife held out in front of me. Taking a deep breath, I swing the door open and look out into the yard, seeing nothing. I can feel eyes on me, like there's someone hiding in my bushes waiting until my back is turned to ambush me, and it sends goose bumps racing across my skin.

I scan the yard again and again, hoping that I see something and praying that I don't all at the same time. The wind whips through the trees lining the back fence, and I can see my breath as I take a step outside, my entire body on edge and poised to attack. Finally, I look to the side of the house and let out a sigh as I realize the crash that I heard was one of my lawn chairs being blown into the side of the house.

"Take a chill pill, Ali," I mutter to myself, feeling stupid for overreacting as I turn and march back into the house. Even though I know it was nothing, I can't help but lock the door and then double check to make sure it's really locked before going back to the island and sitting on the barstool. I slide the knife onto the counter and pick up my phone.

"Sorry, Mom."

"Good Lord, Alison Marie. What the hell is going on?"

I sigh and look back at the doors. "It's really windy tonight, and one of the lawn chairs hit the side of the house. Scared the hell out of me."

"Why are you so jumpy, Honey?" she asks, and I turn away from the doors, unable to brush off the feeling of being watched. I decide not to tell her about the break-in. She's so far away, and I don't want to worry her unless it's something serious.

"It's probably just my new celebrity status that has me so on edge," I joke, and she laughs.

"Oh, yeah? All from going viral, huh?"

I mentally sigh with relief as she goes off asking questions about my article going viral, and I feel better as I tell her all about how my life has changed in the past few weeks.

* * * *

Subtly, I pull the curtains back and peek over into Logan's yard. He climbs off his bike and glances over at my house. I freeze, thinking maybe he saw me but then he turns and goes into his house without another look back at me. Sighing, I let them fall back into place and lean back against the wall, wondering what the hell is going on. Is it really too much to ask that he just give me an explanation? Even if he doesn't want to be with me, I deserve that. My phone buzzes, and I yank it out of my back pocket.

Izzy:
Still on for dinner?

Me:
Yep. Meet you guys there.

Carly:
I'll be there.

I shove my phone back in my pocket and peek out the window again. After checking the time, I push off the wall and try to decide what to do. I need to shower and get ready for dinner but I also want to march over to Logan's house and pound on the fucking door until he answers. Thinking back to the night we spent together, I get the kick in the ass I need to throw my shoes on and march out onto my porch, slamming my front door behind me.

I hate feeling like the fool. It's the way Adam made me feel when he cheated on me, and it's the way I feel now that Logan has seemingly dropped out of my life. God, how could I be such an idiot? He has trouble written all over him but I ignored that, dismissed my better judgment because the connection we have is unlike anything I've ever felt. But that doesn't matter anymore. I promised myself that I'd never let a man put me in a position to hurt me again, and I shouldn't have abandoned that at the first captivating set of eyes and rock hard abs.

Marching up the stairs to his porch, I suck in a breath and pause for just a moment before I start banging on the door. I can hear him moving around on the other side of the door, and his boots sound against the floor as he approaches the door. Silence descends over me for a moment, and then the footsteps start moving away from the door. Is he seriously not going to answer? I pound my fist against the door again, getting angrier and angrier the longer I wait out here.

"Logan!" I yell, not caring one bit that the whole damn neighborhood can hear me. "Open the door."

Silence.

I pound again, some of my fight draining out of me as I realize that he's really not going to answer the door. Well, I guess this tells me everything that I need to know, doesn't it?

I knock one more time, my voice breaking as I say, "Logan. Please."

Still nothing and I back away from the door with tears in my eyes. This is so stupid. I just met this man. I shouldn't be crying over the loss of him but as I turn and start walking back to my house, I do cry. Peeking over my shoulder, I take one last look at the house but I'm not seeing the house anymore - I'm seeing the day we met. I'm seeing future Friday nights cuddled up on the couch as we watch movies and birthday dinners that I spent all day making. I'm seeing his lazy smile as he rolls over in the morning and pulls me into his arms. I'm seeing all the possibilities that I imagined for us that will never happen.

I'm such a stupid girl, and I got so ahead of myself but it just felt right with him. I put so much faith in that feeling – that contentment that seemed to settle into my soul when I met him. As I walk back into my house, I feel absolutely deflated but I've got to put on a brave face and go out to dinner with the girls.

I drag myself to the bathroom, turning on the water before undressing and tossing my clothes in a pile on the floor. Steam fills the room, and I step under the hot water, the tears falling already. It's safe here. I can cry and no one will ever know as the water washes my pain away. I swipe angrily at my eyes, hating that I let him get to me like this. And the short amount of time that he was able to get to me makes it even worse. It's a vicious cycle of pain and anger as I scrub my body clean, wishing I could rinse him from my heart and mind so easily.

When I'm done, I step out and secure the towel around my body as I throw another one on my head and go into my bedroom. I plop down on the edge of the bed and sigh. I'm over this. He obviously didn't even care enough to open the damn door and talk to me so

I'm done crying over him. I'll go back to the way it was before. I'll focus on my work, and I'll be fine. And maybe one day, I'll find someone who won't cast me aside so easily. A man who will give anything to be with me and will be worthy of all I have to offer him. I'm constantly giving readers this same advice so why aren't I taking it myself?

With new resolve, I stand and start getting ready for dinner, doing my hair and make-up before grabbing a dress from my closet. Once I'm dressed, I go to my dresser and look through my necklaces, trying to find the one my grandmother gave me. I don't find it on my first pass of my jewelry so I look again, growing panicked when I can't find it. My hand goes to my throat, and I check to make sure I'm not wearing it as I run into the bathroom and check there. When I don't find it in the bathroom, I run back out to my bedroom, ready to pull the dresser out but my phone buzzes on the nightstand, stopping me. Sighing, I grab it.

Izzy:
Leaving now.

Carly:
OMW

Sighing again, I look over at the dresser and make a point to search for the necklace when I get home tonight. But right now, I've got to get to my girls. I grab my purse and force a smile to my face as I push down anything that will keep me from having a good time with my friends.

* * * *

"We'll take three martinis, please," Izzy says to the waiter.

"Martinis tonight? Looking to get trashed?" Carly asks her as he walks away, and Izzy points to me.

"Home girl looks like she could use something a little stronger."

I let out a curt laugh and cross my arms over my chest. "Do I really look that bad?"

"You look gorgeous but sad," Izzy says, trying to soften the blow, and I sigh. "What's going on?"

"Things are, uh…over with Logan," I say, looking down at my dress and pretending to pick some lint off.

Carly gasps. "What?"

"Since when?" Izzy asks, her eyes narrowing in my direction.

"Today."

Carly shakes her head and takes a sip of water. "No, that doesn't make any sense. I saw the way he was looking at you the other day. Why would he end things?"

"I ended it."

They both give me sympathetic looks, and I'm really starting to hate it. I feel like all I've gotten from people in the last couple days is sympathy. It would be amazing if I could just go back to a few days ago before someone broke into my house and turned my world upside down.

"Why would you end it? I thought you were really into him," Carly says, and I sigh just as the waiter brings our drinks to the table. I take a sip before setting it back down and looking up at them.

"I was. I am. But I'm not into the games, you know? One minute he's there, telling me he wants to be with me, and then he disappears for days at a time without a word. I went over to his house today, and he refused to even come talk to me."

"Maybe he wasn't home," Carly suggests, and I love her optimism and wish that were the case.

"I watched him come home, and when I knocked on the door, I could hear him walking up to the door but he never opened it and he never said a word."

Carly looks over to Izzy, who's staring at me with a faraway look in her eyes, and I can't help but wonder what's going on in her head.

"There's got to be some kind of explanation, right?" Carly asks, and I shake my head.

"Maybe there is, Hon. But look at me. It's only been three weeks and I'm feeling like this? Better to just bail out now before I do something stupid like fall in love with him."

Izzy clears her throat, and I glance over at her as she takes a big gulp of her martini. "You sure it's not already too late?"

Sighing, I mimic her gulp with the martini and shrug. "Not really but the longer I invest in this, the harder it will be when it falls apart."

"Who says it's going to fall apart?" Carly asks, and I shoot her a look.

"He's hiding out in his house and refusing to talk to me. There's no way that this can go anywhere but down."

Carly shoots me a look of annoyance. "You always do this, Ali. I get that Adam hurt you badly but Logan is nothing like Adam. I've never seen a man look at a woman the way Logan looks at you, and I would do anything to have someone look at me like that."

"Sweetie, someone broke into my house and his first reaction was to call me a slut, and then he just up and left me with the detective without saying a word. And I still haven't heard from him four days later. These are not the actions of a man who has any feelings at all."

She huffs, her annoyance with me growing. "I don't know why he left, and I don't know why he hasn't spoken to you since then but he can't hide the look he gives you. He can force himself to stay away but his eyes give him away anytime you're in the room."

"Okay, back to your corners, Ladies," Izzy says, and I sigh, taking a sip of my drink as I glance over at Carly. She avoids my gaze, and I hate it.

"I'm sorry. I just can't invest any more in this if I'm the only one doing it. It's really only been three weeks since I met him, and I got a little too caught up in the idea of a relationship with him but when you look at the reality, it's not as pretty."

"Did you see his face when you got to the house on Monday? He looked like once he saw you he could finally breathe again. How can you doubt that?"

"Then where is he, Carly? Why has my phone not gone off one time with a text from him since Monday? Why did he purposefully ignore me when I knocked on his door? Maybe he does feel something for me but not enough to make an effort."

"I don't know," she snaps, crossing her arms over her chest and looking away from me. This is so unlike her, and I glance over at Izzy, who shrugs in return.

"Are you okay, Car? This really isn't like you," Izzy points out, and Carly sighs, dropping her gaze down to the tablecloth.

"Until I met you guys, I always felt like I was too much for people. I'd meet friends and take to them much faster than they did me, and I'd want to hang out more than they did. It's the same with guys. I want someone that's going to look at me the way Logan was looking at Ali. Like I light up their whole world."

My heart squeezes in my chest, and I reach out, grabbing on to her hand. "You're going to find it someday, Carly. You're too good not to, and those other bitches have no idea the great friend that they are missing out on. We're lucky to have you."

"Oh, Jesus, do not make me cry in public," Izzy snaps, dabbing at her eyes, and we both start laughing at her, the tension melting away.

"I'm sorry for snapping at you," Carly says, and I shake my head.

"Don't mention it. It's already forgotten."

Chapter Twenty
Storm

I watch her in the window as she walks away from my house, each step she takes is like a hit to the chest, and every part of me wants to fling the door open and yell at her to come back. But I can't. This whole thing moved so damn fast, and each time I see her, it's like I'm sucker punched by all the feelings she stirs up in me. I wasn't ready for this, ready for her, and I haven't handled any of this right. None of that matters anymore though. She's mine. And I'll do whatever it takes to keep her.

Bear whines, and I glance down at him. "Yeah, I know, Buddy. I miss her, too."

I fucking hate that I can't be with her right now but I've got shit that needs to be dealt with before I can be with her. If I just threw caution to the wind and did exactly what I'm dying to do right now, her life would be in danger, and that's not something I'm even remotely willing to sacrifice. Not again. I watch her until she disappears into her house, and the dejected look on her gorgeous face breaks my fucking heart. I just need her to hold on for a little bit, and then I'll give her everything she wants.

Moving away from the window, I grab my phone off the table and slip my cut on before stalking out to my bike. I'm jittery as I climb on, ready to end this shit. Straddling the bike, I check my messages.

Ray:
Meet you in the usual spot.

I shove my phone back in my pocket and fire up my bike before pulling out onto the street. My gaze lingers on Ali's house as I drive by, and I promise her that I'll be seeing her soon. The wind whips against my skin as I drive west out of town, the sun sinking into the horizon in front of me. I imagine bringing Ali out on the bike, her arms wrapping around me from behind, and I grin. I've never had someone on the back of my bike, and I'm looking forward to it.

After riding for a few miles, I turn onto the dirt road, only slowing when I approach the edge of the river. Ray climbs out of his truck as I turn my bike off and get off.

"Hey, man, good to hear from you," he says, slapping my hand and pulling me in for a half hug. I laugh.

"No, it's not. No one calls you when it's good news."

He puts a cigarette in his mouth and lights it, nodding. "Well, you're right about that. So, what's up?"

Running my hand over my hair, I look out over the river. "Your friend, Shaun, still doin' time?"

"Yeah."

"He still in the Pen?"

I glance over at him and he nods as he draws on his cigarette. "Sure is. This the same thing as last time?"

"He's got someone following me. Following my girl, too, and someone broke into her house earlier this week but didn't steal anything."

He nods, pulling out a notepad like the cops use. "What's his name again?"

"Ian Blackwell."

"And what's he doing time for?"

I suck in a breath, turning back to the river. "Murder."

"How bad you want him hurt?"

What a loaded question. I would love it if he were just as dead as the woman he killed but Blaze's voice sounds in my head, reminding me that we aren't the bad guys and we can't act like thugs.

"Bad enough to drive the point home. He calls off his brother and stays the hell away from me and my girl."

He finishes scribbling something and tucks the notebook back into his pocket before slapping me on my shoulder. "I'll call you when it's done."

* * * *

"Church in five," Blaze calls just as I walk in the door, and everyone nods at him before turning back to what they were doing before. I slide onto a barstool next to Chance and nod at Teresa when she sets a beer down in front of me.

"Well, don't you look fucking chipper," Chance says, and I laugh, almost choking on my beer.

"That a bad thing?"

He shakes his head and takes a sip of his own beer. "Suppose not. Just different."

He's right; it is different. For the past six years, I've had a dark cloud hanging over me, and it was visible to everyone, but not anymore.

"You just got over it like that, huh?"

"Naw, man. I didn't just get over it but Ali, she makes it all easier, you know. Gave me a reason to smile again."

He snorts and nods. "Yeah, okay. Don't go getting all sappy on me."

"Shut the fuck up, dude."

"Hey, Storm," Smith calls from the back corner of the clubhouse where he and Moose are playing pool.

"What?"

"You and that neighbor of yours serious?"

Red-hot rage blinds my vision as I think about him putting his hands on her. Brother or not, that shit is not happening. Possessiveness wells up inside me, and I stand, slamming my beer bottle down on the bar.

"She's fucking off limits."

Everyone grows quiet, all eyes trained on me. "You claimin' her, then? Officially?"

"You're damn right I am."

Kodiak laughs and jumps up from the couch, slapping me on the shoulder. "Well, it's about damn time."

"Church," Blaze calls from the doorway, a knowing smile on his face as I pass him and take my seat at the table. Everyone else files in and fills the rest of the table as Blaze goes to the head of the table and bangs the gavel.

"All right, let's get down to business. Kodiak and Smith, what do you have from Ali's house?"

"Honestly, boss, not a whole lot," Kodiak says, and Smith nods in agreement, only increasing my suspicions about what really happened.

"The back door looks like it's been jimmied quite a few times so it's impossible to say how many times this guy has been in there. That alone rules out the possibility of this being an attempted robbery," Smith adds, and I shift in my seat. I don't like the fucking sound of this at all.

"And nothing was taken?" Blaze asks, and Kodiak and Smith share a look.

"Possibly some panties but there's no way to know for sure."

"Ali said her bed was made when she left that morning, and it was messed up when we were there like someone had been lying in it," I say, and they all turn to me. This feels so familiar, and it turns my stomach just thinking about it.

"Sounds like she's got a stalker," Fuzz says, and my heart drops.

"It's Ian's brother."

Everyone turns to look at me except for Streak, who just nods in agreement. I glance over at Blaze, and he's studying me. "How do you know this?"

"Had Streak look into him. I never even realized that Ian had a twin brother but it makes sense with the pictures that have been left on my doorstep."

He stares at me for a moment longer before turning to the other guys around the table. "We should put a guard on her."

"That's not necessary. I'm already taking care of it."

Blaze turns his focus back to me. "What the hell does that mean?"

"It means I've got a guy taking care of it."

He slams his fist onto the table, and everyone falls quiet. "I fucking told you not to do anything."

"Honestly, Prez, with Storm claimin' her, it might be the best way to go," Smith says, playing his part as sergeant at arms. "It's been a long ass time since we've had to worry about protecting an old lady, and we don't want to set a precedent with this."

I look to the back of the table where our two older members, Red and Earl, sit. They are the only ones with old ladies anymore so it's not something Blaze has had to worry about in a while.

"We can't just go around killing people. That's part of the reason we got in that mess six years ago."

"I'm not killing him," I say, knowing that will in no way pacify Blaze.

He turns to me and sighs, running a hand over his face. "And if he doesn't get the message?"

"Then we'll be having this conversation again."

"Goddamn it, we have to be careful here. Rodriguez may be a friend but he's a good cop, and he won't protect you if shit goes down."

I nod. "I know. But I'm gonna do whatever the fuck I have to do to protect my woman. This shit is not happening again."

He studies me and I see the moment it clicks, the moment he realizes that I'm living a nightmare all over again, and he nods. "Understood, but we discuss it here before you do anything."

Hopelessly Devoted

Chapter Twenty-One
Alison

Dear Alison,
I've been seeing this guy for a little while, and I'm really into him but I can't tell if he feels the same about me. He's hot and cold, there one minute and gone the next like I mean nothing to him. I really want to be with him but I don't want to waste my time or get my heart broken. What should I do?
Dazed and Confused

Did I write a letter to myself in my sleep or something? Jeez, it's like someone plucked these exact thoughts from my head. Tossing the letter down on my desk, I sigh. It's been over a week since I've seen Logan, and I never expected it to hit me this hard. Taking a deep breath, I shake my head and push those thoughts down. It won't do me any good to wallow in this, and I just keep telling myself that there's a reason for everything even if I'm not sure that I really believe that.

Sighing, I pull up a Word document and look over at the letter on my desk as I formulate a response in my head. Once I have a pretty good feel for where I'm going with this, I start typing.

Dear Dazed and Confused,
It's been my experience that guys are usually pretty direct when it comes to what they want. If this guy truly wanted to be with you, you wouldn't be writing me this letter. I know that kind of sucks, and I'm sorry that I don't have a better answer for you but he's showing you through his actions what he refuses to say out loud. And I think a part of you already knew that. You shouldn't let this hurt you though. Just think, there's probably some guy out there looking for you and he just doesn't know it yet. There's got to be more out there than being someone's second or third priority. Hold on and have faith that when the time is right, he'll find you and you won't have to doubt how he feels because it will shine through in everything he does.
Sincerely,
Alison

I reread through my response several times before looking back over at the letter. It's funny how I can give my readers such sound advice when my own love life is a complete mess. How can I expect people to listen to me when I can't even take my own advice? Because if I did, it would stop hurting so damn bad that Logan just up and left my life without a word.

"Ali, there's someone at the front desk for you," Margie, our receptionist, says over the intercom, and I lean across the desk, pushing the button to respond.

"Thanks, Margie. I'll be up in a second."

I make sure to save my Word document and just as I'm standing to leave, Carly walks into my office with a smile on her face.

"Lunch today? We could try that new Mexican place down the street."

My stomach growls on cue, and I nod. "Yes. That sounds amazing."

"Okay, just let me finish something real quick and then we can go."

I grab my bag off of the floor. "Actually, I have to go up to reception so I'll just meet you there."

She nods and heads back to her office as I look back at my desk, grabbing my phone before walking out and heading to reception. I can't help but smile when I look at everyone running around working. They all seem so happy, and it's such a contrast from the paper that it still surprises me at times. And even though things didn't work out in my personal life, I'm still happy with this change.

As I step around the corner, the smile on my face slowly drains away, and my heart pounds in my chest. Logan is leaning up against the reception desk, talking to Margie. She says something, and he laughs, laying the charm on thick, and my stomach twists. Seriously? He disappears for over a week without a single goddamn word, and then he shows up here and flirts with Margie? I don't want him here because even just looking at him hurts me.

I don't want to love the way his jeans hug his hips or the perfect way his cut hangs off his shoulders. Envisioning walking up to him, grabbing the leather in my hands, and pulling him to me is a sure-fire path to disaster. And yet, here I stand, doing just that as my chest aches.

"What the fuck?" Carly hisses in my ear as she comes up behind me, and I nod in agreement. What the fuck, indeed.

"My thoughts exactly," I whisper back and resist the urge to run back to my office and lock the door. Let's be honest, he'd probably just follow me and make a scene. He turns to us and as soon as he sees me, his smile brightens, and his eyes warm, trailing down my body as he takes a step toward me, almost like he can't stop himself. I shouldn't let it get to me but the way he looks at me does all sorts of things to my traitorous body. I want to jump in his arms and slap the shit out of him all at the same time.

"Hey, Baby," he says, smiling like he has every right to call me that.

"What did I tell you about that word?"

His brow furrows, and his smile drops a little. "What? Baby?"

"That's the one," I say, nodding, and he pushes off the counter, standing tall as he studies me.

"I thought we cleared this up already."

I can hear his words in my head, telling me that I was his and he was mine. I loved that; loved the way that it felt to have someone I could call mine. "That was before you turned into Houdini."

Sighing, he looks over at Margie, who is enthralled by our little display, before turning back to me. "Can we talk in private?"

"No."

"Ali, please," he pleads, and for a moment, I see Logan peeking through the Storm façade. It breaks me and I sigh, looking back at Carly. She's glaring at Logan, and I wonder when she changed her mind about him.

"Outside," I snap, pointing to the glass doors that lead out to the sidewalk, and he nods, following behind me. When we get outside, I pull my sweater tighter around my body and look back into the office. Carly hasn't moved an inch, still shooting daggers at Logan and now Mercedes has joined the viewing party.

"What are you doing here, Storm?"

He shoves his hands in his pockets, and I'm glad because one touch and I'd be in danger of giving in to him. "Don't do that."

There is so much I want to say to him right now. I'd love to just start screaming at him; tell him how much he hurt me even if I was a little reckless with my heart when it came to him. But, I don't say any of that because the only thing worse than him hurting me is him knowing how much he hurt me.

"What are you doing here?"

He opens his mouth and shuts it again, searching my face as he tries to grasp on to something to say to persuade me. "I want to take you to lunch."

"Not interested," I shoot back, turning to walk back inside, and he grabs onto my arm.

"Alison."

I whip back around, letting him see just how fucking angry I am. "What? Where have you been for the last week, Storm?"

"Stop calling me that," he growls, pulling me into his body and sliding a hand into my hair. It feels too good to be good for me. "Logan. You and only you call me Logan."

"Where have you been for the past week, *Logan*?"

His grip loosens but he doesn't release me. "I've been busy."

"Bullshit." My answer is immediate and resounding in the space between us. "Let me go."

"No," he says, locking eyes with me, and we're in a battle of wills. He's not willing to let me go, and I don't want to stay.

"You remember when I told you that I didn't want to play games?"

He nods.

"This is exactly what I was talking about. One minute, you're here and the next, you're gone without a word. Where were you all week?"

He grits his teeth, not taking his eyes off mine as he says, "Busy."

"And that prevented you from texting me?"

He doesn't say a word, only dropping his gaze from my eyes to my lips.

"You couldn't find five minutes in your day to just run next door and say hi to me so I would know that you meant all the shit that's coming out of your mouth?"

He looks up, his turbulent gray eyes meeting mine, and just like that, everything inside me wants to lose myself in him. "If I talked to you or spent five minutes with you, it would just make it harder to stay away, and there was shit I had to do."

"Bullshit," I say again, and his grip tightens, pulling me in, but he doesn't say anything because we both know I'm right.

"Tell you what, Storm," I sneer, tears threatening to fall. I fucking hate that he keeps making me cry. "Why don't you come find me when you're ready to get real. Until then, I'm fucking done."

He releases his grip on me, and I despise the fact that it hurts when he lets me go. Without a word, I turn and march back into the office where Carly envelops me in a hug.

"So, totally a bad time, I know, but who is that yummy man out there?" Mercedes asks, and I laugh through my anger.

"Uh, that would be Logan. You've met him before, right? The day he came looking for me?"

She shakes her head. "No, Honey. I definitely would have remembered him."

I scowl and look behind me where Logan is still staring at me through the glass. Carly nudges me, and I turn back to look at her.

"Let's just order the really yummy soup from the place next door," she offers, and I force a smile to my face as I nod.

"Is he still out there?"

She looks behind us and nods. "Yeah, he is. By the way, I'm totally on your side now."

It's so ridiculous that I just start laughing, and she grins at me as she hooks her arm over my shoulder and leads me away from the door to my office. She closes the door behind her when we get inside, and I sit down on the couch Mercedes insisted I needed.

"I'm so stupid, Car," I sigh, and she spins to me, her phone in her hand, and a shocked expression on her face.

"What? No, you're not."

"I met him three weeks ago. Only three weeks and I was thinking there was something serious between us. I'm an idiot."

Her gaze softens, and she sinks down into one of the chairs in front of my desk. "You can't control your heart, Ali. Three weeks or three years – no one can tell you how quickly you'll fall for someone. And for the record, I think there is something real between the two of you but he's an idiot."

I sniff, wiping away a tear as I crack a tiny smile. "Thank you."

"What are friends for?" She shrugs before turning her attention back to her phone to order our food. I stare out the window and wonder if he's still out there. There was something different about him today. He seemed freer than before, like maybe the things that were holding him back have finally released him. I shake my head and sigh. I can't think like that. It's a guaranteed way to make sure my heart gets broken into a million little pieces.

"You okay, Hon?" Carly asks, looking up from her phone, and I lift my head and nod at her.

"Yeah, I'll be all right."

Hopelessly Devoted

"Is it wrong to say that I'm still kind of hoping that he pulls his shit together?"

I laugh and shake my head. "No, you go ahead and hope for the both of us because I can't."

"Done and food will be here in fifteen."

I nod and start to ask her a question when someone knocks on the door. I call for them to come in, and Margie appears in the doorway holding a single rose in a vase and a teddy bear.

"Someone's popular today," she says, and I force a smile. She sets it down on my desk and hands me a card before leaving. I look up at Carly and then down to the card in my hand.

"Doesn't really seem like Logan's style," she says, eyeing the flower and teddy bear.

"No, it doesn't."

She meets my eyes before looking down at the card that I'd honestly forgotten I was holding. "Well, open it."

I glance down and flip the card over, sliding my finger under the flap, and it comes apart easily. On the front of the card is a bear just like the one sitting on my desk with a little speech bubble that says, "I love you beary much." Uneasiness washes over me, and I look up at Carly.

"What does it say?" she asks, looking as weirded out as I feel. I open the card and read it to myself.

Alison,
I wanted to say congratulations on the column. I've read every single one, and as predicted, you are

brilliant. But you already knew that. My sweet Ali, it feels like it's been forever since I've gotten to see you, and the only comfort I've had is your beautiful words. Why are you hiding from me? You wouldn't even believe how much I miss you. I hope you like the bear and the flower, and I hope they serve as reminders of me while you're hard at work until I see you again, my love.

See you in my dreams, Sweetheart.
Chris

My stomach rolls as I pass the card to her with shaky hands, trying to process what the hell I just read. I'm officially weirded out by this Chris guy, and I don't understand what he wrote at all. He talks like we're in a relationship and I've been ignoring him for work. He talks like he knows me intimately. A shiver works its way down my spine, and I kind of feel like I'm going to be sick.

"You dating someone else I don't know about?" Carly asks, looking up at me when she finishes reading, and I shake my head. "Hey, wait... Chris – isn't that the same guy that sent you the letter and called into the radio show?"

"Yeah, that's him."

She hands me back the card, and I look at the flower and teddy bear on my desk, baffled.

"What should I do?"

She looks over the things on my desk before grabbing the vase and teddy bear. She drops them in my trashcan and takes the card from me and slips it into the paper shredder. "Ignore him. When you don't give him the attention he wants, he'll go away."

I nod, hoping she's right.

* * * *

The doorbell rings just as I'm settling in for some trashy TV with a big glass of wine, and I sigh, looking over at the door as I consider just ignoring it. After everything that happened today, I don't want to deal with anything else except whatever is making Kim Kardashian ugly cry this week. Whoever is on the other side is persistent, though, and they ring the bell again before knocking a few times. Setting my glass down on the coffee table, I climb off the couch and march over to the door, determined to get them out of here as soon as possible. As soon as I fling open the door, I groan in annoyance.

"I'm really not in the mood to do this with you again, Logan."

He steps past me without waiting for an invitation, and all my hopes of going back to my comfy spot on the couch die. "Too bad. We need to talk."

"No, we really don't," I say, even though I'm closing the door.

Instead of responding, he reaches out and wraps an arm around my waist before pulling me into him, hard. I collide with his body, and my eyes close, not willing to give away how good it feels to be in his arms again.

"Open your eyes," he rasps, and I'm powerless to deny him. My eyes blink open, and he stares down at me, all his intensity focused on me. "You are mine, Ali. From the very fucking moment I laid eyes on you, you've been mine. I'll explain everything to you but it doesn't change that fact."

"We'll see."

"No, we won't. You can run all across this world and I'll burn it down looking for you. This is fucking real, and I'm done avoiding it."

I narrow my eyes at him, studying the way he's looking at me and looking for any sign of deception. "I don't believe you."

"Yes, you do. Look in my eyes, Ali. You own me. Can't you see that?"

I shake my head, pushing away from him, and he releases me. "I thought I saw a lot of things that weren't true."

"Don't do that. I fucking know I screwed up before but I'm being real with you now."

I look away from him to the door before reaching over and opening it again. "I want you to leave."

"No." He seems to grow even taller than he already is, and I can see that he won't leave until he's talked to me. Slamming the door, I march over to the couch and sit down, taking a sip of my wine.

"Fine. Talk, then."

He sits down next to me on the couch, and just as I set my wine back on the coffee table, he grabs my wrist and pulls me into his lap so I'm straddling him. I open my mouth to yell at him when his hand smacks against the side of my ass.

"Stop being a brat and listen."

I'm stunned speechless as he wraps his arms around my back, holding me firm on his lap. He hesitates for a moment before meeting my eyes and clearing his throat. "When I met you, I was in a fucking bad place."

Pain floods his eyes, and it's obvious that this is hard for him to say. Something deep down inside me wants to comfort him. I reach out, placing my hand on his chest, right by his heart, and he lets out a relieved breath.

"My life was so dark and bleak for so long, and I'd accepted that. I'd become accustomed to living my life like that but then Bear got out of the yard and found you."

He grins, and I fight back a smile of my own as I remember that day.

"You hit me like a ton of bricks the moment I looked into your eyes. You came out of nowhere, and I wasn't ready for it. I don't deserve you but I couldn't stay away from you."

"Why?" I whisper. He looks away, blowing out a breath before focusing back on me, the pain in his eyes so fresh and so potent that my own chest aches.

"It's been so long since I've done this – been in a relationship. The last time was six years ago, and when it ended, I was destroyed."

"What happened?" I whisper.

"She died."

"Oh." My heart breaks for him, for the pain that I can't even imagine, and suddenly everything makes sense. I get why he was pushing me away and fighting our connection. "I'm so sorry."

He blinks in shock. "You're sorry? For what?"

"If I had known, I never would have…"

He presses a finger over my lips. "You don't have a single thing to apologize for. I handled this all wrong."

"No, it's okay."

He stops me, shaking his head as he grabs my hand and squeezes it. "You fucking terrify me, Ali. I'm scared shitless of letting you in but I can't walk away either. You're mine, and that's the end of it."

"Is it now?"

He grins and slides his hand into my hair, pulling me down to him. "Yeah, it is. You can fight, Baby, but we'll always end up back here. I think you know that, too."

"It scares me to trust you," I whisper against his lips, and he pulls back to look in my eyes.

"Why?"

I force a smile to my face and shrug. "Trust issues. My last boyfriend wasn't all that great."

"I'm not like any other punk ass bitch you've been with in your life, Ali. I did a shitty job dealing with this before but that's done now. You are my woman, and I'll never give you a reason to lose faith in me. Anything you ever need or want, I'll move mountains to give it to you."

Wow.

Hopelessly Devoted

    I honestly couldn't tell you if I said the word or just thought it because he stuns me. He seems so sure of himself now, the hesitation that was always present between us before is long gone. My gaze drops down to his full lips, and I'm consumed with thoughts of kissing him because any other response would pale in comparison. His thoughts must mimic my own because he pulls me to him and claims my lips as the arm wrapped around my back tightens. I wrap my arms around his neck, threading my fingers through his dark hair, and he groans, his grip on the back of my neck tightening.

    His kiss isn't hard or demanding like the last time we were together but it's just intense, hypnotizing me with its slow, seductive rhythm as one of his hands cradles the back of my head and the other massages my ass. His touch assaults me from all angles, a tingling sensation scattering across my skin and shooting between my legs. Grabbing his cut, I grind against him, letting out a quiet moan as I drive myself crazy.

    "Come with me," I whisper, climbing off him and grabbing his hand. He laces our fingers together as I lead him to my bedroom, and even that simple action makes my heart race.

    When we get to my bedroom, I turn his back to the bed and shove him so he falls back onto the mattress. He arches a brow, a wide grin on his face as I reach around to my side and unzip my pants, sliding them down my legs. His gaze falls between my thighs, and he licks his lips, his cock twitching in his jeans. Slowly, in an effort to tease him, I reach down and guide my shirt up my belly, over my breasts, and finally pull it over my head.

    Molten gray eyes trace a path up my body, taking their time to enjoy every inch of me, and I feel sexy and powerful standing before him like this. When his gaze meets mine, I smile and reach behind my back, unhooking my bra, and letting it fall down my arms. He licks his lips again, and I can clearly see his need. Sitting up on the bed, he rips his cut off, tossing it on the chair in the corner of the room before turning back to me and pulling his t-shirt over his head. He unbuckles his jeans and holds a hand out to me. I walk over to him and slip my hand into his, intertwining our fingers again as I climb on top of him and push his shoulders back down to the bed.

    An easy smile curves his lips as he reaches up and wraps his hand around the back of my neck, pulling me down to him as he leans up to kiss me. I follow him down to the bed, releasing his hand to run my fingers over his inked skin. He shudders and wraps his arms around me before flipping me to my back and standing to shove his jeans off, his cock springing free.

    He climbs back over me and grabs my hip as he takes my lips in a scorching kiss, his grip on me so determined. It reinforces his words from earlier. I'm his. I can't doubt that when he's holding me and kissing me like this. Reaching between us, he rubs circles over my clit with his thumb, and I buck underneath him, grabbing his shoulder as I moan. He flicks his tongue against my neck before sinking his teeth into my skin, and I moan again, desire pooling between my thighs.

"Logan," I whisper, a desperate plea in my voice. Although, I'm not all that sure what, exactly, I'm begging for.

"God, I missed you, Baby," he whispers in my ear, pulling his hand away, and rubbing his cock against my lace-covered pussy.

"Please," I whine, and he pulls back, hooking his fingers in my panties before pulling them down my legs.

"Please, what? Tell me what you want, Alison."

I reach out to grab his cock, and he slaps my hand away, shaking his head.

"Tell me what you want," he repeats, and I moan, lifting my hips off the bed in an effort to get the friction I need.

"Sweet Ali, this problem of yours could be so easily solved if you'd just tell me what you want," he teases, a smug grin on his face. Son of a bitch. He's going to make me say it.

"I want your cock."

His grin grows, and he leans over me again, positioning himself at my entrance. "You ask for anything and it's yours," he says, reminding me of his words earlier as he plunges into me and holds himself there.

I gasp, my body quickly adjusting to his size. He remains still, and I start to feel that desperate need again as I try to wiggle underneath him. Pinning me with his eyes, he slowly pulls out and sinks back into me with the same slow pace he kissed me with, and I can't pull my gaze away as he does it again and again. I bite down on my lip, peeking up at him through hooded eyes as he keeps his pace, dragging his cock out of me deliberately before sinking back in at the same casual pace. Moaning, I slide my hands down his body, my nails digging into his skin as the desire simmering in my belly begins to build.

"You like that, Gorgeous?" he asks, and I nod. "Or maybe you would prefer if I flipped you on all fours and fucked you so good that you couldn't stand for a couple hours?"

I moan, and my hips rise off the bed to meet his as he drives back into me while he chuckles.

"I think that was a yes. Was that a yes, Kitten?"

I shoot him a confused look. "Kitten?"

"Well, I was going to call you Ali-Cat but I figured you wouldn't appreciate that."

"Smart move," I half moan as he plunges into me a little harder this time.

"Actually, I think Kitten is kind of perfect after today."

How the hell is he holding a conversation with me right now? The man has nerves of fucking steel and the patience of a saint. It's so hard to concentrate on what's coming out of his mouth when I'm consumed by what he's doing between my legs.

"Why's that?"

"Because you're all cute and sweet, and then all of a sudden the claws come out like they did today when I tried to get you to have lunch with me."

"Clever," I say through gritted teeth as he continues driving me out of my mind. Has he slowed down? I swear he's thrusting slower than he was before.

I claw at his back, desperate for more. He groans through his grin.

"Ah, see, there they are."

"I swear to God, Logan," I say, glaring up at him, "I will show you fucking claws if you don't pick up the pace."

"Like this?" he asks as he pulls back and drives into me hard and fast, just the way I want it. Something between a gasp and moan comes out of my mouth, and I fist the sheets underneath me. He slows down again, and I lose it. I wrap my leg around his waist and use my other foot to kick off the bed and roll us. He lands on his back with a thud and looks up at me in surprise for a moment. I rise up and sink back down, finding the perfect rhythm to send me building toward the orgasm he was denying me.

He grabs my hips, his fingers digging into my skin, and I brace myself with one hand on his chest as I close my eyes and lose myself to the intoxicating sensation of Logan filling me.

"You're so fucking gorgeous, Kitten," he rasps, sounding just as lost as I am right now, and I open my eyes. He's looking up at me, the fire in his eyes hot enough to burn me up. I lean down to kiss him, and he knocks my hand off his chest, pulling me down to him as he starts driving up into me. My mind blanks, and all I can do is ride the wave as I race toward the release that I've been begging for.

"That's it, Baby. I want you to come all over my cock. Give it to me," he growls in my ear. I catapult over the edge, crying out into the room as my body tenses and my pussy grips his length. Wave after wave of pleasure washes over me, and I gasp for air on his chest as he continues thrusting up into me, seeking his own orgasm and prolonging mine.

His grip on me tightens, and he tenses underneath me, groaning in my ear before he collapses back on the bed, his arms splaying out at his sides. We just lie like that for a few minutes before he pulls me off him and moves me to his side, pulling me in close. His breath ruffles my hair as he leans down and presses his lips to the top of my head, breathing me in, and my throat tightens.

"Shit, Baby. I forgot to grab a condom," he whispers.

"I'm on the pill, and I was telling you the truth when I said I hadn't been with anyone in two years."

He looks away from me for a second before meeting my eyes again. "I haven't exactly been a saint but I'm clean."

I nod and cuddle back into his side, images of him with other girls assaulting me, and tears sting my eyes.

"Excuse me," I whisper, untangling myself from his arms and sliding over to the edge of the bed.

"You okay?"

I turn back to him and nod, my eyes burning as tears threaten to fall but I force a smile to my face. "Yeah, just need to pee. I'll be right back."

He nods, looking so right lying in my bed, and I turn away before I lose it in front of him. Hopping off the bed, I rush to the bathroom and close the door, turning the faucet on just as the tears start to fall. I cover my mouth as I start to sob so he won't hear me and press my back to the door. I sink down to the floor and pull my knees to my chest as the tears fall down my cheeks relentlessly.

    I'm such an idiot.

    I heard everything he said earlier and there is a huge part of me that wants to believe him, that's urging me to put my trust in him and give this a shot. But it's the small voice in my head that just made me realize I'm head over heels in love with him and I worry that he won't stick around. He still has so much pain buried inside him, and I wonder if his pain is going to end up breaking my heart, too.

Chapter Twenty-Two
Storm

"You got news for me, Ray?" I ask, answering my phone as I climb off my bike outside the clubhouse. I hang the helmet on the handlebars and turn toward the parking lot.

"It's done. Good old Ian is takin' himself a little vacation to the infirmary."

Kodiak gives me a little chin lift, and I nod at him as he passes, waiting until he's walking into the clubhouse to respond. "And he got the message?"

Ray laughs. "Oh, yeah. Loud and clear."

"You sure?" I still don't feel settled, and I'm not sure that I ever will. As long as Ian Blackwell is still living, that is.

"Yeah, Storm. Shaun made it very clear that it would be a very traumatic day for him if his brother came around you or your girl again."

I sigh, my mind calming a little. "All right. Thank you."

"No problem, man. Just remember, you owe me one."

"Yeah? So that takes one off all the times you owe me, right?"

He laughs. "That sounds about right."

Saying good-bye, I hang up and walk into the clubhouse, ready to get church over with already. I just left Ali not even twenty minutes ago but fuck if I don't miss her right now. It's only been a few days since I told her about part of my past but she's already embedded herself in my soul, and I know there's no letting her go. I don't even care that she makes me watch those stupid fucking TV shows as long as she's in my arms and I get to hear her sweet laugh as I make fun of the people on the screen.

"Dude," Chance says from the couch next to the door as soon as I walk in, "you're not even trying to hide how whipped you are anymore."

"Shut the fuck up, Chance," I growl, shoving him, and he laughs but it's not convincing. Chance may give me a hard time about Ali but I know that he wants to find a good girl and settle down, too. After all the shit he dealt with from his mom growing up, he wanted a family, and even though he's found a sense of family in the club, he still wants more. He's tried a few times but it just didn't work out. That's what happens when you try to turn a hoe into a housewife.

"Church," Blaze barks from the doorway before turning and disappearing back inside. Everyone stares at the spot he just was for a moment before standing up and filing in. I glance over at Chance, and he shrugs. We take our seats as Blaze waits for us at the head of the table, a grim expression on his face. Once we're all seated, he bangs the gavel on the table and clears his throat.

"Listen up, y'all. We've got two jobs this week, and they are both at the end of the week so I want extra surveillance leading up to the transfer. We don't need another situation like last time. Storm's eye is just starting to go back to normal."

"Yeah, fuck you," I half-heartedly say to Blaze, and he barely cracks a smile as chuckles ring out from around the table.

"Now, I plan on takin' both of them over to Emma and Nix's so I want two of you to go out there and beef up security. The last thing we need right now is trouble at their place."

"What exactly are you wantin' out there?" Smith asks.

"Lights, cameras, and motion detectors, at least. Maybe an electric fence along the front and sides, too." Smith's eyebrows shoot up, and he looks over to me for an explanation but I've got no idea what's going on with our president right now. I glance around the table, and the same concern is etched across everyone else's face as they all stare back at Blaze.

"Next Friday is the first job. Her name is Sammy, and she's Biche's girl."

"Shit," I curse under my breath as the men around the table echo the same.

"As you might remember, Biche is the piece of shit that set Henn up and got him locked up. He's moved up the ranks since Henn's arrest, and no doubt he's got guys keeping an eye on Sammy. Her best friend is the one who called us. Sammy is on board and ready to leave but she has no access to a phone or anything. We've got to figure out who's watching her without being seen ourselves and form a plan to get her out of there without alerting the bodyguards."

"Understood, Prez," Moose says, nodding at Blaze. Blaze just nods in response, looking down at the sheet of paper on the table in front of him.

"The other one is on Saturday. Her name is Nadia, and she's got a three-month-old baby girl with her. Husband is a shrimper so he'll be gone all day, and it should be fairly easy."

"You know better than to say that, Blaze," Streak says, and Blaze sighs as he nods. His face falls even more as he looks down at the paper in front of him and runs his hand through his hair.

"This morning, I got a call from the nurse that helped Dina out when she came into the ER."

"She got a new girl that needs help?" Red asks from the back, crossing his arms over his chest as he leans back in his chair. Blaze shakes his head.

"Dina was brought back into the ER last night with a serious brain injury, five broken ribs, and a lot of internal bleeding. They were able to stop the bleeding but when they examined her, it became clear that there was no brain function, and her mother made the decision to turn off life support."

A hush falls over the room, and I feel like I can't breathe as the past tries to assault me. It feels all too familiar.

"It's unclear right now what happened. She may have gone back to him or he may have found her. All we know is that no one can find her boyfriend but Rodriguez is looking for him."

"She wouldn't have gone back," Chance says, shaking his head in disbelief.

"You don't know that, Chance. We've been doing this long enough to know better." Blaze says.

Chance slams his fist on the table, and everyone turns to him. An outburst is completely out of character for him but I know how seriously he takes helping these women. "No. She wouldn't have gone back. He was right there when we were picking her up. He begged her to come back, and if she didn't fold then, she wouldn't have gone back to him."

"Look, Chance," Fuzz says, slapping a hand on his shoulder, "we all want to believe that she wouldn't put herself in that position again but we just don't know."

"Anything else?" Blaze asks, scanning the table, and I nod.

"Yeah, I got a call just before we came in here, and the Ian situation is taken care of. He's got himself an all inclusive five-day, four-night stay in the sick bay."

Blaze turns his gaze on me, and it's obvious how much Dina's death is eating away at him. "You sure?"

"He got the message loud and clear."

He nods, looking down again as he sighs. "Heard. But keep an eye out. The bastard was deranged six years ago so I can only imagine how messed up he is now. If we need to go further with this, we need to do it smart."

"Understood."

He studies me for a moment before nodding and turning back to the table. "Smith and Fuzz, I want you to take care of the security at Nix's place. They're waitin' for you."

"On it, boss," Fuzz says, shooting Blaze a mock salute while Smith nods in agreement. This is what these two live for. Emma and Nix's place will be harder to get into than the White House. Blaze nods and bangs the gavel on the table, storming out of the room before anyone else can even stand.

I'm sure he's taking the Dina situation pretty hard but it's best to let him work it out himself. We all knew when we got started doing this that we wouldn't be able to save everyone, and if she went back to him then we did all we could for her. The memories that it brings up, though, propel me forward. I can't get out of that door fast enough because the only thing that's going to make me feel any better is waiting for me at home.

* * * *

Dusk is falling over the neighborhood, the streetlights just starting to come on as I pull my bike into the driveway and shut it off. The entire drive home, I was swallowed up by memories that haven't plagued me since the day I met Ali, and I'm eager to get back to her. Climbing off the bike, I start toward the front steps, knowing that I can't leave Bear unattended all night or I'll come home to more holes in the drywall. I'm pretty sure the dog's got some kind of separation anxiety, and he loses his shit when I leave him alone.

Opening the door, I call out his name, and a fraction of a second later I hear him barreling down the hallway. He skids into the kitchen and stops, staring at me with his tail wagging back and forth. I take a quick scan of the room, making sure everything is the way I left it, and he doesn't move which only makes me suspicious.

"What have you been up to?" I ask him, and he just fucking grins at me. I never knew dogs could smile until Emma decided I needed this mutt.

"Well, come on, then. You want to go see Ali?"

At the mention of her name, his ears perk up, and he starts running at me full speed like a maniac. I step out of the way just in time, and he hits the wall before righting himself and looking up at me, tongue hanging out the side of his mouth, and his tail wagging like crazy.

"Let's go. You know the way," I tell him, and he walks out the door and down the steps before sitting and waiting for me to follow him. I lock up and as soon as my foot hits the sidewalk, he trots off, leading the way to Ali's house. I swear, he loves her more than me and I'm the one that fucking feeds him.

Not that I can blame him.

I honestly don't know how I resisted her this long. The very moment we met, I felt it. Like a bolt of lightning, she sparked something in me, and I was resurrected. There's still so much shit from my past that she doesn't know, and I'm going to have to tell her someday, but I want to put it off as long as I can. The things I did, while justified to me, may seem wrong to her, and it would fucking kill me if the way she looked at me changed.

I'm addicted to it. The way her blue eyes sparkle in amusement when she tells a joke or the heated look she shoots my way after I kiss her. I need it all. For as long as she'll let me have it. No, that's not even true. I won't ever be able to let her go, and I knew it from the start. Ali is mine until the very moment I take my last breath.

Bear slows in front of me, lowering his chest to the ground as he lets out a low growl, and I stop, scanning the street. He takes a step forward, his gaze locked on an older dark-colored sedan across the street, and I reach for the gun tucked into the back of my pants as I study the car. The window rolls down, and a face I never thought I'd see again grins at me as he pulls away from the curb and races down the road.

I look up at Ali's house, my heart pounding and fury seizing my body. This isn't over, and I don't think I can leave her – even if it would save her life. There has to be another way. I'll find another way to end this and keep her safe that doesn't involve me losing her.

"Bear," I snap as I start jogging up the sidewalk to her house, needing to see her as panic rips me apart. I just need to see her, make sure she's okay before my heart rate will go back down to normal. I pound on the door but she doesn't answer, and I pound again. The door flies open, and she gapes at me.

"Jesus, where's the fire?"

Reaching out, I grab her arm and pull her out onto the porch, into my arms, as I lean down and possess her lips. Everything rights itself as soon as I hold her, and her kiss breathes life into me again. She melts against me, gripping my cut in her fists as she clings to me like her life depends on it. I fucking love it. Eat it up as she kisses me back like the hour I was away was just too goddamn much to bear. When I finally pull away, she looks up at me with a dreamy little smile.

"Oh, there's the fire."

I laugh and hold her tight against my body, breathing in her intoxicating fruity scent as I try to force myself to breathe regularly. She pushes against my chest so she can lean back enough to look up at me with a scowl on her gorgeous face.

"What's wrong?" she asks, and I know there's no way to lie my way out of this. She always sees straight through me no matter how hard I try to hide.

"Let's go inside." I glance over my shoulder, feeling like we've got eyes on us, and I won't relax fully until I've got her locked away safe and sound. She nods and leans up on her toes to kiss my cheek before spinning around and marching into the house. I follow her down the hallway into the kitchen, and she goes straight to the refrigerator as I sit down on one of the barstools lining the island. She sets a beer down in front of me and cocks a brow.

"What's up with you tonight?"

I fiddle with the label on the beer bottle for a minute before standing and walking around the island, pulling her into my arms. "When I was coming over here, there was someone sitting outside of your house watching you."

Her face pales as she stares up at me. "Oh," she whispers, her voice so quiet that I almost don't hear her, and it breaks my fucking heart. I can't believe I brought her into this mess, and I hate myself for it. I should have ended this six years ago. She looks away from me as she starts chewing on her bottom lip, and I try to read her.

"Tell me what you're thinking, Kitten," I say, gripping her chin between my fingers and guiding her gaze back to mine. The fear in her eyes grips me like a fist squeezing my heart, and a huge fucking part of me just wants to lock her away until this is over. He can't fucking have her – not again – and I'll do whatever I have to in order to keep her safe.

"There's been some weird things going on at work, and I just dismissed it all, but if someone was watching me…" Her voice trails off, and my ears ring as I process through what she just said.

"What things? And how long?"

"Since the column went viral. And it's just this guy, Chris. He called in to the radio interview I did, and he's written a couple of letters."

Jesus, of course. I'd totally forgotten about the article going viral, and it would have made it so much easier for Ian's brother to find her. "What did you do with the letters? I want to see them."

"I threw them away."

I blow out a breath and nod. "What did they say?"

She pulls away from me and goes to the sink, grabbing a glass from the counter next to it and filling it up. Glancing over at me, she chugs the whole thing before leaning back against the counter and closing her eyes. I go to her, stopping just in front of her and pressing my body against hers. She lays her forehead on my chest and takes another deep breath.

"What did the letters say, Baby?"

"The first one just said that he loved all my work and he thought I was really talented and that he couldn't wait to read the column," she says, not lifting her forehead off my chest. I want her to be comfortable but I need to see her eyes. I slide my hand into her hair and give it a little tug, urging her to look up at me. She does and it almost guts me. She's so fucking scared right now, and I don't have any way to make it better.

"How many more have there been?"

"Just one more."

I nod, running my fingers across her scalp in an effort to calm her. "And what did it say?"

"He was talking like we were in a relationship, and he was sad that I had been working so much and not seeing him. He sent a teddy bear and a rose with that one."

All of this feels so familiar, and I know that Ian is behind it but I won't be making the same mistakes again. I'll end this before he ever lays a finger on Ali.

"Are you sure he was watching me?" she asks, chewing on her bottom lip again, and I reach up, pulling it free from her teeth.

"Yeah, Baby, I'm pretty sure." The less she knows right now, the better. I don't want to scare her, and I can't protect her if she runs from me.

She shakes her head and pushes me away as she straightens her body and walks over to the end of the island and paces back. "No, this has to be a mistake."

"Ali..."

"No," she says, cutting me off. "This is a mistake. He was just checking his phone or something, and you misinterpreted it."

"What about the letters?" I ask, wondering if I really want to poke holes in her theory right now.

"The letters are just from a fan who's gotten a little carried away in his crush for me. My article went viral so a couple of weird letters are to be expected."

As she passes me in her pacing, I reach out and grab her, pulling her into my body again. Her head drops back as she looks up at me, and I press a quick kiss to her lips.

"Maybe you're right, Kitten. But if you're wrong, I'll never let anything happen to you so you don't need to worry either way."

She searches my eyes for a moment before she buries her face in my chest, and I hold her, mentally promising her and myself that I'll die before I let anyone hurt her. I may have fought this but she's my life now, and I won't lose her.

Hopelessly Devoted

Chapter Twenty-Three
Chris

Rage twists through my veins like heroine as I stare down at the photo in my hands. How? How could she do this to me? Even looking down at the snapshot of them together turns my stomach, and hatred simmers in my soul. I crumple the photo and turn away from it but it doesn't matter. In my mind, I can still see him on top of her, his lips pressed to her neck as her naked body stretches out beneath him. I've been sitting here in my car, watching her house for what feels like hours and yet, I still can't understand why she would betray me like this. I thought we had something real and special but the moment I go away, she's with him. I'll make him pay for this. He'll regret ever touching my girl but what the hell am I supposed to do about her?

Even now, I still love her.

Looking down, I unfold the photo and stare at it again, letting the anger take hold as I look at the way he thrusts into her like he has every goddamn right to. But it's the look of ecstasy on her face that drives the stake into my heart. The anger builds and builds until it feels like I'm going to explode, rising up from the pit of my stomach until I'm forced to scream out into the car, slamming my fist down on the steering wheel.

My perfect angel.

She's been destroyed by this insignificant piece of shit. Who the fuck does he think he is? I glance over in the passenger seat where the rest of the photos of them together are. I threw them in a fit of rage, and now they're scattered across the car, taunting me with the image of my beauty being fucked by the devil from every angle.

I can't wrap my brain around the fact that she would do this to me. We were building something together. Why would she go and destroy it like this? Then again, I suppose she thought she could get away with it. Pain like I've never known stabs at my chest again and again, and I can't believe I trusted her. Leaning back in the seat, I look up at the house again, my heart shattering in my chest.

There is so much that I imagined for us, for our future, but that's all gone now, and someone needs to pay. And I'll start with him.

Just as I'm turning away, I spot a different photo, and my eyes widen as I pick it up. It's my sweet Ali crying on her bathroom floor, and it hits me out of nowhere. Of course! She's not there voluntarily. I stare up at the house like it might tell me the answers. It makes sense, actually. He's in a motorcycle gang, a lowlife. He's keeping her there against her will.

Needing validation, I slip out of the car and creep across the street before sneaking into her backyard, careful not to alert anyone of my presence. The last thing I need is him going off on her if he realizes that I'm here. God, this must be why she hasn't responded to any of my letters and why it's been harder and harder to see her. She was probably trying to save me, and I responded by assuming she cheated on me. I'm filled with remorse as I carefully open the gate and creep along the house.

When I reach the window that leads into the family room, I crouch down next to it and take a deep breath before standing off to the side and creeping over until I can see her. She's there on the couch next to him, and he's got his arm wrapped around her, holding her close to his side. I see red and every cell in my body wants to charge through that back door and rip them apart, but I take another deep breath, reminding myself that I need to be smart here so she doesn't get hurt.

Looking over at her, my heart breaks. She glances up at him and smiles. God, she's putting on one hell of a show but I can see the fear lingering in her gaze when she looks at him. Slipping back to the side of the window, I let out a breath. I can't believe I ever doubted her. Of course she wouldn't cheat on me. Not my Ali. She's a good woman, through and through. This situation presents me with a whole new challenge though, and I have no idea how I'm going to get her out of there.

"I promise I'll save you, Sweetheart," I whisper into the night before slipping back out to my car and driving back to my apartment to formulate a plan.

Chapter Twenty-Four
Alison

"So, since I didn't hear from you all weekend, does that mean things are good with Logan?" Carly asks, standing at the doorway to my office, and I can't stop the smile from spreading across my face as I look up at her from my laptop.

"Yeah, things are good."

She grins at me. "Good. I'm happy for you. You hear from your enthusiastic fan again?"

At the mention of Chris, my face falls and I think back to Friday night and the car that Logan saw outside my house. Carly picks up on it instantly and steps into my office, planting herself in one of the chairs across from my desk.

"What is it? Did you hear from him?"

"I'm not exactly sure."

She studies me for a second. "What does that mean?"

"Well, Logan was coming over Friday night and he saw this car outside my house, and as soon as he noticed it, the driver sped off. He was really on edge about it but I don't know. I mean, it could have been nothing, right?"

"It's either nothing or really, really bad."

I wince and nod. "Yeah, I was kind of hoping you weren't going to say that."

"Miss James," Jeremy, the new intern, calls from the office door, a large box in his hands.

"Yeah, just set them on the couch, Jeremy. Thank you."

He smiles. "No problem, Miss James. There are three more so I'll be back."

He leaves and Carly laughs as she stands from the chair and moves around the desk to hug me. I stand, and she wraps her arms around me.

"Just be careful, okay?" she asks, and I nod as she pulls back.

"I promise I will."

She leaves, and I step out from behind the desk and walk over to the couch to sort through the first box of letters. I grab the first one off the top and open the flap just as my phone rings on the desk. Rushing back over, I grab it and answer as I plop down in my chair.

"Hello?"

"Hey, Kitten, you all right?" Logan's voice comes floating through the phone, and a giddy smile stretches across my face as I fall back into the chair.

"Yeah, just rushing to the phone. What are you up to?"

"Thinking of ways to convince you to call in sick and play hooky with me," he says, and I laugh as I sit up straight and scoot my chair into the desk.

"Any good ideas?"

"Oh, I've got a few but you're not going to like them. We both know how much you hate to wait."

I laugh and pull the sheet of paper out of the envelope. "Don't you have a job to go to or something?"

"Not until later this week and Bear is so lonely here without you."

"Just Bear?" I ask, flipping open the letter and setting it down as I wait for his answer.

"No, but he is the one being the most pathetic about it."

Laughing, I lift the letter and start reading. "Well, I'm very sorry but…" My voice trails off, and my hand starts to shake as I read the words in front of me, my heart pounding in my chest.

"Ali? You still there?"

"Yes. I'm here," I whisper, my voice shaking as tears well up in my eyes.

"What's wrong?" Logan's voice is panicked, and I can hear rustling through the phone.

"I got a letter," I tell him, my voice cracking as a tear falls down my cheek. Why the hell am I crying right now? I shouldn't be feeling like this. I mean, it's a stupid letter except I've never been more scared in my life.

"Read it to me," he demands, his voice tight.

"Okay," I whisper and start reading to him.

Dear Alison,

I'm so incredibly sorry, my love. God, I'm sorry for so much but most of all, I'm sorry for thinking that you would ever leave me willingly for that man. No, man isn't even the right word. Monster. I should have known that you wouldn't leave me for that monster. I should have known better. It was a momentary lapse in sanity, and I can assure you that it won't happen again. And I'm sorry that I ever allowed him to get close enough to you for this to happen. As soon as I saw your face the other night, I knew you didn't want to be there. I don't want you to be afraid, Sweetheart. I have a plan, and I'm going to get you away from him. We'll run far away, and I'll keep you safe for the rest of your life, I promise. Just hang on for a little longer.

Yours until the end of time,
Chris

"Come home now, Alison," Logan growls into the phone, and I stand, nodding my head.

"Okay."

The line is quiet for a moment, and I can almost hear the shit storm going on in his head right now. "Are you okay to drive, Kitten?" he asks, his voice softening, and I love him for it.

"I think so."

"Come straight home, do you hear me? I'll be waiting here."

I nod again even though he can't see me. My brain is so scrambled right now that I'm not really sure if I should drive. "I'm on my way."

"Okay, Baby. I… Just get here safe."

I promise him that I will, and we hang up before I grab my bag and walk like a zombie out into the common area where I bump into Carly.

"Hey, you okay, Hon?"

"Um…no," I say, handing the letter to her that I never put down. She reads through it quickly before looking back at me with wide eyes. "I, uh… I need to go home."

She nods. "Yeah, I'll go explain this to Mercedes. She may know what to do but you just get home, okay? Is Logan waiting for you?"

"Yeah, I was on the phone with him when I opened it."

"'Kay. Go before he freaks out." She ushers me out of the office, and I hurry to my car, parked in the parking garage at the end of the block. I feel like everywhere I go, eyes are watching me as I start the car and drive out of the garage. Even as I drive home, I feel like I'm never quite alone.

The way he spoke about me in the letter makes it sound like Logan is keeping me prisoner. No matter how much I try to process it all, I can't understand how I got here. Did I do something to encourage whoever this is into thinking there was something more between us? Or is he just completely crazy and making up an entire relationship with me? The more I try to answer the questions I already have, the more pop up, and by the time I pull up in front of my house, I'm officially losing my shit.

Logan is sitting on the porch with Bear, and I scramble out of my car as he stands, looking tortured. Bear rushes down to me and leads me back to the porch where Logan grabs me and pulls me into his arms. He buries his nose in my hair and takes a deep breath before kissing my cheek.

"You okay?"

I shake my head. "No."

"Let's get inside." He reaches down and grabs a black duffel bag from the floor before placing a hand on my lower back and guiding me into the house. We step into the foyer, and all I can see are the open curtains on every window in the house. I feel like his eyes are everywhere, watching me as I walk through the formal living room and sit down on the couch.

Logan sits next to me, and I wring my hands together, unable to take my gaze off the window in front of me. I jump up and rush over to it, pulling the curtains closed so no one can see into my house anymore before going to the other window and closing those curtains. I think of the windows in the kitchen and family room and rush down the hallway to close the curtains there, too.

Logan follows behind me and starts helping me close all the curtains. Peeking over at him, I want to cry. I'm acting crazy right now but he hasn't said a word. He just follows behind me and starts joining in on my crazy. Finally, all the windows are blocked off, and I feel like I can breathe again, sucking air into my lungs as I bury my face in my hands and fight back tears.

He closes the distance between us and wraps his arms around me, holding me against his body tight as I lose it, my tears staining his t-shirt. After a few moments, I start to calm down, and my breathing returns to normal as we stand in my kitchen, wrapped up in each other. I pull back and look up at him, wiping my nose with a tissue that he hands me.

"I'm sorry," I whisper, peeking up at him sheepishly, and he shakes his head.

"For what? You've got nothing to apologize for here, Baby."

"How did you get so perfect?" I ask through a watery smile, and he barks out a laugh.

"Oh, Kitten, I'm not perfect at all but it does good things for my ego to hear you say that."

Dropping my head back, I look up at him before leaning up on my toes and pressing a kiss against his lips. It's not passionate or hot like any other kiss we've shared but it's deep enough to convey all the things that I'm so not ready to admit out loud to him. When I pull away, he grins, and I spot the duffel bag on the table.

"What's the bag for?"

He looks over his shoulder. "I'm staying with you until this is over."

"Logan, I…" I start to say, shaking my head, but he cuts me off.

"No arguments, Ali. I'm staying here, and I'm going to keep you safe. End of fucking discussion."

I gape at him as he pulls away from me and grabs his bag. He starts heading for my bedroom, and I follow behind him. "You can't just say end of discussion and expect it to be done."

"I absolutely can with something like this. I'm staying here. End of discussion. I will put a bullet in every single part of his body if this fucker ever tries to come near you again. End of fucking discussion. No arguments because I will not lose you. End. Of. Fucking. Discussion."

　　　I try to think of something to say to him but I've got nothing. Besides, what he just said might be the hottest thing I've ever heard in my life. Can you be terrified and turned on all at the same time? As he starts moving my clothes around and finding space for his own, I have to admit that I like having him here. And not just because I'm scared to even move right now.

　　　"Fine, Logan. But you leave the toilet seat up and I'll be the one with the gun," I say and spin, walking out of the room as he throws his head back and laughs.

* * * *

　　　"You want some more food, Babe?" Logan asks, standing up from the couch, and I shake my head, holding my wine glass out to him.

　　　"I will take some more of that, though."

　　　He laughs and takes it from me. "Trying to get drunk tonight?"

　　　I shake my head as he takes his plate into the kitchen, and I flip around on the couch so I can watch him. In the four days since he started staying with me, I think I've gotten used to having him around. He fits in like he belongs here, and I'm trying my hardest to not fall completely and totally head over heels for him, but I'm afraid it's a losing battle.

"I'm gonna eat the rest of this. You sure you don't want more?" he asks, pointing down to the chicken I made tonight. I shake my head again.

"I'm stuffed."

Just as he's picking up his plate, a sound comes from behind me, and I whip around, half expecting the boogey man to be crouching in the corner. The silence rings in my ears as I look all over for the source of the noise, and my heart starts pounding when nothing is out of place. Bear jumps to his feet and looks at the back door, lowering his head to the floor and letting out a low growl. I turn back to Logan, and he's already got his gun in his hand as he creeps toward the back door.

Standing, I rush over to him, and he cradles my cheek in his hand. "Stay in here and do not open this door unless it's me, you hear?"

I nod and he pulls me in, kissing me quick before he yanks open the French door and steps out into the night. Slamming the door closed, I lock it and pull on it to make sure it's really locked before going to the island and curling up on one of the barstools. Bear sits at my feet, his gaze trained on the back door and his body tight. My heart pounds in my ears as I wait for something to happen, and the quiet is the worst thing I've ever heard in my life. Adrenaline rushes through my body, and I reach over, grabbing the butcher knife out of the knife block, not taking my eyes off the back door as I move.

Once I have my knife, I hold it in front of me, ready to defend myself if I have to, and the seconds stretch into minutes and the minutes into hours as I wait for Logan to come back. Oh, God, what if something happened to him? Am I locked in my house with a madman just outside? The doorknob turns, and I gasp and scramble off the barstool, backing up further into the house with the knife held out in front of me. Bear barks, snarling as he gets between me and the door.

"It's me, Kitten. Let me in," Logan says from outside the door, and relief rushes through me as I race over and unlock it. He eyes my knife as he steps inside and sets his gun on the counter. I spin the knife and give him the handle end, and he forces a smile to his face.

"What's wrong?"

He shakes his head and looks away from me. "Nothing."

"Logan," I whisper, placing my hand against his broad back, and he shudders, "please talk to me. Was someone out there?"

"No," he says, spinning back around. "This is all just bringing up memories, and I'm not fucking handling it well."

"Memories of what?"

He hesitates for just a second before sighing. "This is what I do all the time, protect women from shit like this, and now I can't even protect you."

"It looks like you're protecting me just fine."

"How do you figure?" he asks, motioning around the room. "You haven't opened the blinds since you got that letter, and anytime you hear a noise, you jump sky high. This should have never happened to you. I should have stopped it."

I lean into him. "And what could you have done to stop it? There are some things that are in your control and some things that aren't."

He looks away again, denying me his gaze but it doesn't matter. I already know what I'll find there. This whole thing is bringing up memories of losing his ex, and I feel guilty that I'm putting him through this.

"Don't you get it?" he whispers, whipping his head forward to lock eyes with me as he steps into my space and presses himself against me. "I can't stand to lose anyone else, Baby. Especially you. I can't fucking do it again."

My heart cracks clean down the center for him as he closes his eyes and presses his forehead to mine.

"I'm not going anywhere," I assure him but instead of pulling away at my reassurance, he holds me closer.

"I can't lose you," he whispers, his voice a broken shell of the one I'm used to, and I grip his t-shirt in my fists, hoping to give him even a fraction of comfort. I grab his other hand and press it into my hip before sliding it up my side.

"I'm here, Logan. I'm right here."

He pulls back, and when his eyes meet mine, I gasp at the raw need dancing there. His gaze drops to my lips, and his tongue darts out, wetting his bottom lip as he looks at me like he wants to devour me whole. Without a word, he slams his lips to mine and fists my hair in his hand, yanking me into his body. His other hand slips around my back and holds me against him.

This kiss is different than any we've shared before. It's bruising in his frantic need for me, and instinctively I know that he just needs this right now. He needs to take me right now and feel like he's in control of something so I surrender to him, ready for wherever he takes us. He shuffles us a little and presses my back into the counter, the cold granite making me shiver even through the fabric of my tank top.

Reaching down, he grabs one of my legs and guides it up around his hip as he grabs the other and pushes me back onto the counter. His fingers brush against my belly as his hand slips up under my shirt, and he pulls it over my head. After pulling away long enough to toss my shirt onto the floor, he's grabbing me again and pulling me into his kiss. My nipples pucker in the cold air, and I moan when his warm hand closes over my breast.

"Logan," I moan again as his hand starts massaging me, and he kisses down my neck. By now, I'm used to his dirty talk and the way he loves to tease but I get none of that tonight as he pushes me back on the counter. The cold stone presses against my bare back, and I gasp as he pulls my lounge shorts down my legs and rips my panties away.

Before I even have a chance to move or say anything, he's pulling my legs apart and latching onto my pussy. My hips buck off the counter, and I cry out, my voice echoing a little in this big room. His fingers dig into the tops of my thighs as he holds me in place and laps at me again and again like he may never get enough of me. My entire body is buzzing, sensations stabbing me from everywhere, and I can't focus on one long enough to enjoy it.

He growls against my flesh, and it vibrates through me before shooting straight between my thighs, and a breathy moan slips past my lips. Without warning, he pulls away from me and grabs my hand, yanking me back up into a sitting position. Tingles shoot down my spine as he grabs my hair again and claims my mouth, his tongue plunging past my lips. I can taste myself, and I moan which only makes him crazier.

He yanks his lips away and wraps an arm around my back, holding me up as he stalks into the bedroom, looking at me with the eyes of a predator. Stopping next to my bed, he sets me back on my feet and leans down, kissing me sweetly as he unbuckles his belt. When he pulls away, he shoves his jeans down his legs, and his erection springs free. He grips the base and grins at me.

"Get on your knees and suck my cock, Kitten," he rasps, and I can't drop to my knees fast enough. Peeking up at him, I circle my tongue around the head and watch his face as he sucks in a breath. I like that he doesn't close his eyes as I sink down on his length, using my tongue to massage the underside of his cock as I suck.

He groans, and his eyes flutter like they want to close but he doesn't look away. His gray depths are locked firmly on me as fire dances in his gaze. He threads his fingers through my hair and holds me steady as he pulls out of my mouth before driving back in. He groans loudly, and I plant my hands on his thighs as he does it again. In and out. In and out. Fucking my mouth again and again until his grip in my hair is so tight that I think he'll pull a chunk out. My pussy is throbbing, and I can't deny that I love being used like this. Then he releases me and reaches down to lift me off the floor.

"You're incredible, Gorgeous," he whispers, giving me another sweet kiss that melts me faster than any other. "Now get on all fours on the bed."

My heart jumps, and a grin stretches across my face as I climb onto the bed on my hands and knees with my head facing away from him. He runs a hand from the base of my neck to my ass and groans.

"Put your shoulders flat on the bed," he commands, and I do it, dropping my head and shoulders down to the bed. His hand skims over my ass cheek, and he groans again as he smacks it.

"Yeah, just like that, Kitten. You ready?"

I moan in response, and the head of his cock presses against my entrance. Holding my breath, I push back into him a little, and he surges forward, filling me up and stretching me out perfectly. I moan, fisting the comforter by my head as he pulls out and slams in again. He leans over me and slides his hand into my hair, pushing my head into the bed. It's animalistic, the way he's fucking me, and I eat it up, moaning every time he enters me and trying to back up when he retreats.

"Ali," he groans, kissing my back as he continues his strenuous pace, working us both to an orgasm that will knock us on our asses.

"Yes. Fuck me," I hiss, taunting him a little, and he growls as he pulls back and drives home harder than before. It steals my breath. I pull on the blanket in my hands, my mouth wide open but no sounds coming out.

"Stop being a brat, and come right now or I'll spank your ass raw," he whispers in my ear. It's my undoing. My back arches, and I cry out into the room as my pussy clamps down on his cock. He groans and stiffens behind me before releasing my hair and collapsing on top of me with a sigh.

I giggle. His head pops up, and he looks down at me, all the worry from earlier completely forgotten.

"Thanks, Baby. I needed that."

"Anytime," I reply, winking at him, and he laughs again as he rolls to my side and pulls me into his body.

Chapter Twenty-Five
Alison

I glance up from my laptop, watching as a couple of the guys sit at the bar drinking beer while two others play pool off in the corner. Logan had a job tonight, and he refused to leave me alone, so after a little bit of arguing I agreed to wait for him at the clubhouse. It's different than I imagined it but it fits. As soon as you walk in the door, there's a bar to your right and couches off to the left. Behind the bar is a door that leads to a pretty large kitchen that looks like it could feed fifty easily. The back corner has two pool tables set up, and on the other side is a staircase that leads upstairs to the rooms. I haven't been up there to check them out at all but Logan gave me a quick tour when he dropped me off.

"You mind if I sit?" one of the guys asks, looking at the empty spot next to me, and I grab my notebook, shaking my head.

"Not at all. Go ahead."

He smiles as he sits next to me, and I rack my brain, trying to remember his name. "I'm Chance, by the way."

"Ali. It's nice to meet you," I say, holding out my hand. Logan talks a lot about the club and the guys here so I recognize his name instantly. Chance has been his best friend since they were kids.

He takes my hand, his kind smile permanently in place. "Yeah, you, too. But I think I should be thanking you."

"Why's that?"

He looks out at the two men still at the bar and sighs before turning back to look at me. "He's different with you, ya know?"

"That's what everyone keeps telling me." I can't help but think back to Blaze telling me the same thing on my porch after the break-in.

"He's happy again, and he hasn't been happy in a damn long time."

"Since his girlfriend died?" I ask, and his eyes widen.

"He told you about Fi?"

I scowl in confusion. "Fi?"

"Yeah, that was her name – Sophia, actually. He told you about her?"

I nod. "Yes."

"Wow. I guess I didn't know if he would ever tell you. He keeps all that pretty private. I mean, none of us were even allowed to mention her name for the first couple years." I fidget in my seat, feeling uncomfortable talking about this behind Logan's back. If he wants me to know more, then he'll tell me.

"Hey, don't you usually go on these things with him?" I ask, hoping to change the subject, and it works.

"Yeah, but they needed a different skill set on this one."

"What does that mean?"

He shakes his head. "Sorry, Sweets. Club business."

Just as I'm about to ask him what that means, the door swings open, and Logan walks in, grinning when his gaze lands on me. He walks over to me and braces his arm on the couch as he leans down.

"Hey, Kitten. Ready to go home?" he whispers, and I nod, fighting back my own smile.

"Definitely."

He helps me get my laptop and notebooks back into my bag before he tells everyone we're leaving. They all yell crude comments at him as he leads me outside, and I giggle as a few of them make him turn and glare.

"Bunch of animals," he growls, fighting back a smile, and I laugh again.

"Oh, they weren't that bad."

He drops his gaze down to me as we reach his truck, and he pushes me up against the door. "Careful, Baby. You're going to make me jealous."

Playfully, I bite down on my lip and glance back over to the clubhouse. "You know, one of them was pretty cute. He was playing pool in the back corner… what was his name?"

Possessiveness flashes in his eyes, and I yelp as he yanks the truck door open and ushers me inside without a word. As he climbs in behind the wheel and fires up the truck, I peek over at him and when our eyes meet, he flashes me a wicked smile.

"Don't say I didn't warn you."

My heart skips a beat as he races out of the parking lot and starts toward home, glancing over at me every once in a while with hunger filling his eyes. Feeling bold, I scoot along the bench seat to get closer to him and reach over, trailing my fingers up the inside of his thigh. He tenses underneath me and shifts his gaze to glare at me.

"Alison," he warns, and I hold back a giggle as I pull my hand away and scoot closer. He reaches out with one hand and pulls me into his side, leaning down and kissing the side of my head.

"I'm going to chap your ass for this," he whispers, and I wiggle against him, my core clenching at the thought. When we pull up in front of the house, he shuts the truck off and opens his door, pulling me out with him, and I laugh as he scoops me up in his arms. My legs wrap around his hips, and I lean down, kissing him as he holds me in the middle of the sidewalk.

Pulling back, I smile down at him, and he drops me to my feet before spinning me to the house. "Go," he commands, smacking my ass, and I yelp as I start walking up the sidewalk.

Glancing at him over my shoulder, I wink, and he fights back a grin, shaking his head. I spin back to the front and start up the steps, slowing as something catches the light and sparkles from the welcome mat in front of the door. Stopping on the front step, I suck in a breath.

What is that doing here?

Logan crashes into me and grabs my arms to keep me from falling. "Jesus, Ali. What are you doing?"

My eyes stay rooted to the mat in front of the door where the necklace that I've been looking for these past two weeks sits. Logan comes to my side and follows my gaze before looking back to me.

"What is it, Kitten?"

I open my mouth only to close it again as I look up at him. He runs his thumb down my cheek, and I suck in a breath. "It's my necklace. I haven't been able to find it since the break-in."

He turns back to the necklace laid out perfectly in front of the door, clenching his jaw as he pulls me closer. "Inside."

He grabs my keys out of my bag and opens the door before ushering me inside and leaving me in the foyer as he stomps down the hallway to the kitchen. When he comes back, he's got a Ziploc bag in his hand. He turns it inside out and uses it to pick up the necklace. Once it's safely inside, he zips it up and slams the door before turning to me. The bag is set down on the entry table as he reaches for me and pulls me into him.

He buries his nose in my hair and breathes me in. "You okay?"

"No," I answer, shaking my head. I don't even want to think about it right now. I just want to go back to five minutes ago when we were smiling and teasing each other. The fact that he was in my house and he took my things is something that I don't want to deal with at the moment.

"Go pack a bag. We're going to go stay at the clubhouse." He turns away from me like he expects me to just do as he says but I cross my arms over my chest and wait for him to turn around again.

"No," I say when he does, and his eyebrows shoot up.

"Excuse me?"

"You heard me." I unfold my arms and walk off, down the hallway and I can hear him stomping behind me.

"Ali, this isn't a goddamn joke. I need to keep you safe."

Stopping in the kitchen, I spin around, and he almost runs into me. "Then call the cops but I'm not leaving my home."

He growls and pulls me into his arms, pulling me tight against his body. "Why aren't you taking this seriously?"

"I am, that's why I want you to call Detective Rodriguez."

He lets me go and walks over to the island, bracing his hands on it as he drops his head and takes a deep breath. "The man has told you that he's going to kidnap you and still you fight me on this. You'll be safe at the clubhouse, Baby. I need you to be safe."

"I'll be safe here. You're with me."

"No," he barks.

"Yes," I fire back. He's not making me leave my home.

"I swear to God, Woman. I will throw you over my shoulder and carry you out of here if I have to," he says, his eyes snapping open, and just from the determination in his gaze, I know he's telling the truth.

Arching a brow, I meet his intense stare, not backing down. "And what? You'll just kidnap me like he intends to?"

"That's not fair," he growls.

"I'm not letting him take my home from me, Logan. I won't do it."

Dropping his head, he closes his eyes again and takes a deep breath. He tilts his head and opens one eye as he holds his hand out for me. I go to him without hesitation, and he wraps his arms around my waist. "I hate this."

"I know," I whisper, running my hand down his cheek, and he leans into me. "But I don't want to go hide out at the clubhouse. This is my home, and he's already taken so much from me."

He leans down and claims my lips, pulling me into him tighter before pressing his forehead to mine and sighing. "I'm going to have a heart attack by the time I reach forty, and it's going to be your fault."

"Nothing is going to happen to me," I assure him, my heart beating a little faster with the knowledge that he's thinking long term. I'm ready to fight like hell for this, and I just hope that he is, too.

* * * *

I wave at Mercedes with my free hand as I pass her office, and she glances up from the papers in front of her, grinning as she waves back at me. Writers pop in and out of offices, the gentle buzz of conversation filling the conference area, and I let out a breath, relieved to be back here as I slip into my office. Setting my bag down on the couch next to one of today's boxes of letters, I wonder why we don't just use email as I slip behind my desk and sink into my chair. The coffee warms my throat as I take a sip and lean back in my chair, sighing again. Work and normalcy – it's exactly what I need after this weekend.

Logan spent the rest of Friday night trying to convince me to go to the clubhouse with him, and when that didn't work, he tried to use his mouth to persuade me. I'm holding firm though. I refuse to let Chris, whoever he is, push me out of my home and control my life. I don't care how scared I am, that is not happening. By Saturday afternoon, Logan had given up on the clubhouse altogether but he refused to let me out of his sight for even a moment the rest of the weekend – even following me into the shower. He tried to play it off as sexy and fun, but I know better. This whole situation is really hard for him, and I need to try to be more understanding.

I can't even imagine what he's going through, and I wish he would open up more about his girlfriend. Maybe if I knew *how* she died, I would understand why he's freaking out so badly right now. Then again, maybe it's just the fact that he lost her that's making him act like this now. Maybe even the possibility of something happening to me brings up everything he went through when she died. I wish he could just relax a little though.

We haven't heard from Chris since the necklace showed up on Friday night, and there haven't been any more presents left on the porch. I want to know what it means. Why would he steal the necklace only to leave it there for me to find? A part of me hopes that he's just washing his hands of this and that he'll leave me alone but all I have to do is think about the last letter he sent to know that isn't true. It's too hard to wrap my brain around though. The entire situation sounds like the plot of a movie, and it doesn't feel real. The thing that scares me the most is that I don't know what the best course of action is. If I knew the best way to go, the best way to handle this whole situation, we could make a plan, and it would put my mind at ease, but right now, we're kind of stumbling along in the dark.

My phone rings on the desk, and I roll my eyes at Logan's picture as I pick it up and answer it. "Yes, Logan. I made it safe, and I'm perfectly fine."

He made me promise to call him the moment I walked in the door so he knew I was safe, and I feel a little bad that I forgot. Although, in my defense, he really does need to relax or that heart attack he joked about will be real.

"Come home," he says, his voice cracking, and I shoot up in my chair, setting the coffee down on the table.

"What's wrong?"

He sighs, and I hear something crash on the other end. My heart rate spikes, and I hold my breath as I wait for his reply. "I need you to come home. He fucking trashed my house."

"Oh, Logan, I'm so sorry," I whisper, dropping my head down into my hands. This is all my fault. If he weren't with me, this never would have happened to him. "How bad is it?"

"I don't give a shit about the house, Kitten. I care about you, so please come home."

Sighing, I look up as Mercedes walks in and points to the chair across from me. I nod, and she sits down, pulling out her phone as she waits for me to finish the call. "Logan, I can't just keep leaving my job because you're freaking out about this."

"What has to happen for you to understand how much danger you're in?" he shouts through the phone, and I can imagine him running his hand through his hair in frustration.

"What's going on?" Mercedes whispers, and I pull the phone away from my ear and quickly explain everything that I know. When I finish, her eyes are wide. She stares at me for a moment before looking back down at her phone as she starts typing away.

"Ali?" Logan barks into the phone, and I jump in my seat.

"What?"

"Come home." It's clear that he's not asking me this time, and I sigh.

"Let me talk to Mercedes, and I'll text you."

He grumbles something on the other end of the line and sighs. "Fine. But if you haven't texted me in five minutes, I'm coming to get you."

"Grumpy ass man," I mumble as I hang up the phone and look up at Mercedes. She's chewing on her bottom lip as she reads something on her phone, not paying any attention to me.

"What are you doing over there?" I ask her, and her head pops up.

"I texted the lawyers and asked them what we could do but it's not looking good. Do you know his name?"

I shake my head. "Just Chris but there is no guarantee that it's his real name."

"Shit. Without his name, we can't even get a restraining order. I'll look into beefing up security here but you should go be with Logan today. Just take your laptop with you, and I'll have the letters delivered."

My world is spinning, and I feel like I can't even grab onto anything to keep me from falling into the abyss of this insanity. "Mercedes, I can't just go running back home every time something happens. I need to work. You didn't hire me to never be here."

"Uh, one," she snaps, her voice taking on a bit of an attitude, "you can work from anywhere, and two, you won't be doing anything if this psycho kidnaps you or worse."

I scoff. "Yeah, right."

"You think I'm kidding?" she asks, leveling a glare at me. "Maybe when you're done writing your column, you should do some research on stalkers. I've been reading up since this whole thing started. This is serious, Ali, and I'm sure your man would appreciate it if you started being more careful. Now, go home."

Without another word, she stands and marches out of my office as I gape at her. Her words sunk in though, and I turn to my computer to do some research on stalkers when I remember that I promised to text Logan. My fingers shaking, I grab the phone and fire off a text to him.

Me:
Leaving now.

Logan:
I'll be here.

Logan:
Please be careful, Kitten.

My heart breaks reading his message, and as I pack up my things, I promise to be more considerate of what he's going through right now. Just as I'm about to step out of my office, a large man fills the doorway, and I gasp, slapping my hand over my heart as I take a step back.

He holds his hands up in front of him. "Sorry, ma'am. I'm the new intern. Mercedes sent me to carry a box out to your car for you."

Sucking in a breath, I nod. "It's okay. You just startled me," I tell him, peeking around his wide body as Mercedes stops outside the door and grins at me.

"Lance, here, is going to help you carry the letters out to your car, Ali," she says, a triumphant look flashing across her face. Of course she had to go find the biggest man in the office. He's got to be well over six feet tall, and he's as wide as a linebacker with a shiny, bald head and white smile. His polo shirt is stretched so far around his massive arms that it looks like it's going to burst at any moment.

"It's that box there," I instruct, pointing to the box on the couch, and when he steps into the office to grab it, I glance over at Mercedes and roll my eyes. She practically skips back to her office as Lance follows me out of my office.

He's quiet as we step out of the building and walk down the sidewalk to the parking garage. Even with him next to me, I start to feel like someone is watching me, and I pick up my pace, ready to get away from here and back to Logan all of a sudden. My heartbeat pounds in my ears, and it takes every ounce of restraint I have not to run the rest of the way to my car.

By the time we reach my car, my nerves are shot. I'm shaking, and my breath is choppy as Lance puts the box on the floor of the passenger seat and comes back around to stand in front of me.

"Thank you," I say, my eyes darting all over the garage floor like danger might jump out at any second. He smiles and nods.

"No problem. Do you need anything else?"

I shake my head, and he tells me to have a good day before turning and walking back out of the garage. As soon as he's out of sight, I climb into the car and lock it twice before grabbing the wheel and trying to force air into my lungs. No matter what I do though, it

doesn't help, and I know there's only one thing that will make me feel better right now.
　　Logan.

Chapter Twenty-Six
Alison

Tentatively, I walk up the sidewalk to Logan's front porch, eyeing the open door before glancing around me. "Logan?"

As soon as I got home, I ran into the house to find him but he wasn't there. His bike is in the driveway, and his truck is parked along the street so he's got to be here. Glass crunches under my feet as I step inside the front door, and tears sting my eyes at the sight before me. Logan is on his knees in the middle of the living room, picking up broken picture frames and tossing them back into a box. There are large holes in the drywall above his couch like someone took a sledge hammer to the wall, and his leather couch has a huge rip right down the center like whoever broke in here tried to cut it in half. My gaze travels up, and I gasp at the message written on the wall in blood red paint.

SHE IS MINE.

"Ali," Logan growls, jumping to his feet and stomping over to me, not even noticing the photos that he's stepping on. He yanks me into his chest and hugs me hard, his large arms binding around me like a vise as he kisses my forehead and lets out a breath.

"Logan," I gasp, tears threatening to fall as I look at all the damage I've caused in his life. All of this – his house and the emotional toll this is taking on him – is all my fault and I can't help but wonder if he would be better off without me. "I'm so sorry."

"Look at me," he says, pulling back, and I peek up at him, the guilt mounting inside me and making me feel two feet tall. "I don't care about this house, Ali. It's just a house. The most important thing is that you're safe."

He doesn't wait for my reply before pulling me back into him. I shuffle and my foot hits something on the floor. Glancing down, I pull away from him and grab the photo off the floor, brushing the glass off it. When I look up at him again, his gaze is firmly on me.

"Is this her?" I ask, wondering if I should really broach this topic with him right now but he doesn't seem bothered as he nods.

"Yeah. That's Sophia."

I glance down at the photo again, a small smile forming as I see how happy he looked in this photo, and I wonder if there will ever be a time when we get to that place. He's been around more lately, and he hasn't run again, but I still don't know what he wants from me. I guess I just preferred to live in the moment instead of questioning his motives.

"You look happy."

He clears his throat. "We were."

Sucking in a breath, I pluck up my courage and meet his eyes. "What happened to her?"

"I already told you, she died."

I nod, offering him a comforting look. "I know but I was just wondering *how* she died…"

He studies me for a long moment, indecision filling his gaze. Oh, God, maybe I shouldn't have asked that. I have no idea what the protocol is here. Am I supposed to ask about her or just leave it alone? Finally, he drops his head and releases a breath. "She was murdered."

I gasp and stare up at him but he refuses to meet my gaze, and after a few moments, I give up, handing him the photo. "I'm so sorry, Logan. I shouldn't have asked."

He takes the photo and clears his throat again, looking over at the box in the corner. "It's okay. To be honest, it's probably well past time that I get rid of this stuff."

"Why do you say that?"

"It's holding me hostage. All of it – this house, the photos, the damn truck outside."

I reach for him, grabbing his hand and pulling him into me. This is one time that he needs my comfort, and I'm damn sure going to be there for him. "How do you mean?"

"It was all for her. I bought this house for her, and I fixed up that truck for her. I took the pictures off the wall but they've been sitting in that box in the corner for years, and it's all keeping me from moving on."

He turns to throw the picture in the box, and I grab his hand. "Stop. You loved her. You can acknowledge that you loved her and move on with your life. You don't need to hide her photos in a box because she'll always have a piece of your heart and that's okay."

He turns his gaze back on me, something new and different in his eyes as he pulls me into his body and claims my lips in a kiss that has me clinging to him. When he pulls away, he runs the tip of his nose up mine, and it's so sweet and tender that I lose another piece of my heart to him in this moment.

"Let's get out of here," he whispers, guiding me outside as he pulls the door closed behind him. I wait for him to lock up, and then he laces his fingers with mine as we walk back to my house. With each step we take, my guilt grows as I think about all he's been through in the last month because of me. How can I do this to him? If everything that Mercedes, Carly, and Logan have been telling me are true, this will get worse before it gets better. What kind of person does it make me to drag him along with me?

"Kitten," he says softly, getting my attention as he opens my front door, and I look up at him. His gaze flicks over my face for a moment, studying me before he reaches up and grazes my cheek with his thumb. "What's going on in your head?"

I shake my head and whisper, "Nothing."

As I step into the house and kick my heels off, I can feel his eyes on me, boring into me like he's trying to tear me apart piece by piece until he finds the answers he's looking for. Bending down, I grab my shoes and walk down the hallway, resisting the urge to peek over my shoulder at him, but no matter how far I get from him, I can still feel his gaze. The front door shuts, and the lock clinks into place before I hear his boots stomping against the hardwood floors as he comes after me.

I don't want to do this but I have to. "You should leave."

He stops, and the house grows deathly silent, the only thing I hear is my heavy breath as I wait for him to respond. "That's not going to fucking happen."

"I want you to leave," I respond, sucking in a breath because I've never told a bigger lie than that in my life. I want to see him but if I turn around, I'll be finished.

"That's too goddamn bad because you're stuck with me."

Why won't he just listen to me and leave? Latching on to my frustration, I spin around and level a glare at him. "I don't need your help, Storm, so you can leave. Go back to your life."

"Again with this Storm shit," he growls, closing the distance between us and slipping a hand into my hair. He gives it a tug, forcing me to drop my head back to look up at him. "Why don't you get fucking real, Ali? What's your real problem here?"

Staring up at him, the anger melts away, and I frantically grasp at it, needing it to keep this up. My lip trembles, and I look away from him as tears sting my eyes. He's still got a hold of my hair though, and he tugs it again, forcing my eyes back to him.

"Spit it out, Baby. What do you want?"

YOU.

My heart is screaming out his name from the depths of my soul, begging me to stop doing this, pull him in instead of pushing him away. But the mental image of him, dressed in all black as he watches a casket being lowered into the ground has been plaguing me since we left his house. I can't do that to him. I won't. Maybe I shouldn't think like that. Maybe I should try to be positive but it seems that whenever I look around lately, it's just darkness and chaos surrounding me. How can I pull him into this? How can I ask him to risk his beautiful heart one more time when I have no guarantees that I'll survive this?

"What do you want, Ali?" he asks again through gritted teeth as he pulls me closer, his lips hovering above mine. I don't have the strength to force the words out of my mouth anymore, though. I'm such a coward.

"I can't do this to you," I whisper, and he jerks back, searching my eyes.

"What can't you do?"

A tear slips down my cheek, and I shake my head. "All of this. All the bad shit that's happened to you lately has been because of me. I can't put you through something like this after all you've been through. You have to leave."

"No," he forces out, his eyes closing as he takes a deep breath. When he looks at me again, I'm almost knocked off my feet by the powerful emotion in his eyes.

"Just leave, Logan," I beg, pushing against his chest and stepping away from him. "Please just leave me."

He shakes his head, his gaze locked onto mine. "I can't do that."

"Yes, you can," I shout, my mind racing as I try to think of anything to make him leave. "Go. The door is right there. Just fucking leave."

Tears are pouring down my face by the time I'm done, and he takes a step toward me. I back up, shaking my head but he advances again. "Logan!" I scream. "Leave me."

"I can't," he says again, his voice so sure that deep down, I know there's no way I'll convince him to leave. What the hell is keeping him here? Is it some sense of loyalty that he feels he owes me since we've been seeing each other for a while? Or is it the work he does with the club that's keeping him rooted in my kitchen?

"Leave!" I yell again, and he shakes his head.

"No." He takes another step toward me, and I back up again, my back hitting the wall.

"Fucking leave me!" I scream at him, louder than ever before, and he blows out a breath as he shakes his head and presses his body up against mine.

"I can't," he snaps, his voice full of anger but his eyes telling me something completely different. "I fucking love you, Ali. From the moment I met you, my fate was sealed, and I'm not going anywhere, no matter what you say to me. And I will end this fucker, do you hear me? I will make him pay for the hell he's put you through, and you will never have to be scared again because you're mine, and I will rip apart anyone that gets in between us."

I gape up at him, my mind racing, and somehow still blank as the air punches out of my lungs again and again.

"We clear, Kitten? I love you, and I'm never walking out of that door. End of fucking discussion."

Slowly, I nod. His words ring in my head again and again as what he said sinks in, and finally, a little smile teases my lips. He reaches up and cradles my face in his hands as he runs his thumbs over my bottom lip.

"What?"

"I love you, too," I whisper, grinning, and he chuckles.

"I know. Every single emotion that you feel shows on your face. You can't hide from me."

Leaning up on my toes, I wrap my arms around his neck and press my lips to his as he lifts me in the air, and I wrap my legs around his waist. He pushes me back against the wall before pulling away from my kiss.

"We done with all this yellin' shit?"

I laugh and nod. "Yeah, I think we're done."

"Good, 'cause I've got plans to make you do a whole different kind of yelling," he says, grinning at me as he pulls me away from the wall and turns into my bedroom.

"That's presumptuous of you," I tease, and he shakes his head as he tosses me down on the bed. I giggle as I bounce a couple times before he slowly climbs over me, pulling my blouse up with his teeth and kissing my belly before continuing his journey to my mouth.

"Not presumptuous. We just had our first fight, and I'm pretty sure that means I get a whole night of make-up sex."

I arch a brow and fight off a grin as he kisses up my neck. "Who says?"

"Shit, I don't know. There's got to be a handbook or something, somewhere. You started a fight with me, and now you gotta make it up to me."

With a seductive smile on my face, I push on his shoulder and he rolls to my side and lays flat on his back. I straddle his thighs and trail my fingers down the front of his t-shirt. "I hope you're prepared, then."

"Don't tease me, woman."

I plaster an innocent look on my face, and he laughs. "Who's teasing?"

"Get to work," he says, smacking my ass, and a thrill runs through me as I climb off him and strip next to the bed. He moves to the middle of the bed and props a pillow behind his head as he watches me, his eyes growing hungry with each new strip of skin revealed to him. As I slip my skirt and panties down my legs, he licks his lips and holds a hand out for me.

Taking it, I climb back on the bed and position myself between his legs, peeking up at him as I unbuckle his belt. He sits up enough to pull the shirt over his head and tosses it to the floor. Once I have the belt undone, I press my lips to his stomach, just above his jeans, and brush my breasts against his jean-covered erection as I slowly start kissing up his body.

"Kitten," he groans, grabbing my arms and pulling me up his body. He steals a kiss, holding me captive as his tongue tangles with mine, and I moan. He releases one arm to smack my ass again as he pulls away. "Get back down there."

I slide down his body, unbuttoning and unzipping his pants before slowly pulling them down his thighs. He lifts his hips off the bed to help me, and his cock springs free, bobbing in front of my face as I shove his clothes the rest of the way down. He kicks them off and grabs the base of his shaft, pointing it toward my lips.

"Open your mouth, Baby," he rasps, the gravel in his voice more pronounced than just a moment ago, and it sends a shiver down my spine. I follow his instructions and close my mouth around the head as I tease him with my tongue, and he groans softly, dropping his head to the pillow. I brush his hand out of the way and grab his length, gently stroking him up and down as I work him further and further into my mouth.

"Spin around," he says, reaching down for my legs, and I release him long enough to position my pussy over his face before taking his cock in my hand again. He groans, louder this time as I take him into my mouth and he grips my ass tightly. After a moment, he starts kissing up the inside of my thigh and bites down. I yelp but he quickly soothes the sting with his tongue, and I sigh until he latches onto my pussy. He circles my clit with his tongue before dipping into me, and I moan around his length. Pulling away, I prop myself up on my hands as he slowly eats at me, slowly building me toward release.

His hand slips up my back, and he pushes down on my shoulder, directing me back to his cock, and I smile as I suck him between my lips. Focusing on what

I'm doing, I press my tongue to the base of his shaft before running it up toward the tip, and he groans against my pussy. His fingers dig into my skin as he grips my ass and sucks my clit into his mouth.

I buck on top of him before taking him all the way, the head of his cock pressing against the back of my throat. I'm able to hold it for a few seconds before gagging. He groans and pushes my hips off him, moving over me as I fall to the bed. Grabbing my ankle, he pulls me under him and lines his cock up with my entrance.

"Look at me, Ali," he says, his voice soft again, and I meet his eyes. He smiles, a brilliant smile that lights up his entire face and takes my breath away. "I love you."

"I love you, too," I whisper as he slides home, and I fall into this perfect little piece of heaven where only he and I exist.

* * * *

"Stop making that face," I say, glancing over at Logan next to me on the couch.

"You're making me watch *Pitch Perfect*, Baby. I'm gonna make a face."

I scoff and playfully shove his shoulder. "Whatever. I watched *Mad Max* without any complaining."

"Well, yeah, 'cause *Mad Max* is the best movie ever made."

Laughing, I roll my eyes and push him again. "You're delusional."

"So?" he laughs, and I can't help but smile at him. He's like a completely different person since he confessed his feelings for me a few nights ago. Or maybe we're both just finally comfortable in this relationship.

"So nothing, I guess."

"If I'm delusional and you love me, what does that make you?" he asks, his gray eyes sparkling with playfulness.

"Certifiably insane."

He growls and pulls me into his arms, swooping down and claiming my lips in a passionate kiss. I sigh and reach up, cradling his face in my hand as I kiss him back, unable to believe that I'm this happy. He pulls back and grins before gently biting my bottom lip.

"That's okay, Baby. We can be crazy together."

"Aww," I say, patting his face. "I love it when you get all mushy."

He scowls at me, trying to cover up his smile but failing. "Careful or I'll be forced to show you all the things about me that aren't mushy at all."

"Don't make promises you can't deliver on, Storm," I purr, straddling his lap and pressing my hands to his chest.

"You trying to get me riled up? I can't think of any other reason you'd call me Storm. Unless you want me to spank this gorgeous ass." He grabs my ass through the cotton shorts I'm wearing, and I gasp, grinding down on his lap. "You know the pizza's gonna be here any minute. Why are you teasing me now?"

"Oh, that reminds me – did you remember to get extra mushrooms on the pizza?" I ask.

He sighs and moves his hands up to my hips. "Kitten, give me a little credit here. I know how you like your pizza."

"Well, how am I supposed to know that?"

"Just assume that if it's about you, I already know the answer."

My brow arches, and I study him for a moment. "What did you do? Have someone dig up information on me?"

"Yes," he says, nodding. I can't believe that he doesn't even bother trying to deny it.

"I don't know if I should be worried or flattered."

Reaching up, he brushes his thumb over my cheek. "I told you, Baby, the moment I met you, you owned me, and I had to know everything about you."

"Well, when do I get the dossier on you?"

"I'll tell you anything you want to know about me, Ali."

I watch him, skeptical of his statement. I'm not sure that he would tell me anything I wanted to know. In the past, getting him to talk about things has been like pulling teeth.

"All right, we'll start off easy. How old are you?"

He laughs. "That was your big burning question? I'm thirty-one."

"Oh, man, you're so old," I tease, and his fingers dig into my sides. I squeal and wiggle in his lap, trying to get away as he tickles me.

"Anything else you'd like to know, nosey?" he asks as he stops tickling me, and I let out a breath.

I'd love to ask about other things but I'm still not sure that he'd tell me. I open my mouth to test it out and ask him something when the doorbell rings. Bear lifts his head and barks once before rolling onto his back and falling back to sleep.

Logan scoffs. "Some guard dog he is."

"I'll get the pizza," I say, hopping off his lap, and he stands, handing me his wallet. I start to argue with him but he gives me a look, and instead, I snap my mouth shut and go over to the door. I swing the door open and scowl. There's no one here.

Scanning the street, I step out of the door, and my foot hits something, drawing my eye down. I suck in a breath and back into the house, my gaze fixed on the two dolls lying on the welcome mat. Logan's wallet falls to the floor, and my hand covers my heart as it beats against my ribcage.

"Ali?" Logan's voice comes from behind me but it sounds far away somehow, like I'm underwater, and I don't move, frozen to the spot as the rest of the world fades in and out of focus. Each breath I take rings in my ears, drowning out everything else except the sound of my heart frantically pounding in my chest.

Breathe in.
Boom-Boom.
Boom-Boom.
Breathe out.

Again and again as I stare at the two dolls that look like exact replicas of Logan and I. My doll is delicate with golden blonde hair piled up on her head and striking blue eyes, her hands folded in front of her as she smiles in a white satin wedding dress. Logan's doll looks just like he does now – t-shirt, jeans, and boots – but there's a pocketknife sticking out of his chest and X's drawn over his captivating eyes.

I whimper, my body shaking violently as I struggle to draw air into my body.

"Kitten, look at me," Logan says, louder this time as he slips into my field of vision, and I blink up at him as I gasp for air. "Just breathe, Baby. It's okay. You're going to be okay."

Still gasping, tears fill my eyes and slip down my cheeks as I look at him, pleading with him to do something to make it stop. I don't even know what to do. My body is frozen but inside I'm being pulled in a hundred different directions. I can't move, and suddenly I know what it feels like to be a deer stuck in the road as a car blares its horn and barrels straight for you.

I whimper again, my knees wobbling, and Logan's face twists with agony as he pulls me into his body and crushes me to him. "Shh, Baby. I've got you. It's okay."

Reaching up with one hand, I grip his shirt in my fist, squeezing it tight as I sob into his body, and he whispers in my ear, running his hand over my hair again and again. The smoothing repetitive motion does begin to calm me but I still cling to him, my mind racing with all the bad scenarios that I read about after Mercedes told me to research stalkers.

"Come here, Kitten. Come sit down while I deal with this shit," Logan whispers in my ear, and I grip his shirt tighter and shake my head.

"I don't want those things in here."

He pushes me away so he can look in my eyes as he wraps his hand around the back of my neck. "I know, Baby. But we have to close this door, and I've got to make some calls."

I stare up at him for a few seconds before nodding my head. "Okay."

He kisses my forehead before releasing me and turning around to grab the dolls from the porch. I look away as he picks them up and shuts the door. When I glance back at him, he's holding them off to his side so I can't see them. He smiles and nods his head toward the hallway.

"Let's go in the kitchen."

I nod, and he walks in front of me, careful to keep the dolls out of my view as we walk into the kitchen. He stands by the sink in the island, and I climb on a barstool, watching him carefully.

"I'm going to put them on the counter, okay?"

I nod and take a deep breath as he pulls the dolls up from under the counter and lays them on the granite. My stomach rolls, and I can't take my eyes off the doll that looks like Logan as tears well in my eyes. In all his letters, Chris has never once shown violence or been angry at me but it hits me all of a sudden as I sit in my kitchen with tears streaming down my face that, quite possibly, it's not my life we need to be worrying about.

Logan watches me closely as he pulls out his phone and dials a number before holding it to his ear. I tune him out, trying to think about all this clearly, but my mind is still bogged down by fear, and I can do nothing but sit here and freak out. Logan ends the call and dials another number, and I think back to the research that Mercedes insisted I do. I wish I would have paid more attention when I was reading but I was still at a point where I was dismissing all of this as not that big of a deal. But not anymore.

"Hey, Mercedes, it's Logan," he says, and my gaze flies to him. He's staring right at me, love and determination in his eyes. "Not great, actually. I was actually calling to ask if Ali could work from home for the time being."

I start shaking my head at him but he turns away from me. "Yeah? That'd be awesome. Thank you so much. I'll tell her to call you."

"What the fuck do you think you're doing?" I snap as soon as he hangs up the phone, and he sighs as he turns to me.

"Keeping you safe."

I climb off the barstool and cross my arms over my chest as I glare at him. "You don't get to dictate my life."

"Right now, I absolutely do. I will keep you safe, Ali. No matter what it takes."

"I'm not the one with a knife sticking out of my chest," I yell, gesturing to the dolls lying on the counter, and he glances down at them. "Are you going to stay locked up in the house with me?"

"If that's what you want, yes."

I huff and shake my head, pointing down the hallway to the front door. "I want you to leave."

"No."

"I'm fucking serious this time, Logan. I don't want to see you right now. Leave."

He shakes his head and stalks over to me. I meet his glare as he leans in closer, hovering just above my lips. "Get over it, Princess. I love you, and I'm not going anywhere."

"Get the fuck out of my house, Logan," I growl, anger spiking inside me.

"Uh… bad time?" someone asks, and I turn my glare to Chance and Kodiak as they stand in the entrance to my kitchen, uncomfortable expressions on their faces.

"Nope," I snap and spin, marching into my bedroom and slamming the door, making sure it's locked before I crawl into bed and silently cry myself to sleep.

Chapter Twenty-Seven
Chris

"Fucking idiots," I mutter to myself as I watch the guard they put out in front of my angel's house turn the corner and head back to the front porch where his equally stupid partner waits for him. Hopping the fence, I try to push down my anger because I only have twenty minutes with my girl before they make their rounds again, and I don't want to waste it on any of these fuckers. It figures that Storm would call in his crew though. He's probably got my sweet Ali under lock and key – anything to keep her away from me.

The hatred twists in my gut as I creep through the trees that line the back of her property, my heart pounding with each step. It's been close to two days since I've been able to see her at all, and I feel like I'm losing my mind. My whole plan was almost shot to shit when I pulled up tonight and saw those criminals posted outside. I was so close to marching up to them and sinking a knife into each of their throats so I could go get my girl.

But I've got a plan.

Storm is going to know the hell he's putting me through right now, and he's going to know that I'm coming for her. Every day, he'll wake up and wonder if today's the day that he'll lose her. That's what my little gifts are all about. I feel terrible because I'm sure it's starting to scare my angel a little bit but Storm is going to suffer for what he did. Each time he looks out the window of her house, he's going to know that I'm coming for her, and his stomach is going to twist with the knowledge that he's going to lose her. Forever.

I honestly can't wait. The enjoyment I'll get from watching his life fall apart will be unparalleled – until I end his life. In the beginning, I toyed with the idea of leaving him alive, making him watch as Ali and I built a life together, but in the end, I couldn't risk losing her again. He's in a gang, and no doubt he's got connections that could make life difficult for me. So, I'll kill him but only after he reaches his lowest point and wallows there for a little while. It's a delicate balance. He needs to be in agony but not long enough to work up the strength to come after her. A smile stretches across my face as I sneak through her yard, imagining the depths of his despair.

Sweet, sweet revenge.

Reaching the back of the house, I creep along to her window, constantly scanning my surroundings just in case one of those fuckers decides to make his rounds early. That would be just my luck lately. When I get to her window, I peek in, and air rushes into my lungs as I suck in the first satisfying breath I've been able to take since the last time I saw her. She's alone in bed this time, and my smile widens as I wonder why Storm isn't with her. Well, this night is certainly looking up.

Thoughts of her captor are completely forgotten as my eyes roam down her body, over the curve of her hips, and down to her little toes poking out of the end of the blanket. Red nail polish covers her toenails, and I grin again, knowing she did that for me. She knows that red is my favorite color. I look over her again and again, committing her image to memory so that when I have to leave here, I can take her with me. It's the only thing keeping me going right now.

My heart pounds as I press my hands to the glass, wishing I could be in there with her but I'm not stupid enough to assume that Storm left her. He knows I'm coming, and he would never leave her unguarded. Closing my eyes, I imagine that she's back with me – under me – as my hands freely roam her perfect body. I miss the softness of her skin under my fingertips and the fruity, sweet scent that I get when I bury my nose in her hair.

With my eyes closed and my hand pressed to the glass, I let my mind wander. Leaning in close, I kiss her softly – letting her feel the depths of my love for her – before I take her hard, my passion controlling me. She lets out a little sigh as I slide into her, and she and I both know that we're home. She gazes up at me, love shining in her hooded eyes as I pull out and drive in, again and again – never able to get enough of my angel. I hiss when her fingernails dig into my shoulder; urging me to go harder, give her more because she needs this just as much as I do. Anything she asks, I'll do. She gasps, her body tensing underneath me as her pussy clamps down on me, and I can't hold back any longer, spilling into her.

Opening my eyes, I groan as my cock presses against the inside of my zipper. I lean in and press my forehead to the glass, my chest aching so badly that I consider calling an ambulance for a moment. Slamming my hand over my heart, I just watch her as she sleeps. I'll have to leave soon, and it's going to kill me to do it. I need her. Without her, my life is completely empty and each day is a burden. Waking up without her next to me gets harder each morning, and I honestly don't know how much longer I can do it.

My anger toward the fucker that stole her from me only increases, renewed by my desperation for her. The only thing that calms me is imagining the look on his face when I take her back. Well, that and sinking a knife into his body again and again until he is no more. Looking back to my angel, I press my lips to the glass.

"I love you, Ali," I whisper, hoping that she at least feels me here. "I'm coming for you soon, Sweetheart. I promise."

With one last look, I pull away from the window and creep along the back of the house as I check my watch. I should have another ten minutes with her before they do their rounds. Maybe I could just sneak in and spend a couple minutes with her. It would go a long way to calming me down right now. When I reach the French doors that lead to her kitchen, I peek in and mutter a curse. The object of my rage is asleep on one of the dining room chairs that he moved right next to her door. Keeping a close eye on her, no doubt. His stupid mutt is sleeping on the floor next to him, and I know that I'll never make it to her.

Fuck!

I want her back in my arms. The need is clawing at me, stripping pieces of me away with each day that he holds her hostage. The only thing that will calm this beast that I'm turning into is my angel. I have to speed up the process, get her out sooner, because if I wait too long, we both may be lost. Sighing, I glance over at her closed bedroom door and decide that this weekend will have to do. As much as I'd love to torture Storm some more, it's not worth giving up my Ali.

A.M. Myers

Chapter Twenty-Eight
Alison

    I sigh, tapping my finger on the table as I stare at the blank Word document on my screen, and my frustration builds.
    "Just write something," I whisper to myself, glancing down at the letter I decided to answer this time. With another heavy sigh, I grab it and read through it again.

Dear Ali,
My son has been acting out lately – getting into trouble with the police and giving his father and I attitude. It's nothing too serious with the police but he keeps pulling these little stunts to gain our attention, and we're at our wits' end. His latest exploit is that he told us he's gay. Now, I am a good Christian woman, and this is not who I raised my son to be. I'm worried with how far he'll take this to hurt us and that his soul will be damned to hell. We've talked about kicking him out of the house until he gets his act together, and

unless you can give us another idea, I'm afraid that it's what we'll have to do. Please help us.
 Sincerely,
 Devout and Disgusted

 I read through it a second time, shaking my head as I set it down on the table. This has got to be a joke, right? I've got several responses to this lady but I'm not sure that any of them are appropriate for an advice column. Grabbing my phone, I fire off a text to Mercedes.

Me:
Do I have any restrictions on this column?

Mercedes:
Nope. Write whatever your heart desires.

 Laughing, I reply to her, already formulating my response in my head.

Me:
You may regret this.

Mercedes:
Ooh, now I'm intrigued. Can't wait to read it.

 Setting my phone back down, I crack my knuckles and smile as I start typing.

Hopelessly Devoted

Dear Devout and Disgusted,
I'm quite disgusted, too, but it's not your son who is making my stomach roll right now. It's you. You say your son has been acting out recently, and yet, you never stopped to consider that his acting out was covering very real emotions, like fear. Fear that you wouldn't accept who he is, fear that you would do something so drastic like kick him out of the only home he's ever known. You claim to be a good Christian woman but you're filled with so much hate for your own son, your flesh and blood. You want some advice? Because I do have a suggestion to turn your life around. There's a children's hospital downtown, maybe you should take a little trip over there and walk the halls, looking at all the children there fighting for their lives. Look at the parents with tears in their eyes as they beg God to save their baby, because I promise you, they wouldn't care if their son or daughter were gay as long as they were alive. Then, go home, look at your beautiful, brave son who took a chance and revealed who he really is to you and apologize for the way you've been acting. Life is short and if you're not careful, you're going to miss out on being a part of your son's.
Sincerely,
Alison

I read it over, feeling satisfied but concerned that I may have gone too far. I snap a picture and send it to Mercedes, and she replies back almost immediately.

Mercedes:
Savage. I love it.

Grinning, I grab a few more letters and start reading through them, not feeling inspired to respond to any of them. Opening a new Word document, I try to come up with a single response to any of the letters I've read today but I've got nothing.

The front door opens as I set my phone down, and I peek over my shoulder, watching Chance as he walks down the hallway and opens my fridge like he owns the place. Chance is quite a bit shorter than Logan but he is just as built, and his genuine blue eyes and friendly smile fascinate me. You wouldn't know it by just looking at him but I get the distinct feeling that he's got a pile of pain that he keeps buried.

"You done staring at me?" he asks, shutting the fridge door and popping the top off the beer. He turns and watches me as he takes a sip.

"Sorry. I was just having trouble writing today so you were a welcome distraction."

He walks over to me and pulls out the chair next to me, the legs scraping against the tile floor, before he sits down and stretches his legs out in front of him. "Why can't you write?"

"Stress, probably," I say with a sardonic laugh. He nods, looking at me thoughtfully for a second before taking another sip of his beer.

"Maybe you should go make up with your man."

Rolling my eyes, I turn back to my computer and stare at the Word document like somehow the words will magically jump from my head onto the screen. It's been two days but I'm still so pissed at Logan. It's not fair, and I know that, but this whole situation is hard, and it's even harder when he just makes decisions and expects me to go along with them. It's my life and so much of it has been taken away from me. I should get some say.

"Don't be so hard on him, Ali," Chance says, and I turn back to him.

"Why not?"

He sighs, looking down at his beer bottle before meeting my eyes again. "If you know about his past, then you know how hard this is for him. He's going through hell, and he's handling it as best as he can."

I open my mouth to respond but the front door opens again, cutting me off. Peeking over my shoulder, I smile as Izzy and Carly walk down the hallway toward me.

"I'll let you all talk but just think about what I said," Chance says, standing from the chair and nodding at the girls as he pushes it in and passes them. Carly's gaze lingers on him as he stomps off down the hallway, and when she finally looks back to me, my brow arches.

"Hey, Car, see somethin' you like?" I ask, a smile stretching across my face, and she shakes her head.

"Shut up. We're here to talk about you. Not me."

I laugh and nod, kicking out one of the chairs next to me. "By all means then, have a seat."

"How are you doing, Hon?" Izzy asks, looking at me with a concerned expression as she sits down and crosses her arms on the table.

"Well, let's see. I'm locked in my house because some psycho is leaving dolls on my doorstep, and I'm not talking to my boyfriend since he thinks he can run my life but he won't leave me alone so we just walk around the house, not speaking to each other."

"Ali, he's just trying to protect you," Carly says, and I nod.

"I know that but I wish he would just cool it a little bit. If he had just talked to me about it, I probably would have agreed with him, but he didn't. He bulldozed over me and started barking orders."

"Sounds a little bit like you're taking shit out on him," Izzy says, giving me a look. "This is hard for both of you, and there is no handbook. Hell, even the cops can't do much right now. Maybe you should just cut him some slack."

I bite down on my lip as I mull over what she said. "Yeah, you're right," I whisper, and she nods, standing.

"Then, our work here is done."

"What? You're leaving?" I ask in a panic. I hate being cooped up in this house, and I don't want them to leave me yet.

"Sorry, Hon. We just swung by on our lunch break and traffic was awful. We'll stop by tonight if you want," Carly offers, and I nod.

"She'll be busy," Logan says from the end of the hall, and I jump, pressing my hand over my chest as my heart pounds. Jeez, where the hell did he come from? Carly and Izzy give me sympathetic looks as they hug me and duck out of the kitchen. Logan stomps down the hallway and sits in the chair next to me. When the door closes, he holds out his hand.

"Come here, Kitten."

After a moment of hesitation, I stand, deciding to let it all go as I grab his hand. He tugs it, pulling me into his lap, and moving me so I'm straddling his thighs. "We done with this fighting bullshit, Darlin'?"

I sigh and press my hands to his chest. "Maybe."

"Just maybe."

"Are you done acting like a Neanderthal and ordering me around and running my life?"

He wraps his arms around my waist and pulls me closer, dropping his head back to look up at me. "Ali, I'm just trying to protect you."

"I know that but you've got to talk to me, too. I'm an adult, and you're treating me like a child. Chances are I would have agreed with you if you had just had a conversation with me before you went and called my boss. I was terrified that night, and then you just steamrolled me."

He watches me for a moment before sighing. "I'm not going to apologize for the things I've done to keep you safe but I am sorry for not talking to you. This shit is so hard on me, Babe, and I get tunnel vision. I can't stop thinking that I'm going to lose you just like I lost her, and I can't do it. I can't lose you, too."

"I know," I whisper, pressing my hand to his face.

"I don't know what I would do if I lost you, Baby," he whispers, his voice raw, and it reaches into my chest and squeezes my heart.

"Well, it's a good thing you'll never have to find out then, huh?"

He forces a smile but I can tell that he's not buying what I'm selling. "Are we good?"

"Yeah, Logan," I say, leaning in and hovering over his lips. "We're good. Always."

* * * *

"Wake up, Kitten," he whispers in my ear, his breath fanning out across my skin as he cages me in with his arms and legs. Groaning, I turn my head into the pillow, trying to get away from him, and he laughs. "Uh-uh, Darlin'. It's time to get up."

"It's Saturday," I say, trying to roll over, but he stops me.

"Yeah, but we got somewhere to be."

I peek open my eye and look up at him, his dark hair messy from sleep and a sly grin on his face. "Where?"

"It's a surprise," he says, smacking my ass, and I jump. "Come on, get up."

Rolling over to my back, I shoot him a skeptical look but he just laughs. "What are you up to?"

"Guess you'll just have to get up and find out."

I lift my hips off the bed, pressing into his erection, and he fights to keep his eyes open.

"But there's so much more fun we could have here," I tease, batting my eyes at him as I reach down and wrap my fingers around his cock.

"Kitten," he rasps, his eyes glowing with a primal need that sends a shiver down my spine, "you're getting in that shower one way or another. How quickly you do it, however, determines if you get this cock or not."

He thrusts into my hand, and I moan before pushing him off me and jumping out of the bed as he laughs. Glancing back at him, I pause and turn to just look at him. He's sprawled out across my bed, naked as the day he was born with his hand on his chest as he looks back at me with love shining in his eyes. Happiness swells up inside, me and it feels like I may just burst from it.

"Hey, Logan," I whisper, and a soft smile pulls at his lips.

"Yeah, Gorgeous?"

"I love you."

His smile slowly melts away as he just stares at me, the intensity in his eyes overpowering as he meets my gaze and holds it there, like he can't physically look away. There's so much that passes between us as we look at each other across my bedroom, and I can't believe that I ever doubted this. Our connection is present in every single look, every little touch, and I hate that we wasted time skirting around each other.

He sits up and scoots to the edge of the bed and holds his hand out to me. I go to him without a drop of hesitation and straddle his lap as he wraps his arms around my waist. As he smiles up at me and pulls me closer, I wrap my arms around his neck and lean down, gently pressing my lips to his. He trails his hand over my hair, cradling the back of my head as he takes control from me and teases my lips with the tip of his tongue.

I sigh, melting into him, and he runs his tongue slowly along the roof of my mouth, and I tremble in his arms. Humming his approval, he stands with me in his arms and starts walking to the bathroom without pulling away from my lips. It's a little awkward but we make it to the bathroom, and he presses one last sweet kiss to my lips before pulling away just enough to turn on the water.

"Was that your way of saying, 'I love you, too'?" I ask, and he smiles.

"No."

I scowl and he laughs, reaching up and smoothing the crinkle in my forehead.

"I can't find the right words for what you mean to me, Ali. Every time I think I've got a grip on this emotion, you do something and my feelings for you grow, eclipsing the sensation I just felt moments before. Each time I think I couldn't possibly love you any more, you go and prove me wrong, and a simple word like 'love' just doesn't do it anymore."

"Well, that'll do," I whisper, unable to catch my breath after his beautiful words, and he laughs. I've never felt more loved than I do in this moment, and I throw up a massive thanks to the universe that all the stars aligned when they did and brought Logan and I together. He kisses me again and walks us into the shower, careful not to stick my face under the water, and I grin at him.

His brow arches, and I reach behind me, cupping my hand so it fills with water. He starts shaking his head. "Don't do it, Kitten."

"Or what?"

"Or I won't spank your ass this time since you seem to like it so damn much."

I pout and the water falls out of my hand. He laughs and leans in, biting my neck. "Don't pout, Sweetheart. I can think of lots of other things that we can do to cheer you up."

"Such as?"

He smiles, sliding me down the front of his body, and my breath catches as my feet hit the tile, and he spins me around, pressing my chest up against the tile wall. I gasp, and he circles his tongue on my neck before kissing the same spot, and my gasp turns into a moan.

"Press your hands to the wall above your head," he whispers in my ear, and I suck in a breath as I do as I'm told. He nudges my feet apart as his hands slips around my body, and he pulls me away from the wall so he can cup my breasts. I move my hips back, pressing against his cock, and he softly groans in my ear, sending another shiver twisting down my spine.

"You want something, Sweetheart?" he asks, and I nod. "You think you're ready for me?"

I nod. "Yes."

His teeth sink into my ear as one of his hands travels down my body, slipping between my legs. I moan when he brushes against my clit, and he growls, his finger sliding into me with ease.

"Oh, you're so wet, Baby. You feeling a little desperate?" He slowly pulls his finger out and slides it back in – too slowly – and it feels like a form of torture.

"Yes, Logan," I moan, rocking my hips as I try to get some friction. He pulls away from me, and I cry out as he spins me around and presses my back to the wall. With wide, needy eyes, I watch him as he grips my chin in his hand, hard, but not enough to hurt me, and leans in, moving my head to the side as he presses his lips to my neck. My eyes flutter closed, and he bites a line up my neck all the way to my ear, my body shaking violently in his grasp.

"God, you're so responsive," he mumbles, kissing behind my ear as he takes one of my nipples between his thumb and finger. "You have no idea how hard you get me. Everything you do turns me on but watching you come undone beneath me, shaking as your need takes over your body and you lose yourself in me – nothing is better than that."

"Please, Logan," I gasp, reaching out and wrapping my fingers around his cock. He drops his head back as I move my hand up and down his shaft, trying to drive him crazy enough that he doesn't feel the need to endlessly tease me today. "I need you."

His head falls forward, and his eyes snap open, boring into me as he takes a step toward me. My hand falls away, and he grabs my wrists, pinning them above my head. "Say that again."

It takes me a moment to remember what I just said but when I do, I smile up at him. "I need you."

His hand cups my cheek, and he leans in, pressing his forehead to mine and closing his eyes. I watch him, wondering what's going on in his head right now but I don't get long to speculate. Gray eyes blink open, and in the next second, he's spinning me to face the wall again as he grips my hips in his hands.

"Hands on the wall, Alison," he barks, and my heart jumps in my chest as I obey his command. I need to figure out what the hell I just said and do it again – often. He kicks my feet apart and lines his cock up at my entrance before driving forward. I gasp, my fingers pressing into the tile harder as he stretches me open and holds himself there for a moment. Just when I'm about to glance back and ask if he's okay, he lifts my feet off the floor so he doesn't have to crouch down and pulls out of me.

"Hold on to that goddamn wall," he growls as he drives in and pulls out, and one of my hands slips. He takes a step closer to the wall and it's a little easier to keep myself upright, and he pulls me back at the same time that he thrusts forward. Something between a gasp and a moan slips out of my mouth, and my mind blanks, only able to focus on holding myself up and his cock plunging into me.

I lose track of time. It's only him and I as he fucks me better than anyone else ever has, and I know that I'll never find another man like him. I'm addicted to every little thing about him from the way he smells to the way he is only with me, and I know that I'm ruined. There will never be a man that reaches the depths of my soul like Logan does. He fills in all the gaps and erases the loneliness that I hadn't even realized was there until the day I met him.

"Logan," I cry out, my voice bouncing off the tile walls of the bathroom as my body tenses and my pussy grips his length.

"Fuck," he groans loudly, setting me back on my feet and pulling out of me. "On your knees, Kitten."

I spin around and drop to my knees as he wraps his hand around his cock, pumping up and down. His eyes are on fire as he gazes down at me, licking his lips. I open my mouth and he groans, slipping his fingers into my hair as his breathing quickens. Leaning forward, I suck the tip into my mouth and he groans loudly, his head falling back as I start to suck. His grip in my hair tightens and cum splashes against the back of my throat as his cock jerks and he continues to groan.

I release him with a pop, and he reaches down, pulling me to my feet as he buries his head in my neck and sighs.

"God, I fucking love you, Ali," he says, and I grin as I hold him tighter and nod in agreement. This is forever.

Chapter Twenty-Nine
Alison

Gazing out the window as the trees blur past us, I sigh, relaxed for the first time in weeks. Just being out here on this deserted highway, I feel free. I don't have to worry that someone's watching me or that this isn't going to end well. I still have no idea where he's taking me but I can't say that I care all that much right now because I just want to stay here for a while – in this safe space where life is easy. The truck slows, and I glance over at Logan as he turns onto a gravel road almost completely engulfed by trees on either side. We bump along for a few feet before Logan stops and throws the truck in park.

"Where are we?" I ask, and he just smiles as he opens the truck door and runs down the road a couple more feet to unlock and swing open a large metal gate. I watch him through the windshield as he makes his way back to the truck.

"Where are we?" I ask again as soon as he slides into the truck, and he grins, looking like a mischievous boy instead of the hard man I'm used to.

"We're almost there."

Letting out a huff, I turn back to the road in front of us and cross my arms over my chest. "Almost where?" I grumble to myself as I rest my forehead against the window and watch the trees go by again. The forest is so thick here that I can't see more than six feet into the brush. I'm usually not an "outdoorsy" person but I can't deny that I like the feeling of safety that this place settles over me – whatever it is.

We pass the gate and he stops the truck again, jumping out, and I peek behind me as he closes the gate and locks it before double-checking that it's secure. Is it normal to get mushy about stupid stuff like that? I mean, it must be because watching him make sure that we're safe here warms my insides and only makes me love him more. He climbs back in the truck and glances over at me, laughing when he sees the look on my face.

Well, I'm glad he thinks this is amusing.

I promise myself that I will get some retribution as he grabs my hand and laces our fingers together, lifting our hands and pressing his lips to my skin. I melt, and he winks at me before pulling me closer and laying my hand on his thigh. As I cuddle into his side, he wraps one arm around me and starts off down the road again, the gravel crunching under the tires.

He gives me a little squeeze as the trees open up, revealing a clearing that's almost a perfect circle with the forest fencing us in. The dirt road leads to a cute little log cabin in the middle of the meadow with a little porch attached. Two white rocking chairs sit on either side of a bright yellow door, and I smile as I peek up at him. Without looking at me, he leans down and kisses my forehead as he pulls to a stop in front of the house.

"What is this place?" I ask, my voice soft as I look around in wonder. I don't know what it is about this place but being here, something settles inside me.

"It was my grandparents'. They left it to me when they died," he says, grabbing my hand and lacing our fingers. He tugs on my arm and pulls me into his lap as I shake my head at him.

"It's gorgeous," I tell him, peeking over my shoulder at the cabin before looking back at him.

"No one knows about this place," he whispers, trailing his fingers down my cheek, and I lean into him as my eyes drift shut. "You'll be safe out here but if you don't want to stay, that's okay, too."

My heart warms at the fact that he's giving me a choice, and I lean down, gently pressing my lips to his. "I want to stay."

"I was really hoping you would say that." His lips brush mine as he speaks, and I let out a breath before his hand slips into my hair and he claims my mouth. I moan and wrap both hands around the back of his neck as he nips at my bottom lip, and his tongue slips past my lips and teases me. He pulls away, breathing hard as he pushes down on my hips and lifts off the bench seat, grinding up into me.

"There's no one around for miles, you could just go naked all day," he rasps, his voice deeper and more gravelly than a moment ago.

"Noted. Why don't you give me a tour?"

He groans, and I giggle as he pushes me off him with a glare. "Well, let's go then but you're gonna pay for this later."

"Looking forward to it."

He climbs out of the truck and holds his hand out for me, helping me down before he goes to the back and lowers the tailgate. When he comes back, he has a bag and big cooler in his hands. Bear trots along beside him, his tongue hanging out of the side of his mouth, and I chuckle at him.

"Wanna check out the house first?" He's got a wicked grin on his face, and I shake my head as I try to fight back my own smile. I know if we go into that cabin, there will be no tour. Laughing, he nods and sets the stuff down on the porch before grabbing my hand again and lacing our fingers. As we walk away from the cabin, I peek up at him, unable to believe just how happy I am. It hits me out of the blue sometimes. I'll just be going about my day then I'll look at him and it blindsides me, a giant rush of happiness, and it's hard to believe that this is my life. And yet, it's hard to remember how it was before he waltzed into my world. Or even who I was.

He's changed me but it's for the better. All the parts of me that used to be closed off and guarded are now wide open, and he owns each of them. There isn't a single piece of my heart and soul that doesn't belong to Logan, and that doesn't scare me anymore. It's thrilling, and I'm excited for what our future together brings.

"So, basically, it's just trees," Logan says, chuckling, as we stop a little ways from the cabin, and it takes me a moment to remember what we were doing.

"How far does your property go?" I ask when I realize that he's showing me the land.

"Uh, let's see. It goes all the way to the road and about two miles on each side. And then three or so miles past that lake down there." He points to one end of the clearing where I can just barely make out the glint of sunlight reflecting off the water.

"How long have you had it?"

He tucks me into his side and leads me over to the back of the house where another little porch sits with matching rocking chairs. He sits down in one and pulls me into his lap as we look out at the water which is much more visible from this angle.

"My granddad bought it in fifty-one, and he built this house for my grandma. My dad was raised out here, and then Grandma passed away when I was ten but Granddad couldn't stand to leave this place so he stayed here until he died eleven years ago."

I let my gaze wander over the land again, his story adding a richness to it that wasn't there before. "That's beautiful."

"I always thought so. They were crazy about each other even when I was a kid. I spent so much time out here since it was just Mom and me and she worked so much. My old man wasn't around much, and when he was, he usually dropped me off here, too. They were good to my mom though and babysat me for her even though their son had kind of abandoned us. Actually, I think they kind of felt guilty about the way he turned out."

"You aren't close?" I ask, cuddling closer and laying my head on his shoulder.

He lets out a sardonic laugh and shakes his head. "No, not really. He's in my life but just barely."

"That's terrible." My heart aches for him once again. I can't imagine my life without my parents.

"It's probably better that he was never around. He's kind of obsessed with money, and he's always looking for the next get-rich-quick scheme. Toxic is what the shrink called him when he took my mom to court for custody."

I sit up and look in his eyes. "I'm sorry, Babe. That sounds awful."

"I think I turned out all right," he says, an easy smile on his face, and I nod.

"Yes, you sure did."

"So, about that tour of the cabin now?" he asks, his eyes heating, and I wiggle in his lap. My stomach growls, and he sighs as I throw my head back and laugh.

"I don't know. I'm kind of hungry," I joke, and he shakes his head.

"Yeah, I heard that," he grumbles before standing with me in his arms. He sets me on my feet and points to the back door. "Inside that door is a blanket. Will you grab it and meet me over by the lake?"

"Uh, sure," I say, glancing back at the door. "What are we doing?"

He starts off toward the front of the cabin. "I packed some food for us."

"What? Like a picnic?" I ask, scrunching my nose up in confusion. I try to imagine Logan setting up a cute little picnic, and the picture is so absurd that I laugh.

"Yeah, something like that. Just grab the blanket, Kitten." He disappears around the corner, and I shake my head as I open the back door and grab the blanket that's folded up on top of a dryer.

"Well, you're just full of surprises," I mutter to myself as I close the door behind me and start off toward the lake.

* * * *

Crickets chirp and frogs croak as the fire crackles and dances in front of us, warming my skin as night descends. I cuddle into Logan as we lie next to each other, stretched out on a blanket in the grass just off the back porch of the cabin. Stars begin to pop out in the clear sky above us, and I roll to my back, staring up at them. Today was absolutely perfect in every way imaginable. After we ate lunch down by the lake, Logan showed me the old tree house that his granddad built for him on one side of the meadow, a couple of feet into the forest. Then we spent the afternoon fishing down at the dock, and not once during that whole time did I think about the situation back home or the mess we're going back to tomorrow.

"Are you sure we have to go back?" I ask and turn my head to look at him as he grins.

"Yeah, Kitten. We gotta go back but we can come here anytime you want."

I nod and turn back to the stars. "I'd like that," I whisper, and he slips his arm around my waist and pulls me closer.

"Me, too."

I love this new side of Logan that I get to see lately. The rest of the world sees him as Storm – dark, unapproachable biker, but when he's with me like this he's just Logan – the sweet, sexy man who completely owns me. No one else gets to know him like I do, and I love it.

"Tell me about your grandparents," I say, so curious about them for some reason that I can't quite figure out.

"Well, they met when they were little kids. He said he knew from the moment he saw her kick a bully in the shins that she was the love of his life."

I smile wide. "That's sweet."

"Yeah, they were amazing people separately but there was just something about the two of them together that was extra special."

"When did they start dating?"

"Not until they got into high school. Granddad never had any doubts that she was the one for him but they were just friends until she got stranded at some diner by her friends on a Friday night. She called my granddad and that was it. They were inseparable from that point on."

I place my hand over my heart and look up at him. "That's such a sweet story."

"It is."

"When did he build this place for her?"

He looks over at the house. "After he got out of the Army. He bought it off this couple that had moved down from New York or something. They bought it sight unseen and then got here and hated it. I think he got a pretty good deal on it."

"How could you hate this place?" I ask, glancing over at the still water of the lake reflecting the night sky.

"Who knows? But I'm glad they did. This place is my home."

I smile and close my eyes, trying to imagine him as a little boy running through the trees but I just can't. "I can't picture it."

"What?" He laughs.

"You as a kid here. I can't picture it."

He sits up and pulls me up, positioning me between his bent legs as he sits facing the lake. "Okay, imagine me except smaller."

"And less muscly?"

Laughing, he nods and bites my earlobe. "Yeah, real scrawny."

"Okay, I'm getting it now," I say, closing my eyes, and he laughs again.

"So, over there," he says, and I open my eyes as he points at the lake, "I went fishing almost everyday with my granddad. He gave all sorts of advice about life and girls, and then when it was lunchtime, Grandma would call to us from the back door."

Smiling, I lean back into him, and he wraps his arm tighter around me.

"I played in the tree house a lot, and Granddad taught me how to fix cars in the driveway. If it was rainy or cold, Grandma would teach me how to bake and she taught me how to dance."

"Shut up," I spit out, sitting up and turning to look at him. "You can cook and dance?"

He just winks, and I shake my head with a scoff. "I don't believe it."

"Baby, there are lots of things about me that you haven't discovered yet."

A thrill runs through me and he hops to his feet, leaving me sitting on the blanket as he runs into the house. He comes back out a moment later with a radio in his hand. Setting it down on the porch railing, he flicks it on, and a slow, soulful melody floats out of the speakers. I stand as he comes down the stairs and holds his hand out to me. As soon as I take it, he gives it a tug, spinning me into his arms, and a startled laugh spills out of me.

"Okay, maybe I believe you."

He just grins as he puts his hand on my side, and he starts leading me back and forth through the grass. My heart thumps in my chest, happiness shooting out of it with every beat.

"So, why did you move away from here?" I ask, and he tenses for a brief second before sighing.

"Because I bought the house next to you for Sophia."

"Did you guys come out here a lot?" I ask, and he shakes his head, looking uncomfortable.

"No."

"Why not?"

"I don't know, actually. I never even felt like bringing her here, and I never thought that was weird. Now, though, I don't know."

I pull back and look up at him. "You don't know what?"

"It feels wrong to even say," he says, almost to himself, as he looks away.

"You can tell me anything, Logan."

His gaze meets mine again, and the sorrow in his eyes is overwhelming. "I loved Sophia, I swear, I fucking did, but being with you and the way I feel now, I don't know if it would have lasted. I don't want to tarnish her memory but if I'm being honest, maybe we weren't right for each other. She came into my life at a time when I really fucking needed her, and I fell in love with her but it's not the same as what I feel for you, Ali."

What the hell do you say when the man you love compares you to his dead fiancée? Apparently, nothing, since I just stand here and gawk at him for a moment before getting my bearings.

"Shit. Forget I said that."

I shake my head. "Did you mean it?"

"Yeah."

"Then, I won't forget it. It's okay that you loved her, Logan, and it's okay that you love me. You don't have to explain anything to me, and loving me doesn't cheapen what you had with her. Plus, you're a different person now than you were then. Her death changed you, and maybe that's why you found me."

"I think I fell in love with you the moment I met you but I felt so goddamn guilty about it, like moving on and being happy again would mean I didn't love Sophia, but I'm willing to live with this guilt for the rest of my life because it's better than living for a hundred years without you."

Tears sting my eyes, and I reach up, pressing my hand to his chest. "Please don't feel guilty. If she truly loved you, she would want you to be happy again. It's the only thing in the world that I would want for you if something happened to me."

He blinks, and pain crosses his face. I hate it but I know he needs to hear this, even if it reminds him that he could lose me.

"You know, you're kinda good with the words," he says finally, looking at me as happiness overshadows the pain that was just clouding his gaze.

I burst into laughter and shake my head at him. "God, I hope so."

"You see me, Kitten. Past all the stuff that's just on the surface, you get me and you accept my past. When I was being pulled under by pain, you pulled me out and around you, I could finally breathe again. I had no fucking choice but to fall in love with you because you stole my fucked-up heart the moment you looked up at me from your front lawn. That's why I'm doing this," he whispers, pulling a ring out of the pocket of his jeans as his smile melts away. My mouth pops open, and I stare up at him before my gaze falls to the ring pinched between his thumb and finger.

"What are you doing?" I ask, even though I've already got a pretty damn good idea what he's doing.

"Askin' you to marry me," he says, his voice full of nerves, and I suck in a breath as I look at the ring. I meet his eyes again, shaking my head, and he starts to pull away. I grab him and keep him from backing away from me.

"Nothing sounds better than a lifetime with you, Logan, but I can't say yes right now."

His brow crinkles, and the hurt in his eyes kills me. "Why the hell not?"

I have no idea how Chris would react if he saw a ring on my finger, and as much as I hate the fact that he's controlling my life, I can't let anything happen to Logan. He's everything to me. I just hope he understands. "Because I'm afraid of what will happen to you if I put that ring on my finger. I can't lose you."

He studies me for a second before understanding dawns on his face, and he cups my cheek. "You're worried about me?"

"More than you know. If I can do this one thing to try and keep you safe, I will."

"But you're saying yes?"

I nod, fighting back a smile. "Yes, I guess I am. Only you and I can know about this, though. And I need you to hold on to that ring for me."

"Kitten," he says, his voice soft as he pulls me into him with a smile on his face, "I don't give a shit about anything else as long as you promise that I get to make you mine forever."

"Oh, that ship sailed a long time ago. You're stuck with me."

"Perfect," he growls, his face a mask of possessiveness as he claims my lips and grabs my hand, rubbing his thumb over my left ring finger, marking me as his.

Chapter Thirty
Alison

"I'm sorry we couldn't stay there longer, Kitten," Logan says as we pull up in front of the house. I turn my head to look at him and smile.

"I'll forgive you if you promise to take me back there often."

He grins and grabs my hand, lacing our fingers before he lifts it and presses his lips to my skin. "Anything you want, Sweetheart."

"You keep saying that and you're going to be very good at this marriage thing."

He laughs and pulls me across the seat, tucking me under his arm. "Yes, Your Highness."

"It's Your Majesty," I correct him, and he actually looks contrite.

"My mistake, Your Majesty. Please forgive me." He places our joined hands over his heart and practically gives me puppy dog eyes.

"Ooh, a quick learner, too. A plus, Mr. Chambers."

His eyes heat, roaming my body like I'm prime rib as he licks his lips. "Have I ever told you that I've always had this sexy teacher fantasy?"

"No," I say, shaking my head as I reach up and brush my lips against his, "but I'm very interested."

With a growl, he claims my lips in a vicious kiss, pulling me onto his lap in the cab of the truck as his hand squeezes my ass. He pulls away, breathing hard as his gaze lights a fire across my skin.

"Inside," he barks, opening the door, and I scramble off him as fast as I can, excited to see where this is going to lead. He goes to the back to let Bear out, and as I walk up the sidewalk, I hear his boots slapping against the pavement behind me. The next thing I know, I'm being tossed over his shoulder.

"Hey!" I squeal, laughing, and he smacks my ass. "I thought we were doing a school teacher bit not a caveman bit."

"Change of plans. In fact, anytime that you offer to do the school teacher bit I might just get so fucking hard that it turns into a caveman bit."

"We should get you a club," I tease.

"Don't tempt me, Ali."

Laughing, I smack his ass as he unlocks the door, and he turns his head into me, sinking his teeth into the side of my ass. Just as the front door opens, the roar of bikes fills the air, and I look up as two of them stop in front of the house.

"Hey, what are you two doing here?" I ask as soon as they turn off their bikes.

"We interrupting something?" Kodiak asks, laughing as he climbs off his bike.

"Yes," I say at the same time that Logan tells them no and I turn, scowling at the back of his head.

"We're here for bodyguard duty," Smith says, crossing his arms over his chest and leaning back on his bike.

"Well, could you come back later?" All three guys laugh at me, and I huff as I struggle to hold myself up to look at them.

"Sorry, Darlin', no can do. But if y'all are into role-play, we could act out *The Bodyguard*. Really get me motivated to lay my life on the line for you," he says, winking at me, and I shake my head.

"Dude, what the fuck are you talking about?" Kodiak asks.

Smith sighs. "It's a movie. Haven't any of you idiots ever had a girlfriend? It's a girl classic like *The Notebook*."

Kodiak and Logan both start laughing as Smith and Kodiak start walking up to the porch. "Wait, are you telling me that you've watched *The Notebook*?"

"Whatever. Shut the fuck up," Smith grumbles before turning back to look at me. "What do you say, Sweets? You play Whitney and I'll play Kevin?"

"Only if you have a death wish," Logan growls, and Smith grins at him. "Why don't you just go to a bar and pick up some pussy that won't cost you your life?"

I smack Logan in the back of the head for the pussy comment, and he sighs. "Not talkin' about you, Kitten."

"Whatever, man. Don't mind us. We'll just sit out here and listen to the show."

"That's not fucking happening," Logan growls, setting me down on my feet before pulling me into his side. Kodiak and Smith join us on the porch, sitting down in the rocking chairs on either side of the door.

"Don't worry about a thing, Miss Ali. You're safe with us here," Smith assures me, and I smile through the sudden panic that hits me as I realize that I'm back where Chris can find me. Logan ushers me inside and pushes me up against the entryway wall before the door even closes all the way. Warm lips press against my neck, and I sigh, gripping his shirt in my hands.

"Babe," I whine, pushing on his chest. He pulls back and looks at me like I've lost my mind. "I need to go take a shower. I smell like fish." I make a face, and he laughs as he pulls away from me.

"All right, you get in the shower and I'll join you after I check out the house, okay?"

I nod, biting my bottom lip as I trail my fingers down the front of his body, stopping just above his cock. "Don't take too long."

"Devil woman," he whispers, smacking my ass as I skip off toward my bedroom with a smile on my face. Bouncing into my bedroom, I sit on the edge of my bed and fall back, spreading my arms out on either side of me as I sigh, so blissfully happy that it almost hurts.

I hear Logan moving around the house and I sit up, wanting to beat him to the shower. The look on his face when he walks in and I'm already all wet and soapy is one of my favorites. As I push off the bed, I reach for my shirt and start to pull it up as I turn to face the bed. It gets halfway up my stomach before I freeze, my breath catching in my throat. I stare at the window, my heart pounding like a bass drum in my ears, and peer into the darkness, trying to see if anything is out there. I could have sworn that I just saw someone there. Or maybe one of the guys passed by on their rounds.

It's probably nothing...right?

Each second that I stare at that window, the harder my heart beats, and I feel like I could jump out of my skin right now. But there is nothing, only darkness and my own reflection. Giving up, I chalk it up to my eyes playing tricks on me as I start to lift my shirt again. Slowly, almost like in a dream, a face appears in the glass. Yelping, I drop my shirt back down my body and take a step back as the face inches closer to the window. I want to scream but it's stuck in my throat, the fear choking me. Every breath that I take rings in my ears as tears fill my eyes, and I take another step back, hitting the wall.

The man raises a hand and presses it against the window like he's trying to touch me and smiles up at me, a sinister little grin that seems to reach into my body and fill me with terror. Oh, God, I need to call for help but as I open my mouth, nothing comes out. Where is Logan? He has to be coming in here soon. Right? He drops his gaze down my body, and I sink down the wall, pulling my knees into my chest. As I shake on the floor, he steps closer, his face almost pressed against the glass, and his grin widens as he mouths, "My Ali."

I can't speak.
I can't move.

I'm powerless as I stare into a face that is so familiar and yet, so foreign.

I know him.

Where do I know him from?

Where have I seen him?

I stare at him and all of the sudden it hits me. He looks like...

"Logan!" I scream as loud as I can, tears streaming down my face, and my heart beating against my ribcage like it wants release. The face in my window disappears seconds before Logan bursts into the room, gun drawn. His gaze wildly flies around the room before landing on me, huddled up in a ball on the floor. Quickly tucking the gun back in his jeans, he crouches down and pulls me into his arms.

Kodiak and Smith burst into the room, looking around for the danger as I start to hyperventilate, gripping Logan's shirt like his mere presence will keep me from spiraling into the abyss of my fear.

"Go search outside," he barks at them, clutching me tighter, and I sob into his neck. "I've got her."

The guys rush out of the room, and Logan rubs his hand down my back, trying to calm me, but nothing is working. It's one thing to know that someone is following you but to see him actually staring in your window and feeling that powerlessness is another thing altogether. It feels monumental in this moment. How will I ever come back in this room? How will I ever look in a window again without my heart kicking in my chest? I'm consumed by the fear, shaking uncontrollably in Logan's embrace.

"You're okay, Kitten," he whispers in my ear, kissing my cheek gently, and my sobs gradually settle into hiccups as a few more tears streak down my face. "I've got you."

I don't know how long he just holds me, whispering soothing words in my ear, but eventually Kodiak and Smith come back into the room with grim expressions. My stomach knots. "There are boot prints in the mud outside Ali's window but other than that, nothing."

"I need one of you on each door. I'm taking her to the clubhouse as soon as I can get her calmed down."

They both nod, and Smith claps his shoulder. "You got it, Brother."

When they leave, Logan cups my cheek and pulls my gaze up to his. "What happened, Baby?"

I start to breathe heavily again as I replay those sixty seconds in my head. God, was it really only that long? Tears form in my eyes again as I try to tell him. I can see it so perfectly in my mind, each tick of the clock exaggerated by fear and the adrenaline coursing through my body, but I can't seem to get the words out.

"He's gone, Gorgeous. We're not going to let anything happen to you. I love you."

I peek up at him and take a deep breath. "I started to get undressed, and when I turned toward the window, I thought I saw someone there but then I thought I was just imagining things."

"Okay, and?"

"I was about to turn away to get in the shower, and then he was there," I say, tears starting to fall again as my body trembles against him. He nods and leans down, gently kissing my lips, and surprisingly, it helps.

"Did you get a good look at him, Kitten?"

I nod, my lip trembling.

"What did he look like?"

I start shaking again, my eyes watering as his face appears in my mind once more. "He kind of looked…like you."

He blinks and pulls away from me, his brow furrowing in confusion as he gazes down at me. "What?"

"He looked like you. The same clothes, the same haircut, same hair color, and even had the same scar but it looked fresh," I say, touching the thin scar that runs through his eyebrow. "Except his eyes were all wrong. They were brown and lifeless."

"And there wasn't anything else?" he asks, and I shrug, my mind blanking.

"I don't know."

"Okay," he says, pulling me close again and tucking my head under his chin. "We're going to go to the clubhouse, and I don't want to hear any arguments. It's safe there, Baby."

"I'm scared," I whisper, feeling small as I admit my feelings to him.

"I know but I'm never going to let anything happen to you."

I pull back and look up at him, wanting to look in his eyes when I say this. "I love you, Logan."

He nods and cradles my face in his hands as he leans in and kisses me gently. "I love you, Ali, and I'm going to end this, I promise you."

Hopelessly Devoted

* * * *

"Sweet, Ali," the voice says, echoing off the dark barren room, and I spin around, looking for the source, but all I see are reflections of myself. Taking a tentative step forward, I reach out and press my fingers to smooth glass.

Mirrors.

They're all mirrors.

They surround me. Everywhere I look, my own terrified face stares back at me, and I don't know which way leads to my salvation and which leads to my demise. The voice laughs, a chilling sound that creeps down my spine and raises the hair on my arms.

"I'm not there, my sweet, Ali. Come find me."

"No," I whisper, my head whipping back and forth as I search for the voice.

"Yes."

"No!" I scream out into the space, my voice magnified by the echo, and he laughs again.

"I've missed you so much, Sweetheart. Why would you leave me?" Pain overshadows his voice, and I look around, feeling like I'm losing my mind.

"I didn't leave you. We were never together."

The sound of glass shattering swells around me, and I spin around, looking for a broken mirror, but I can't find one anywhere.

"Why do you do this to us? To me!" he roars, and I spin again, searching for him as my skin prickles from his gaze. He's here. And he can see me but no matter how hard I search, I can't find him.

"You're delusional. I was never yours."

"Lies!" he screams, followed by the sound of more breaking glass, and I back up, my paranoia overwhelming me. "What we had was special, and you just threw it away."

"I don't even know you," I spit, my eyes flying wildly around the space but he's still hidden from me. My gaze lands back on the mirror directly in front of me, and I back up as his face appears.

Arms wrap around me from behind, covering my mouth as he leans down, whispering in my ear. "Sweet, sweet, Ali. You should know by now that I'm never going to let you go."

Screaming, I shoot up in bed, and Logan is at my side a second later.

"Shh, Kitten. You're okay. It was just a dream," he whispers, rubbing a hand down my back, and I collapse into him as I start sobbing.

"I saw his face," I say, reliving it in my head all over again. "He got me. He grabbed me from behind."

Logan lifts me up and pulls me into his lap, moving my legs to straddle him as he reaches up and cups my cheek. "That's never going to happen, Baby. Do you hear me? I won't ever let that happen."

The door flies open, and I scream as Logan binds his arms around me and mutters a curse, pulling the blanket up over us to cover our naked bodies. "Don't fucking look at her. It was just a nightmare."

Hopelessly Devoted

I peek over at Fuzz and Blaze as they both give me sympathetic looks. "You guys need anything?" Blaze asks, and Logan shakes his head. They mutter an apology before leaving and closing the door behind them. As soon as they're gone, my nightmare is in the forefront of my mind again, and I start to shake.

"Look at me, Alison," Logan says, nudging me to lift my head and meet his gaze. His gray eyes are fierce as he stares up at me, giving me a little bit of strength as I take a deep breath and nod.

"Do you feel this?" he asks, pulling my hand toward him and placing it over his heart. My fingers dig into his broad chest as the steady thump of his pulse pounds against my palm, calming me. "It beats for you, and someone will have to put a bullet through this heart to get anywhere near you. I promise that nothing is going to happen to you, Darlin'."

"I love you," I whisper, leaning down and kissing him softly before pulling away again. "Each time you vow to protect me, I'm overwhelmed by how much I love you and how much you mean to me, but please remember as you fight that you are just as vital to my survival as the air that I breathe."

He nods, hooking his hand behind my neck and pulling me closer as he claims me with a kiss. It feels like I'm being branded with his name on every part of my body for the entire world to see so they'll know whom I belong to. If you had told me I wanted to be claimed by someone only a couple of months ago, I would have laughed you right out of my life, but now I crave it. I want him to mark me, and I want everyone to know that this man owns my heart.

I sink into his kiss, wrapping my arms around his neck as his grip around my waist tightens, and he pushes me down on his erection as he thrusts up off the bed. Moaning, I place one hand on his chest, my fingers digging into his skin as I grind on top of him, and he lets out a long, low groan that sends a shiver rushing through me. My core clenches, and I run my nails down his back. He pulls away from my lips, his chest heaving as he gasps for air.

"You sure this is what you need right now?"

I nod, rocking my hips over him. "Please, Logan. I need to feel you."

"You know I can't deny you, Ali," he whispers, capturing my lips again before scooting us up the bed so he can lean back against the headboard. I rock my hips, and his cock brushes against my entrance. I reach down between us and grab the base as I lower myself a little, rubbing the head against my clit. He hisses, and a soft moan spills out of my mouth as I do it a couple more times.

"You keep teasing me," he growls, "and I'm gonna take over and fuck your sweet little cunt until you can't walk anymore."

I shiver and push his cock back until it's brushing against my entrance before I sink down slowly. Once I get about halfway, I pull up again and slowly sink to the same halfway point before I pull up.

"Kitten," he warns, and I grin as I sink to the halfway point again. He reaches for me but I manage to grab his hands as I lean forward and pin them to the bed. I won't be able to hold him for long but I should be able to tease him a couple more times. Sinking down to the halfway point again, I hum and let my eyes drift closed as I pull back up. Growling, he tries to thrust up into me but I pull away, letting him slip out of me completely.

"This is your last warning," he says, the gravel in his voice sending sparks across my skin as he looks at me with pure fire in his eyes. I wrap my fingers around his cock and line him up again before slowly sinking all the way to the base. He throws his head back, gripping my hips firmly in his hands as he groans.

Leaning forward, I press my lips to his neck, tears forming in my eyes when his stubble scrapes against my nose but I love it. With a soft moan, I stick my tongue out and drag it up his neck, and his grip on my body tightens, his fingers digging into my skin. I lift my hips, pulling off him slightly before sinking my teeth into his neck and dropping back down. Repeating the same motion a few more times, I kiss up to his ear and nibble on his earlobe as his hand slips into my hair. He fists it and gives it a tug, pulling my head back as I place my hand on his chest and rise up and sink down again and again.

"Sweet Jesus," he groans, palming my breast as I ride him, my head thrown back and eyes closed.

"Look at me, Gorgeous," he orders, and my head snaps forward, hooded eyes meeting his as I continue bobbing up and down on his length. He groans, releasing my hair but holding me captive with his gaze as his swallows me up. I lose myself in his gray depths, and there's nothing else anymore. Just us. He reaches up and hooks his hand around the back of my neck, pulling me down to kiss him.

His arm tightens around my waist, and he flips me onto my back in the middle of the bed. I gaze up at him with wide eyes as I suck air into my lungs. He plunges into me, and I gasp, my back arching off the bed as he pins my hands above my head.

"Is this what you wanted, Baby? You wanted to get me so worked up that I would fuck you like this?" he asks, pulling out and driving back into me with a desperation that I've never felt from him before, and I love it.

"Yes," I hiss.

"You want me to fuck you so good that any other man just has to be near you to know that you fucking belong to me?"

I nod, my body arching off the bed again as he continues thrusting into me ferociously. He keeps the same pace as he leans down and runs his tongue up the side of my neck, and I cry out, sensations assaulting me from every angle. He releases my hands and props himself up over me as my body hurtles toward a release that I so desperately need.

"Say it, Kitten. Tell me who owns this sweet pussy?"

"Oh, God, you do, Logan," I gasp, my eyes squeezing shut as my fingers dig into his shoulders.

"Damn fucking right, I do," he says, smirking. "No one else can make you come like this."

He leans down and bites my neck as his thrusts speed up, and he slips a hand between us to rub my clit. I black out, stars exploding behind my eyes as my release rockets through me. I scream his name, clutching the sheets beneath me as I writhe underneath him, and he groans, tensing over me as his cock jerks inside me. Gasping, he drops his forehead to mine for a second before rolling off to my side. I'm exhausted, and it's a struggle to keep my eyes open. He pulls me back up to the pillows and tucks me into his side as he slips his arm under my head.

"Go to sleep, my gorgeous girl. I've got you," he whispers against my temple, and I sigh, sleep already claiming me.

Chapter Thirty-One
Storm

"I'm going to go try and find some food in this place," Ali says, and I smile.

"I think you're forgetting something, Kitten."

Her brows rise in question, and she glances around the room, only making me grin wider. "What?"

Holding my hand out, I give her an expectant look, and she smiles as she skips over to my chair and braces her hands on the arms, dipping down to kiss me.

"Is this what you were looking for?" she asks, and I nod.

"Yeah, this is almost perfect."

She jerks back and glares at me. "Almost perfect?"

Nodding, I push her hands off the arms of the chair and pull her into my lap. She straddles my legs and huffs as her stomach growls.

"It might be a little chilly in hell today," she quips, challenging me with just a look, and I laugh.

"Why's that?"

"Because I'm hungry, and you're not feeding me."

"Careful, Darlin'. That's like challenging my manhood."

She crosses her arms over her chest and smirks at me. "Well, then I guess you should do something about it."

"You're just askin' for trouble today," I tell her as I pull her closer and capture her lips. She melts into me, a little hum rising up from the back of her throat, and as badly as I want to pin her to the bed and make her sorry for going up against me, I'm not gonna let her starve. Pulling away, I smack her ass. "Why don't you go see if there is any food downstairs, and if there's not, we'll go out?"

"Is it safe?" she asks timidly, and it breaks my fucking heart. I never wanted any of this to touch her. I never wanted her to know this fear.

"Yeah, Baby. We'll take some of the guys and make them sit somewhere else."

She smiles and leans in, kissing me again before she jumps off my lap. "I love you," she says, smiling as she walks away from me backward.

"I love you, too. I just gotta talk to Streak, and then I'll be down there."

She blows me a kiss and leaves the room. I stay in my seat, watching her leave until she disappears from my sight before sinking back into my chair for a second. My mind has been working overdrive since Sunday night, trying to figure out what the hell is going on. It seemed so straightforward until she told me that the man in her window looked like me. Why the fuck would Ian's brother do that? Is it part of the game?

Shoving out of the chair, I slip out of my room and go down to the end of the hall where Streak's office is set up, knocking on the door twice before I open it. He glances up from one of the three computer screens in front of him with bleary eyes.

"Yeah?"

I close the door and sit in the chair next to his desk. "Did you find any social media profiles on the brother when you searched him?"

"No. He's probably one of the only people in the world without Facebook."

"Shit," I curse, running a hand through my hair.

"Why? What's going on?"

I shake my head, trying to work it all out in my mind but it's just not adding up for me, and that makes me uneasy. "The other night when Ali saw that guy in her window, she said he looked like me. He even had a scar through his eyebrow but his looked fresh."

"That's awfully coincidental," he muses, and I shake my head.

"Or not."

"You think someone made themselves look like you?"

I shrug. "It's either that or it really is a coincidence, and I don't really believe in those."

"Yeah, me either," he says, turning back to his computer and typing. "Well, this is interesting."

"What?"

"I've been trying to access some of Ian's medical records since you asked me but it's been difficult. I just got one this morning from right after he was sentenced. It's from a psychologist."

I lean forward, trying to look at the screen, but I have no idea what I'm looking at. "What does it say?"

"It says that Ian is perfectly normal mentally except mental illness does run in his family." He stares at the computer screen again, and I can see the wheels turnin' in his head.

"What are you thinking?"

"Well, Ian is just an abusive narcissist, we know this, but what if his brother has other mental issues? What if the brother started following Ali and became obsessed with her himself? Whoever is sending those letters and presents clearly thinks that he and Ali were or are in a relationship."

I drop my head into my hands and let out a breath. Jesus Christ, did I do this to her? Did I lead a crazy person straight to her door? Maybe I should have just stayed away, but even thinking that makes me feel like I'm being ripped apart. Sighing, I stand and slap Streak's shoulder.

"Keep diggin', yeah?"

He nods. "You got it."

I leave his office, needing to get my hands on my girl for just a second so I can breathe again. Goddamn it, if anything happens to her, I'll never fucking forgive myself. Stopping in the middle of the hallway, I press my forehead to the wall and pound my fist against it. How was I supposed to stay away from her? It was impossible, and now she might pay with her life. My stomach lurches violently as I think about that possibility, but I pull away from the wall shaking my head.

No. I'll do anything to keep that from happening. My phone rings, pulling me out of my thoughts, and I answer without even glancing at the screen.

"Yeah?" I bark.

"Hey, Storm. It's Ray. I...uh, I heard some shit, and you're not gonna like it, man."

The other shoe comes crashing down, and this is the bad news I've been expecting since the moment I gave into this. I just know it is.

"Tell me."

"Shaun, my guy up at the prison, just heard Ian boasting that he hired some guy to take out your girl. I don't know many details but I know he's got enough money to make it happen."

"Fuck!" I roar, slamming my fist into the drywall as my entire world crashes down around me. I can't erase the picture of Ali in a pine box out of my mind. I can't fucking do this again. I can't lose her. This time, I won't survive it. "I gotta go."

I don't even wait for his reply as I hang up the phone, and the door to Streak's office opens. "You okay?" he asks, and I glance back at him before stalking off toward the stairs. I'm not thinking as I fly down the stairs and scan the room for Ali. She walks out of the kitchen with a plate of fruit, a huge smile on her face, and I suck in a breath. Glancing up, she spots me and her smile fades as she looks me over. She hands the plate off to Smith and practically runs across the room to me.

"What's wrong?" she asks, running her hands down my arms. I suck in a breath, breathing a little easier now that she's in my grasp.

"I need you to listen to me, okay?"

She nods, her eyes vulnerable as she looks up at me.

"I have to go handle something, and I need you to stay inside this building, no matter what. You can't go outside, you hear me?"

She shakes her head. "What's going on, Logan? You're scaring me."

"Kitten," I whisper, pulling her into me and pressing my lips to her forehead, "I promise to tell you everything when this is over but right now, I need to go. I'll fill in the guys, and I need you to stay here. Please?"

She nods, reaching up to kiss me. "I love you. Please be careful."

"I made you a promise, Baby, and I intend to keep it. I'm going to end this, and then I'll tell you everything. I just hope you don't hate me when it's over because I don't know how I would survive losing you."

"I could never," she says but I cut her off with my lips, kissing her with all the love and pain and desperation that I feel in this moment, and when I pull away, she wipes a tear from her cheek. Planting one last kiss on her forehead, I walk toward the door and throw it open, bright sunlight almost blinding me.

"Want to fill us in?" Blaze asks, waiting by my bike.

"Ian hired someone to kill Ali."

"Shit," Blaze spits as Fuzz runs a hand over his hair.

"What's your plan?" Fuzz asks.

I stop and look at them because honestly, I hadn't even thought about it. My girl was threatened, and I just jumped into action without thinking over my options.

"I'm going to take your silence to mean that you have no fucking clue," Blaze says, and I nod. He glances over at Fuzz, who shrugs.

"When this all started, Fuzz came to me with an idea that might be our best option."

"All right, well, let's hear it."

Blaze sighs and shakes his head, looking off in the distance. I know he hates this situation coming to this since they all left the violence behind six years ago, but there isn't anything I wouldn't do to protect Ali.

"I've got this friend up there, who is a guard. I'm going to give him a call, and he'll meet you outside the prison on his break at five. Slip him a note to give to Henn, telling him to call you. When he calls you, tell him to recruit someone to take Ian out, someone who has no chance of ever getting out, and we'll deposit two grand into their account over the next six months as payments," Fuzz says, and I just stare at him for a moment, thinking through his plan. It might just work.

"I don't fucking like this," Blaze says, turning back to look at us. "But we ain't gonna let your girl get hurt. It may be time to rethink some things if y'all are gonna start settlin' down. Smith was right. We can't let people think they can hurt our women."

I nod. "We're not regressing here, Blaze. Maybe just tweaking a few things."

He nods and slaps my shoulder. "You should take Fuzz with you."

"You ready to go?" I ask Fuzz, and he nods. Blaze heads back inside with a promise to keep my girl safe, and Fuzz and I climb on our bikes before pulling out of the parking lot. The entire way to the prison, I'm assaulted by memories of six years ago and everything that this worthless motherfucker did to Fi and I. I can't stop them this time, and I stop trying, letting them come so I'm prepared to face him as we drive up to the prison. It feels so damn good to know that I'm ending this for real this time; that Ian Blackwell will never bother me again. Then, Ali and I can move forward and start planning our life together. There's nothing I want more.

* * * *

I shift in the chair, waiting for Ian to appear on the other side of the Plexiglas so I can get this over with and get back to Ali. Fuzz's plan didn't require that I come here and confront him but I needed it. I needed to look in his eyes and let him know that he doesn't get to win. He doesn't get to take anything else from me. And then I see him. He limps into the room, a guard on either side of him and his wrists and ankles cuffed. When he looks up and sees me, a wide smile stretches across his face but his eyes look like death.

"Well, well, well," he says as soon as they sit him down in the chair, and he grabs the phone on his side. "Gotta say, never thought I'd see you here."

"This isn't a social visit, asshole," I snap into the phone but it only makes him smile wider.

"Ah, are you here about your new little toy? Let me ask you something, how could you do that to our sweet Sophia?"

"Shut up," I growl, dropping my head and taking a deep breath to calm me. He laughs, and my head shoots up as I level a glare at him.

"No, I'm not going to stop. Do you know how much you would break her poor heart if she knew that you were with someone new?"

I shake my head, keeping my glare trained on him. I really just need to know who he hired to kill Ali, and then I can leave. "No, it wouldn't because she's dead. You killed her, remember? You just couldn't let her go, and even now, you're still obsessed with her."

He leans back in his chair, a smug smile on his face. "I don't know. I guess looking at sweet, sweet Ali, I can understand how you moved on. Maybe I'll try and get me some of that."

I lunge forward, and the guard behind me puts a hand on my shoulder. Gritting my teeth, I release a breath and shrug him off as I sink back down. Ian laughs. "You won't ever fucking touch her."

The smile slides off his face, and he leans forward, getting close to the glass as he looks me straight in the eye. "You're right. I won't and neither will you because you're going to pay for everything you did. You took my beautiful Sophia away from me, and now I'm going to take Ali. It's just a shame I don't get to test drive her before I crash her into a pole."

Rage simmers just under my skin, and I toss the phone down, kicking my chair back as I stand. I've heard enough. Turning to the guard, he opens the door, and as I leave the room, I can still hear Ian's laughter. My only regret is that I can't be the one to choke the life out of him. But knowing that very soon he'll be six feet under eases that desire slightly.

As I stomp back out to my bike, I try to calm myself down because I feel like I could rip someone apart with my hands right now, and I don't want to go back to Ali like this. Fuzz jumps off his bike when he sees me coming, quiet as he studies my face.

"How did it go?"

"He confirmed it."

Fuzz watches me for another moment before nodding. "My guy should be here any minute. You sure you don't want to talk about it?"

"What are you? A chick? No, I don't want to fucking talk about it," I snap at him and instantly feel bad about it. Crossing my arms over my chest, I lean back against the bike and just stare at the prison, trying to get my anger under control.

"Sorry, man," I mutter a moment later.

"Don't worry about it. I can't even imagine how I would react after talking to my fiancée's murderer. Yell all you want. Hell, I might even let you hit me."

I snort a laugh and shake my head. "No, you wouldn't."

"Yeah, you're right, but it's the thought that counts."

"Bullshit."

A guard crossing the lot to us interrupts us, and Fuzz climbs off his bike and meets him, shaking his hand. He slips a piece of paper into his pocket, and they both walk over to me.

"Hey, thanks for this," I say, extending my hand, and he nods, shaking it.

"Fuzz told me about what happened, and I'm of the thinking that some people never need to leave this place. I'll get this where it needs to go," he says, patting his pocket, and I nod, standing up straight. "Besides, I've spent the last six years listening to that fucker boast about what he did to your girl. I'd stick a shank in his neck myself if I could."

"Thanks, man," I tell him, my face burning with the knowledge that Ian's spent the last six years proudly telling everyone in there what he's done. Fuzz pulls him off to the side and says something to him but I'm not paying attention, ready to get out of here. All I want to do is get back to my girl and forget about this shit-tastic day.

* * * *

My phone rings, rattling around on the table next to the bed, and I untangle myself from Ali, scooping it up as I pull some jeans on and slip out into the hallway.

"Hello?"

"You have received a collect call from," an automated voice says, cutting out when Henn says his name, "at Dixon Correctional Institute. Do you accept these charges?"

"Yes."

It rings once more before connecting to the other line.

"Storm?" Henn asks.

"Yeah, I'm here. Thanks for getting back to me, Brother." I lean back against the wall and run my hand over my face. I haven't slept in over twenty-four hours, and I'm not sure that I will until this is over.

"Don't mention it. Shelby filled me in on what's going on."

"Shelby?" I ask, and he chuckles.

"Yeah, Officer Shelby. Fuzz's friend."

I nod. "Oh, right. Didn't realize his name was Shelby."

"It's not something he advertises," Henn says, laughing, and I grin, shaking my head.

"All right, my girl's gonna wake up soon so here's the deal, Ian's gotta go, and Blaze wants you to find someone to do the job. Someone who is never gonna get out of there and would be willing to do it."

"What kind of compensation are we talking here?"

"We'll deposit two grand in their account over the next six months."

He's quiet for a minute, and I worry that our plan will fall apart. "I think I can make that happen. I've got a couple of guys in mind."

"Thank you for doing this."

"Don't mention it. There isn't anything I wouldn't do for my woman. I get it."

"Give me a call when it's done?"

He sucks in a breath, and I pause. "Yeah, you got it. Listen, there is a favor I need to ask you for."

"What is it?"

"I'm looking at getting out in the next year, and I need to find my girl."

I push off the wall and walk down the hallway a little bit. "What do you mean 'find' her?"

"Fuck, I don't know, man. The night I got pinched, I was supposed to pick her up, but of course, I couldn't, and ever since then, Blaze says she disappeared. I haven't seen her in six years, and it's fucking killing me. She's my world, you know?"

"Yeah, Brother, I get it. I'll look into it."

He thanks me, and we hang up before I slip back into my room and climb into bed, pulling Ali into my arms. Weight lifts off my shoulders as I realize that this is almost over, and a smile stretches across my face as I close my eyes.

A.M. Myers

Hopelessly Devoted

Chapter Thirty-Two
Alison

"Oh my god, I missed you so much, bitch," Izzy squeals as she runs across the parking lot and practically jumps into my arms as Carly follows behind her, shaking her head. Laughing, I hug her, and she pulls back before looking over my body. "Are you okay? What happened?"

When we left my house Sunday night, there wasn't much time to explain everything. I did tell them that I had to go to the clubhouse for my safety but I couldn't give them details. "It was crazy, Iz."

"Well, tell me everything."

I glance over my shoulder to the picnic tables that surround the fire pit. All the guys are on one side, drinking beer as they talk and stare into the fire. I point to the table across from them. "Let's go sit down, and I'll tell you everything."

We move over to the table, and as they sit down, I take a deep breath and begin explaining the whole weekend to them – telling them about Logan's cabin and how amazing it was. Then I start telling them about when we came home. When I finish, Carly has tears in her eyes, and Izzy looks murderous.

"I can't imagine how terrifying that was, Hon," Carly says, and I nod.

"I've honestly never felt fear like that. I was frozen, and I couldn't even scream for Logan. I thought my heart was going to literally burst."

Izzy blows out a breath and looks up at me from the table. "What are we doing to end this son of a bitch?"

"Logan is handling it."

"Well, what is he doing?"

I shrug, peeking over my shoulder at him. He smiles and winks at me, and my cheeks heat. "I don't know, Iz. He promised to tell me everything when it was over."

"And you're okay with that?" she asks, incredulously.

I turn back to her and nod. "I am. If there is one thing I know for certain, it's that Logan is madly in love with me. He would do whatever it takes to keep me safe, and if me being in the dark for a little bit helps him deal with this, then I'm okay with that. But he will be telling me every little detail when this is all over."

"I don't know how you do it," she grumbles, and I laugh as the boys surround the table.

"Ladies," Chance says, his gaze lingering on Carly, and I arch a brow as his eyes shift to me. He looks away without a word but I swear, he was blushing. The guys fill in the tables around us, and

Logan lifts me off the bench, sitting down in my spot as he pulls me into his lap and presses his lips to my neck.

"Wait, I'm gonna need you all to tell me your names again," Izzy says, forgetting her earlier mood as she bats her eyes at the guys. I laugh, and Carly just shakes her head as they start telling her their names. When it's Moose's turn, he tells her, and she holds up her hand.

"Hold on. Moose?"

His brow arches. "Yeah?"

"How in the hell did you get a name like Moose?"

All of the guys start cracking up, and Smith slaps him on the back. "Yes, Brother. Please tell us how you came to be known as Moose."

"No," he snaps, looking away from the group.

"Ah, come on, Buddy. If you don't, I will," Kodiak says with a teasing grin on his face. Moose turns to glare at him.

"Don't you dare."

Kodiak smiles wider and turns to us. "It happened like this, ladies. Good old Moose here was dating this girl, a real psycho, but she sucked better than a hoover."

I snort out a laugh, and Izzy smiles like the cat that ate the canary as she props her chin up on her hand, enthralled in the story.

"Anyway, Moose, in his infinite wisdom, recognized that this was the type of woman that would cut your balls off in your sleep and decided to end it with her. To say she didn't take it well would be an understatement. She just didn't want to let our sweet Moose-y go so she devised this plan to kidnap him."

"What?" Izzy sputters out, and all of the guys are snickering at this point as Moose's cheeks burn.

"Right?" Kodiak asks. "Moose is a big boy. I have no idea how she was planning on getting him out of here but we had a party one night and she showed up. She spent the night flirting with all of us but always keepin' an eye on our boy here, and when Moose went upstairs to get something, she followed him. We heard the crash and went running up there. Home girl had shot him with a tranquilizer, and he was lying on the floor, moaning like a…"

"Moose!" Izzy shouts, cutting Kodiak off, and the entire table erupts in laughter, nudging him as he looks away, blushing harder.

"I fucking hate you all," he growls, and Kodiak pats his head.

"Oh, no, you don't."

Izzy sighs and shakes her head. "Well, now I'm just more intrigued about all of your names."

"Let's see. Fuzz was a cop," Kodiak says, pointing to Fuzz, who tips his hat at us, and Izzy smiles. "Smith is just because that's his last name."

"Super unoriginal," she says to him, and he shrugs as he takes a drink of his beer.

"Storm here was named by Red's old lady. She said he always looked like he had a storm brewing in his mind because of his eyes."

Izzy glances over at us and nods. "Yeah, I could see that. Not so much anymore."

I grin and Logan squeezes me tighter, kissing my cheek.

"Aw. It makes me want to barf," Streak says, and the guys laugh as someone nudges Logan.

"Ah, Streak got his name because he's the luckiest son of a bitch you've ever met. Seriously, don't ever play cards with him."

"I've just got skills, Bro," Streak says, and Kodiak shakes his head.

"No, what you've got is like some crazy voodoo magic that I want no part in."

"I've got to go with Kodiak on this one, Streak," Blaze says from the table next to us. "I've never met a guy who finds more money layin' on the ground than you do."

"Whatever," Streak mumbles, a smile still on his face as he sips his beer.

"Who's left? Oh, Chance – also just his name. Super unoriginal. And Blaze is because he used to like to play with fire a little too much."

"Keywords there, used to," Blaze says, and Kodiak nods.

"Wait. What about you?" Carly asks, and when I glance over at her, I smile. Chance is also staring at my best friend like he can't drag his eyes away.

"Mine is 'cause I'm from Alaska."

"Wait, hold on. That's only part of it," Moose says, his cheeks finally returning to their regular color. "You know how grizzly bears in Alaska are so much bigger and meaner than ones you find in the lower forty-eight?"

"Yeah," Carly says, nodding. Moose motions to Kodiak, who just rolls his eyes.

"Oh, please, I'm just a big teddy bear."

"Is that why you almost got arrested when you went home last year and saw that guy talking to your baby sister?"

Kodiak growls and takes a sip of his beer. "Whatever. That little fucker had it coming."

"I feel like we're forgetting someone," Smith says, leaning forward and looking around the circle.

"Henn," Logan says from behind me. Kodiak snaps his fingers.

"That's right. Blaze tells that story the best though."

Blaze chuckles and leans forward, placing his beer on the table. "When Henn was prospecting in, we had a party one night. The guys had been riding him hard cause some of them didn't think he belonged in the club and he wanted to prove himself. He drank so much goddamn Hennessey that he just ran around the clubhouse naked screaming, 'I am Hennessey!' at the top of his lungs." He shrugs. "The name stuck."

"Oh, man, that's great," Izzy says, sighing as she stands. "Now, which one of you is gonna show me where the booze is?"

Kodiak jumps up and smirks at her. "I got ya, Darlin'."

"Mmhmm," she hums, walking off with Kodiak following behind her with his tongue wagging. I lean into Logan's arms, giggling as I watch my friend lay it on thick as she disappears into the clubhouse.

"Let's get some music going," Streak says, hopping up and pulling a remote out of his pocket. He pushes a button and *Thunder Kiss '65* by Rob Zombie starts playing. The guys all break off into different groups, talking and laughing as they drink, and when I glance around, I realize that Carly is gone.

"Did you see where Carly went?" I ask, and Logan nods.

"She disappeared with Chance."

I laugh and shake my head. "I can't say that I'm surprised."

Before he can say anything, his phone rings and he lifts me off his lap for a second to grab it. I half-heartedly listen as he talks to whoever is on the other end of the line, and when he hangs up, he squeezes me.

"You want to go home, Kitten?"

I whip my head around to look at him. "What?"

"That phone call I just got was from a buddy who is helping us deal with our little situation. It's over. We can go home."

The news slowly sinks in, and a smile stretches across my face. I'm free. "Yeah, I wanna go home."

He nods and stands, setting me on top of the table. "Wait right here. I just need to go talk to Kodiak for a second."

I watch him disappear into the clubhouse, feeling one hundred pounds lighter knowing that this is really over and Logan and I can move on with our lives.

* * * *

Logan nervously glances at me from across the cab of the truck, and I turn to face him, studying him as his gaze remains firmly on the road. He's been antsy since we packed up and left the clubhouse but I can't figure out why. He should be happy right now.

"Are you sure we're safe?" I ask, watching his reaction closely. When he looks at me, I can see the certainty in his gaze.

"Yeah, Baby. You never have to worry about this again."

His grip tightens around the steering wheel as we pull up in front of my house and he throws the truck in park. "Then why are you agitated?"

"Let's go inside," he says, opening his door and avoiding my gaze.

"No. Tell me what's wrong." Anxiousness descends over me, and my mind works in overdrive, trying to figure out what is bothering him so much. Why isn't he happy that we're finally free?

He runs a hand over his face, fear filling his eyes. "Kitten, we've got a lot of talkin' to do tonight. Please, can we just go inside?"

Eyeing him warily, I scoot across the seat and hop down. He grabs our bag out of the bed and grabs my hand, lacing our fingers as we walk up to the house. I can't help but glance around, looking for any hidden threat that may be lurking in the shadows, and I don't think that habit will go away anytime soon. How could it? I'm a completely different person than I was before.

It's a lot like how I changed when Adam cheated on me. Before this whole mess started, I walked around with this naïve sense of optimism but not anymore.

Now, I know what kinds of things lurk in the shadows.

Logan unlocks the door and steps aside, motioning for me to go in first, and he steps in behind me, shutting and locking the door behind him. Looking around my house, everything looks the same but it feels so different – tainted by the memories of someone stalking me.

"Do you want to sit?" he asks, and I peek over my shoulder just as he runs his hand over his hair.

"Why don't you tell me what you want since you look like you're about to fall apart?"

He looks down the hall before his gaze flicks to the living room. "In here is fine."

I nod and march into the living room, ready to get this conversation started because he's driving me crazy with his nervous tics. Sitting down on the couch, I fold my legs underneath me, and turn to face Logan as he sits next to me.

"I haven't been completely honest with you," he whispers, clearing his throat as he looks up at me.

"You lied to me?" My heart beats a little faster, the pain poised on the edge and ready to invade my body as I wait for his answer.

"No. I never lied to you. I just never told you the whole truth. Maybe you would have understood me better through this whole thing but I've done things, and the thought of losing you because of that…well, I couldn't stand it."

I nod. "I'm listening."

He glances up at me and the uncertainty in his eyes breaks my heart. What could he possibly have to tell me that would make him so scared? Reaching out, I grab his hand and pull it into my lap, giving it a squeeze to encourage him.

"I met Sophia about a year after I was discharged from the Army. When she found me, I was in a dark place, Baby. I had lost friends over there and seen things that I thought would haunt me forever. I blamed myself for the death of my best friend, and she made it easier. She helped me work through it and deal with it all. I guess we needed each other because she had gotten out of an abusive relationship, and we helped each other heal."

I nod, my eyes watering. I hate hearing about his pain, and if I could do anything to take it away, I would.

"Her ex, Ian – he was a nasty son of a bitch but his family came from old southern money, and he could put on a show better than anyone else I've ever met. She tried to get help but no one would believe her because he was just that good of an actor. One night, he beat her so bad that she could barely stand but somehow she stumbled out of their house and ran to a gas station that was just down the road. She barely made it in the door before she passed out in Blaze's arms."

I nod, the entire picture starting to come together in my mind.

"Blaze took one look at her face and carried her out to his truck. He knew he had to save her. Ian pulled up to the gas station and when he got out, not a hair was out of place but he had hit her so hard that his knuckles were bruised and swollen. Blaze told him that if he ever came around her again, he would put a bullet between his eyes, and believe me, back then he would have without a second thought."

"I can't even picture him like that," I say, trying to imagine Blaze the way Logan is describing him.

"Yeah, he's definitely changed a lot. That was close to when he decided to turn things around, and it's because of the fact that he wouldn't have hesitated to take a man's life."

"Is that how you met her?"

He shakes his head. "No, I met her about seven months later. I was working in the motorcycle shop owned by the club, and she came in to talk to Blaze. As soon as I saw her, that was it. We moved fast and soon I was living with her, and I was planning our future. What I didn't know at the time was that Ian had been keeping an eye on her. He watched her, watched us together, and waited for the right moment."

"Oh," I whisper, suddenly understanding some of Logan's reactions as we dealt with the same issue.

"It started off simple enough. Fi would see him somewhere but she didn't think anything of it. Then, when we'd been together for six months, I proposed to her. She said yes and I was the happiest I'd ever been. But things started escalating quickly. Things were left at the house for her, and we got notes in the mail that scared her so bad that she'd just sit in a ball on the floor and shake."

"Oh, Logan, I'm so sorry."

"It's okay. It's not your fault. And back then, I didn't realize how serious it was. To me, they just seemed like a guy trying to get back with his ex but every time we got something from him, it scared the hell out of her. She never told me about her past, either. It wasn't something that she ever wanted to talk about and I didn't push her. Blaze told me everything, after the fact. One night, about a month after we got engaged, she called me. I picked up the phone but it was just static so I hung up and called her again."

My stomach knots up, and my chest aches because I know this story isn't going to end well, but all this time, I assumed that she had died in a car accident or was hit by a drunk driver. I never thought it could be something like this.

"Instead of Fi answering, it was Ian. He told me that he had my girl and that if I came to face him like a man, he would let her go. I was at the shop and Blaze insisted on coming with me with a couple other guys, including Chance. When we got to the field where he told us to meet them, he had her on her knees in front of his car with a gun to her head."

His breath hitches, and I climb on his lap, straddling his legs as I press my lips to his cheek in an effort to be there for him but I have no idea if I'm doing any good. His hands slip up my sides, and he holds me as his eyes drift closed for a moment.

"I begged him to let her go, to take me instead, but he just laughed. He said if he couldn't have her, then I couldn't either and he…" He chokes on his words, and tears slip down my cheeks as I imagine what he's going to say next. His hold on me tightens, and he takes a deep breath.

"He shot her right there in front of me. I'll never fucking get that picture out of my head. I ran to her but she was already gone," he says, his voice cracking, and I hold him tighter, sobbing into his shoulder and wishing there was more I could do for him.

"I love you," I whisper, because honestly, I can't think of anything else, and he holds me closer. "I'm so sorry, Logan."

I can't even imagine the hell that my situation has put him through, and it all makes sense now. Every single look and every single reaction makes perfect sense, and I regret that I put him through this again.

"Wait. There's more I have to tell you, and if I don't say it now, I don't know that I ever will," he says, pulling his head back to look at me as he blinks away the tears that were filling his eyes. I run my hand down his cheek, and he shudders.

"The guys, they grabbed Ian and threw him in the back of someone's truck while Blaze called his buddy at the police station, who happened to be Fuzz. Fuzz came out with a couple detectives, and as they took Fi away, he promised me that I would get my retribution."

My stomach sinks, and I wonder just what he did to this man.

"God, Kitten, please don't leave me for what I'm about to tell you. I fucking love you, and I can't lose you."

"Go on," I whisper, wondering if I could leave him even if I wanted to.

"They kept him in the county jail until his arraignment, and Fuzz got Ian in a room by himself and let me in the back. I spent a couple of hours in there, doling out what I thought was justice. I messed up his knee so bad that he had a permanent limp and he couldn't hear out of his right ear. I lost count of the number of cuts I made on his body but to this day, I still remember his screams as I poured my pain into him."

I'm frozen in his lap, trying to process what he just said and think of something to say in response. I'm bothered by just how much I don't care. I should, right?

"Please say something, Ali," he says, that fear in his voice again.

I meet his eyes and open my mouth but nothing comes out. I close it again and shake my head. "I know I should probably be repulsed by the things you've done and I'm trying to find even a shred of disgust, but I can't. I know you, Logan. I know the man you are in here," I say, placing my hand on his chest, over his heart. "I know that anything you did was for the ones that you love so how can I fault you for your total devotion to those lucky enough to find themselves in your heart?"

He glances up at me and swallows. "You don't think I'm a monster?"

"I think under the right circumstances, anyone can temporarily become a monster but you have a good heart. I think the fact that you still feel this guilt over what you did means that you aren't the monster you seem to think you are."

"I would do it again. If I had to go back, I would do it all over again and probably finish the job this time."

My fingers dig into his skin, and he hisses. "Are you trying to run me off?"

"No. I just need you to understand who I am."

"Who you are is the man who threw himself into a situation that caused him immense pain to keep me safe. Who you are is a man who every day helps women escape a hell I can only imagine. Who you are is the man who I know would lay down his life to protect me, the man that I trust completely with every part of me. That's who you are, Logan, and I love every piece of you. Even the ones you think are broken or damaged."

"Have I mentioned that I fucking love the shit out of you, Kitten? You are everything that I ever wanted and all the things I didn't even realize that I needed."

I nod, leaning down and pressing my lips to his softly before pulling back just enough to let them brush against his as I speak. "I love you, too, Logan. Until the day I take my last breath."

He hooks his hand around the back of my neck and pulls me onto his lips. I pull away when he wiggles underneath me, and when I look down, he's holding out the engagement ring.

"I say it's about time you put this on," he says, and I grin as I hold my hand out. He slips the gorgeous antique ring on my finger before pulling it up and kissing it.

"It's gorgeous," I whisper, admiring it.

"It was my grandma's, and I know that she'd be thrilled that I gave it to you."

I beam at him, leaning down and kissing him before pulling back. I look at him and back down to the ring. "Wait. How does the story you told relate to me being safe now?"

He sucks in a breath and wraps his arms around my waist again like he's trying to keep me from leaving. "It was Ian, Babe. He had a guy, his twin brother actually, following me, and when Ian saw the photos of you and I together the day we met, he set out to get his revenge. He knew doing all the same things that he did all those years ago would set me off, and he was right. It also led me right back to him."

"Is he dead?" I ask, and he watches me for a moment before nodding slowly. "Good."

"That day that I ran out of the clubhouse and told you to stay inside, I got a call from a friend of mine. He heard that Ian had hired someone to kill you, and when I went up to the prison, he confirmed it."

"But, wait, if it's the brother, how am I safe?" I look over my shoulder, panicking as I think about someone watching me again.

"Relax, Ali. Do you really think I'd bring you back here if you were in danger? Kodiak is out picking him up right now."

"What are you going to do to him?" I ask, my heart pounding as I think about someone getting hurt because of me – even if they are a bad guy.

"That really depends on how reasonable he is."
"What do you mean?"

He sighs. "Well, Streak thought that some of the letters sounded like he was really in love with you. It's possible that he developed his own obsession as he started following you for his brother, and if that's the case then we'll end this."

"And what if he's not obsessed?"

"Then it will depend on how hell-bent he is for revenge for his brother's death."

I don't like this one bit.

"I know you're probably not comfortable with this, Baby, and trust me, we're not too excited about the idea either, but if he's obsessed or out for revenge, you know it's gotta be this way."

I watch him for a minute before letting out a breath and nodding. I hate it but he's right. We can't let him go if he's going to be a threat to us or our life together.

"All right. You know how I feel about it but I know you won't do this unless it's your only option."

"Hey, Kitten?" he says, and I arch a brow at him. "I can't fucking wait to marry you."

Hopelessly Devoted

Chapter Thirty-Three
Alison

"Kitten?" Logan calls out from the kitchen, and I look up from my book.

"Yeah?"

He walks into the living room and grins when he sees me curled up on the couch with a book. "You're cute as shit with those glasses on, Baby."

"Noted," I say, laughing, and he sits down on the edge of the couch.

"So, my mom just called and she's having some electrical issues over at her house. You good here if I run over there real quick?"

I nod, smiling at him. "I am. You should invite her over for dinner next weekend so she can meet me and you can tell her we're getting married."

"You got it, Baby," he says, standing up and leaning over me, caging me in with his arms. He leans down and gently presses his lips to mine, kissing me with such tenderness that I just want to melt into the couch.

"The prospects are outside, just in case. Okay?" he says as he pulls away, and I shake my head.

"Logan, I'm safe now. I don't need the bodyguard detail."

He smirks and leans in again, hovering over my lips, and my eyes drift closed as I reach up for him. "Just humor me," he whispers, his breath brushing over my parted lips.

Opening my eyes, I pin him with a glare. "Fine. But by the end of the week, I want them gone for good."

He seals his lips to mine and strokes my cheek with his thumb before pulling away. He backs up and turns to head for the door before glancing over his shoulder at me. "We'll discuss it."

"Hell, no, we won't discuss it. By the end of the week, Logan. I'm serious," I call after him, and he just laughs as the front door opens.

"We'll see." He winks and leaves before I can say anything else, and I sink back into the couch with a sigh as I try to fight back a smile.

God, I love that irritating man.

I sigh, enjoying the feeling of just being in my house again after everything that happened. It feels like my little piece of heaven again, and I know a big part of that is because of Logan. Grinning, I set my book down and pull out the bridal magazine that I hid in here the other day. I had to hide it because if Logan had seen it, he would have insisted that we just run off to the courthouse and get married. I don't want anything big or crazy but I definitely want to have a wedding.

Hopelessly Devoted

As I flip through the magazine, I toy with the idea of having it out at his grandparents' property. It's such an integral part of his childhood and the man he is today. Plus, I love it out there, and after listening to his grandparents' love story, I want to honor that and maybe get some good juju for our own marriage. I just hope he's on board, too.

I flick to a page with an ad for wedding dresses and gasp as the perfect dress stares back at me. Oh, I so want to get married in that. It's a white tulle ball gown with a sweetheart neckline and a band of diamonds around the waist – not too big, not too small, not too flashy. It's perfect. Bear trots into the room and stops in front of the couch, plopping his drool-covered face down on my magazine – right over my beautiful dress.

"Bear," I gasp, shaking my head as I rub behind his ears. "Is this a sign? Here I was thinking we'd make you ring bearer but you might just drool all over everyone."

He lets out a lazy woof and looks up at me with pleading eyes.

"What do you want? Hungry?" I ask, and he just continues staring at me with his big brown eyes.

"Want to go outside?"

He woofs again, and I laugh as I pull the magazine out from under him and lay it open on the coffee table so it can dry. He follows along at my side, nudging my hand with his nose as I walk down the hallway and open the back door for him. He shoots out into the yard, swallowed up by the darkness, and I laugh at him as I cross my arms over my chest and wait for him to come back. The wind whips through the yard, sending a chill down my spine, and I shake my head. The weather here is crazy. It was eighty degrees yesterday, and tonight I'm seriously considering starting a fire.

"Bear," I call, shaking from the cold, but he doesn't come back. Sighing, I turn back into the house. "Fine, Pup. Freeze to death."

He'll come back when he's ready; he always does. Personally, I think he likes having a bigger backyard to run around in. The yard at Logan's house was barely enough room for Bear after the previous owners built the huge deck on the back.

Shivering, I go to the fridge and grab a bottle of wine and two glasses before slipping into the family room and setting them down on the table. After I start a fire, I'll go see if my magazine is dry yet.

Once I've got the fire roaring, I sit down on the couch and pour myself a glass of wine, glancing over at the back door, wondering where the hell that dog is. I'm just about to go check on him when the front door opens and closes.

"That was quick," I call, grabbing the remote to turn on the TV. Logan promised me he would sit through one chick flick this weekend, and I intend to make him keep that promise. "How was your mom?"

"My sweet, Ali," a voice I've only heard in my dreams says, and the glass of wine slips out of my hand, a dark purple stain spreading across the carpet. My heart pounds in my ears as I stand and slowly turn. He smiles at me, the same sickening smile that's haunted me since I last saw him staring in my window. "My sweet, gorgeous girl. I'm here for you."

I move backward, creeping along the couch toward the hallway so I can run, and his brow furrows as he moves toward me, holding his hands out. "Don't be afraid, Sweetheart. I'm here to save you."

"No, you're not." My voice is soft as I continue creeping toward the hallway. I'm so close, maybe I can just make a run for it. I turn and start running but I don't make it far before his arms are wrapping around me and pulling me into his body. He spins me around to face him, and I open my mouth to scream but he covers it with his gloved hand, the leather cold against my skin.

"Shh, Sweetheart. What has he done to you, my love?" he whispers and pulls his hand away. Before I can scream, his lips are closing over mine, and I fight against him as he thrusts his tongue into my mouth. Tears leak out the corners of my eyes as I struggle in his arms. He tastes like tobacco, and it makes me gag. Pulling away, he rubs his hand over my hair and down my face again and again as he shushes me.

"You're all right, Ali. I'm going to keep you safe from that animal."

"No!" I yell, still struggling as I try to free myself from his grip. "Help!"

"Why are you doing this? Besides, no one is here to help you. I personally delivered those demons straight to hell for keeping you from me."

"No," I gasp, picturing the two young men that I'd only had the chance to meet briefly. Miles was fresh out of the Army and Logan had sponsored him in, while Cody was from the wrong side of town and looking to better his life. Now they were gone ,and it was all my fault. Tears stream down my face, and he wipes them away.

"Don't cry for them, my love. They got what was coming to them. I'll kill anyone that gets in between you and I. You're mine."

I shake my head, looking him right in the eyes as I say, "No, I'm not." I finally manage to connect my knee with his groin, and he falls to the floor as I start scrambling down the hallway. It feels like I'm walking through a fun maze, the walls moving and distorting as my body fills with adrenaline, my heart pounding a rapid beat in my ears. I turn the corner, and I can see the door. I'm almost free.

Air punches out of my lungs as he tackles me from behind, knocking me down to the floor and lying on top of me.

"Don't make me do this to you, Sweetheart," he pleads, and I scream and swing my fists, hoping to connect with some part of his body, but it's impossible to do with him behind me. He sighs and stands up, grabbing onto my ankles. He starts pulling me down the hallway, back toward the kitchen.

I scream.

I kick.

I try to hang on to the floor, my nails ripping away against the hardwood, and pain shoots up my arms as he continues dragging my body down the hallway.

Tears stream down my face in torrents as he pulls me into the kitchen and flips me to my back, straddling my waist as he reaches for my hands. I fight him, constantly moving so I'm harder to latch on to, and one hand connects with his cheek. He roars in anger, slamming his body down on me, and I struggle to breathe as I continue trying to fight him. Sitting up, he wraps his hand around my throat, and my eyes go wide as I reach for him.

"You'll thank me for this some day," he whispers. "Fifty years from now, when we're still happily married and our grandchildren are running around the house, you'll thank me."

"No!" I scream, my throat aching from the strain as he grabs one hand and pins it to the floor. I swing at him and scratch his cheek. He releases me with a hiss, bringing his hand up to his face before looking back down at me with wide eyes.

"Why are you doing this? I'm saving you."

"No, you're kidnapping me!" I yell, spitting in his face, and he growls as his fist slams down on my face. It stuns me long enough that he's able to grab both of my hands and tape them together before doing the same to my ankles. As he picks me up from the floor and carries me over to the kitchen table, I glare at him.

He sets me down in a chair and crouches down in front of me, running a hand over my face. "Why did you make me do this, Sweet Girl? What did he do to you to make you think I was the evil in your life?"

"He didn't have to do anything. I saw it all on my own," I spit, and he stands, sighing as he starts pacing through the kitchen.

"It's gotta be like some kind of Stockholm syndrome, right?" he mutters to himself, glancing at me. He comes back over to me and kneels in front of my chair. "You have to remember, Baby."

When I don't say anything, he sighs and drops his head.

"Remember when we first met, Angel? We sat across from each other on that deck, and our connection was so strong."

I'm about to tell him that he's delusional when a memory hits me, and I tilt my head as I look at him. There's only one person that I can remember sitting on a deck with in recent memory but he doesn't look anything like him. I squint, trying to imagine him with a mop of light brown hair instead of the straight dark hair he has now, and he smiles.

I gasp.

"Zach?" I ask, my mind racing as I think over my entire dinner with him. What on earth is he talking about though? He was nice but there was no connection. None at all.

"Yes, Baby," he exclaims, grabbing my face in his hands. "You remember, don't you? The very moment we met; I knew what we have is so special."

I shake my head. "We didn't have a connection. I had dinner with you once, and I haven't seen you again."

"No. That's not true. We were inseparable until *he* took you away from me."

I glance up at him, and the earnest look on his face makes me rethink my approach. I just need to get away from him. Maybe if I play along…

"I remember," I whisper, and he smiles, his entire face lighting up.

"You do?"

I nod, forcing a smile to my face as I peek up at him. "Yes, I do."

"Oh, Angel," he says, leaning forward and caressing my cheek. He leans in to kiss me but stops. "Let me clean you up, Baby. I'm so sorry that I had to do this."

"It's okay, I understand," I say, choking back the bile that is fighting its way up from my little act. He comes back with a wet washcloth and starts cleaning the blood off my face. I hiss as he brushes my nose, and I already know that it's broken.

"I'm so sorry, Angel. When we get out of here, we'll get you fixed up. But we have to hurry."

Once I'm clean, he leans down and smiles as he presses his lips to mine. My body retches, desperately wanting to get away from him but I take a deep breath and force myself to kiss him back. It's the only way it will work.

"Why did you use a different name?" I ask, the question nagging me as I watch him.

"I had to, Sweetheart. If you had known it was me, you wouldn't have been scared and he would have known. I had to keep you safe."

"And your hair?"

"I had to make myself look similar to him so the neighbors wouldn't question me coming and going from your house. Everything I did was to keep you safe, Ali." He pulls away and stands me up, leaning down and cutting the tape around my ankles.

"Baby," I whisper when he stands back up, reaching up and brushing my fingers over his cheek.

His whole body shudders, and I want to scream. "This is hurting me."

He looks down at the tape around my wrists and nods. "Of course, Angel. I'm so sorry that I hurt you."

He cuts the tape and peels it away from my skin, leaning down and pressing kisses against my wrists as my stomach rolls, and I close my eyes. He grabs my hand.

"Let's go home. Okay?" he asks, and I nod, looking toward the front door. If I can just get outside, I can make a run for it. I'll scream the whole damn neighborhood down if I have to. He wraps an arm around my shoulders and starts leading me outside. I take a deep breath as I fiddle with my ring, and he glances down.

"What the fuck is that?" he seethes, grabbing it and pulling it up to his face to inspect it. "He was forcing you to marry him?"

I squeeze my eyes closed, and tears slip down my cheeks as I nod. He'll think I'm crying because I'm scared of Logan but denying my love for him even when my life is in danger is the real reason for my tears.

"Take it off," he says, trying to grab it, and I yank my hand away, taking a step back as I shake my head. "What are you doing? Take that fucking ring off, Ali."

"No," I whisper, backing up again. He reaches out and wraps an arm around my waist before I can get away and pulls me into his body.

"Where the hell do you think you're going? I want his ring off your finger."

I shake my head. I don't care what he does to me – I won't take Logan's ring off. "No."

His eyes narrow, and he studies me for a second before his gaze goes cold, taking on an evil quality that makes me tremble in his arms. Reaching behind his back, he pulls a gun out of his waistband, and I gasp. "You were lying to me the entire time, weren't you?"

"No. No, I wasn't," I gasp, shaking my head as I hold my hands up. He presses the gun against my head and spins me around so my back is to his front as he pushes us toward the front door.

"We're leaving, and I swear to God, if you try to get away from me, I will shoot you."

"So much for loving me," I mutter, my filter completely shut off right now. He presses his cheek to mine, his lips brushing against my ear as the cold barrel of the gun presses into my forehead.

"I do love you, Angel, but I'd rather lose you to death than to that piece of shit. Besides, if you go, I won't be far behind you, and then we can be together again. Forever."

My blood runs cold, and my stomach rolls. The only thing worse than hell is forever with him, no matter where that forever is served.

Glancing over at the gun that's digging into my forehead, I notice that the safety is still on, and his hand is wrapped firmly around the grip. I let out a breath, sending a giant thank you to my dad for teaching me about guns as I elbow him in the ribs and spin away from him, running down the hallway. I can hear him wheezing behind me, and then his boots are slapping against the floor as he follows behind me.

"Don't make me do this, Ali!" he yells behind me just as I make it into the kitchen and glance behind me. He fires the gun. A burning pain tears through my arm, and I cry out as I spin around to face him. I cover the wound and blood bubbles over my fingers, running down my arm and dripping onto the floor. He creeps into the kitchen, gun trained on me as his gaze flicks down to my arm. I use it to my advantage, charging toward him and tackling him. We fall to the floor, and he quickly rolls on top of me, pointing the gun to my chest.

As I fight him, I imagine my life with Logan. Our wedding, the kids we'll have, raising them out on the property, and tears sting my eyes as I realize I might lose all that.

No.

That's not an option.

I can feel myself getting weak, and I know I'm losing a lot of blood. With my last bit of energy, I bring my knee up, slamming it right into his balls. He gasps, and his body jerks, allowing me some leverage on the gun. We struggle for it, fighting for our lives, and it goes off once more. My ears ring, and I feel a heavy pressure on my chest as darkness descends over me.

Hopelessly Devoted

Chapter Thirty-Four
Logan

Climbing out of the truck, I sigh and slip my keys into my pocket, worrying about my mom. When I got to her house and went around back, it was clear that the lines had been cut. It could have just been some punk messing around but I don't take chances like that anymore. Whatever it is, it's a problem for tomorrow. I'm anxious to get back to my girl. Even knowing she's safe, I still hate being away from her for long.

"Bear?" I ask when I come around the truck and see him sitting in the shadows on the porch. "What the hell?"

The side gate is open, and he comes running to me, whining, and prancing around like something is wrong. I pat his head and creep over to the side gate but stop short, cursing. Just inside the gate are the bodies of our two prospects, one of which I sponsored. Crouching down, I look them over before a gunshot has me shooting to my feet.

I'm thrust back to that night, and it feels like everything is crashing down on me. I can see Fi so perfectly in my mind, kneeling in front of Ian's car, the fog billowing around us as his headlights shined in my face, preventing me from seeing her face. And then she was gone, slumped over in the dirt like the prospects. I pound my fist into the wooden fence, and my mind jumps to Ali.

Oh, God, Ali.

No.

A second gunshot snaps me out of my daze. I jump onto the porch, hopping over the railing as Bear runs around to the steps, and I practically rip the front door off the hinges. I stop in the foyer, scanning the front room and the hallway, but she's not there. Bear whines next to me, and I run down the hallway to her bedroom, flinging the door open as my gaze flies over the space.

Where the fuck is she?

Spinning around, my heart stops beating, and I fall to my knees. She's on the floor at the end of the island, so pale and lying in a pool of blood. A man dressed all in black is on top of her, and I pull my gun out of my waistband, push off the floor, and rush over to them. Kneeling down next to her, I shove him off her, ready to unload my clip, but just one look and I know he's already gone. Brown, lifeless eyes stare back at me, and I toss him aside, more concerned about my girl.

Digging my phone out of my pocket, I dial nine one one as I feel for a pulse. It's faint as fuck but I think it's there.

"Nine one one, what's your emergency?" the monotone voice says, and I take a deep breath, my heart smashing against my ribcage, pain radiating through my body with each beat.

"My fiancée. She's been shot. I need an ambulance." My voice doesn't sound like my own as I stare down at the love of my life and run my hand over her hair, begging a God I'm not sure that I believe in to not take her from me, too.

"Yes, sir. What's the address?"

I rattle off Ali's address, and she instructs me to stay on the line but I don't care. I end the call and toss my phone aside, and I grab her hand and hold it in mine.

"Logan," she whispers, her eyes still closed, and my heart jumps.

"Yeah, Baby. I'm right here. You're going to be okay," I tell her, hoping that I'm telling her the truth. I can't do this without her.

"I love you." Her eyes crack open, allowing me a split second of her gorgeous blue gaze before they flutter closed again.

"I know, Sweetheart. The ambulance is going to be here soon. You're going to be okay."

She moans in pain, and I mutter a curse, looking over her body as I wonder if I should be doing anything. Blood is still oozing out of her arm, and I reach up onto the counter, grabbing a towel and tying it as tight as I can around her wound. She jerks and cries out in pain, and I apologize again and again as I make sure it's tight enough.

"You have to say it back," she says, and I shake my head.

"I'll say it when they get you all fixed up."

She cracks open her eyes, a single tear slipping down her cheek as she looks up at me. "You have to say it now. If I don't... You have to say it."

"Shh," I say, leaning down and cradling her face. "You're not leaving me, do you hear me? You're staying right here, and we're spending the rest of our lives together."

She nods, her eyes drifting closed again.

"Look at me, Baby. Keep looking at me."

"I'm cold, Logan," she responds, and I can barely hear her. Desperation taking over, I lift her into my arms and apologize again as she cries out.

"Is that better?" I ask when she's securely in my lap, and she nods. She peeks up at me again, and I can tell that I'm losing her. Where the fuck is that ambulance?

"I found my wedding dress," she whispers, and I smile through the tears building in my eyes.

"You did? I can't wait to see you wear it, Kitten."

A dreamy little smile stretches across her face as her eyes close again. "I think we should get married at the cabin, down by the lake."

"Yeah, Baby. That sounds perfect."

"Can't wait to be your wife," she says, her voice fading, and I panic, shaking her a little.

"Ali! Baby, you gotta keep those gorgeous eyes on me. I need you to stay with me, Sweetheart. I need you."

She opens her eyes and reaches up with her good arm, running her fingers down my cheek. "The moment I met you, I knew you were going to steal my heart."

"Don't you dare say good-bye to me right now, Kitten. Do you hear me? I'm going to still be spanking your ass when we're eighty and you decide to give me lip."

She tries to smile but she can't quite manage. "I like the sound of that."

Fuck! Where is that goddamn ambulance?

"Logan," she whispers, and I nod. Her eyes flutter closed again, and her hand falls away.

"Ali. Open your fucking eyes!" I yell, tears spilling down my cheeks, and darkness lurking in the corners, waiting to swallow me up again.

"If I don't make it," she says, sighing like even that sentence was too much for her, and I start shaking my head. I don't want to fucking hear this. She's not leaving me. I won't allow it. I finally found her, and I was finally able to live again. I can't lose her. "You have to try and move on."

"No, Ali."

"Please, Logan. All I want is for you to be happy."

I shake her again, and her eyes open slightly. "You make me happy. Do you hear me? I'm fucking delirious when I'm with you so you fight. You're not leaving me."

Her eyes close again, and this time when I shake her, she doesn't move. Pain crashes down on me, and I struggle to breathe as I shake her again.

"No. Ali. Don't leave me, Baby. You gotta stay with me. I need you. I need you," I say, holding her to my chest as I rock back and forth, demons dancing in the wings, chomping at the bit to get their hands on me.

"I'm scared." Her voice cracks as she forces the words out of her mouth, her skin against mine. Pressing my hand to her face, I lean down and kiss her forehead, a tear falling as I struggle to breathe.

"I'm right here, Kitten. You've got absolutely nothing to be afraid of."

"Love you," she whispers. "So much."

And then the darkness descends.

* * * *

Beep.
Beep.
Beep.

That steady beeping – it's the only thing that confirms she's still here. That I get one more moment with her on this earth because the doctors can't tell me anything. They say she'll wake up when she's ready. If she ever wakes up – that's what they're not saying. She may not ever open her gorgeous blue eyes and smile at me again. I'm so close to losing everything all over again, and if I thought the pain of my past was torture, I was fucking wrong. I'm hanging off the edge of an abyss, my fingers digging into the rocky cliff as fire burns below me, waiting to consume me.

She lost so much damn blood, and it felt like hours as I waited for the paramedics to come in and start working on her. But nothing has ever felt as long as the two days that I've waited for her to just open her damn eyes as her final words ring in my ears. She's here – her heart is still beating, and her lungs still suck in air and push it out again but it all means nothing if she never opens her eyes.

This is my fucking fault.

I can't stop looking at the situation from other scenarios, trying to see where I went wrong. God, I was so stubborn and determined to end it that I didn't even consider another possibility, and it just might cost me her. I can't help but think of all the things I did wrong. Why didn't I ever consider that it could have been someone else? There are still so many unanswered questions but one thing I know for sure is the dead man in our kitchen was not Ian's twin brother, Tristan. How is it possible that she was in even more danger than I realized? Not that it matters if she doesn't open her goddamn eyes.

"Kitten," I whisper, grabbing her hand and bringing it to my lips. "You gotta wake up for me, okay? I need to know that you're still in there."

Tears gather in my eyes again as I just look at her, her creamy skin so pale and cold, and her hair greasy as it sticks to her face.

"The last time I said this to someone, I was young and thought I knew everything, but this time is different. With you, it's all different. I won't survive losing you, Baby. I know it. You're the only woman on this earth for me, and we have a whole life to live together so you can't leave me."

Stroking the back of her hand with my thumb, I imagine the wedding she described to me as she lay in a pool of blood on the kitchen floor. I picture her walking toward me in a white dress with a brilliant smile on her face and her blue eyes twinkling. I miss her eyes. I'm addicted to the way she looks at me and that little sparkle I get when she smiles at me. My knee starts bouncing, and I kiss her hand again before I look up at the ceiling.

"What the fuck did I ever do to you? You do this to me not once but twice? Don't you dare fucking take her from me, too. You don't get to take her," I rage at God, and the door to Ali's room opens as I wipe my eyes and turn back to my girl.

"How's our girl doing?" Janice, Ali's mom, asks. As the ambulance drove Ali to the hospital and I followed them, I called her parents. I knew she would want them here, and if she's not coming back to us, they need to be here to say good-bye to their daughter. Just that thought has me choking back tears again.

"She's the same," I answer, my voice rough as I stare up at Ali's face.

"Why don't you go get some food, son," Peter, her father, says, patting my shoulder but I just shake my head.

"I'm not leaving her."

As soon as they showed up, they hugged me and welcomed me into their family like it was meant to be. In fact, Janice has kind of been mothering all the guys as they stop by to check on Ali every so often. I didn't even know that she knew about me, and I don't really understand how she can be so accepting after I put her daughter in this situation but all my focus is on Ali right now.

"Well, all right, then. We'll go down to the cafeteria and get you something to eat. Any preference?"

I shake my head, and she sighs before patting my shoulder just like Peter did. When the door closes behind them, I stand up and lean over the bed, pressing my forehead to Ali's as I just breathe her in, missing the mango scent of her soap more than I ever thought I would.

"I need you, Baby. You've got to come back to me. You've got to fight. I love you. Do you hear me? I fucking love you, Kitten, so you've got to come back."

The door opens again, and I clear my throat as I sit back down, holding her hand tight between my own.

"Hey, Man," Kodiak says, coming up behind me and slapping my shoulder. "How's she doing?"

"Same."

"It'll work out, Brother. That girl loves you too fucking much to leave you. She'll wake up when she's ready."

I nod, unable to speak as I think about the opposite of that happening. I squeeze her hand and press it against my forehead as I close my eyes.

"I've got some news for you."

"Let's hear it then," I snap without looking at him. I know I'm being a colossal dick but I can't even bring myself to care right now.

"Picked up Tristan, Ian's brother. Turns out, Ian was blackmailing him to follow Ali. He wants nothing to do with any of this. We gave him enough money to start over somewhere new and drove him out of town."

I nod, lifting my head and staring at Ali again. "Well, at least one thing worked in our favor."

"Man, you couldn't have known that it wasn't Ian. Everything pointed to him."

My gaze flicks up to him, and I shake my head. "I should have known. I promised to protect her and look what I fucking did to her."

"You didn't do shit to her. We still don't even know who the hell this guy is to Ali. This isn't on you. Sometimes, bad shit just happens."

"Yeah, because of me. Every time."

He sighs and pushes off the wall. "Like when my pops died. That your fault, too? Or when Moose's dad shot his mom right in front of him and then shot himself. Was all that your fault?"

I don't say anything, my knee bouncing harder as I keep my gaze trained on Ali.

"Yeah, didn't think so. Bad shit happens and yes, Brother, you've had more shit piled on you than a lot of people, but that girl is wakin' up. I know it."

"No, you don't, actually."

He shoves my shoulder, and I stand, ready to slam my fist into his face. "Man, knock your shit off and pull your head out of your ass. She needs you right now so be the man that she needs you to be. And have a little faith. I'll be back later to check on you."

Without another word, he leaves, and I sink back into my chair, holding her hand to my lips again.

"I'm here, Ali. I'm right here, and I'm not leaving until you come back to me. Just come back, Baby. I miss you so fucking much."

I close my eyes and start telling her ideas for the wedding, really hoping that I'm not setting myself up for disaster here as I allow a flicker of hope to light inside my chest.

Hopelessly Devoted

Chapter Thirty-Five
Alison

Beep.
Beep.
Beep.
The constant rhythmic beeping cuts through the fog, fading in and out as I try to fight through the feeling of something weighing down my body. Sucking in a breath, I try to open my eyes but nothing happens, and I want to cry. Why the hell can't I open my eyes? What's happening to me?

"How's she doing today?" a voice asks, and it takes me a moment to realize that it's Carly.

"Same," Logan responds, his voice gravelly and tired. He runs his thumb across the back of my hand, and warmth washes over me. I'd know his touch anywhere.

"Have the doctors said anything?" another voice asks, and I smile. Izzy.

"They've said the same shit for three days. She'll wake up when she's ready."

Three days?

Have I really been out for three days?

"She lost a lot of blood, Logan. She needs rest," Carly says, and he growls.

"Well, I need her."

"And she needs you so she will wake up. I know it."

"We've got to get to work but we'll stop by again tonight, okay?" Izzy adds in, and Logan makes a sound of approval. Someone squeezes my foot, and then the door to the room opens and closes.

"Kitten," he whispers, and I try to reach for him but my arms don't work. "You can't leave me. I need you, Baby. Every day for the rest of forever, I need you by my side so you can't go leaving me yet."

I want to scream that I never want to leave him but nothing works. I can't speak, I can't move. All I can do is listen as he pleads for me not to give up.

Never.

I'll never give up – not when I have Logan waiting for me.

"I bet we could get married in June if we hurry. It's so gorgeous out there in the summer. We could put lights in the trees and get married under the stars. Would you like that, Kitten?"

YES!

This is torture. I'm entombed in my own body, my subconscious clawing at my skin, trying to break free so I can let him know that I love him and that I'm not going anywhere.

Come on, Ali.

Fight.

"Baby?" he asks, hope in his voice, and I try to reach for him again. "Can you hear me, Ali? I swear I saw your finger move."

Yes!

Yes, I'm here.

I try to reach for him again but I can see the darkness creeping in from the edges of my vision, and I know I'm going to lose this battle.

* * * *

Someone is snoring.

That's my first thought as I slowly drift back into consciousness, nerves hitting me as I remember the last time. Will I be able to open my eyes this time? Or will I be frozen in my own skin again? My eyelids flutter open, and I hiss as I slam them shut again, the bright morning sunlight spilling in the window too much for me.

"Kitten?" his sleepy voice asks, squeezing my hand, and I squeeze back. He shoots up next to me, yanking my arm in the process, and my entire body aches. I moan, and he kisses my hand before releasing it and leaning over me. "Let me see those gorgeous blue eyes, Baby."

"It's bright," I whisper, my voice cracking, and my throat aching.

"Hold on." He's gone, and then a few moments later, he's back. "Try now."

I slowly open my eyes and look up at him. He beams before leaning down and kissing me with such tenderness that a tear slips down my cheek. "There's my girl," he whispers against my lips, and I place my hand on his cheek, my eyes closing again as I just breathe him in.

"I missed you."

He nods. "You never get to leave me again. It's a new rule. Like, I won't even let you take a damn shower by yourself."

"I like the sound of that."

He smiles against my lips, and I can just picture that cocky little smirk he flashes me sometimes. "That's real good, Kitten, 'cause I wasn't askin'."

"Such a charmer," I mutter, leaning back into my pillow to look up at him. He pulls back slightly but his lips are still hovering over mine. "I suppose I'll let you get away with it if you marry me under the stars like you promised."

"You heard me?" he asks, his grin replaced with a boyish smile that melts the stress off his face. I nod.

"I did and I'm so making you do it."

"Alison James, you should know by now that I'll give you absolutely anything you want. You only have to ask."

"Am I interrupting?" someone asks from the doorway, and Logan says yes without even looking at them. I laugh and peek over his shoulder. Detective Rodriguez stands in the doorway, and I wave him in.

"Come on in."

Rodriguez chuckles and walks into the room, sitting down in the chair on the far side of my bed. "I didn't realize you had woken up. I was just coming to check in on you."

"She's only been awake for a couple of minutes," Logan tells him, and he nods.

"Let me go grab the doctor, then." He stands and leaves the room, coming back a few moments later with a gorgeous woman with bright red hair.

"Hi, Ali. I'm Doctor Brandt. How are you feeling?" she asks, shining a light in my eyes and looking me over. Rodriguez leans back against the wall and begins taking notes.

"Tired," I answer, and she nods.

"The bullet nicked an artery, and you lost nearly your entire blood volume. If it hadn't been for the towel your fiancé wrapped around your arm, you might not be here with us now."

I glance up at Logan and smile. "You saved me."

"Promised you I would," he answers, pressing his lips to my hand.

"Other than that, you'll probably be quite sore for a while. We also need to keep bandages on your hands since some of the nails were ripped out."

"What?" Logan asks, his voice horrified as he looks down at me. "He ripped your nails out?"

I shake my head and bite my lip. "He dragged me down the hallway, and I was just trying to grab on to anything."

"They look good, and I'm sure they'll heal up just fine. We want to monitor you for a couple days but once you go home, you'll still need to get lots of rest. Will you have someone there to take care of you?"

Logan clears his throat and nods. "Don't worry about that, Doc."

She nods and offers me a smile, telling me she'll be back to check on me later before leaving. Logan sits in the chair next to the bed and holds my hand as he closes his eyes and takes a deep breath. Rodriguez steps forward and sits in the chair on the other side of my bed.

"Are you feeling okay to go over a few things?"

I nod.

"Okay, so why don't you tell me what happened?"

I sigh and begin reliving that night for him, feeling stronger than I expected as I retell it. Rodriguez takes notes, and Logan's grip tightens on my hand periodically. I'm sure this is hard on him, too.

"And did you know the assailant?"

I nod, and Logan growls. "What? How did you know him?"

"Do you remember when I told you how my boss made me go on those dates?" He nods. "Zach was date number two."

"And you had no indication that he was the one stalking you?" Rodriguez asks, and I shake my head.

"I didn't even recognize him at first. He'd changed his appearance to look more like Logan, and he used a different name."

"Looking back at his file, this isn't the first time he's become obsessed with someone. There was a girl in college who filed a restraining order against him, and he went to counseling for a while."

"Oh," I whisper, thinking over our date again but I can't think of anything that would have raised a red flag.

"We shouldn't need anything else from you, Ali. Based on the crime scene and what we found in his apartment, this is an open and shut case." He stands, and I reach out for him.

"Wait. What did you find in his apartment?"

He hesitates, his gaze flicking between Logan and I. "Trust me when I say that the two of you are better off not knowing. Move on with your lives and put this behind you."

He holds our gazes for a moment before we nod and he tells us good-bye. When he leaves, I glance over at Logan, and he kisses my hand.

"I love you," I tell him, and he nods. I want to say it every second of every day.

"I want you to tell me everything again."

"No."

He opens his mouth to protest, and I shake my head again.

"It's in the past, and I'm not going to allow you to torture yourself with the details. I want to move forward. With you."

He studies me for a second before nodding and standing. He reaches into his pocket and pulls out his grandmother's ring. He slips it down my finger, and I beam, happiness settling into my heart as I look up at him.

"June. Under the stars?" I ask, and he nods.

"If that's what you want."

"The only thing I really want is to be married to you," I tell him, and he flashes me a grin.

"That's good, Kitten, 'cause there was no other option for us. You're mine until the day I take my last breath." He leans over me, and I press my hand to his cheek as he presses a soft kiss to my lips.

"I'm the luckiest girl in the world."

Hopelessly Devoted

Epilogue
June

"You look gorgeous," Carly says, beaming as she brushes her hands down her own dress and looks at my reflection in the mirror.

"I feel gorgeous," I murmur, twisting back and forth as I take in the stunning mermaid sweetheart dress that we found when we all went to New Orleans with my mom.

Izzy steps up beside us and grins. "Logan's going to lose his shit."

I can't help but giggle because that was the whole point of this dress – get my soon to be husband all worked up so that when everyone leaves and we disappear into the cabin for our honeymoon, he can't control himself. Looking at the three of us lined up in the mirror, love wells up inside me, and I feel so incredibly lucky.

"I honestly don't know what I would do without you two. You're the best friends a girl could ever ask for," I whisper, taking each of their hands in mine, and Izzy looks up at the ceiling while Carly fans her eyes.

"Jesus, don't make me cry," Izzy shouts but her voice lacks conviction.

"We love you, too," Carly says, smiling through the tears gathering in her eyes. I grab a tissue off the table and pass it to her. As she dabs at her eyes, Izzy takes a couple deep breaths and meets my eyes again.

"I'm so lucky that you got stuck with me freshman year," she says, and I laugh.

"Yeah, I am."

She wraps her arms around me just as someone knocks on the door.

"Okay to come in?" Mom asks.

"Yeah, come on in, Mom."

"Oh my gosh," Mom whispers as she steps into the bedroom and covers her mouth with her hands, tears building in her eyes.

"Don't start, Mama. If you cry, then I'm going to cry."

She fans her face and looks up at the ceiling, trying to dry her eyes, but when she glances down at me again, her lips tremble. "Oh, I just can't help it. My only baby is getting married today, and you look absolutely gorgeous."

"Thank you," I sigh, a slight blush staining my cheeks as I turn back to the mirror. Well, here's the blushing bride. Let's go find a groom. "Are you sure you guys are okay with all this?"

They were pretty surprised when I told them I was getting married but they loved Logan from the moment they met him.

"What?"

"All the guys in leather out there?" I joke, pointing out the window where guests are milling by the back deck.

"Those sweet boys? I couldn't be happier. It seems like you're getting a whole family."

I laugh. Only my mother would refer to a group of big, tatted up bikers as sweet boys.

"Are we ready to get this show on the road? They're ushering people down to their seats," Dad says, stepping into the room and pausing when he sees me. "Good Lord," he whispers, his hand over his heart.

"Now, don't go having a heart attack until your daughter says, 'I do'," Mom says, scolding him, and I laugh, which seems to snap him out of his trance. He shakes his head and smiles.

"I swear, just last week you were my baby girl and riding around on my shoulders."

"Dad," I whisper, tears welling up in my eyes, and Mom rolls her eyes.

"Oh, for heaven's sake. Let's get her in the golf cart before you both start blubbering like babies," she scolds us like she wasn't just doing the same thing. "Carly and Izzy, go on now. There's a second golf cart waiting for you."

They duck out of the room and I smirk as I put my shoes on and slip my arm through Dad's. He tucks his arm in and pats my hand as he leads me out to the front of the cabin where a golf cart is waiting for me. There is a large white tent down by the edge of the lake where Logan is waiting for me, and I can't wait to get to him. After the attack, this day couldn't come quick enough, and we almost gave in and just eloped but Logan was adamant about giving me my dream wedding.

I slip into my seat, and Mom hands me my bouquet before hopping on the back as Dad sits beside me. "Ready to do this, Sweetie?"

I nod, no hesitation. "More than ready."

He smiles and starts the golf cart, butterflies flapping around in my belly as we drive across the meadow, toward the edge of the lake where my man is waiting for me. The frogs croak, and crickets chirp as the entire yard is lit up by thousands of white twinkle lights hanging from the trees all around us. They reflect off the water as the stars wink at us from above our heads, and I can't think of a more perfect way to marry him.

Dad stops the cart at the end of the aisle and climbs out, walking around the back to help me out. *Home* by Blue October starts playing, and Dad holds his hand out for me. As I slip my hand into his, he helps me out of the golf cart. My eyes meet Logan's at the end of the aisle, and he beams, smiling through the tears in his eyes, and I clear my throat, feeling a little choked up as Dad takes my hand again, and we start off down the aisle.

When we reach the end, Dad passes my hand over to Logan and slaps him on the shoulder. "I would tell you to take care of her but you've already saved her life, so just make sure that she's happy."

"Absolutely, Sir," Logan vows, nodding, and Dad smiles before joining Mom in the front row. Logan looks back to me, and a soft smile stretches across his face. "You look stunning, Kitten," he whispers, and I blush again.

I didn't think Logan could get more attractive but in a tux with his dark hair in his face, he looks so good that it hurts. He takes my hand and nods to the pastor, who steps forward.

"Welcome, friends and family. We're here this evening to witness the love between Logan and Ali as they commit themselves to each other forever in Holy Matrimony."

Several loud whoops come from the audience, and I giggle as I look out, getting a wink from Kodiak and Chance. As my gaze rakes over the guests, Emma catches my eye, and I smile. It was certainly a surprise to realize how connected we all are, and I'm happy that Logan has someone else in his corner. Her husband, Nix, wraps an arm around her shoulder and pulls her closer as he leans down and whispers something in her ear. Her smile changes as she peeks up at him, and I turn back to Logan as he shakes his head and squeezes my hand.

"They wanted to keep this short and sweet so we're going to jump right into the vows. Logan," the pastor says, stepping back, and Logan smiles at me.

"Ali… what on earth could I say to the woman who brought me back to life? You came into my life and chased away the darkness, you made me want to live again, and you healed my broken heart just before you managed to steal it for yourself. There won't be a moment that you're on this earth that you won't know how much I love you. That's my promise to you here today. That you'll always know how precious you are to me, how appreciated you are, and how lucky I am to have you. The only thing I want to do is make you happy, and I'll move mountains to do just that. Until the day they put me in the ground."

I sniffle, dabbing underneath my eye as I take a deep breath.

"Ali," the pastor prompts, and I smile up at Logan.

"I knew you were going to say that," I start, and a few chuckles ring out around us. "Which is why I thought it was important to tell you that you brought me back to life, too. You woke me up, and you made me feel when I hadn't for a long time. There's this story in Greek mythology that humans were originally created with four arms, four legs, and a head with two faces. When Zeus saw this, he feared their power and separated them, condemning them to spend their lives searching for their other half. The day I met you, I stopped searching because I found my other half, and I was a whole person again. And with you, I know that I can do anything. Together, we have the power to overcome any obstacle, and I'll love every second of it with you by my side. We have so many years in front of us, and I look forward to the good ones as well as the bad because there is no one else in the entire world that could compete with you, and I'm damn lucky that you had a shitty fence and a mischievous dog."

Everyone laughs, and Logan smiles, dropping his head and shaking it. When he looks up at me again, he mouths, "I love you," and I repeat it back to him.

"Who has the rings?" the pastor asks, stepping forward again, and Chance stands and hands them to him. He gives us each one. "Logan, place this ring on Alison's finger and repeat after me: I, Logan James Chambers, take you, Alison Marie James, to be my lawfully wedded wife, through sickness and health, for richer or poorer, in good times and bad until death do us part."

Logan slips the ring on my finger, fitting it perfectly against my engagement ring and repeats after the pastor. When he's finished, he pulls my hand up and kisses it.

The pastor clears his throat and turns to me, repeating the same phrase, and I copy him as I slide the ring on Logan's finger. I can't help but grin as I look down at his hand, loving the ring that tells the rest of the world that he's mine. Forever.

"Now, by the power vested in me by the state of Louisiana, I now pronounce you man and wife. You may kiss your bride."

Logan's arms wind around my waist, and he dips me as he claims my mouth in a fierce, possessive kiss that steals my breath. When we come back up, he pulls away but refuses to release me.

"Now, there's one more thing we need to get out of the way first," Blaze says, standing up and handing a gift bag to Logan. I arch a brow in question but Logan just grins, pulling a black leather vest out of the bag. I scowl, and he holds it up to me.

Property of Storm is stamped across the back, and I squeal as I rip it out of his hands, and slip it on over my wedding dress. The guys all laugh, and he pulls me in for another kiss.

"Now, you're mine in every way, Kitten," he whispers, and I beam.

"You know, you're such a softie under all this leather and attitude," I tell him, and he throws his head back and laughs.

"I fucking love you, Woman."

I grin at him. "You better 'cause you're never getting away from me."

The End

I want to say a huge thank you for going on this crazy ride with me and I hope that you enjoyed this story. Through the course of writing this book, Storm and Ali stole my heart and I hope they did the same to you. If you're wanting more from the Bayou Devils, have no fear because all of their stories are coming. Next up is Chance. His book, Addicted to Love, has a tentative release date of July 2017 but you can follow me at any of the links below to stay up to date on all that.

Author Page:
www.facebook.com/authorammyers/

Newsletter:
http://eepurl.com/cANpav

Fan group:
https://www.facebook.com/groups/585884704893900/

Printed in Great Britain
by Amazon